He would
travel to the
ends of the
earth, to see
love blossom
in her eyes...

continued . . .

DAY DREAMER

When Celine Winters exchanged cloaks—and futures—with a stranger, she hoped to find a destiny greater than any daydream.

"Not since *Jade* has Jill Marie Landis delved into romantic suspense with as much verve and skillful storytelling as she has done in *Day Dreamer*."

—*Romantic Times*

LAST CHANCE

Rachel McKenna shocked everyone when she danced with legendary gunfighter Lane Cassidy. But she knew he could be her last chance for happiness . . .

"Readers who loved *After All* . . . will be overjoyed with this first-rate spin-off." —*Publishers Weekly*

AFTER ALL

The passionate and moving story of a dance hall girl trying to change her life in the town of Last Chance, Montana.

"Historical romance at its very best."

—*Publishers Weekly*

UNTIL TOMORROW

A soldier returning from war shows a backwoods beauty that every dream is possible—even the dream of love . . .

"Landis does what she does best by creating characters of great dimension, compassion, and strength."
                                        —*Publishers Weekly*

PAST PROMISES

She was a brilliant paleontologist who came west in search of dinosaurs. But a rugged cowboy poet was determined to unearth the beauty and passion behind her bookish spectacles . . .

"Warmth, charm, and appeal . . . *Past Promises* is guaranteed to satisfy romance readers everywhere."
                                        —Amanda Quick

COME SPRING

Winner of the Romance Writers of America's
"Rita Award for Favorite Novel of 1993"

Snowbound in a mountain man's cabin, beautiful Annika learned that unexpected love can grow as surely as the seasons change . . .

"A beautiful love story."   —Julie Garwood

continued . . .

JADE

Her exotic beauty captured the heart of a rugged rancher. But could he forget the past—and love again?

"Guaranteed to enthrall . . . an unusual, fast-paced love story."
— *Romantic Times*

ROSE

Across the golden frontier, her passionate heart dared to dream . . .

"A gentle romance that will warm your soul."
— *Heartland Critiques*

WILDFLOWER

Amidst the untamed beauty of the Rocky Mountains, two daring hearts forged a perilous passion . . .

"A delight from start to finish!" — *Rendezvous*

SUNFLOWER

Winner of the Romance Writers of America's
"Golden Medallion for Best Historical Romance"

Jill Marie Landis's stunning debut novel, this sweeping love story astonished critics, earning glowing reviews including a Five Star rating from Affaire de Coeur . . .

"A truly fabulous read! The story comes vibrantly alive, making you laugh and cry." — *Affaire de Coeur*

The Orchid Hunter

Jill Marie Landis

JOVE BOOKS, NEW YORK

THE ORCHID HUNTER

A Jove Book / published by arrangement with
the author

PRINTING HISTORY
Jove edition / March 2000

All rights reserved.
Copyright © 2000 by Jill Marie Landis.
This book may not be reproduced in whole or in part,
by mimeograph or any other means, without permission.
For information address: The Berkley Publishing Group,
a division of Penguin Putnam Inc.,
375 Hudson Street, New York, New York 10014.

The Penguin Putnam Inc. World Wide Web site address is
http://www.penguinputnam.com

ISBN: 0-515-12768-X

A JOVE BOOK®
Jove Books are published by The Berkley Publishing Group,
a division of Penguin Putnam Inc.,
375 Hudson Street, New York, New York 10014.
JOVE and the "J" design
are trademarks belonging to Penguin Putnam Inc.

PRINTED IN THE UNITED STATES OF AMERICA

10 9 8 7 6 5 4 3 2

The Orchid Hunter

The Island

Chapter 1

1850

Joya Penn stood on the valley floor, staring up high mountain walls lush with vegetation, up into the cloud of mist that had settled upon the upper slopes of Kibatante. The mountain was inhabited by a great, hulking spirit of the same name who *was* the mountain and at the same time, was a god who existed *within* the volcanic, igneous rock.

As long as the spirit of Kibatante slept in the heart of the island, everyone knew that all would be well on Matarenga.

One of her sandals had come untied, so Joya bent down and quickly rewrapped the woven hemp thong around her ankle. As she straightened, she brushed a cockroach off of the coarse, yellowed fabric of her shin-length trousers.

Her shirt, a soiled castoff of her father's, was knotted at her midriff. She found the garment a nuisance, but the year that her breasts had developed, her parents had demanded she cover herself. She would prefer not to be burdened with so many clothes, but her father still insisted. She argued that Matarengi women felt no need to cover their upper bodies. Why should she? She was perfectly comfortable with or without clothing. Still, she bowed to her father's will.

Joya sighed, feeling adrift as she wiped perspiration from her brow with her forearm. Wishing that Kibatante's spirit would slip inside her heart and ease her unsettled feelings, she touched a pouch tied to a thong around her neck. The small leather sack was filled with good-luck charms that kept her safe. She opened the bag and looked at the objects inside—a feather, sharks' teeth, a shining piece of rock. The largest among them was her mother's silver hair comb, which she had pressed into Joya's hand on the day she died. She had begged Joya not to forget her. As if she ever could.

Eight Matarengi bearers, their skin glistening with sweat, were scattered over the hillside gathering moss and plant fibers used to pack around orchid specimens to be shipped to London. Joya had been in charge of leading the men today and the search had gone well. Tomorrow morning, the hunting party would start back over the mountain trail to the native village and the house that she and her father shared on the beach.

Even knowing that her life was full, she wished she could lose the heaviness that she carried in her heart. She had the breathtaking beauty of the island paradise and the lifelong friends she had made among the Matarengi people. She had the orchids that she and her father hunted, gathered, and packed. They were the loveliest of flowers, fragile in appearance, yet hardy enough to grow in the wild and even survive being shipped all over the world.

The work she shared with her father was fulfilling

and, over time, she had recovered as much as a daughter ever can from the loss of her mother. Despite the fact that she was no man's wife, and the fact that she had seen little of the world, she realized that she was a very lucky young woman.

But ever since she had been a child, there had been a shadow of sadness haunting her, a notion that there was something vital, something she could not explain, missing from her life.

According to Matarengi custom, she should have been a bride long before now, but her white, English parents had strictly forbidden her ever marrying into the Matarengi tribe. She was to marry one of her own kind— something that had proved to be nearly impossible, for no suitable white man had ever come to the island for any length of time. Even if she chose to ignore her parents' dictates, there was not a single Matarengi male on the island, save Umbaba, her closest friend, who was even comfortable around her.

She was beginning to lose hope of ever leaving the island or marrying anyone. She wondered if there was anything in the least desirable about her by English standards. How would she ever find out, when leaving the island to search farther afield was something her father refused to allow?

Uncomfortable with the direction of her thoughts, she began to climb the mountainside, keeping to the trail the men had hacked out with huge, lethally sharp machetes. In the lower regions of the valley floor, where the sun rarely fought its way through the dense growth, the ground was perpetually damp. She took care not to fall, for her sandals were caked with mud and slippery. Occasionally she had to pause and chop away branches that intruded across the trail with her own blade.

She passed two of the men, stopping to direct three others to take rooted samples from various plants in a deep ravine on the mountainside. She took a specimen from one of the men, held it close, and examined the root structure. It was a fine orchid, a soft lavender-rose in color.

She wished she could accompany the next shipment of flowers to England, walk along the crowded streets and byways, see the River Thames. She longed to experience the sights and sounds she had only learned of from her parents' stories or seen in the prints in her books.

Whenever she closed her eyes and thought of London, somehow she easily imagined herself already there. Sometimes she would dream of England in vivid detail, scene upon scene, with such complete clarity that the images seemed very real.

Sometimes her dreams were haunting. Like Kibatante, the spirit of the mountain, it was as if she could be in two places—in the dream itself and outside of it, watching it unfold. She always dreamed of a girl, very much like herself, but *not* herself, in and about London.

Whenever she awoke from such a dream, it would take her a moment or two to realize she had actually been safe in her bed asleep and that she had never really left Matarenga.

The odd sensation of these dreams-within-dreams had begun when she was a child. More curious than frightened, she would tell her mother about the experience and ask for explanations her mother could not give.

Joya could still recall the way deep frown lines appeared upon her mother's brow whenever she tried to explain about the other girl who *was* her and yet was *not* her.

"Do not dwell on such things, child," her mother, Clara, would always say. "Dreams are only that. They aren't real." Then her lovely mother would smile, but the smile would never reach her eyes. Afterward, Joya would feel more confused than ever.

Eventually, she took up sketching, using bits of charcoal and odd pieces of paper, bark cloth, whatever she could find, as she wrestled with the images in an effort to understand. At first the drawings were only the scribbles of a child. As she grew, she amazed her parents with her skill, but they believed that the girl portrayed in the sketches was Joya herself.

Only she knew differently. The young woman in her drawings looked like her, but was definitely not her. She knew that as well as she knew the names of all the shimmering, rainbow-hued fish in the lagoon and the orchids on the hillsides. Drawing what she dreamed about sometimes left her feeling even more adrift than ever.

One day she had called upon Otakgi, the oldest, wisest man on Matarenga, the man her father called a witch doctor. From what little she knew of either, Otakgi was neither a witch nor a doctor. He was a man of magic, a healer, keeper of Matarengi legends and age-old tribal lore. Even when she had been a young girl with a head full of strange dreams and a heart full of questions, even then he had seemed ancient.

Otakgi's skin was blue-black, thin and wrinkled, as withered as the dried blossoms of the flame tree. His hair was tightly braided with colorful beads among the woven strands. He looked as old as the island itself, and it was whispered among the natives that he was almost as old as Kibatante, as timeless as the turquoise lagoon that surrounded Matarenga.

Alone, more frightened of her dreams than of the old

man, she had slipped into the shadowy interior of his small *fadu*, a native dwelling made of coconut fronds and bamboo. He was seated cross-legged on a tightly woven mat of pandanus, staring through the open door, toward the reef and beyond.

She sat in silence and tried not to wiggle until he came out of his trance, looked over, and found her waiting.

"I have strange dreams, Otakgi. Dreams of myself and not myself. I am very confused." She spoke in Matarengi, a language she knew as well as, or better than, English.

She was forced to remain still, even though it was a while before he looked at her again. When he did, his eyes burned like hot black obsidian. He stared through her, as if she had no more substance than smoke. When he finally spoke, his voice reminded her of the rustling of the leaves when the Kusi trade winds blew gently over the land. He raised both hands, palms up. His long fingers, gnarled with age, lifted skyward.

"It will be many, many seasons yet before you know the meaning of these dreams. Do not be frightened, even if they seem strange, for one day you will find your other self. You will know the secret of this second spirit, the lost spirit of your soul."

When he paused, silent again, she was afraid that he would say no more, that she would be no wiser, no more satisfied than when she had entered the *fadu*.

But the old man eventually stirred. He hummed quietly to himself and rocked back and forth on his bare, bony buttocks.

"There is no need to fear," he had said, louder now, his voice firm, as if trying to impress her with the truth. "Be patient."

And so, as the years passed, she continued dreaming and drawing and trying to be patient. She locked her questions away rather than make her lovely mama frown. Her papa, who had always worked so hard exploring the uncharted interior of the island for new orchids, certainly had no time for questions.

She had endured until one day she discovered she was no longer a child, but a woman—and everything changed. She was no longer allowed to go half naked, like her Matarengi friends. Soon, none of the young men, save Umbaba, would speak directly to her. Slowly, she began to feel more and more isolated.

She went to her parents and begged them to take her to England, to let her experience life off of the island. Since she could not live a full life as a Matarengi, she wanted to live among her own kind for a while. They gently refused her outright, but then debated in hushed whispers behind their bedroom door.

Not long afterward, her mother died.

Months eased into years. She tried to lose herself, her questions, her needs, in her work with the orchids, but late at night, she was forced to battle her aching loneliness.

Perhaps, if she could get to London, she would not only find that part of her she felt was missing, but even meet a suitable man who would find her desirable, someone who would want her enough to marry her.

She had not argued with her father about leaving Matarenga in a good while, but today, almost as if the Kusi winds were charged with change, as if her skin no longer fit, Joya found herself thinking about what Otakgi had said to her so long ago: *"One day you will find your other self."* She was determined to leave the island. She would demand that her father make some arrangements to send her along when the boat came to pick up the orchids. She would make her demands when they returned home from the hunt.

Suddenly, the ground began to tremble. Her hand closed around the orchid plant as rocks began to tumble down the mountainside. She was grazed by flying gravel. The Matarengi became frightened. They shouted to each other, and to her, to take cover.

Kibatante was stirring. The god of the mountain, keeper of the island, was disturbed.

Chapter 2

I'll be damned if I die now. Not when I'm so close.

Dangling high above the valley floor, Trevor Mandeville clung with bare, muddied hands to the twisted,
exposed root of a jacaranda tree. The gnarled root was
his lifeline, his only hope.

He cursed and prayed that it would hold his weight
until he was safe on solid ground, until the idea that he
could fail became a memory and the reality that he was
mortal had faded back into his subconscious.

The muscles in his back and arms screamed as he
strained to save himself. A heavy pack on his back
weighed him down. His rifle swayed from the strap over
his shoulder and slapped him in the side. His face was
inches from the scarred, loose earth of the mountainside.

He spat at the dirt, cursed fate, then himself, and even
Dustin Penn, the man he had journeyed halfway around
the world to find. He closed his eyes, imagined staring
Death in the face. Skeletal, hollow-eyed, the Grim

Reaper tempted him to ease the muscles burning in his arms and shoulders.

"Let go," Death whispered, urging him to give up, to feel the cool wind rush past him as he floated through the abyss, down, down through the tangled canopy of treetops that hid the valley floor.

He was raised never to leave a job unfinished, never to walk away from responsibility. His sister, Janelle, had accompanied him to Africa. She was awaiting him off the mainland coast, on Zanzibar. He refused to abandoned her on foreign soil.

So Trevor clung tighter, strained harder. Pulling himself up hand over hand, he fought for a toehold in the crumbling earth. Death was something he would not even consider in this instance, for death meant failure. He always did everything in his power to avoid failure.

An hour ago, as he was hiking a barely discernible jungle trail no wider than his shoulders, a cloud of heavy gray mist had taken him by surprise. Fog settled in, camouflaging the landscape. Thick as rain, it rendered the trail dangerously slick.

Around midday he had stripped off his sweat-soaked shirt and shoved it into the top of his pack, and so when he fell, his skin was scraped by the rough stones embedded in the mountainside. Now his bare chest, scratched and bleeding, stung.

Sweat mingled with dampness from the fog trickled down his spine. His knee-high leather gaiters were covered with trail mud, their crossed laces caked with it. His khaki pants were filthy and torn, the toes of his leather shoes scratched from kicking the mountainside.

In the heavy mist, looming palms and acacia trees around him became hulking dark shapes. Their leaves swayed with the rhythm of the trade wind. Green parrots dived and squawked, taunting him. Howler monkeys screamed with the shrill sound of demented laughter.

Again, Death whispered in his ear, *"Just let go."*

A coarse sound burst from Trevor's throat, one that might have sounded like a laugh, but was really a shout of defiance. It echoed against the face of the mountain and carried to the treetops.

Failure was not an option. The jungles of the world were already littered with the bones of hapless Englishmen who had lost their lives for their orchid-crazed patrons. Hunters had drowned, been lost or murdered, or fallen to their deaths—men who loved to gamble, men of adventure willing to die while searching for beautiful flowers in terrible places, to discover rare, exotic plants that would grace some wealthy aristocrat's home.

Sweat slipped into his eyes and made him blink. He tightened his grip. Hand over hand, Trevor heaved himself upward, using the rough, twisted root to bring him even with the raw, broken edge of the trail. Gritting his teeth, he swung side to side like a pendulum until he dared to let go and grab for a place to land.

He hit the edge and clung. Before he started to slip again, he quickly scooted his upper body along with his elbows and forearms, grunting with effort as he dragged himself along, kicking with his legs. Soon he propelled himself to a secure patch of smooth, level ground.

Not until he drew his legs up and crawled a few feet away from the precipice did he allow himself to breathe. His heartbeat was ragged and wild.

A pair of noisy red-beaked parrots swooped down for a closer look. Beneath him, the earth trembled again, but gently this time, as if settling into place.

His hands shook. He took off his sun helmet, wiped his brow with his forearm, replaced the headgear, and then adjusted the rifle strap. Unfastening the canteen at his waist, he took a long pull of water. As his breath settled into an even cadence, Trevor scanned the sky and tried to see the sun through the tangle of branches and leaves that canopied the trail.

There was no indication it might burn through the fog before nightfall. If he did not start walking again soon, darkness would catch him on the side of the mountain and he would be forced to either bed down there or crawl along the narrow path on hands and knees, feeling his way out.

Pushing himself to his feet, he ignored the swell of weakness in his legs. Resettling his rifle strap, he took note of the superficial scratches on his chest and arms. His right cheek stung. He touched it and his fingers came away smeared with blood.

Starting out again, he concentrated on the trail, searching for any sign of weakness in the earth. Around the bend, where the mountainside was less eroded, he came upon crude steps set into the downhill slope. Flat rocks had been buried in the earth to form stepping-stones. He experienced a surge of relief when hiking became easier.

Every few yards, he could make out an outline of a bootprint amid scattered prints of bare feet in the thick mud along the side of the trail. Trevor smiled with satisfaction. The shock of his close call slowly ebbed, soothed by the promise of success. Months of relentless work could finally yield the desired result. By nightfall, he could actually come face to face with Dustin Penn, the world's most elusive and most renowned orchid hunter.

For years Penn had been shipping notable quantities of rare and unusual finds to London from different ports in Africa, while somehow keeping his whereabouts a secret. Over the last twenty years, Penn's reputation as well as the mystery surrounding him had grown.

In the highly competitive business of orchid hunting, hiding the locations of one's finds was perfectly normal. An amateur orchidologist and part-time hunter himself, Trevor kept meticulous notes and maps that he shared with no one. But hiding from the world, as Penn had done, was not the norm.

Unconsciously, his hand smoothed the butt of his rifle as he wondered how Penn would react to discovery. Would the man resort to violence to keep his whereabouts secret? Had he become a deranged recluse? How would he react when surprised?

As for himself, Trevor hated surprises. He always took great pains to make certain his own life was well ordered, that he consistently stayed on schedule. Everything that he could control always went according to plan.

He had learned at his grandmother's knee that strict routine was necessary to success and that discipline kept one's life from falling into chaos. He was well prepared to face Penn and whatever challenges came with finding him. Hopefully, there would be no surprises.

Although he had never set foot on Matarenga before, Trevor had often trekked over similar ground. If he had learned one thing, it was that jungles were filthy, humid, primeval places where nothing was easy or predictable and a man was never entirely safe. Still, he never felt as fully alive as he did whenever he was on a hunt. Perhaps it was the challenge of the very unpredictability of the jungle that attracted him.

He often thought that if it were not for his responsibilities to Mandeville Imports, to his grandmother and his family name, he would choose to spend all his time hunting orchids in the far corners of the world.

Dusk had poured shadows between the trees by the time Trevor had reached the valley floor. The air was thick enough to drink, close and stagnant. Moss grew on the trees, as did many epiphytic vines and plants that eventually destroyed their hosts.

It was too dark to see the trail now, but the scent of wood smoke had begun to beckon him. He had slipped his shirt on and left it hanging open until he could clean his wounds. Beneath the cuts and bruises, his heart raced with excitement. He hacked away at the undergrowth with his machete until he could see firelight flickering through the trees.

Caution was of the utmost importance now, so he moved with stealth. As he edged closer to the light, he slipped his rifle off his shoulder. Primed and loaded, it would give him only one shot. Then, if attacked, he would be forced to fight hand to hand until the end.

He had never killed another human being before. He did not relish the prospect of doing so now, but he would fire in self-defense if he had to. After what had happened on the trail, he was determined Death would have to work very hard to claim him.

Shoving aside a thick vine that blocked his line of vision, Trevor recoiled when his fingers touched the cool, dry skin of a huge snake as thick as his biceps. Face to face with the reptile, he watched its tongue flicker and its eyes close down to slits. It seemed suspended in air as it hung inches from his face until, without a sound, it slithered down the trunk of the tree and away.

He crouched low and focused on the small, nearly circular clearing ahead of him. A low fire glowed in the center of the encampment. Two small tents had been pitched off to one side.

Three male natives hunkered by the fire while a few more worked together on the far edge of the fire's light. Trevor let go a soft sigh of satisfaction when one of the men moved to reveal a tall packing crate. Further stirring in the group gave him a clear view of three large barrels. Piles of dried moss and coconut husk, packing material for orchid shipments, were heaped on the ground at their feet.

Trevor's gaze shot around the camp. If not Penn, then someone else was hunting orchids here. Firelight shimmered on slick, green leaves knitted into a backdrop. To the right he heard rushing water. Trevor wiped sweat from his brow as he studied the shadowed jungle landscape, recalling the topography of the last few yards so that he could commit them to paper when he logged his notes.

Suddenly his eyes picked up flashes of white against the dark foliage. It was a moment before he realized that what he was seeing was not reflected firelight, but thousands of stark white orchid blossoms scattered like countless stars against the dark backdrop of jungle growth.

His breath left him in a rush.

Not only did he hunt and import orchids, but he had inherited his father's extensive collection. He knew the breathtaking beauty of one single bloom, but nothing he had ever seen before could compare to the sight of hundreds of orchid blossoms exploding across the hillside.

A deep, gravelly laugh diverted his attention. There was movement in the camp. One of the natives called to another, then all of them laughed, sharing some joke in their own language.

A white man, illuminated by the firelight, stepped out of one of the tents. Tall, broad-shouldered, with a full head of long white hair, he looked about the right age to be Penn—somewhere between forty-five and fifty. He wore no sun helmet. His shirt was linen, stained down the front; his pants, muddied khaki, were tucked into worn gaiters. His fist was wrapped around the neck of a whiskey bottle. Three gold earrings dangled from his earlobe to flash in the firelight's glow.

The orchid hunter was unarmed. He spoke to one of his men, then laughed boisterously again, secure in the false belief that they were alone.

Trevor reminded himself to be calm, clear, concise. He would show no threat. He straightened to full height. Every muscle protested. He slipped his rifle strap off, pointing the barrel down. He had traveled halfway round the world for this moment. He would introduce himself, then present his proposition to Penn.

He stepped out of the shadows into the shimmering ring of the campfire's glow and watched as the man across the fire froze stock still and stared back at him in shock.

"Are you Dustin Penn?" Trevor called out.

The native bearers around the fire jumped to their feet. Those near the packing crate swung around. In their own tongue, they murmured among themselves. Their dark eyes shifted to the man he assumed to be Dustin Penn, and then back to him. The Matarengi were tense, ready, awaiting Penn's orders.

Trevor knew he was already a dead man if Penn wanted him dead. He tightened his grip on the rifle.

"Who wants to know?" the orchid hunter shouted back.

Penn, if it was Penn, had not moved a muscle, although he appeared less guarded than his men. His voice was rough as the rocky mountainside, his bulk more muscle than fat. In sharp contrast to his shoulder-length white hair, his skin was bronze, sun-damaged, and leathered. His eyes were light blue and piercing.

"I'm Trevor Mandeville. I'm from London."

Everything seemed to be going according to plan until one of the bearers beside the crate shifted to his left. A young white woman stepped out from behind him into Trevor's line of vision and walked into the clearing.

"And I've come to—" Trevor's gaze touched upon the girl and he was arrested. He could not take his eyes off her. Somewhere in the back of his mind he heard the orchid hunter demanding answers, but for the life of him, he could do nothing but stare at the young woman across the campsite.

Medium height. Round blue eyes, clear as a mountain lake. Bracketed by deep dimples was an evenly drawn, pouting mouth, the lower lip slightly fuller than the upper. Her long hair was blond, thick, tangled, and untamed. Her clear skin had seen much sun, but she was not as darkly suntanned as her father. Her cheeks were radiant.

He was shocked when he realized that not only was she wearing shin-length trousers, but her shirt was tied below her full breasts, leaving nothing to the imagination. Her midriff was bare and trim, her navel exposed. She was not soft, but sleek and finely sculpted, her flesh golden tan.

"Who in the hell are you, sir?" The man was yelling at him now.

The girl quickly crossed the clearing and stood beside

the man. Up close, her features were even more remarkable. Hers was a face Trevor knew as well as his own.

Suddenly, he found his voice.

"*Janelle?*"

Chapter 3

A chill went through Joya as she stared at the white stranger who had materialized from between the trees without warning, like a *jimbwa*, a ghost. She knew that when the god Kibatante had stirred, shaking the mountain this afternoon, that something momentous was going to happen. Here, then, was proof.

The white man was young and very, very pleasing in appearance, with something hauntingly familiar about him, something in his serious dark eyes that made her think she had gazed into them before—and seen herself reflected there.

Impossible thought. Especially since she had never been beyond the protective reef surrounding Matarenga. Few white man had ever come here and definitely not one such as this. He was strong and tall. His hair was black as the night sky. His direct gaze warmed her to her bones. She would surely remember *this* man.

Had Kibatante answered her prayer? Had he sent this man to her?

"Janelle?"

He repeated the word he had said before, but louder this time as he watched her expectantly. Confused and curious, she smiled back, but did not move or respond. Without even looking over at her father, she could feel his simmering anger.

"Are you Dustin Penn, the orchid hunter?" the stranger asked her papa.

"I am. How in the hell did you find me? Who are you and what do you want?" The way her papa was rudely demanding answers, Joya hoped the white stranger did not end up dead.

"Who is *she*?" The stranger pointed at her. "Where did she come from?"

The stranger's voice was stronger, surer now, as if his initial shock had faded.

She started to reply, but her father cut her off when he said, "That's none of your damn business! For the last time, who in the hell are you?"

Her papa shoved the half-full whiskey bottle at one of the Matarengi and stepped around the fire, bearing down on the stranger. Joya quickly followed, reaching up and clutching the small amulet bag in her hand.

"I'm Trevor Mandeville. I've come all the way from London with a proposition for you." As he spoke to her father, the stranger barely took his eyes off of her.

Then the man appealed directly to her, "Please, tell me your name."

Was he foolhardy or oblivious of her father's anger?

"I am Joya . . . Joya Penn." She was tempted to reach out and touch his face just to see if he was real. Dried blood smeared his cheek, a dark crimson crescent upon golden skin. She tried to look away, tried to break the hold of the man's intense stare, but she failed.

"She's my daughter." Not until her father grabbed the white hunter by the shirt collar and forcibly turned the man around did the stranger's eyes leave her.

"Your daughter?" The man sounded baffled.

Joya gently touched her father's arm. "Papa, he's bleeding. He needs help."

The man's shirt hung open, revealing raw cuts and scrapes all down his muscular chest and abdomen. His face and arms were streaked with blood and dirt and sweat.

She calmly appealed to her father again. "Papa, please."

Penn walked him to a low, flat rock. "Sit down."

Glancing around, the man's gaze touched each of the Matarengi in turn. The natives remained solemn, silently watching the exchange. Joya turned to the bearers and spoke in Matarengi, sending some to continue packing the crates and barrels and others to finish preparing the evening meal.

Her father stood beside Trevor Mandeville with his fists planted on his hips. His blue eyes burned with fury. Mandeville slipped his rifle strap and pack off and set them aside. Then he slowly lowered himself to the rock as if his entire body pained him. He glanced at Joya again before he turned back to her father.

Trevor Mandeville.

She committed his name to memory, let her mind tumble it over and around like a child playing with a pretty seashell.

Her father turned to the Matarengi holding the whiskey bottle and snapped his fingers. The bearer handed it to her father, who passed it on to Mandeville.

She saw the Englishman's hand shake slightly as he

lifted the bottle to his lips and took a long swill. He wiped his mouth and then handed the whiskey back to her father.

"I'm sorry. Seeing your daughter has given me quite a shock."

"Why?" Joya stepped closer, heart pounding.

Her father ignored her. "What are you doing here, Mandeville?"

"I am an orchid hunter—"

Her papa snorted. "How did you find me?"

"It took me almost two years. I own Mandeville Imports, of London. We've an auction house, too." He glanced at Joya, frowned. "I've come to make you a business offer, Mr. Penn."

Her father threw back his head and laughed.

"*You* would like to make *me* an offer? Look around, Mr. Mandeville." He swept his arm in a grand sweeping gesture. "You are on *my* island. At *my* mercy. And you think you can offer me anything I need or even want? My only desire is to see you walk out of here."

Joya frowned. She had never seen her father as angry before. He had often been stubborn, but never, ever had she seen him behave this way, in such a rage.

"Papa, he is wounded. He needs our help."

Almost as if he had forgotten she was there, her father suddenly turned to her. It was then that she noticed that there was something lurking in his eyes besides anger. Something she had never seen in them before.

What could her father possibly have to fear from this man?

"Go and see to the men, Joya. Get those last plants packed. We'll head back at first light." He issued the order in Matarengi and quickly dismissed her. Joya did not move, for Mandeville was speaking again.

"Mr. Penn, what I've come to say can wait. Right now, I want to know more about the girl."

"*My daughter* is none of your concern. Forget about her."

"I am afraid that is impossible."

Joya felt her skin tingle. Why was it *impossible* for this man to ignore her? Why did he stare so intently?

"Why do you ask about me?" She had to know.

"Because, Miss Penn," Mandeville said, "you are the image of my sister, Janelle, right down to the dimples in your cheeks."

Joya shivered. A chill fluttered through her again, one that even the moist, close heat of the jungle could not dispel.

"You have a sister in London who looks exactly like me?" She wanted desperately to believe him.

The hunter shifted uncomfortably on the rock. "Actually, she's not in London at the moment. I left her across the channel, on Zanzibar."

"Joya, there is still much work to be done tonight," her father interrupted, reminding her gruffly. "See that it gets finished, girl."

Her entire world had suddenly shifted and her papa was denying her a chance to talk to Trevor Mandeville and learn more.

"But, Papa, you heard him. If there is a girl who looks exactly like me, then don't you think that we should—"

"I'm certain that if he had the two of you side by side, Mr. Mandeville would find that he is mistaken."

"I'd stake my life on them being identical," Mandeville assured them.

"Don't tempt me to take the bet," her father mumbled. "Leave us *alone*, girl. See that the men finish."

"But, Papa . . ."

"Go!"

She stared into Trevor Mandeville's dark eyes and tried to plumb the depths of his soul for answers. She found nothing but more questions. Joya walked slowly across the encampment, feeling his intent gaze. She had to find a way to ask him more about the girl from London, a girl exactly like her who was as close as the island of Zanzibar.

The bearers already had three barrels filled and the crate half finished. Umbaba stepped closer. The yellow, orange, and deep blue glass beads woven into the wide collar that draped his shoulders shimmered in the firelight.

"Who is he?" Umbaba indicated Mandeville with a nod.

"A man from London, England. The place on the other side of the sea where Papa sends his orchids." She spoke softly in Matarengi.

"What does he want?"

"I don't know. Something about business."

"Why does he upset you?"

She looked up, felt his concern. "He says his sister looks exactly like me."

"Then he is a fool. The sun has baked his mind."

How could she explain something to Umbaba that she could not fathom herself? That she had seen strange things in dreams that she had never told him about?

Joya shook her head. "How much of a fool can he be? He found my father when no other English man ever could, didn't he?"

"And made your father as angry as the volcano."

"My father is more than angry. What I wonder is why? Why should this stranger upset him so? My father is many, many times more than angry." She watched the two men as they spoke to one another. Her father gestured toward the dark mountain trail. Mandeville shook his head no.

Studying Trevor Mandeville at a distance, she had the same odd sensation she had experienced when she first laid eyes on him, almost as if she had seen him somewhere before . . . and yet . . .

She closed her eyes.

"Are you all right?" Umbaba lightly touched her shoulder, then quickly withdrew his hand.

Joya opened her eyes and shivered again. Across the campsite, her father and Mandeville had not moved. They were still talking in low, unintelligible tones.

She thought she knew where it was she had seen this white stranger, but only Otakgi, the Matarengi shaman, would believe her. Trevor Mandeville had appeared in one of her dreams.

Trevor, still reeling with shock, looked at Penn. "I beg of you, tell me about your daughter."

"She is no concern of yours."

"I am afraid you are wrong. Unless I've lost my mind, she's my sister's twin." Trevor could see the man's control was about to snap. Penn closed his fists, shifted his stance and refused to say more.

"Why aren't you arguing that it's impossible?" Trevor wanted to know.

Penn looked away. "Joya is my daughter."

"Who is her mother?"

"My wife, Clara, was her mother, but Clara's dead now, God rest her soul. Joya is no kin to you."

"But technically, neither is my sister. She was adopted as an infant."

"I don't give a good Goddamn who your sister is or where she's from!"

"Why not? If I were in your position, I would at least be curious." *Unless*, Trevor thought, *I had something to hide*.

He watched Dustin Penn fight to calm down. The man took another swig of whiskey. His eyes were hard and cold when he finally offered, "Have some food. It's too dark to go back up the trail. You'll have to stay the night. Tomorrow at dawn, you'll hike out of here with the rest of us. Once we reach the village, I'll have you hauled off the island by force, if I have to."

"You haven't even heard my proposition yet."

"Nor do I want to. I want you off my island. My men will take you to the mainland by sailing canoe."

"*Your* island? *Your* men?"

"The Matarengi high chief, Faruki, and I have had a fine business agreement of our own going on for years. That's why I'm not interested in anything you have to offer, Mandeville."

Trevor tried to sort things out in his mind as he watched Dustin Penn walk away. He needed to carefully assimilate what had just happened in the same way that he always identified and catalogued his orchid finds by genus and species.

He had not only tracked down Dustin Penn, but more to his amazement, he had come face to face with a young woman who was nearly identical to his sister Janelle in every physical way: the same height, weight, coloring and features. But a *twin*? *How?* Being a logical man who was never given to flights of fancy, he knew there had to be some rational explanation.

One of Penn's bearers brought him food: baked bananas, meat, rice, all piled on the thick end of a banana leaf. He ate with his hands, ignoring the dirt under his nails and the mud caked in the lines and creases of his knuckles as he shoveled food into his mouth.

With his arms resting on his knees, he hung over the makeshift plate and unabashedly watched Joya Penn as she supervised six Matarengi natives packing orchids. Each man was well over six feet and although they towered over her, she moved among them with familiarity and ease, speaking in Matarengi.

Joya Penn, *not* Janelle, he reminded himself.

The girl moved with natural seductive ease in a way that Janelle, raised under strict English social mores, would not dare. His sister liked to believe she was a Bohemian, but he doubted Janelle would even walk around alone inside her room in the limited amount of clothing that Joya Penn was perfectly comfortable wearing.

Janelle was headstrong and independent. She considered herself a free thinker. He had never seen her display an ounce of flirtatiousness and most certainly none of the exotic sensuousness that Joya Penn exhibited. The island girl possessed an alluring, natural grace.

As he watched her lift a heavy machete, he noted there was not a spare ounce of flesh on her. The blade flashed in the firelight as she swung it across a low hanging branch. Though there was nothing soft about her body, she was still curvaceous and surprisingly feminine. Uncomfortably alluring. The fact that he even found her attractive when she looked so like Janelle made him very, very uncomfortable with his physical response to her.

He licked his fingertips and took another bite.

Usually not one to give in to emotion that would cloud his thoughts or temper his plans, Trevor forced himself to look away from the girl and ponder the mystery rationally.

Janelle had just turned twenty. He needed to learn Joya's birth date and age. She had seemed more than willing to talk to him earlier.

As he thought back to her reaction when he had first told her that his sister looked exactly like her, he recalled she had appeared shocked, but not incredulous. *Why not?* He wondered.

Tossing the empty banana leaf far into the underbrush, Trevor wiped his hands on his pants and stood up. Because of his fall, every part of him ached. He reached for his shoulder and rotated the joint. Then he rolled his head on his neck, trying to ease his strained muscles.

He looked around. No one was staring at him, but he knew by the surreptitious looks he was getting from the natives that Penn had ordered him watched. The orchid hunter was nowhere to be seen, so Trevor surmised Penn had retired to his tent for the night.

Would he be risking his neck if he tried to approach Joya later?

His pack seemed three times heavier than it was as he carried it to the far edge of the clearing, opened it, and took out his hammock. He was as comfortable in it as in his bed at Mandeville House. After hanging the hammock, he rummaged around in the pack for a small washcloth.

"Do you need help?"

He spun around at the sound of Joya's voice. Unlike his sister's, it had a low, seductive timbre, and a slight trace of inflection that came from the Matarengi language.

"I was going to wash these cuts," he told her.

She took the washcloth from him, walked over to a

basket-covered gourd and brought the water vessel back in her arms. He found it arousing to watch her walk in trousers. They fit her snugly, defined her hips and strong legs and derrière, and left little to the imagination.

He quickly turned around, made certain his hammock was secure, and tried to convince himself he was no pervert. After all, she was *not* Janelle.

But who the hell *was* she?

He jumped with surprise when she placed a hand on his forearm. He turned and watched her dip the cloth in tepid water, then set the flat-bottomed gourd on the ground. Without hesitation, she reached for his shirt, eased the front open, and gently touched the cloth to his wounds.

He caught his breath at both the stinging sensation of the cool, wet muslin against his skin and her forwardness. No proper young woman in England would ever think of gazing upon a man's naked chest, let alone touch him so intimately. He reminded himself that she was no sheltered English miss, but a hybrid, a combination of both worlds.

She was standing so close to him that he could feel the warmth of her breath against her collarbone. She was watching him intently, almost if judging him and weighing his character.

"You can trust me," he said, going on instinct.

"You are not lying? About this other girl?"

He shook his head no, glancing across the camp. The natives were watching them.

"No, I'm not lying. Why should I?"

"Somehow, I have always known that something, perhaps someone, was missing from my life." She spoke quickly, as if she expected her father to come charging after her at any moment. "My mama and papa never understood my strange dreams, my feeling of . . . loss. This is the only home I've ever known, and yet sometimes I feel as if part of me is wandering in the world somewhere. Do you think I am mad?"

"I'm beginning to think myself mad."

She was quiet for a moment, lost in thought as she wiped his wounds, dipped the rag in water, and wrung it out. Her eyes were shadowed with questions and a wistful sadness.

"Many times I asked my parents to take me to England. I could never understand why they refused. I think that there is something they were hiding from me, something Papa continues to hide. Where does your sister live when she is in England?"

"In London."

"What is London like?"

"Imagine this entire island covered with people standing shoulder to shoulder. London is probably larger than Matarenga."

She frowned. "I have seen pictures in books."

He felt as if there was much more she was not saying. Fearful of frightening her away, he did not press her.

"What is you sister like?" she asked.

"She looks like you, but she is very different."

"English."

"Yes," he said. "English. Very smart. Very stubborn."

"Like Papa." She sighed.

"She has always been very serious. Very much her own woman."

"Please. Take your shirt off."

"What?"

"I cannot reach the scratches on your shoulders."

After a moment's pause, Trevor stripped off his shirt and sat on the ground. She worked quickly, efficiently, without any sign of embarrassment. He glanced over at the Matarengi men. A bare back was nothing new to her. There was probably not a single part of the male anatomy that she had not seen.

"All done." She handed him the rag.

Trevor stood up and smiled. She was looking into his face with something akin to awe. Then one of the Matarengi swiftly moved up behind her and spoke to her in his native tongue.

"What did he say?" Trevor asked.

"One of the men has gone to get my father. I must go."

"But—"

"My father is madder than a monkey with his hand stuck in a coconut. He will not listen to reason tonight."

She pushed her wild blond hair back off her face with both hands and tried to dismiss the strongly built, striking native with a smile, but he would not leave her side.

"Your father has ordered me off the island, but before I go I must speak to him about you, and present the business offer I came all this way to make."

He hoped that when the shock of discovery had worn off and Dustin Penn's anger had cooled, there would be an opportunity for discussion.

"I'll try to talk to him." Joya seemed hesitant to leave, but finally she turned to walk away.

Unfortunately, she had lingered a moment too long. Dustin Penn came steaming toward them, his long hair untied, flaring out around his head as if he had been running his hands through it. His face was florid with drink. Or anger. Probably both, Trevor decided.

"I told you to stay away from her!" Penn shouted.

Dustin Penn moved with surprising speed and agility.

Trevor braced for attack, when suddenly Joya stepped between them.

"Papa, stop it. Mr. Mandeville is hurt. I only wanted to help him. That is what Mama would have had me do. Surely there is nothing wrong in that? Umbaba has not left my side."

At the sound of his name, the young Matarengi man stepped up beside Joya. Penn glowered at each of them in turn and then pinned Trevor with a cold, hard stare.

"Stay away from her, Mandeville," Penn warned. He said something to the Matarengi, Umbaba, before he turned to Trevor again.

"If you talk to her again tonight, this man will kill you."

Exhausted, Trevor had climbed into his hammock and fell asleep, half-expecting to awaken and find himself on the breakfast menu, but the night passed without incident.

At dawn, light filtered through the treetops. Mist sifted through wide shafts of golden sunlight, evaporating before it reached the valley floor. There was no sign of Penn or his daughter in the camp.

Trevor rolled up his hammock, again thankfully ate what the Matarengi offered, and then crossed the clearing to get a better view of the slope covered with white orchids. The view of the overwhelming array of cattleyas with huge stems of blossoms was spectacular. By the light of day he could see that the flowers flourished in a rainbow of hues and were not only white, as he had assumed last night.

Trevor paused to touch the frilly edge of a waxy dark green flower, amazed to see that some of the plants had grown to three feet in height.

He drew back when the sound of Joya and Dustin Penn's voices filtered through the trees. The girl and her father remained out of his line of vision as they descended a nearby hillside path and paused somewhere on the trail. Although he could not see them, he could hear them quite clearly.

"If Mama were alive she would agree with me," Joya said.

"For the first time in three years I'm thankful she is not here."

"Papa! How can you say that?"

"Because it is true. This would upset her no end."

"You're being unreasonable. You should at least listen to the man. Hear him out."

"He's mad, raving on and on about some girl who looks like you. Why should I believe anything he says after hearing such mad talk?"

"Why would he lie?"

"You believe him because you *want* to believe that nonsense. All of those bloody notions of yours . . ."

As they drew near, Trevor hurried back toward the center of the camp. The bearers had everything ready; the heavy crate and the barrels were already tied to stout poles that they would carry on their shoulders. The tents had been struck, the camp equipment and staples packed.

Trevor buttoned the front of his shirt and gingerly shouldered his pack and rifle, careful not to scrape the straps over his wounds. Until he could persuade Penn to hear him out, he would bide his time, keep his mouth shut, and try not to further infuriate the man. He would rely on Joya Penn to argue his case and hope she succeeded.

He did not want to leave Matarenga without some answers about Joya or a contract agreement. He regretted more than anything that his revelation about Janelle had upset the other girl, but he was certain that there was a definite link between Joya and his sister.

He would not give up. Not when the truth was waiting to be told.

Chapter 4

Joya took her place in the line of bearers not far behind
Trevor Mandeville. From there she could study him as
the party snaked its way along the trail that wound its
way up from the valley floor. She was tired, suffering
from lack of sleep and the riot of emotions still warring
inside.

For so long had she been at odds with her father and
with her feelings that it had been a relief when Trevor
Mandeville made his surprise appearance and then his
startling revelation. Even though the truth still eluded
her, it glimmered in her future, flirting with them all.

Umbaba walked behind her, a constant shadow and
protector. Her best friend. Countless times they had
laughed and swam together, fished in the lagoon, shared
meals with his family in their *fadu* and in her home.

She had grown up with many close Matarengi friends,
but then, when they all began to mature, everything suddenly changed. One by one, her childhood companions
were taken to the initiation hut—the girls, as soon as

they began to bleed in rhythm with the moon; the boys, when their voices hummed with the timbre of a man.

When signs of her own womanhood had come upon her, when she proudly announced to her mother that she was ready for initiation, her mother, Clara, forbade her going to the Matarengi women to prepare for the ceremony. She told Joya that it was time to give up her childish ways, to cover her budding breasts. She would not be allowed to run wild with Umbaba or the other Matarengi boys and girls anymore.

The ceremonies, her mother said, were not for her. Joya had become upset, and had asked why she was not told this before. Clara only sighed and said wistfully, "You have grown up so fast. The years slipped by so quickly."

Joya could still recall lying awake that night, despondent, confused, listening to her parents as they argued in hushed, rough whispers. She heard her mother tell her father that she had warned him this day was coming.

"I fear we've let her run with the Matarengi far too long already. She is almost more native than English," Mama whispered.

"I don't need civilization. You've been content with our life here." Papa's voice was a deep, raspy hush.

"But it was our choice to leave England. Joya had no choice. What sort of future will she have if we keep her here? If not to England, perhaps we could send her to one of the colonies. Or would you condemn her to a lifetime alone?"

"She has everything she needs."

"For now." Her mother had lowered her voice so much that Joya had been forced to press her ear against the bamboo wall. ". . . a woman . . . needs . . . fear that she will grow too close to one of the young men . . . the unthinkable."

"Spoken . . . the high chief . . . already made certain . . ." The sound of her father's words had drifted away. Then, louder, he begged, "Please, Clara. Not yet. Wait a year. I could not bear to lose either of you. I can't let my girl go yet."

They sounded so scared that she became afraid for them, and for herself. Time passed, as time does, and after her mother died of fever and the weeks slipped into years, there were long periods when she forgot exactly what she had heard that night.

She and her father both missed her mother sorely. In unspoken agreement, together they threw themselves into the hunt for more orchids. Dustin Penn was much revered on Matarenga, not only for his wisdom but for the shipments of supplies and goods he provided the Matarengi: tools, tea, and all the other items they could not produce. Even Faruki, the high chief, deferred to him.

Over time, Joya had finally convinced herself that she had misunderstood the fearful tone of her parents' argument that night long ago. What could ever touch them here?

Then, last night in the camp, when she had seen the fear in her papa's eyes, all of it had come back to her. What in the world was he so afraid of?

The party stopped beside a stream rushing down from the mountaintop. As the men drank from water gourds, Joya watched Trevor Mandeville refill his canteen.

She did not know what to expect of a proper Englishman. The only white men she had ever seen had been among a group of German missionaries or the occasional trader or boat captain who came to pick up one of the orchid shipments. None of them had ever been bold enough to stand up to her father, even if they had wanted to stay. She could still see the shock on the German preacher's face when her papa had told him to take his religion and get off Matarenga. He said that the natives had plenty of gods of their own. They did not need to import any more.

Near the stream, Mandeville stood with one foot on a rock, the other firmly on the trail. He put the lip of the canteen to his mouth, tipped his head back, and took a long drink. She watched his throat work as a drop of sweat trickled down the corded muscles in his neck.

When he lowered the canteen, he caught her watching him. She smiled. He did not. With his dark eyes shaded by his sun helmet, she could not read what was in them. She longed to talk to him alone again, to be near him and listen to his finely accented speech, to look deep into his eyes.

The head man shouted orders to the others. Her father, at the front of the line, was already on his way again. She had never known him to set such a breakneck pace.

Trevor waited until Dustin Penn disappeared around a bend in the trail before he stopped and shifted his pack. Motioning the bearers around him, he lingered until Joya caught up to him and then fell into step directly behind her.

The trail was too narrow to walk side by side, so he contented himself with watching the way she held her shoulders, the way her hips swayed. He tore his gaze away and looked around, studying the trail. If his recollections were correct, they were almost to the top of the grade where he had nearly lost his life.

He raised his voice over the sound of the trade winds. "Warn them the trail is out just before that next turn. That is the place where I fell."

She called out to the Matarengi in front of her. Word quickly passed through the line and the party halted. The men put down their burdens. Some squatted in the middle of the trail; others stared out toward the horizon where the sea disappeared into sky.

Waves broke at the edge of the coral reef that surrounded the volcanic island. Between the open water and the beach, a clear turquoise lagoon sparkled in the bright sunlight. There was no sign of a sizable Matarengi village hidden by the palms and other trees growing along the shoreline. The only indication a settlement was there at all were wisps of smoke rising from cook fires.

Trevor took off his helmet, wiped his brow with his shirtsleeve, and took comfort from the slight breeze. His hair was matted, his scalp sweaty. He was in need of a shave, a long soak, and an opportunity to convince Dustin Penn that the man needed Mandeville Imports as much as it needed him.

As Trevor put his hat on again, Dustin Penn called his name. The bearers stepped back, forced to lean into the hillside to let him pass. He worked his way to the head of the line, to find Penn staring at the spot where the mountain trail had given way beneath him.

The jacaranda root that had saved him still protruded from the earth like a scarred and jagged bone. Trevor's stomach lurched when he looked down into the valley.

Penn stood with his back to him and shook his head. "How in the hell did you make it?"

"I refused to die before I presented you with my offer."

Penn made no comment. Trevor took the silence as an opening.

"If I agree not to mention my sister's likeness to your daughter again, will you listen to my business proposal?"

Penn's face grew florid. He squinted against the sun but at least he did not erupt.

"You really don't give up, do you, Mandeville?"

"No, sir. Not if I can help it. It's a family trait."

Dustin Penn looked at him with something akin to grudging admiration. "If you leave my girl out of it, I'll hear you out when we get home. But I won't make any promises."

Trevor thanked him but made no promises either.

The broken trail gaped like a yawning pit. Penn stared down into the abyss, then up the mountainside.

"We'll have to wait while the men cut a new trail." He called over his shoulder, "Umbaba!"

The young man who had protectively stood by Joya last night separated himself from the other Matarengi and joined them. Penn quickly explained what he wanted done and Umbaba started gathering a crew.

"Don't they speak English?" Trevor asked.

Penn seemed to have set aside his anger for the moment. "No. I thought it a waste of time to teach them English when they have a perfectly good language of their own."

Trevor wondered if the man kept the Matarengi as isolated as he had his daughter in order to keep his own whereabouts a secret.

"You don't have to like me, Mandeville. I could not care less." Penn was watching him closely.

"No, I don't," Trevor agreed. "But I need your expertise and I think you'll like the money you stand to make when you agree to my offer."

Men were shouting directions to each other from the hillside, sweating profusely as they cut a new section of the trail into the side of the mountain.

Trevor looked back and saw Joya sitting alone on the edge of the old trail with her legs dangling over the side of the precipice. The sun beat down upon her golden hair and turned her cheeks an even brighter shade.

He tried to imagine Janelle sitting on the edge of the narrow mountain trail, casually swinging her bare legs over a thousand-foot drop as she feasted on dried fruit and coconut.

He had always admired his sister for her intelligence, her stubborn grit and intuitiveness, but hard as he might try, he could not imagine her ever adapting to Joya Penn's way of life. Janelle enjoyed her painting, her colorful and eccentric friends, and her discussion groups and salons far too much to give them up.

As if she felt his stare, Joya looked his way, lifting her hand in a discreet wave. After he nodded in acknowledgment, she turned her gaze to the open sea, shielded her eyes from the sun's glare, and looked over the lagoon toward the far horizon.

Toward the mainland of Africa. Toward the island of Zanzibar.

Chapter 5

Time is running out.

Trevor's impending departure was all Joya could think about on the way down Mount Kibatante. As the hunting party headed along the road to the beach, she found herself trying to memorize every detail of the Englishman's appearance and dress, his haunting dark eyes, the way the sunlight glistened in his black hair, the way he moved.

She continually found herself drawn to him in an inexplicable way, and not only that, but whenever she looked at him, she felt a curious need unraveling inside her. The thought of telling him good-bye so soon filled her with mounting panic.

They came to a fork in the road where the Matarengi village lay off to the right. She could see it in the distance, a gathering of *fadu* that blended into the trees bordering the beach. Monkeys chattered high above them, announcing their return. A dog barked. Naked children chased loose hens and roosters as they darted between the huts. A few older boys and girls ran along the beach, carefree, laughing, teasing the water where it lapped against the shore.

An old fisherman walked along with a bundle of fishnet slung over his shoulder. Here and there, a few Matarengi women moved about, ducking in and out of low doorways. Some carried infants in colorful, woven cloth slings as they engaged in what Joya suspected was the same women's work all over the world: weaving mats, preparing food, collecting water, and tending small garden plots behind the *fadu*.

Everything was so tranquil, so normal. Almost too quiet.

How much longer would Mandeville be allowed to stay? Would her father hear him out or would the next few minutes be his last on the island? If she asked him to do so, would he consider taking her to London? Would she ever see this sister of his if he refused?

The bearers followed her father to the left, toward the main house with long greenhouse sheds beside it. As they all walked beneath the trees, dappled shade sparing them the heat of the blazing sun, she was very aware of Trevor walking ahead of her.

He was constantly watching her as if there were nothing else of interest on the island. Her cheeks burned whenever she caught him staring, but she could not look away. If only she knew what he was thinking, or what to say to a man so foreign in every way—and yet a man who seemed so familiar.

When she saw her house through the trees, she tried to set aside her anxiety, but for some reason, today she did not enjoy the comforting sight of home. Instead, as she looked at the house, she felt an intense surge of emotion that she could not name.

Thick stemmed frangipani trees lined the stone path, abundant with creamy white blooms; their sweet, cloying scent perfumed the air. Doum and coconut palms grew around a once-semiformal garden, gone wild without her mother to tame it. Usually parrots were shrieking in the trees, but today they were silent.

Concentrating on the house, she didn't notice that Trevor had fallen back a few paces until he was suddenly walking beside her. Her stomach was making a habit of fluttering wildly whenever he smiled down at her. A huge, iridescent dragonfly hovered in the air between them for a second and then flitted on.

"It appears there's a welcoming party to meet us," he said.

With no little regret, she looked away. A gathering of Matarengi waited in the side garden. When she noticed they were surrounding the porch, her anxiety mounted.

Just then, a youth of twelve spotted her father and the lead bearers. A cry went up as he came running along the path. Drums started beating. The boy stopped before her father and began to speak excitedly, loud enough for Joya to hear. He gestured toward the house, pointing as he spoke, his words punctuated with fear.

Her father listened, staring at the crowd. Slowly, his face drained of color. The lines etched on his suntanned skin seemed to deepen, almost as if he were aging before her eyes.

Joya's heart pounded as hard as storm waves upon the reef. She grabbed Trevor's hand and whispered, "She's here!"

"*Who's* here?"

"Your sister. It must be her. The boy just told my father that a *jimbwa*, a spirit, *my* spirit, stepped out of a canoe a while ago, even though everyone saw me go up the mountain. They were afraid when I suddenly appeared on the beach without my father. She is waiting on the porch." She shivered as a chill ran down her spine. "Everyone knows, only a spirit can be two places at once."

Her heart was still matching the rhythm of the drum. Joya looked at the house again and knew where her unsettled feelings had come from, just as she knew that from this day forward, her life would never be the same.

Surely she has misunderstood, Trevor thought.

He had left Janelle safely ensconced in their lodgings on Zanzibar where, she had assured him, she would await him, content to finish her latest painting. He should have suspected his sister was planning something. Now that he thought about it, she had acquiesced far too easily.

He watched as Dustin Penn spoke to the Matarengi boy. Penn was staring at his home as if loath to take another step.

Beside Trevor, Joya did not move a muscle. She, too, was staring at the house. Trevor's gaze swept the yard, taking in the natives gathered there—a few women, some children, but mostly silent, solemn-faced men holding shields made of sea turtle shells and long spears. As the drumbeat intensified, the air became charged with anticipation.

An unsettling feeling came over him. He scanned the shadows of the veranda. A woman stood so far beneath the wide overhang of the porch that her features were cast in shadow, but he recognized the embroidered fabric of her full skirt and the way Janelle sometimes planted her hands on her hips. He could not tell whether his sister had seen the hunting party yet, but from where he stood, she appeared to be watching the Matarengi in the garden.

Dustin Penn started down the path, his heavy boots pounding along the volcanic stone walkway. Trevor took off after him at a trot. He doubted Janelle would back down, even if confronted by Penn.

The drums suddenly stopped.

Trevor shouldered the natives aside as he and Penn reached the garden at virtually the same time. It was not until then that Trevor realized Joya had not kept pace. He glanced over his shoulder and saw her standing alone at the far end of the garden walk, framed between the profusely blooming frangipani.

Then Janelle called out to him from the veranda.

"Trevor! Thank God. I was beginning to think I was never going to see you again."

Beside him, Dustin Penn had gone still and white as a corpse.

"What in God's name were you thinking?" Trevor kept his voice down and his temper under control as he cleared two low steps to stand beside Janelle. "How did you get here?"

"The same way you did. I hired a sailing canoe and I have to say, I have never seen a more motley-looking captain or crew." She waved her hand toward the crowd. "Trevor, these people have been staring at me since I arrived. It's quite disconcerting."

She frowned as she pushed the wire frame of her spectacles up the bridge of her nose.

He grabbed her by the shoulders and gave her a cursory once-over. She looked fit, although her cheeks were stained with high color and her face a bit paler than usual. She blinked her wide, blue eyes, which always appeared owlish behind her thick spectacles.

"Are you all right?" he demanded.

"Of course, but this has been a little unnerving. The natives don't seem to want to get near me, although they haven't left me alone. If I take a step forward, they all step back." She paused to demonstrate for him. "It's very curious, really. I tried speaking a few words of the dialects that we have learned, but they don't seem to understand me at all."

"They think you are a ghost, a *jimbwa*."

"Why?"

"It's a long story. Where is your maid?"

"I was sick of Betty crying with homesickness day and night and when she refused to come with me, I thought to myself, what's the use of torturing her any longer? There was a ship departing for England and so I bought her a ticket and put her aboard." She shrugged as if it were that simple. "And here I am. Did you find Dustin Penn?"

He could not believe he had ever wasted a moment worrying about how his sister might fare if left alone.

"And a bit more, I'm afraid."

Before he could tell her about Joya, Dustin Penn walked up to them and stared at Janelle, his expression deeply grave.

Janelle smiled at Penn and held out her hand without waiting for Trevor to introduce them.

"You must be the famous orchid hunter my brother has spent the better part of two years talking about. I'm Janelle Mandeville."

When Dustin Penn did not even acknowledge her introduction, Janelle turned to Trevor. He was still furious at his sister for putting her safety at risk, but in a way, he was also relieved that she was here. Seeing her removed all doubt about Joya's likeness to her.

Instant concern for his sister came over him when he suddenly realized that he had no idea how she would react to seeing Joya. Or how Joya would react to her.

How would he feel, were he to suddenly come face to face with a man who was *his* double in almost every way?

He took his sister's hand, giving it a squeeze before he looked out over the garden, searching for Joya again. He spotted her nearly hidden in the midst of the bearers. Like the others, she was staring at Janelle in silent wonder, but tears glistened on her cheeks.

Beside him, Dustin Penn turned. Trevor realized that he, too, was searching the crowd for Joya.

"Trevor?" Janelle whispered. "What's wrong?"

Trevor turned to his sister, squeezing her hand again. Staring down into her upturned face, he felt none of the attraction he had for Joya. Although Janelle's features were the same, although he cared for her because he thought of her as a sister, Joya emanated a radiance, a sense of being and an essence that moved him in a far different way.

"I have someone to introduce you to. I have no explanation as to who she really is or how she came to be here. I don't even know how to tell you about her."

"You are scaring me." Janelle glanced at the crowd.

Trevor followed her gaze. His sister was watching a well-fed man wearing an ornately woven headdress adorned with orange sunbird feathers as he stepped out of the crowd. The man's regal bearing gave away his status as chief of the tribe. He carried a polished turtle shield and tall spear.

A murmur went through the crowd as the man walked past Janelle. He did not take his eyes off her as he went directly to Dustin Penn and said something in Matarengi, but the orchid hunter did not look up.

As Trevor led Janelle down the steps, the crowd parted. The Matarengi spoke among themselves, falling back as they passed by. Joya was now standing at the edge of the crowd. She was no longer crying, but staring intently, motionless. His sister, who was studying each of the Matarengi in turn, had not yet noticed her likeness among the others.

Trevor suddenly wished he could take Janelle home and leave whatever secrets were buried here on Matarenga alone, but it was too late now.

Too late for all of them.

Joya could not swallow the lump in her throat. She had been trembling ever since she had been close enough to the veranda to see Janelle Mandeville clearly.

Everything Trevor had said about his sister was true, but there was so much he had not told her. In feature and form, Janelle Mandeville was exactly like her, but Joya marveled most at her skin, for it was as creamy white as a delicate frangipani blossom and appeared to be just as soft and fragile.

Joya ran her dirty hands over the rough material of her trousers as she took in every detail of Janelle's clothing, the intricate design sewn into the deep violet fabric, the touch of lace at her collar and cuffs. Small, golden earbobs dangled from her ears. Ribbons that matched her gown held perfectly wound curls beside her face, where they bounced prettily. Round, silver-framed spectacles perched upon the end of her nose.

Never had Joya dreamed what it would be like to see a real English lady come to life. Looking at Janelle was even more curious, for it was like seeing herself transformed.

Suddenly, Trevor's sister looked directly at her. Joya heard her gasp, saw her face drain of color. Janelle quickly turned to Trevor, but before he could say a word, she let go of his hand and walked away.

Joya held her breath. Janelle Mandeville did not stop until she stood directly in front of her, then reached out and touched Joya's cheek.

"How can this be?" Janelle whispered. *"How can this be?"*

She did not cry, but stared back intently, touching Joya's face and then her hair. She ran her hand down Joya's arm.

In an impulsive gesture, Joya threw her arms about Janelle's neck and cried, "You are my lost spirit, the likeness of myself I've seen only in dreams! I *knew* one day I would find you, but you have found me first."

She loosened her hold on Janelle and stepped back, anxious to hear what her likeness had to say.

Janelle Mandeville fainted dead away at her feet.

Chapter 6

Joya knelt beside Janelle, demanding that the Matarengi step back while she chafed the girl's wrist. Trevor hovered over his sister with a dark scowl on his face, as if it were Joya's fault that Janelle had fainted.

"Take her inside," Joya ordered.

He immediately scooped up Janelle as if she weighed next to nothing and started back toward the house.

Joya reached the veranda first. Her father was there, staring over the garden toward the open sea, his rugged face devoid of color. He looked like an old, old man.

Joya turned to Trevor and bade him take Janelle inside again.

Before she could talk to her father, Faruki, the Matarengi chieftain, was there demanding explanations. He wanted to know why, since his people had always been good to Dustin Penn, had the white hunter summoned a ghost into their midst? When her father did not answer, she tried to tell Faruki that Janelle was no *jimbwa*, but she had no idea how to appease the chief, for she had no explanation. If anyone knew the truth, it had to be her father.

"Papa, send these people home and come inside with me."

Her father shook himself out of his stupor and quickly tried to reassure the chief that the strange woman was no *jimbwa*, but flesh and blood.

Hadn't she just fainted? her father asked Faruki. What ghost fainted in the noonday sun? He told the man to take his people back to the village. Finally, grudgingly, Faruki left the porch and the others followed. Then her father turned around and walked inside.

When they crossed the threshold, the cool, comfortable room settled around her like a familiar, worn shirt. Her mother's touches were everywhere: in vases of bamboo where Joya still placed cut flowers, in the way the furnishings, all made of island woods and woven coverings, were arranged.

The shutters were open to the breeze off the sea. An ancient ylang-ylang tree grew just outside the window. Its heady perfume scented the air.

Trevor laid his sister on a low platform daybed built against the wall beneath a bank of windows. He fussed over her, smoothing out her full skirt, and then threw a worried glance Joya's way.

She had an odd twinge, envying their closeness. She looked to her father across the room. He was pouring himself a whiskey.

Joya crossed the room and felt a distinct sensation of familiarity as she knelt down beside Janelle and took her hand again.

"Has she stirred?" she asked Trevor.

"No." The word was clipped by his tension and worry. "She had no warning."

"I should have planned this better."

"You did not even know she was here."

"But I should have warned her the moment I saw her."

Joya let go of Janelle's hand. Her father was staring at them.

"Drink, Mandeville?"

At Trevor's nod, Joya felt safe enough to leave them alone and scooted quickly out of the room to get Janelle some water. When she came back a few minutes later, she was relieved to find Janelle somewhat dazed, but sitting up.

Joya paused on the threshold between the two rooms.

"I am all right," Janelle said to her with a weak smile. "Trevor can vouch for me when I say that I have never succumbed to the vapors before."

Joya had no idea what succumbing to vapors meant. She smiled anyway, just thankful that Janelle Mandeville had not died of fright.

"Here," she said, thrusting the water glass at Janelle. The liquid splashed over the rim. Joya watched the moisture splat and fan out into a dark stain on Janelle's skirt.

"Oh, no," Joya whispered.

Janelle graciously accepted the glass. "Please, don't worry about a little water. It will dry."

Janelle's gaze, filled with bewildered curiosity, swept her from the tip of her muddy toes to her tangled hair. When she stared at Joya's pants, a smile lifted the corner of her lips and a dimple exactly like Joya's own appeared in her cheek.

Janelle was so perfect, so clean and lovely, that Joya wanted to crawl beneath the woven floor covering.

The English girl took a long drink and then settled against the bank of pillows along the wall. "I can't stop staring at you," she said when she was comfortable.

"Nor I you," Joya admitted, relieved that the color had returned to Janelle's cheeks.

"It is incredible," Trevor added, looking back and forth between the two girls. "Unbelievable."

"Trevor told me that your name is Joya. It's a beautiful name," Janelle said softly.

"My mother always said I was her joy," Joya whispered.

Trevor downed the whiskey in his hand, then looked over at her father. "Mr. Penn, now that you have seen my sister, now that she and your daughter are side by side, you can't deny that I was right about their likeness. Janelle and Joya are nearly identical. I have every right to hear everything you can tell us that will shed light on this situation."

"*We* have a right to hear," Janelle added.

After all her years of strange dreams and doubts, Joya was suddenly afraid to hear what her father might say. An intense pain squeezed her heart when she realized that anyone else in his position would have been questioning Trevor and Janelle, hounding them for answers. Unless, of course, he already knew the answers.

Her father's eyes were suspiciously bright. Unable to stand, Joya sank down and sat cross-legged on the floor beside Janelle Mandeville's feet, careful not to let her dirty clothing touch the lovely fabric of the girl's gown.

Her father sighed, ran his hand through his hair. Then he cleared his throat, setting the whiskey glass down on a bamboo table beside his favorite chair.

Joya looked at Trevor, who was watching both her and Janelle intently. Long, silent seconds passed. Her gaze caught and held his. She could not tell what he was thinking behind his rich, dark eyes.

Joya jumped, startled when Janelle suddenly took her hand. She found the gesture comforting. When her father began to speak, his voice was low and husky. The deep timbre easily drifted to them on the Kusi trade wind.

"It began almost nineteen years ago on the night of a terrible storm in London. I was twenty-five then, about your age, Mandeville. I had been in London a week, having gone there on some unpleasant business.

"Professor Osmond Oates was a young botanist who had died while on expedition with me here in Africa. When I went back to England to break the terrible news of his death to Oates's widow, she was about to give birth to their first child. She hadn't been having an easy time of it anyway, and the shock of her husband's death proved to be too much for her. When she heard he was dead, she went to bed with grief and never recovered."

"My mother," Janelle said. Her hand tightened on Joya's.

Penn nodded. "That's right. Her name was Stephanie Oates."

Joya bit her lower lip to keep it from trembling. She closed her eyes, terrified to hear what he was going to say next.

"The weather was so bad the night she delivered that the doctor did not arrive in time for the birth. My Clara was the Oates's housekeeper back then." He looked off, focused on something distant. "She was lovely. Young, buxom, had the most beautiful, thick russet hair." He brought himself back, looked at each of them in turn.

"She delivered you," Penn told Janelle. "And then, it was obvious Stephanie Oates was going to die. In accordance with your mother's dying wish, Clara handed you over to an amateur orchidologist, a very close friend of Osmond Oates." He looked at Trevor. "That man was your father, James Mandeville."

Joya could not imagine her mother, who had never

lived without servants here on Matarenga, working in an Englishman's household. She glanced over at Trevor again. His handsome features were set in an intense scowl. Her father continued.

"Clara said that after she gave Mandeville the newborn and went back into the room, Stephanie was delirious. Clara tried to comfort her, told her she had given birth to a lovely girl, that the infant was safe with the Mandeville's. A few minutes later, Clara realized there was another babe on the way."

Janelle gasped. Joya, numb, watched her father through a wash of tears. His image wavered like a mirage. If he was not really her father, did he really exist at all?

"Clara sent the upstairs maid to get me, told me to wait for her in the kitchen. When she came downstairs, she spoke to me alone, begging me to take her with me to Africa, to ask no questions."

He looked down at his hands—scarred, rough, timeworn, strong. The hands of a man unafraid of hard work. Then he met Joya's eyes, looking directly into them. "She was holding a basket full of linens tight in both arms, as if it held a great treasure. I wondered why a woman who had already rebuffed my obvious attention had changed her mind and was suddenly begging me to take her to Africa." His voice lowered. "She said she would do anything if I took her away. Then a soft cry came from the basket. Before Clara could stop me, I pulled back the covering and there . . ." He paused, cleared his throat, and looked at Joya. "There you were. So tiny. So helpless."

Joya felt the pressure of Janelle's hand tighten. Trevor sat apart from them, listening intently.

As her father told the terrible, astounding, shocking truth of her birth, it seemed as if she and this man she knew only as Papa, this man who had raised her, were the only two people on earth. With her free hand, Joya wiped away her tears as he continued.

"Clara had already told me that James Mandeville had taken the first twin. Things became very clear to me the minute I laid eyes on you, Joya. Clara was going to keep you no matter what I said or did. I wanted her desperately, and I could see that she would never leave you behind. I took you both, and found a ship that sailed the next morning. We made our way to Africa and then, after I made certain no one was tracking us, I brought you both here to Matarenga. You have been my daughter ever since that night."

"Is that why you would never take me to England?" Joya's voice broke. She buried her face in her hands.

"Yes. Knowing you had a twin in England, we feared discovery. If we had returned and met with any of my contacts in the Orchid Society—to which James Mandeville also belonged—we feared someone might recognize that you looked like the Mandevilles' adopted child."

Joya could not raise her head. She heard him approach, and knew that her father was kneeling before her. When he took her hand, she choked down a sob.

Trevor watched Penn with mixed emotions. The man was broken, on the verge of tears. Brought low, humbled on bended knee before the girl he had raised as a daughter, the man knelt with his shoulders bent, his expression mournful. The orchid hunter looked as if he had just lost everything he held dear.

"I'm begging you, Joya, look at me, girl," Penn said softly. "Look at your papa."

Trevor realized he was holding his own breath, waiting for Joya to take pity on the man. How would he feel right now if his entire world had just been torn apart?

"Please, Joya," Penn whispered.

Finally, she raised her head and looked into Penn's eyes.

"How can it be that you are not really my father? That you never were?"

Penn seemed to fold in on himself. Trevor could see that Joya was in shock, shaking her head in disbelief.

"That Mama . . . Clara . . . was not my mother? How can it be that she stole me from my home and family?"

"You were orphaned. She had to keep you. She said she had given James Mandeville enough. We *loved* you, girl," Penn said, threading hope and apology in his tone. "We gave up our pasts for you. We loved you more than anything else in this world. In my heart you are, and always will be, mine."

Trevor watched as Joya turned to Janelle. Were they seeing each other as sisters, as twins? He wondered how different their lives might have been if they had all grown up together at Mandeville House.

Then Joya looked at her father.

"Papa, I had a *sister*. A *twin!* Why didn't you at least tell me that much? If I had known the truth, then perhaps I wouldn't have been so haunted by my dreams. I would have understood why I have always felt as if a part of me were missing."

Janelle suddenly turned to Trevor. Her eyes were red from crying, too. She had slipped off her spectacles and was drying her tears with the hem of her skirt.

"Oh, Trevor, this explains so much, doesn't it?" she cried.

He nodded. It did, indeed, explain so very much.

Chapter 7

Janelle Mandeville watched Dustin Penn rise and leave the room. Sometime during his revelation, she had stopped shaking. Shock, initiated by her first sight of Joya Penn, had quickly been replaced by astonishment, wonder, and an odd sense of inner peace.

Unlike Joya, she had always known that she had been born an Oates, even though she had been legally adopted by James Mandeville. Even without blood ties, she always considered Trevor her brother and Adelaide Mandeville her grandmother. When James died, she had mourned him as a daughter would a father, but in the back of her mind, there had always been that underlying, defining truth—she was Janelle *Oates* Mandeville.

The only shock she had been dealt today had come from finding out she had a twin sister, whereas Joya had just learned that her entire life had been built upon a lie. It was impossible for Janelle to put herself in her sister's place. She could not even begin to fathom the emotional upheaval that Joya must be going through.

The glorious color had drained out of Joya's face, leaving her tanned skin a pale, jaundiced shade. Her eyes were stark, filled with confusion, reddened by tears.

"Should you go to him?" Janelle stared at the open doorway. There was no sight of Dustin Penn on the veranda.

Joya shook her head. "I can't."

An awkward stillness lengthened. Janelle was just debating whether to sit on the floor beside Joya and comfort her when Trevor suddenly stood.

"Do you need some time alone?" he asked Joya.

Janelle saw that while Trevor stared into Joya Penn's eyes, his face was filled with an expression of deep concern.

Joya turned to her and asked, "What did you mean when you said, this explains so much?"

When she hesitated to answer, Trevor began, "My sister has had terrible nightmares since she was a child. Dreams in which she found herself alone and abandoned in the jungle, wandering, helplessly lost."

Janelle added, "Trevor was always the first one there and would try to comfort me. Father, that is, James, tried to understand, but our grandmother, Adelaide, believed I was just demanding attention." She looked at her hands. "As I grew older, the dreams became less terrifying, but they always confused and sometimes frightened me. I took up painting at an early age, committing to canvas the scenes I saw in my dreams. I thought it might help me understand."

Janelle could see that Joya now had a death grip on the fabric of her trousers. Her hands were clenching the rough woven material so tightly that her knuckles were white.

"But it did not help you, did it?" Joya was staring up at her intently.

She frowned, shook her head. "Only a little. I became more and more compelled to paint, almost as if I were being drawn into the work itself."

Trevor added, "We thought perhaps the stories she had heard about Osmond Oates's death, stories told when she was a child, might have frightened her enough to inspire her nightmares. It did not help when I began going on orchid-hunting expeditions myself. She began to worry that I would meet the same end."

"I began to believe the dreams might be prophesies of Trevor's fate," Janelle added. "When he planned this expedition, I told him that I wanted to come to Africa because I hoped that seeing the jungles I have dreamed of might put my mind at rest."

"I finally agreed to let her come along with me."

"Only after I begged him unmercifully," Janelle quickly added.

Trevor went on. "I had hoped that a tour of Africa would bring her nightmares to an end."

"Instead, the dreams only intensified," Janelle quickly added.

"You didn't tell me," Trevor said.

Joya whispered something neither of them heard.

"I beg your pardon," Janelle turned to her twin. "What did you say?"

"He died here," Joya said softly. "Osmond Oates died *here*, on Matarenga. He is buried near my . . . my mother . . ." She shuddered and corrected herself. "Clara Penn."

"Osmond Oates . . . my father? Buried here?"

"*Our* father. I will take you to his grave," Joya told

them. "But not today. There has been enough for one day."

She rose, pausing as if uncomfortable in her own home. She looked around as if seeing the room through the eyes of a stranger. This was, indeed, Janelle thought, the first few moments of a whole new life for her twin.

"Wait here . . . please." Joya quickly walked to the far side of the room and exited through a narrow doorway.

Trevor watched Joya disappear. Then he looked down at Janelle. "Are you all right?"

"As right as anyone can be who just came face to face with herself." She tried to laugh, managing a smile, at least. "She is so very brave," she added. "Trevor, can you imagine what she must be feeling right now?"

"Penn should be strung up."

By stealing Joya, the man and his wife had robbed the girl of everything his own father would have given her. She would have grown up with Janelle, been raised at Mandeville House. She would have been taught how to walk and dress and act the part of a lady. Like Janelle, Joya would have been no more than a sister to him.

And as such, she might not have fascinated him with her every move, not triggered such gut-wrenching confusion each time he looked at her.

"I have a sister," Janelle said softly. "Can you believe it, Trevor? I not only have a sister, but a *twin*. Of course, she can't stay here now. We'll simply have to take her home with us."

He had walked over to look out the window. Penn was nowhere in sight. Suddenly, he realized what Janelle had just said and turned around.

"What are you talking about?"

"Joya, of course. We have to take her home."

He had not even thought about taking Joya Penn back to England. Hell, he had not anticipated any of this. He ran his hand through his already tousled hair, disturbed by the hopeful look in his sister's eyes.

There was barely manageable uneasiness building inside him. He was certain, without knowing how, that the ramifications of Joya's existence would surely spread like ripples on a pond.

For a man who valued planning and order, it was hard to imagine what to expect from such a major upheaval.

As his father's heir, he had assumed responsibility for Janelle. He had always acted as her older brother and guardian. His father had promised to see to Osmond Oates's offspring. Was he now responsible for Joya, for seeing her taken care of and settled, too?

So many questions only intensified his unease. He did not enjoy being out of control of any situation. He prided himself on being a man who took great pains not to let anything of the kind happen.

Before he could comment to Janelle, Joya had reappeared, but paused instead of coming forward into the room. She watched intently from the doorway. The color had not yet returned to her face. If anything, she looked even more pale and forlorn. In one hand she held what appeared to be various-sized pieces of paper.

Without thinking, he crossed the room and found himself beside her, compelled to try to help, to be near her. To catch her should she fall.

It took a moment, but she finally managed the barest hint of a smile. One corner of her mouth lifted and the dimple in her cheek appeared.

"I have something to show you," she said. "Both of you."

Then she walked over to where Janelle sat on the day-bed.

Joya held the pages out to Janelle, who took them and lowered them to her lap. She lifted the top page, staring down at it.

Trevor viewed the page upside down. It appeared to be a somewhat smudged charcoal rendering of the Tower of London with a female figure standing in the foreground.

Janelle stared at the drawing, then quickly began to leaf through the others. "You did these?" she asked without looking up.

"Yes."

"All scenes of London."

"Yes."

Trevor saw Janelle's hand tremble.

"What is it?" He saw no reason mere drawings should upset her. "It's not surprising she can draw, is it? You are an artist. Osmond Oates painted beautiful water-colors of many botanical species. You both inherited artistic talents."

"It's not that," Janelle told him. Joya stood there mute, as if she expected Janelle to make some further discovery.

"You have never been to London, have you?" Janelle asked.

"No." Joya shook her head. "I have only seen drawings in my mother's books."

"Some of the details in these scenes are missing or misplaced, but overall, these scenes are quite good. Very recognizable." Janelle slowly looked through each page again.

Trevor sensed some form of silent communication taking place between the twins. He was a bystander watching an exchange he couldn't fathom, a discourse between two individuals speaking another language. He felt not only left out, but highly uncomfortable.

"You drew yourself in each scene," Janelle mused.

"No. That is not me. It was *never* me in the drawings. It was another girl, one who looked like me. I knew it in my heart each time I drew her and every time I looked at the drawings afterward. That is *not* me."

"Then it must be me," Janelle whispered.

"Yes," Joya agreed. "I know now that it was you."

Trevor shifted, beyond uncomfortable with the direction of their talk. He was not one to believe in such esoteric nonsense. He could not acknowledge anything beyond the concrete, physical everyday world. He believed in a world of order, of genera and species, of classification.

What the twins were hinting at, what Janelle obviously accepted so easily, was beyond explanation, beyond anything he could define. Seeing was believing. He wanted no part of such talk.

Still he lingered, feeling shut out, yet unwilling to leave either of them.

Janelle stared at the drawings spread over her lap and then looked at Joya. "While I was in London painting the jungle, wandering in dreams of the terrifying, wild darkness of this place, you were here, half a world away, drawing scenes of London. Drawing me."

Then Janelle looked at Trevor. "It's incredible, isn't it? We may have been separated on the night of our birth, but we have been seeking each other without even having knowledge of what we were searching for."

"Incredible? It's impossible." He folded his arms and thought about helping himself to Penn's whiskey.

"Then how do you explain these?" Janelle picked up

some of the drawings and waved them at him.

"I have no explanation."

Joya was arrested, listening to their exchange, marveling at the way the deep sound of Trevor's voice seemed to slide along her backbone. Whenever their eyes met, she experienced sensations as intimate as a touch.

As Trevor and Janelle spoke quickly, in such a clipped, fast exchange, she found it hard to understand everything they were saying as they talked of taking her with them to London, of Mandeville House and their grandmother, Adelaide.

Suddenly Umbaba appeared in the doorway, calling her back to reality, to Matarenga. Trevor and Janelle both stopped talking at once.

"What is it?" Joya spoke in Matarengi as she crossed the room.

"Your father."

"Where is he?"

"At the place where your mother lies in the ground."

There was no Matarengi word for *grave*. She had been right in guessing that Dustin Penn would have gone to her mother's grave.

She assured Umbaba that she would leave immediately. He did not move off the porch, but waited to walk with her. She turned back to the Mandevilles.

"I must go to my father. He needs me."

She had to tell her father what was in her heart, and this was something that she must do alone. She quickly explained to Umbaba and asked him to have his wives bring food to the strangers.

"Is she a *jimbwa*?" He pointed to Janelle.

"She is no ghost. She is my sister." The reality of the statement startled Joya as much as it did Umbaba. The truth had barely begun to seep into her. She had a sister. She had family other than her father—and Trevor Mandeville was a part of that family now.

"When are they leaving?" Umbaba continued to eye both whites with suspicion.

"Soon." Mixed emotions swept through her. Chilled her. She looked through the open door, across the lagoon, the reef, the open sea. Was she really ready to leave this place, this island that had been her paradise and her prison?

She tried to hide her hesitation when she told Janelle and Trevor, "Umbaba's wives will bring you food. Our house is yours. Be at ease."

She walked away, lost in thought as she tried to find the words that would help ease not only the pain inside her own soul, but the sadness she had seen in her father's eyes. He, too, was suffering.

"Joya?"

She heard Trevor say her name and paused at the bottom of the porch steps.

"Are you sure you don't want me to go along?" he asked.

"I am sure." Silently, she blessed him for showing his concern. She wished that she did not have to confront her father at all, but things could not be left the way they were.

She walked away from her house clutching her small charm pouch, headed toward the low hill where her mother and Osmond Oates lay buried. No matter what happened between her and her father, she now had a sister who would be awaiting her return.

And Trevor Mandeville would be waiting as well.

Chapter 8

Joya found her father alone on the hillside, his back pressed against the trunk of the flame tree, his legs stretched out before him. The muddied, trail-worn soles of his shoes faced the sea. The Kusi wind lifted his hair. He was staring at her mother's grave and had not seen her yet.

Joya looked over at her mother's grave and thought, *I know now, Mama. I know what you did and my heart is breaking for it.*

Her mother's grave lay near that of Osmond Oates. Joya realized the irony of it all, how she had grown up unaware that her true father lay buried on the hill behind her home. She had often stared at the mound of earth with the crooked cross made of two sticks lashed together at one end.

She stepped toward the tulip tree. "Papa?"

He slowly turned and looked at her. She crossed the clearing and waited for him to say something. When he didn't, she asked, "May I sit with you?"

She would have never thought to ask before. Doing so broke her heart even more. Such a little thing, and yet it showed just how great the tear in the fabric of their lives had become.

"Sit." He patted the dirt beside him.

Help me, Mama, she prayed. *Let me know the right words to say.*

They sat in strained silence as her father continued to stare over at Clara's grave. Joya took a deep breath. She began to smooth down her hair, but when she saw that her hand was trembling, she dropped it into her lap.

"Can you understand, girl? Can you understand at all?"

She nodded, fought not to cry. "I'm trying. I know you didn't want Mama to be punished for . . . for taking me. I can understand your not wanting to take me to England when I was little. But when I grew older, when you made me put aside the Matarengi ways, you should have told me then. You should have given me a choice."

"It's too late now," he said sadly.

"Yes. Too late. With or without your permission, I will go with them to London."

He sat up straight, pushing away from the weathered tree trunk.

"I would give you the moon, girl, if I thought it would put the stars back in your eyes."

Her father's expression hardened. "Mandeville came here to talk business. I'll listen to what he has to say and see if he will be willing to have you in London— for a time." He cleared his throat.

"Thank you, Papa." She got to her knees and wrapped her arms around his neck. Her papa enfolded her in his embrace, rocked back and forth and held her as he had not done since she had been a child.

"Can you forgive me, Joya? Can you forgive your mother and me for what we did?"

"I love you, Papa. What would I be forgiving you for? For loving Mama enough to let her keep me? For loving me too much to let me go?"

Joya gazed over his shoulder at her mother's grave. *Thank you, Mama. Thank you for your help.*

The cooling breeze wafted through the house, carrying the sensual scent of ylang-ylang blossoms. The pungent, heady fragrance stirred Trevor's blood, made him feel restless and unsettled. He had no idea what had gone on between Joya and her father, but Penn had come to him and seemed ready to listen to what he had to say. Janelle had asked Joya to show her where to freshen up so that he and Dustin Penn could have some privacy.

Now, alone with the orchid hunter, Trevor quickly put Joya out of his mind and gathered his thoughts. For the first time since he had been rocked by the sight of Joya Penn, he felt back in control. To him, running Mandeville Imports was as simple as breathing. He prided himself on his business success—it was a job he had been trained to do. He bore the responsibility of generations.

His grandmother had groomed him to guide the family-owned concerns in a way that his own father had never wanted to do. She had instilled in him a deep responsibility to the family import company that his paternal great-great-grandfather had established. The daughter of an impoverished, once-wealthy and titled family, his grandmother had married into the Mandevilles with little hesitation.

Her own son, James, had been an endless disappointment to her. A widower from his young wife's death until the day he died, his father had cared for his orchid collection, his designs for glass conservatories in which to house them, and little else. He had left the overseeing of the business as well as Trevor's upbringing to Adelaide.

A woman unlike any he had ever known, Trevor's grandmother had assured him that she saw her own business acumen in him. Not only had she agreed with this plan to persuade Penn to go into partnership with them, but she had encouraged him to travel to Matarenga to seek out the man in person.

Now had come the moment he had been planning for two years.

"Another drink, Mandeville?" Penn had already refilled his own glass.

"No. Thank you." Trevor shook his head, wanting to keep a clear mind.

"Sit down." Penn indicated a chair directly across from his own.

Trevor sat. Afraid Penn might suddenly change his mind and refuse to hear him out, he began without preamble. "It took me two years to discover your whereabouts, Mr. Penn. When I began my search, I had only one proposition to put to you. Now I have two. I've come to solicit your business for Mandeville Imports. We want exclusive rights to broker your orchids in London and around the world."

Penn took a healthy sip of whiskey, wiping his mouth with the back of his hand. "Tell me why, after all these years, I need a broker?"

"Because I have seen some of the greatest orchid finds of the decade—*your* finds, Mr. Penn—undervalued by other auction houses."

"I make enough to keep me *and* the Matarengi happy."

"Have you planned for Joya's future? What if something were to happen to you?"

Penn appeared thoughtful as he stared out the open doors. Beyond the veranda, the water in the lagoon had gone from turquoise to red-gold in the light of the quickly lowering sun.

"There is an account in London in her name," Penn informed him. A frown marred his features. He looked as if he would rather be anywhere else, discussing anything else. "It holds a considerable sum already, one that would be a small fortune most anywhere in the world."

"Does Joya know?"

"No." The orchid hunter shook his head. "No. I have never discussed it with her."

Trevor wanted to ask him why he thought he was so invincible, why he had never considered that he might suddenly die and Joya would never learn the truth of her background or that her father had provided for her future most amply. Then he reminded himself Joya was not the issue now.

"You are out of touch with current orchid prices. I am not," Trevor said. "Did you know that one recent new find was sold for over five hundred pounds?"

At that Dustin Penn sat up straighter, leaned forward in his chair, and dangled the empty whiskey glass in his hand.

"Five hundred, you say?"

Trevor felt the excitement of a firm commitment in the making. He too, scooted to the edge of his seat.

"Since your name has become synonymous with rare finds, you could be making much, much more for every specimen. For the privilege of buying just one of your orchids, collectors would be willing to pay tremendous amounts. If you deal through Mandeville Imports exclusively, I would raise the price of your plants to six hundred pounds and even hold some back for the most wealthy collectors. I can foresee bidding wars that will put more money into both of our pockets." Trevor paused, then added, "And, of course, more money to put away for your daughter's future."

Penn said nothing. In the awkward silence, Trevor tried to think ahead, to answer any questions before Penn could pose them.

"If you are wondering why you should trust me, let me just say that Mandeville Imports is generations old and has an impeccable reputation," Trevor added.

"No need to assure me of that," Dustin Penn said. "I know of your company. I haven't completely cut myself off from the world. I have a network of dependable bearers and shipping firms already in place, Mandeville."

"Not that dependable, or I wouldn't have been able to find you."

"I've sent plants to Italy, Germany, Belgium, to all the countries where men have gone mad over orchids. I have kept up with the bulletins from the Orchid Society whenever I could get them. Mandeville Imports' reputation is no secret. I knew of the work your father did before you, of his designing conservatories and collecting on his own. I recognized the Mandeville name the night you first told me who you were. That's why I wanted you off the island. I knew Clara had given Joya's twin to your father. I was afraid that somehow the truth had come out, that someone unknown to us knew of Joya's birth and that you had come for her."

Trevor nodded. "I had no knowledge of her. With or without Joya and Janelle's connection, you can rest assured that I would see to it that our contract with you is more than generous."

"You said you had another reason for coming here."

"Word is just out. Prince Albert has conceived of and is planning a Great Exhibition. He intends to bring together the nations of the world to show the very latest in industrial processes and art beneath great glass domes designed by Joseph Paxton. He was a friend of my father's and the creator of an outstanding glass conservatory at Chatsworth.

"The Prince has also challenged the Orchid Society, orchidologists, and hunters around the globe to find an orchid worthy of Queen Victoria's name. The first man or company to bring in the most spectacular, the most exotic orchid discovered to date will be given a royal appointment. There is less than a year left before the exhibition opens."

"What do I need with a title when I'm as good as king right here on Matarenga?"

"Forget about the title then. Think of the additional money you would make. You do have a daughter to think about, Penn. One that will not be content to live here forever."

"You stand to gain as well, Mandeville, or you would not have come all this way to find me."

"As our partner, should you discover the orchid, Mandeville Imports would receive much acclaim, which would assure our position as one of the world's leading import companies for another generation or two. As your sponsor, I would also be eligible for a title, which is something that would mean a great deal to my grandmother."

"But not to you?" Penn was watching him intently. Trevor knew he could not risk denying the truth.

"I can't say that I would turn down such an honor."

"I see folks in London haven't changed much in the

twenty years I have been gone. Still hold to titles, do they? Still look down on the common man?"

"The Mandevilles are not aristocracy, Penn. We come from a long line of traders and merchants. My grandmother, on the other hand, is the granddaughter of an impoverished earl. It has always been her secret wish that somehow a title might be bestowed upon a Mandeville. This is my chance to give her that, as well as further the company's reputation."

"If I agree to become your partner, then it will be up to me to find the Victoria orchid, is that it?"

Full of pent-up energy, Trevor stood, stretched, and walked over to the open door. He did not know Penn well enough to know for certain whether the man was about to agree to his offer, but if he was any judge of men, Penn was close.

He stared out at the burnt orange sun flaming just above the horizon. Within moments, it would be dusk. He turned around again, crossing the room toward Penn.

"I intend to continue my search for the orchid as well. I've had some great success in Venezuela and am eager to return. What I would ask is that you divulge some of your own knowledge. Teach me a little of what you have learned and refined about orchid hunting over these past years."

"Why aren't you a professional orchid hunter instead of trying to run a business at the same time?"

"I fancy myself both, but you are the best in the world, Penn. While you continue to search here on your island, I intend to make one last trip, this time to Venezuela. Armed with some of your secrets about altitude, climate, and growing mediums, I'll search the other side of the world on my own. Hopefully one of us will come up with Queen Victoria's orchid by next spring for the exhibition."

"In other words, you want it all."

"What do you mean?"

"You want my business, my expertise, my daughter."

Trevor stiffened. "I want nothing of the kind."

"You don't want my business, then?"

"I want a percentage."

"My expertise?"

"Yes. In exchange you will receive my brokerage expertise and what Mandeville Imports can bring you."

"And my daughter? Do you want *her*, Mandeville?"

"No, I do not want your daughter. Not in the insulting way I think you mean."

Trevor knew he sounded harsh, but Penn had touched a nerve by stepping too close to the raw emotion, the need Joya threatened to awaken in him. Penn's words conjured up unnerving images.

The man completely surprised him when next he said, "For Joya I will go into partnership with Mandeville Imports. I will sit down and try to tell you something of what I've learned."

Trevor kept his excitement in check. His long trek had been worthwhile. He would soon be privy to Penn's secrets and have a signed contract.

"But before I sign any agreement, Mandeville, there is something I must ask of you."

"What is that?"

"Take Joya to London with you and your sister for an extended stay. Give them time to become acquainted."

As much as Trevor wanted to refuse, he knew that he couldn't. Not only because Penn might renege on their deal, but because of what having Joya with her would mean to Janelle. His sister would have his head if he refused.

"How can I say no?"

"I want you to swear you will see to her safety. Promise me that you will protect Joya just as I would. I want your word that you'll keep your hands, and those of every other swain in London, off her."

Chapter 9

While her father and Trevor discussed business, Joya led Janelle around to the back of the house, found a piece of soap in a wooden box near the back steps, and took a cloth from the hemp clothesline strung between two trees.

Then she lit a torch and walked her twin to a natural stream with a deep pool in the volcanic rock not far from the house. Surrounded by a grove of palms and a wall of bamboo, it was a secluded, tropical oasis.

Twilight had deepened by the time they reached the water's edge. The torchlight shimmered on the opaque surface, creating long spears of light that wavered in the rippling water. The breeze inspired the bamboo to sing with soft, hushed sighs.

"It is so beautiful!" Janelle spread her arms wide, taking in the scene. "Absolutely lovely."

Joya felt proud and happy to have so easily pleased her sister. She shoved the torch handle into the soft sand near the edge of the pool and then indicated the soap and towel.

When Janelle finished with her face and hands, Joya led her over to a large, flat boulder beside the stream. Time and water had worn the volcanic rock smooth. She sat down and Janelle sat beside her.

"Do you know what they were like, our true mother and father?" Joya asked, longing to know something of the man and woman who had been their parents.

"Our father was a scientist, a botanist. A man who studies plants. Stephanie, our mother, was very young when they married. Trevor's father once told me that she loved to read poetry and tried her hand at writing. Stephanie and Osmond were very much in love. Our mother died shortly after she heard that our father had fallen to his death. I believe she didn't wish to live without him."

Joya stared at ripples on the water and wondered what it would be like to love someone so much that life itself dimmed in comparison to that love. She was very aware of her sister, seated so close. The nearness gave her a feeling of comfort and familiarity. Her fingers touched her amulet pouch. There was magic at work here. Magic of a kind she could not define.

"Do you feel it?" she whispered.

"I feel so peaceful inside. Is that what you mean?"

"Yes. Even if I never see London, if I never leave Matarenga, I know now that you are real and not part of my imagination. I feel a strange sense of peace, the way I feel whenever I float in the lagoon on a warm day."

Janelle took hold of both of her hands.

"I cannot wait for you to see London. You have no need to worry about anything while you are there, either.

Our parents left me an inheritance as well as an old manor house in the country. The place is much in need of repair, but it belongs to both of us now. You'll never have to worry about money, or anything else for that matter. Trevor is concerned that you will have a hard time adjusting to our way of life." Janelle laughed at that.

Joya smiled, not because she understood, but because the sound was an echo of her own laughter.

"He is afraid of what I might teach you," Janelle explained. "He thinks of me as something of a bluestocking—a woman with intellectual interests. Men in England don't care much for women who admit to being able to think for themselves. I, on the other hand, have a perfectly capable mind and I use it. I love art. I love to read and discuss all the latest notions on politics and philosophies and I have an odd assortment of Bohemian friends."

Joya nodded, fascinated, as she watched the reflected torchlight play on the lenses of Janelle's spectacles. She had little understanding of what her sister was going on about.

"Grandmama, that is Adelaide Mandeville, thinks I should be settled and married by now. We have always disagreed on most everything. I fear she has always loved Trevor more, for he is her flesh and blood, but she has always provided for me and let me be as independent as I have wanted to be."

When Janelle paused, stretched, and yawned, Joya realized her sister was tired.

"Why don't you go back to the house while I bathe? You can slip into my room from the side door and sleep with me." Joya could not bear the thought of being separated from Janelle now that she had found her.

'Will you be all right out here alone?"

"This is my home. I have nothing to fear here."

As soon as Janelle left and walked back toward the house, Joya pulled her shirt over her head and tossed it aside. Night shadows had cooled the close, humid air. She felt a chill ripple over her exposed breasts. Her nipples tightened.

She stood up and shucked off her trousers, stepped out of them, and dove beneath the surface of the chilly water.

After a long hike down the mountain, she always relished a long soak in the pool. With all that had happened today, she found the kindred spirits of the water a godsend. She closed her eyes, touched her amulet pouch, and gave thanks for all of her blessings.

She dove under again, surfaced, and shook her hair back off her face. Then with long sure strokes, she swam back. A dark shadow shifted behind the torchlight.

Someone had come to share the pool.

Trevor heard a splash over the whisper of the bamboo and the sound of the waves breaking on the far reef. He paused on the narrow stone walkway leading from the house to the pool, where Dustin Penn had suggested he look for the twins.

The glimmering torchlight reflected off Joya's golden skin. At the sight of her rising from the water like Botticelli's Venus, he froze, bewitched as she waded toward the edge of the pool.

Her skin, slick with water, sparkled in the torchlight. No siren, no practiced courtesan could have been any more seductive. She was as naked as the day she was born, lithe, supple, perfectly formed. Her breasts were full, her nipples puckered into tight buds. The small leather pouch on a cord around her neck dangled between her breasts.

Obviously she felt no shame. How could she, he wondered? She had been raised by a housekeeper and a father who had gone native, and was far from drawing-room material. He had seen her in the wild blithely directing a work gang of half-naked Matarengi, hacking her way through the jungle swinging a machete. She was a combination of what her father and mother had told her of the world they had left behind and what she had learned from the Matarengi.

He wondered if he should backtrack, uncertain that she had even seen him in the shadows, until she suddenly said, "Hello, Trevor. Did you come to bathe?"

Speechless, he was mortified to be caught staring, but she was not at all bothered by his presence.

"Do you *always* do that?"

"Do what? Bathe? Yes."

"No. Swim. Without . . . clothes."

"Why would I get my clothes wet? Besides, I am bathing."

"Well, I . . . it's just that . . ."

"Do you bathe in *your* clothes?"

"No, but I bathe in a tub."

"A tub?"

He waved his hands around, trying to give her an idea of something large and low to the ground. "A tub is a container that holds water and you . . . you take off your clothes, in private, and climb into it to bathe."

Realizing he was still staring at her naked form, he looked away, scanning the dark edges of the jungle beyond the torch's glow. "Aren't you worried that someone might come along and *see* you?"

"Everyone bathes here. Everyone sees everyone."

"Indeed."

He heard a splash and turned around. Joya was across the pool now, up to her waist in water, scrubbing her face, her neck and shoulders. She lathered her hair before she dove in to rinse off. When she began to swim back, he faced the other way.

She was quiet for so long that he was finally forced to ask, "Are you dressed?"

"Yes."

When he turned around, she was close enough for him to feel the warmth emanating from her. Her long hair, pulled to one side, curled over her shoulder. Even with the rise of her breasts showing above the edge of a colorful woven fabric, she looked perfectly at ease.

He swallowed hard around the lump in his throat. His blood was running hot as molten lava, and it wasn't from the humid tropic heat.

Obviously Joya's ignorance of the rigid standards of propriety and her complete lack of modesty was fueling his physical reaction. Why else would he be so inexplicably drawn to her? So quickly aroused?

She stood there bare from her toes to her ivory thighs, wearing no more than a piece of bright, native woven cloth that revealed the soft curve of her hips, her narrow waist, the rise of her firm breasts.

"You should cover yourself decently." He realized that he had sounded a bit too harsh when the words slipped out of him almost of their own volition.

"This is much more than the Matarengi women wear." Joya shook out her hair. Her fingers caught in the tangles of her curls as she tried to separate them. She had no idea what she was doing to him.

"In case you have not noticed, you are not a Matarengi woman. Did you see my sister's gown?" he asked.

"It exposes only her neck and shoulders, her wrists, the slightest glimpse of the toes of her shoes. Her skirt is shaped like a bell, to disguise the shape of the lower half of her body. In England, *that* is how far a lady will go to cover herself. Society's rules dictate our dress."

"It must feel strange to wear so many clothes all the time. How do you keep from getting hot?"

He was getting hotter with every heartbeat. He called upon the composure that served him so well in both his business negotiations and in dangerous situations in remote corners of the globe.

"We should go back."

Joya was staring up at him expectantly. "Your talk with my father . . . was it successful?"

His gaze was drawn to her eyes, her breasts, the amulet pouch hanging between them. He had to force himself to look away. Once he did, he found it easier to concentrate while staring at the wall of tall, golden bamboo.

"Your father has agreed to do business with our import house and to teach me some of his orchid-hunting secrets. We will be leaving in three days. Your father has asked me to take you with us."

He heard her gasp, a small, breathy sound. Then there was a long pause before she asked, "Why are you talking to the bamboo?"

He gave up trying and retrieved the torch from the water's edge. Trevor took a deep breath, drinking in the tranquil beauty of the pool, the soothing sound of the stream as it poured over the rocks, and the glow of the torch as it lit the frangipani, orchid, ginger, and bird-of-paradise blooms. He took a deep breath, calmed by the peace of the idyllic setting, and his heartbeat settled back into place.

Until he felt Joya's light touch upon his forearm—
then he lowered the torch, watching the firelight shimmer
on her golden hair.

"Do you find it beautiful here?" Her voice was soft
as a caress.

"Yes." He shifted uncomfortably, catching himself
just as he was about to tumble into the depths of her
intent gaze.

"This is one of my favorite places."

He turned toward the water and took a deep breath.
Instead of clearing his head, the heady, sensual fragrance
of the tropic flowers only added fuel to the fire.

"We should go back," he said.

Completely unaware of the effect she was having on
him, she rubbed one bare foot atop the other as she
combed her fingers through her loose, waving hair.

"I cannot wait to see London."

He felt compelled to look down into her eyes, feeling
very much the same way he had during the earthquake
when the ground had fallen out from under him.

"Nothing you have seen or read about in books can
prepare you for the reality of London."

"The hub of the world, my father calls it."

"It is a far cry from Matarenga."

A nightbird called to its mate, a shrill, high sound that
cut the air. The breeze lifted the ends of her hair, caressing
the waving curls. His fingers itched to touch the
golden strands. She took a step forward and was within
his reach.

They were alone in the semidarkness. Alone without
a chaperon and Joya only half dressed. Her open, innocent
expression told him that she had no notion of
what sort of precarious position she had put herself in,
no idea what her nearness was doing to him.

The jungle that was London would hold far more danger for Joya Penn than the wilds of Matarenga. Janelle might think she could help her twin adjust to English society, but he doubted Joya would ever learn how to be circumspect in every situation. Because of her isolation and her father's powerful hold on the island people, she had existed in a sheltered world where she had very little to fear.

Almost as if she had read his thoughts, she said, "I will do my best. I promise not to bring shame to your family."

And I, he thought, *have given your father my word that I will keep you safe.*

"Perhaps, then, you had best go back to the house." He allowed his irritation with himself and his thoughts to show by commenting in too sharp a tone.

"Have I displeased you, Trevor?"

Her safety in London was of the utmost importance. She had to learn sometime. Now was as good a time as any.

"In England, a young woman is never alone with a man who is not her husband or her fiancé. Ever."

"Is it a rule?"

"Yes, a very important rule. Perhaps the number one most important rule of all."

"Rule Number One is never be alone in the dark with a man who is not my fiancé or my husband." She instantly disarmed him with a smile.

"Exactly. Now go back to the house," he said.

"You aren't coming with me?"

Trevor glanced at the house and sighed. "No. I'll be along. First, I think a long soak in the pool is in order."

"I should see to your cuts. Do you need help removing your clothes?"

"Joya, I just told you that a young woman should not be alone with a man."

"Yes. Rule Number One."

"Which means you, an unmarried young lady, should not be here in the dark, alone with me." He glanced toward the house again, half-expecting Dustin Penn to come charging down the path waving a long, sharp machete in one hand and brandishing a spear in the other.

"But we're not in England," she reminded him. "There is no such rule here."

"Perhaps because the Matarengi are much freer in their relationships."

"What do you mean?"

Suddenly his shirt felt too tight around the collar. Despite the cool night breeze, he had begun to sweat.

"What I mean is, Matarengi society allows them to follow their natural inclinations . . ."

"Their what?"

"You see, between a man and a woman . . . surely your father has told you . . ." Frustrated, he shoved his hand through his hair. She was tying him in knots.

"Just go back to the house. Ask Janelle to explain."

Chapter 10

Trevor rarely saw Joya over the next three days as he sat closeted with Dustin Penn taking copious notes, making drawings and maps, absorbing as much as he could about the environments and altitudes conducive to orchid growth.

He soon came to admire Penn, not only for the man's expertise, but for his self-assurance and blunt honesty. He found himself envying the orchid hunter's freedom, especially the way he had turned his back on the rest of the world to live life exactly the way he wanted.

Finally the day had come to depart. Trevor, on his way to summon the twins to the dock, paused on a path that led up a hill behind the house. Far below he could see the pier stretched toward a deep channel in the lagoon.

Two large sailing canoes were tied up at the end of the pier, the Matarengi sailors ready to sail them to the island of Zanzibar to collect their things. His gear was already stowed, as was Janelle's small traveling case.

The orchid shipment was loaded in the second boat.

He continued on and soon reached the top of the low rise. Beneath a towering flame tree that showered the ground with bloodred blooms, Joya and Janelle stood side by side, looking at two graves that lay a few yards apart.

The sight gave him pause. Joya had donned one of the gowns Janelle had brought over to the island. Her hair was done up in matching bows. Seeing both young women from behind, there was a moment when he could not tell them apart—until Joya turned around. Her eyes were suspiciously bright and there was a wistful sadness about her, a waiflike quality that Janelle never let show. Joya's demeanor made him want to take her in his arms and put the sunshine back in her eyes.

Outwardly, she appeared every bit an English miss except for her glowing, suntanned cheeks enhanced by the butter-yellow shade of her borrowed gown. Janelle had taken Joya's unruly blond curls and artfully gathered them up with bows to frame her face and set off her eyes.

Thankfully, today there was not one immodest inch of Joya showing. The transformation was amazing, but Trevor had the feeling something inexplicably fascinating had been lost. He had an urge to tug the ribbons from her hair and watch it tumble into wild curls again.

"You look like an English miss," he told her.

"Thank you." She flashed a smile and then bent over. He thought she was trying to execute a curtsy, but instead she grabbed the hem of her gown, lifting her skirt to reveal her bare legs up to her thighs. "I am not a proper English miss, yet. I have on my own sandals." She fairly beamed.

Trevor was rendered speechless. Janelle turned and noticed Joya with her skirt thigh-high.

"I'm sure he is not interested in your footwear, Joya." Janelle went blithely on, as if her sister's behavior were nothing out of the ordinary. "Trevor, come see my father's grave," she said.

Disturbed by the unexpected view of Joya's shapely bare legs, Trevor quickly joined Janelle and lowered his voice.

"What are you going to do if she does that in front of Grandmother?" he whispered.

"I can't help but think what fun that would be."

"You have to teach her some comportment before we get home."

"She is charming and entirely natural. I would hate to ruin such spontaneous behavior."

"That is exactly the problem." His gaze flashed back to Joya. "We can't predict what she will do next."

"Do not spend an inordinate amount of time worrying about that, Trevor. Almost as soon as we return to London, you will be setting sail for Venezuela and Joya and I will be on our own with Grandmama. I'm convinced she will manage very well."

With her skirt properly in place, Joya joined them.

"That's Osmond Oates's grave." She pointed it out to Trevor. "Over there lies my mother . . . Clara Penn."

Trevor heard the twice-felt loss of her mother—once in death, and now having learned Clara was not really her mother at all.

The name Clara Hayworth Penn was crudely carved into a large, flat stone beside two Matarengi fetishes. What kind of a woman, a lowly housekeeper at that, would have the nerve to steal a newborn child? What had driven her to do it?

He decided Clara Penn must have wanted a child very desperately, so much that she had been willing to leave civilization behind just to keep Joya.

"My true father's grave," Janelle whispered with a shake of her head.

"I hope that this hasn't upset you," he said.

"Fate has led us here, Trevor. I am sure that finding Joya, visiting this island grave, these are the reasons I have dreamed of African jungles all my life. Perhaps my father's spirit lured me here so that I would find Joya and we would be reunited."

"Blind luck. Nothing more." He was uncomfortable with the direction of her talk.

"Oh, Trevor, I know you don't believe in anything so esoteric, but what if it *were* true?"

Joya frowned and looked up at him as she asked Janelle, "What do you mean, esoteric?"

"If Trevor cannot see something or have it proven to him, he doesn't believe in it," Janelle said.

"The Matarengi believe that the spirits of our ancestors move in the world around us. The rocks, plants, and animals, all of them have spirits, too. How else would we be guided? How else could we survive without their help?" Joya asked.

Janelle turned to him. "Yes, how else, dear brother?"

"You cannot see love," Joya added. "But you believe in love, don't you?"

Trevor shifted uncomfortably. Believe in love? He had never been in love. With all of his responsibilities to the family business and his interest in orchids, he had no time for love. When he looked down at Joya he found her awaiting an answer, yet he had none to give.

"I believe the boat is ready to leave," he said.

"I should take you both to see Otakgi, the wise man

of the village. He speaks with spirits every day." Joya glanced up to watch two small green parrots fly over.

Janelle was excited by the prospect. "Do we have time?"

"No, we don't." Trevor was glad he was along to be the voice of reason. "I don't need spirits to tell me that we should be on the pier." He turned to Joya. "Your father will be waiting to say good-bye."

She suddenly looked so sad at his reminder that he found himself excusing a need to hold and comfort her and tried to convince himself that it was a purely innocent reaction, one that came from years of playing older brother to Janelle.

"Wait for me at the pier. I want to make certain I did not leave anything in the house." Janelle went hurrying down the trail alone.

Joya lingered, silently staring at her mother's grave. When he saw her reach for her bag of charms, he realized she had not put aside her Matarengi amulet pouch with her other clothing.

"Are you all right?" he asked.

"Do you really want me to go to London with you?"

Her question surprised him. He did not know whether she was looking for an excuse to stay or for reassurance that he held no concern.

"Everything is settled."

"But do you want me there?"

"Janelle has her mind made up. She is looking forward to having you with her."

"But do *you*, Trevor Mandeville, want me to come with you to London?"

His first impulse was to be absolutely truthful and say no. He could not shake the terrible feeling that she was about to upset his life like a tempest out of control. But as he looked into her open, ingenuous face, he realized with astounding clarity that leaving her behind would fill him with more regret than would taking her with him.

"Yes, I want you to come with us," he said softly. "But I'll be perfectly honest, I still have reservations. You have no idea what you are walking into."

Chapter 11

Trevor spent much of his time on the voyage home studying his copious notes and wrestling with his growing attraction to his sister's twin. Unlike Janelle, who suffered from seasickness, Joya was amazed by the ship. She spent much of her time tending to her sister, as well as sketching the sights they saw in Africa and on the open water.

After a tearful good-bye to her father, Joya settled in and seemed content, so much so that Trevor let her entertain herself—until early one gusty morning when he could not sleep and decided to take a turn around the deck before breakfast.

Spying a gathering of crew members, he walked closer, curious to see what they might be discussing so intently. Much to his chagrin, he found Joya seated cross-legged on the deck, locked in deep conversation with one particularly unsavory character whose bare upper torso and arms were covered with tattoos.

"That ain't quite the way of it on New Guinea," the

tattooed man was saying. "Out there, the men take the virgins and they . . ."

Trevor did not wait to hear more. Shoving aside the men who were standing idly by, he stepped inside the ring of Joya's admirers.

Thankfully her skirt was tucked beneath her feet and her bare legs were covered, but standing over her, like many of the others, he had a clear view down the low-cut neckline of her gown. Underwear, it seemed, was something she had not quite adjusted to.

He liked to pride himself on his control, but just then he had none. He offered his hand and prayed she would take it and follow him without question.

"Trevor!" Thankfully, she jumped to her feet when she saw him. "I didn't expect you to be out so early. Mr. Tuck and I were just talking about the differences between fertility ceremonies on Matarenga and New Guinea."

"I need to speak to you." He took her hand and held on tight. "Come with me."

She might not have recognized the anger simmering beneath his thin veneer of control, but the sailors did. He hoped he would not have to challenge the lot of them to move aside.

"Is Janelle all right? Does she need me?" Joya asked.

"Janelle is just fine." He was barely able to get the words out. He turned and saw her shrug at the colorful, bare-chested Mr. Tuck and then smile at each of the other men encircling them.

"Mr. Mandeville needs me," she explained. "Perhaps we can continue our talk tomorrow morning." Then she blithely waved good-bye to the sailors.

When the men saw that she was in no danger and more than willing to leave with Trevor, the circle parted and the sailors dispersed. Trevor towed her across the deck and did not stop until they reached a deserted area near the bow.

"Don't *ever* do that again."

"Do what, Trevor?"

What he had seen had so shaken his control that he did not know exactly where to start.

"Let's see. Where should I begin? One, never sit on the deck cross-legged . . . or anywhere else for that matter. Two, never converse with the crew."

"Why not?"

"Because you are a respectable young woman and they are unsavory characters."

"Oh, no they weren't. They were very friendly."

"Don't you remember Rule Number One?"

"Of course. Never be alone with a man."

"So. There you have it." He crossed his arms, satisfied.

"But I wasn't alone with a man. There were at least six of them."

"Which makes what you did six times worse." And she had been in six times more danger. He did not want to even think about what might have happened.

"Is that why you're so angry?"

"I promised your father I would see to your safety. I'm responsible for your well-being and I never take my responsibilities lightly."

"My well-being is just fine, thank you, Trevor."

"You have absolutely no idea what danger you were in, do you?" Before he knew what he was about, he reached out and tucked a stray curl behind her ear. When he realized what he had done, he was thankful that she did not seem to notice.

"I have lived with danger in one way or another every

single day of my life. There are poisonous snakes and slippery trails on Matarenga. The lagoon is filled with sharks of all sizes and even poisonous fish. Why, once we were even attacked by fierce Indonesian pirates. Don't tell me I have no idea when I'm in danger, Trevor."

"But you aren't aware of the customs *off* your island."

"That doesn't mean you can treat me like a child. Don't you see that's what you did back there?"

He saw that quite well and nodded, but he would do it again to see her safe.

"I know you are only keeping your promise to my father, but I see no harm in what I was doing," she argued.

"The harm was not in what you were doing, but in what might have happened. When you act so . . . so relaxed around men like that, with *any* man for that matter, you give the wrong impression."

"What do you mean?"

"I mean . . ." Totally frustrated, he ran his finger around his collar. "I mean that they may get the idea that you are the type of woman who might . . . the sort of woman who would let a man . . . that you might want to . . . let them . . ."

"*Mate* with them?"

With three words she rendered him speechless again.

Joya was staring at him in shock. "I don't think they were thinking any such thing. Besides, I do not believe myself to be a highly desirable woman."

"*What?* Why on earth would you think that?"

"I am twenty years old, far older than any Matarengi bride would ever be. Not one Matarengi ever offered for me, even the men who could afford a high bride price." She looked out to sea as she went on. "I know Papa would have refused them, but still, no one even offered. Neither did any of the white sailors who came to the island. I am certain that they must have found me unappealing."

Trevor sighed, wondering whether he should risk the problems that might arise if she knew how desirable she really was.

"The men on Matarenga were *ordered* by their chief not to touch you. One day during our discussions, your father told me he made it quite clear that the penalty for as much would be death. You were protected on your island. These sailors don't give a hoot who your father is, nor do the men in England. I have a business to see to when I return, and I cannot be everywhere at once playing bodyguard. Not only that, but I've planned an expedition to Venezuela. You are going to have to take some responsibility for yourself and try to abide by the rules of English society."

When the light in her eyes dimmed, he almost wanted to take back every last word. He reminded himself that his warnings were meant for her own good.

That did not make seeing unshed tears shimmering in her eyes any easier.

"My father actually *threatened* the men on Matarenga?"

"Through their head man, Faruki."

"All this time I thought I was undesirable." She spoke in a voice barely above a whisper.

They were under full sail. She reached for the rail and leaned against it, watching the water rush by. The wind blew her hair back off her face. Like spun silk, it tangled and tempted.

"Joya, I am sorry if I have hurt you by telling you the truth." He started to reach for her hair again, to pull it back away from the side of her face. When he realized he was about to touch her again, he dropped his hand. How could she truly believe she was undesirable?

"You needn't feel sorry," she told him. "I would rather hear the truth than continue to live a lie. You have not hurt me, Trevor."

"But you look so sad."

"I grew up hating my white skin because it made me different from the other children. One by one, I watched my friends marry. My parents forbade me to even consider marriage to one of the Matarenga. Do you have any idea what it was like for me growing up? My mother and father and I existed on two islands; one was Matarenga and the other was inside our white skins. For as long as my parents would allow, I tried as hard as I could to be one of the tribe. If I do not know your English rules or customs, it is because I grew up trying so hard to be something I could never, ever be. I rebelled against the white English ways. Now, I must learn to be something entirely different."

She pushed her hair back off her face. Her skin was damp with mist from the sea spray.

"Perhaps I don't belong anywhere," she sighed.

He reached for her, gently touched her shoulder, and urged her to turn around.

"You will learn. You are an intelligent, capable young woman. All you need is time."

"Time to learn the rules, you mean? If I do, do you think an Englishman would find me desirable enough to want to marry me and do the things that husbands and wives do together?"

He shook his head. It was hard for him to believe he was actually having this conversation.

"What do you know of what husbands and wives do together?"

"Everyone on Matarenga knows what happens between a man and his wives, but I am twenty years old and have never even been kissed. I still hold little hope of ever finding a mate. And I think you are wrong, Trevor, I doubt any Englishmen will be attracted to me."

"Of course they will." He did not think he sounded very reassuring at all, especially when he hoped that for his own peace of mind they would not.

"But Janelle and I look alike and she is still unmarried. Is that because men do not find her desirable, either."

"Janelle is unmarried because she is headstrong and opinionated, not because she is undesirable. She has refused so many marriage proposals that no one in our circle of acquaintances will approach her anymore."

"Opinionated?"

"She says exactly what she thinks."

"Being headstrong and truthful is not an admirable trait?"

"Not in English drawing rooms."

"Then I suppose I will not be any more desirable than my sister in English drawing rooms." She laughed, but it was hollow, not joyous. "I am beginning to think that life plays cruel tricks, like Bimjuu, the trickster spirit. I grew up with a mother and father who truly loved one another. I saw their love for one another and I was certain that somewhere in the world, that kind of love existed for me. But now I have learned they weren't even my true mother and father. They loved me, but not enough to tell me the truth about my past. How do I know what is real anymore? Especially love?"

He could name the genus and species of over twelve

hundred orchids. He had survived some of the world's most formidable jungles. He could outbid a business competitor without flinching. But he had absolutely no idea what to say to her about love.

How could he convince her that there was such a thing as a deep abiding love when he had never experienced it himself, nor even witnessed it? How could he convince her that enduring love existed, when he wasn't at all certain that it did?

"These are things you should really speak to Janelle about." He wished he could say something, anything to help.

She tipped her face up, pulling a stray curl away from her lashes. "I've embarrassed you."

"No."

"You look as if you have eaten a bad beetle, Trevor. I have spoken of the wrong things and I'm sorry." She took a deep breath and squared her shoulders. "I must go and see how Janelle is this morning. Thank you for trying to help me."

He stood there mute as she bid him good-bye.

After that day, Trevor spent many long nights aboard ship lying awake, reliving their strange conversation and trying to forget just how desirable Joya Penn was.

Finally the long voyage ended. As they stood at the ship's rail for her first real glimpse of England, Joya plied him with questions. She wanted to know where the palm trees were, why there was no lagoon, and if it was summer, why was it still so cold?

Because she had never seen a moving vehicle in her life, it took a quarter of an hour to convince her that she would survive a coach ride. In the carriage on the way to Mandeville House, the twins were so excited, so lost in an ongoing, high-pitched conversation about where they would go, what they would see, that he felt left out.

Surreptitiously he took sidelong glances at Joya as they mounted the steps to Mandeville House. She gasped at the size of the house, touched the brickwork and the brass lion holding the door knocker in its mouth. Trevor watched her straighten her borrowed bonnet and the bow beneath her chin. She patted her hair into place and smoothed her skirt. Then she fell silent and touched her breast where her amulet pouch lay hidden beneath the bodice of her gown. When she glanced up at him, he saw that there was fear in her eyes.

"Janelle has told me about your grandmother. I don't want to offend her," she confessed in a hushed tone.

Janelle was still beside the carriage, gossiping with their young coachman, Joshua.

"Grandmother's bark is worse than her bite," he said offhandedly.

"She *bites*?" Joya stopped dead still. She stared in horror at the front door.

"That is just a figure of speech," he said.

By now Janelle had rejoined them.

"Oh, Trevor, Joshua just told me that Darcy has had a little boy. She and her husband moved to the country."

"Who in the world is Darcy?"

"Mrs. Billingsley's eldest daughter."

"Who is Mrs. Billingsley?" Joya asked.

"Our housekeeper." Janelle and Trevor answered at the same time.

Trevor opened the door and stood aside while Janelle swept in. He waited as Joya followed cautiously, carefully stepping over the threshold into the entry hall. The foyer was a crowded affair, filled with an array of large mahogany pieces that included a large hall tree off to one side and a huge circular table in the center of the room. The floors were marble, the walls covered in gilt and scarlet. Colorful paintings hung from thick tasseled cords anchored just below the ceiling. An ancient Saxon sword, generations old, was on display near the staircase.

Trevor found himself taking a deep breath as he watched Joya walk to the center of the room, where she placed one hand on the table and then curiously bent to peer beneath it.

Sims, their butler for as long as Trevor could recall, descended upon them as if he had been lurking behind the door, hiding in wait for someone to appear. Ageless, he was tall and still as straight as a lamppost with thinning silver hair.

"There you are, Sims, just as I expected. Do you know, when I was a lad, I thought you lived here in the foyer?"

"I do, sir," Sims said without pause. "Welcome home." Then he turned to Janelle. "Welcome home, miss. You are looking well."

"Thank you, Sims. I must say I'm much better now that I'm on dry land."

"How is my grandmother?" Trevor inquired. When Sims did not answer, Trevor realized it was because the butler was staring at Joya, who had righted herself.

"Sims?" Trevor had never known the man to be at a loss for words. By now, Joya had begun to wander slowly around the room. She walked over to a near-life-sized statue of a winged Mercury and began to run her palm slowly up and down its smooth marble thigh. Trevor had to look away.

Sims blinked rapidly and then turned back and forth from Joya to Janelle, who had paused to strip off her gloves.

Trevor tried to distract Joya's attention from the statue.

"Miss Joya Penn, this is Sims, our butler. Miss Penn is Janelle's twin sister."

"Her . . . twin. Ah, that explains it, then . . . of course." Sims began to direct the footman who was carrying in the luggage. He turned to Trevor and added, "Perhaps, sir, you and the young ladies would like to join Mrs. Mandeville in the drawing room where she is taking tea. I'll have Cook prepare more."

"Thank you, Sims." Trevor was finally forced to guide Joya away from Mercury.

"I thought you told me that the English did not go about naked," she whispered.

"*That* is not an Englishman," he informed her. "Take off your hat and gloves and hand them to Mrs. Billingsley, that charming older woman bearing down on us from the stairs."

The housekeeper fluttered into the room to greet Janelle with a hug. She was about to welcome Trevor when he stepped aside and she had her first glimpse of Joya.

"Oh, my. Oh, *my*!"

"Miss Joya Penn, this is Mrs. Billingsley, our housekeeper."

Joya smiled. "Hello, Mrs. Billingsley. My mother was a housekeeper, too."

Trevor sighed. "Miss Penn is Janelle's twin sister," he explained.

By now, Mrs. Billingsley had dropped her hands from her cheeks to her apron and had begun to twist the material into a knot.

"Every happiness to your recently married daughter, Mrs. Billingsley." Joya added. "May Kibatante keep her as fertile as a hen and her man's rod as straight and strong as a spear made of ebony wood."

Trevor closed his eyes and bit the inside of his cheeks. Sims emitted a strange wheezing sound, somewhere between a bark and a gasp. By the time Trevor recovered, Janelle had Joya by the arm and was leading her toward the drawing room.

Before Trevor could race across the hallway to intercept the butler, Sims had sidestepped the twins, opened the drawing room door and announced, "Madam, the adventurers have returned!"

Chapter 12

At last, my grandson is home.

Adelaide wanted to box Trevor's ears for being away so long, but she had not been able to reach his ears for quite some time and had given up boxing them years ago.

Upon hearing Sims's announcement, she set down her teacup and saucer and turned in anticipation. But it was not Trevor she saw coming through the door, but Janelle, who appeared to be walking arm in arm with . . . *herself*?

Immediately, Adelaide put her hand to her forehead, certain that she had taken her last breath. She had never wanted James to adopt the Oates girl in the first place. Was this, then, her punishment for never truly loving her adopted grandaughter as much as she did Trevor? Was her last earthly vision to be that of *two* Janelles?

A small moan escaped her. Thankfully there was only one of Trevor bounding through the door, quickly skirting the two Janelles. With his long sure strides, he rushed to her side.

"Grandmother, you are looking wonderful."

"Don't be foolish. I think I'm dying," she snapped.

"You look perfectly healthy to me." He kissed her cheek.

She pressed both hands to her temples. "Why then, am I seeing double?"

Janelle tugged her likeness closer. "You aren't seeing double, Grandmama. I have the most wonderful, most fantastic surprise."

Adelaide turned to Trevor. "Please tell me, what is going on here?"

Trevor shot a dark glance at Janelle, then another at Sims, who hovered in the open doorway.

"I had planned to tell you myself, not surprise you like this."

Behind her little round spectacles, Janelle was smiling like a cat in the cream. The young woman beside her, who Adelaide had decided upon closer inspection was not *exactly* Janelle at all, had the nerve to rudely stare back.

"Someone had better explain this and very quickly." She was an old woman. She did not need a shock like this. She reached for Trevor's hand.

Janelle pulled her likeness closer and said, "Grandmama, this is Joya Penn. Joya *Oates* Penn, my twin sister. I can hardly believe it myself, but we found her on an island off the coast of Africa, where we also discovered Dustin Penn. *And* my father's grave!"

"You are telling me this girl . . . this *twin* . . . has existed all these years without anyone's knowledge? Surely, Trevor, your father must have known, for he was there the night Janelle was born." She looked back and forth between the young women. "There must be some reason he did not want to keep them together."

She frowned. It was highly unlikely that James would have separated the sisters unless this new one was deformed, or perhaps mad. Even so, she would not have put it past James to have kept the second girl anyway. He would have felt compelled to raise both infants.

Her dear Trevor had seated himself beside her on the settee and began to explain.

"Father had no idea that Janelle had a twin because one of the Oates servants secreted her out of the house and ran off to Africa with the orchid hunter, Dustin Penn."

"The man you were searching for, dear?"

"Yes."

"Joya, say hello to Adelaide Mandeville." Janelle gave the other girl a nudge. "You may call her Grandmama."

"She may not," Adelaide snapped.

The chit stepped closer. Adelaide looked her up and down. She recognized the girl's gown as one of Janelle's. She supposed the rest of the ensemble belonged to Janelle as well.

On closer inspection, she saw obvious differences between Joya Penn and Janelle. Her eyes were huge, round, and blue, and filled with an ingenuousness Janelle never exhibited. Her sun-darkened skin was an acute embarrassment. Her hair was shades lighter than Janelle's, far thicker and curlier. One of her ribbons had come untied and was dangling precariously against her cheek.

She fidgeted where she stood, looking around the room with undisguised curiosity and wonder. At a glance, she appeared to be neither deformed or mad. Only time would tell.

Then, of a sudden, Joya Penn's gaze met and held

Trevor's, and Adelaide saw more in that brief exchange than she wanted to see. Beside her, Trevor stirred and shifted positions.

Adelaide quickly turned to him and caught a brief, unmistakable flicker of carnal heat in his eyes. It was immediately extinguished, but the fact that the spark was there at all ignited her determination.

She had *not* molded her grandson to become the man he was, to make the strides he had made, the connections—not to mention a fortune—to have him throw everything away on the orphaned twin of his adopted sister.

Oh, how she wished James were alive. She would look him in the eye and say, "I *told* you nothing good would come of you bringing that Oates child into our home."

"Grandmother?" Trevor had laid a hand on her shoulder. His touch startled her back to the moment.

"Yes, dear. I'm fine. This is all quite a shock, you know." She forced herself to smile at Joya Penn, to appear civil. "Welcome to our home, Miss Penn. I hope you have a pleasant holiday here."

The girl stood there like a simpleton. Janelle's smile instantly faded. "She's not here on holiday, Grandmama. Joya has come to live with us."

For Adelaide, staying calm suddenly became an effort.

"How nice. Step closer, Joya Penn. Let me get a look at you."

The girl made an awkward, bobbing motion, something between a curtsy and a bow. She moved no closer.

"I am pleased to meet you, Mrs. Mandeville. You have the eyes of a cobra."

"A *what*?"

Sims, who had tucked himself inside the door, began to wheeze. Adelaide dismissed him with a cold nod. He hurried back to the foyer and closed the door behind him. The wheezing faded along with the sound of his footsteps.

"I believe that is a *good* thing, Grandmama," Janelle said quickly. "Isn't it Joya?"

"Oh, yes. They are cunning and wise and it's very hard to trap one."

Adelaide was beginning to wonder whether the girl was as simple as she seemed, or whether perhaps she was playing them all for fools.

"Where are you from again?"

"I am from Matarenga, a small island off the coast of Africa. It's a very beautiful place."

"And your father is the famous Dustin Penn. How did he come to raise you on an African isle?"

"My mother, Clara, was a housekeeper who worked for the Oateses." Joya smiled at Janelle. "She delivered us. My father says that when she saw there were two babies born that night, she decided to keep one for herself."

Adelaide's heart stopped. Her head began to swim.

"Clara. A housekeeper who worked for the Oateses."

Slowly, Adelaide turned to Trevor, terrified of what he might already know. Suddenly she wished she had forbidden his going to Africa. She wished she had feigned illness, begged him not to leave, anything to keep him from discovering the dark secret she had guarded all his life.

There was nothing in his expression that told her anything had changed. She prayed he still knew nothing.

"This woman, this Clara . . ." She fought to choose her words carefully. "Did you meet her, Trevor?"

"No." He shook his head. "She passed away a few years ago."

Safe. The secret was still safe. Or was it? And for how long?

Adelaide began to breathe a bit easier. Her heart recovered. How in God's name could this have happened? Out of all the islands in all the world, all the jungles where her grandson might have searched for an orchid worthy of Queen Victoria's name, how had he found the very place to which the maid, Clara Hayworth had disappeared?

She wanted to scream at the injustice of it.

Instead, she held her piece and tried to decide how much the Penn chit knew about her "mother," Clara Hayworth.

Only two things were certain at this point; that Janelle, thrilled to have found her sister, would be of no help at all, and that Trevor was half smitten already.

It would be up to her, Adelaide, to make certain Joya Penn was soon out of their home and out of Trevor's life.

Joya let Janelle usher her to a chair. Mimicking her sister's every move, she sat down carefully, folded her hands in her lap, and tried to make herself unobtrusive.

Everything about London and Mandeville House was overwhelming. She knew nothing of London manners, but even she could sense when she was not welcome. She felt it each time she locked gazes with Adelaide Mandeville and the woman's eyes would narrow. But then, what else could one expect from a woman who bit people?

As Trevor and Janelle conversed with their grandmother, Joya settled back, thankful to be forgotten. She sipped the rich, dark tea and was content to look around. Even though it was the beginning of summer, a low fire burned in the fireplace. Long windows lined the room, but heavy draperies blocked much of the sunlight. The drawing room was shadowed and crowded, filled with tables and chairs and settees upholstered in lush, dark fabrics. The walls were covered with shimmering gold material. A multitude of paintings of horses and dogs and vases full of flowers vied for wall space with gilt-framed mirrors. There seemed to be something amazing everywhere she looked.

When her gaze met Adelaide's, she instantly realized the older woman had been watching her. Despite the fire, she shivered with a chill. There had been a change in Adelaide the moment that Trevor had mentioned Clara Penn, one that neither Janelle or Trevor seemed to have noticed. Joya tried to convince herself that perhaps she was imagining Adelaide's dislike. Perhaps the woman stared at every newcomer with such cold calculation.

"Please pour more tea, Janelle," Adelaide requested. Then she turned her attention to Trevor once more. "Now, tell me all about your trip. Don't leave out a single detail."

While Trevor, Janelle and Adelaide talked on and on, Joya paid scant attention and let her thoughts wander. She longed to be outdoors, for she wanted to see more of London than she had during the exhilarating and frightening carriage ride through the crowded streets, but there would be plenty of time for that. She contented herself with finishing her tea. The chair was deep and comfortable. Soon she found it hard to keep her eyes open.

"Joya?"

She had no idea how long she had dozed before Trevor woke her. Through the lingering haze of sleep she thought his voice one of the finest sounds she had ever heard.

"I must have fallen asleep." She smiled over at him.

As she attempted to straighten, the china cup and saucer began to slide off of her lap. When she made a grab for them, she accidentally clapped the two pieces together.

Tea and china chips flew off both delicate floral pieces. A long crack neatly halved the saucer just as the cup broke into three pieces. Joya closed her hands over them and, in an effort to keep the china from hitting the floor, slid off the chair onto her knees.

Kneeling on the stained carpeting, she looked up and whispered, "I'm sorry."

Adelaide gently set down her own cup and did nothing to hide her disgust. "That was my aunt's china. It was very, very old."

"You've cut yourself," Janelle exclaimed, ready to rush to Joya's aid, but Trevor was already there.

"Here," he said softly, kneeling down before her. He took the broken pieces from her and passed the china fragments to Janelle, then gently took both of Joya's hands in his, turned them up, and inspected her wounds. There was a shallow cut in her left palm, a bit of china stuck in her right.

Joya bit her lips together as he carefully pulled out the sliver and handed it to Janelle. Then he took his linen napkin and gently daubed both her wounds. He pressed the napkin against the longest slice and helped Joya to her feet.

"That is just the sort of thing I was talking about," Adelaide said.

Trevor's hand tightened slightly, but not uncomfortably, on Joya's arm. "Grandmother, I think we should discuss this later."

"It was just an accident, Grandmama." Janelle carried the broken cup over to the tea tray and set the pieces down. "It could have happened to anyone."

"I won't have this family embarrassed in front of our closest friends and business associates. She is simply *not* ready."

"Not ready for what?" Joya looked to Janelle and then Trevor.

"Grandmother was concerned that you might be uncomfortable in a formal situation," he said.

"What formal situation?"

Adelaide set her cup down, occupied with very precise, careful movements. There was a great rustling of black silk whenever she moved, and afterward the scent of wilted flowers filled the air.

Janelle stood beside the fireplace. "Knowing we were due back, Grandmother had already planned a gathering of friends, which is to take place in a fortnight. She is concerned that you might need more time to become accustomed to . . . well, everything. But I think it would be a wonderful way to introduce you."

"Trevor, please reason with your sister," Adelaide said.

He was already leading Joya across the room.

"Right now, I'm going to take Joya upstairs. Janelle, please tell Mrs. Billingsley to have a look at these cuts. She may need to send for a doctor."

Joya tried to pull her arm free. "I do *not* need a doctor. My mother told me all about doctors. They bleed people to make them well. I do *not* want a doctor to cut my throat."

He kept walking, and so she was forced to walk with

him. "No one is going to cut your throat."

"I do not need you to drag me across the carpet, either."

Adelaide called sharply, "Trevor, we have yet to discuss your schedule. Everyone in the Orchid Society is quite excited about the search for the Victoria orchid. You will need to leave in the next few weeks if you are going to be the first to find it."

"After I have Joya settled, I'll return and you can tell me everything that's happened while we were away."

"I'm sure Janelle would be happy to see her sister upstairs. You needn't—"

Before Adelaide could finish, Trevor had already pulled Joya out of the drawing room and across the foyer toward the staircase.

It's already started. Just as I feared.

Trevor tended to agree with his grandmother that Joya was not ready to be formally introduced. She had barely set foot inside Mandeville House and she had already caused a disturbance.

What disturbed him even more was the fact that he felt compelled to see to Joya himself, to get her away from his grandmother's disapproving stare and see to her well-being.

"I think we should go back," Joya said. "Your grandmother sounded upset."

"She'll recover."

They started up the staircase.

"Where are we going?" She paused, looking dubiously up the long flight of stairs.

"I'm taking you to your room. It's right next to Janelle's. You will feel more comfortable there."

"I am already comfortable." She stopped every few

steps to look down the steep stairwell. "This is very high."

"Mrs. Billingsley took care of all of our bumps and bruises when we were children. She'll see to your cuts."

"Your grandmother did not tend you?"

"No, definitely not Grandmother." He smiled, unable to imagine his grandmother dispensing warm milk and medical aid. Her forte was business advice.

"She doesn't like me." Joya stopped at the top of the stairs, looked back down again, and then followed him along the seemingly endless hallway.

Joya's observation was far more perceptive than he would have thought. He had noticed as much, too, and attributed his grandmother's seeming dislike to a genuine concern for the repercussions and speculation that would come of Joya's sudden appearance. He could have denied his grandmother's behavior, but feared Joya would see through the lie.

"The notion that Janelle has a twin is a bit of a shock for everyone. It will take Grandmother time to get used to your . . . ways."

Joya stopped again, this time to inspect the wall covering, which depicted a forest scene. She touched it lightly, reverently, with her fingertips. She was so uninhibited and spontaneous—traits that hardly seemed offenses when he thought about them. He shook his head. Heaven help him if he starting thinking like Janelle.

They continued down the hall, turned a corner.

"It's very dark up here," she whispered.

It was dim inside, but the day itself was gray and dismal. Showers were imminent. Little light filtered through the layers of lace and velvet window coverings.

Portraits of grim-faced Mandeville ancestors glared back at them as they passed by.

"Who are all these old men?" She paused again, leaned close to one portrait, stood on tiptoe, and touched the nose of one especially dour-looking gentleman.

"Those are my ancestors. Great-grandfathers and great-uncles. Great-great ones, I suppose. All Mandevilles through and through."

"Why are they so great?"

"Do you plan on bleeding all over the carpet or will you please come along?"

She held her hands up, inspecting them by the weak light.

"I'm not bleeding at all." She glanced over her shoulder. "How do you keep from getting lost?"

"We drop bread crumbs."

"The entire Matarengi tribe could live here."

That pronouncement conjured up images best left alone, he decided. The sound of their footsteps echoed hollowly in the hall. When they reached the door to her room he opened it and ushered her in.

At least here, with corner windows, the light was better. As she walked past him, Trevor caught the satin hair ribbon that had slipped off her shoulder.

"Why, there is my trunk." She turned to him, clearly amazed to find her little trunk waiting at the foot of the bed.

"The footman brought it up."

"How did he know where I was going to sleep?"

"Sims told him."

"How did Sims know?"

"Because Janelle told him." He handed her the ribbon. She set it on the nightstand.

"My hair has fallen apart," she said mournfully. "Perhaps that is why your grandmother doesn't like me."

"I told you not to take offense. Grandmother can be difficult at times. I greatly admire her, for it is due primarily to her efforts that Mandeville Imports has grown and thrived—no small feat for a woman to succeed in business, which is still very much a man's world. She has always put the family first, even though she married into the Mandevilles. Now, please, sit down and let me look at your hands again. Where is Mrs. Billingsley, I wonder?"

Joya appeared thoughtful for a moment, then ignored his request and walked over to the window fronting the street. She pulled aside the heavy, gold drapery, lifted the edge of the material, and rubbed it against her cheek.

"So soft." She turned to him again. "What is the name of this cloth, Trevor?"

"Velvet."

"I like it very much."

"I'll tell Janelle. She can see that you have a gown fashioned out of it."

"Oh, but I would hate to have her cut up your window covering." She dropped the drapery and turned to him again. "Why are you looking at me like that?"

"Like what?"

"Like you ate—"

"Another bad beetle?"

"Yes." She walked to the edge of the bed and sat down. The curls on the ribbonless side of her hair had fallen to her shoulder. He knew it was not the style, but he still liked her hair better that way; it seemed more like Joya.

She held up her hands. "You see. No blood."

Trevor took a deep breath and crossed the room. He took both her hands in his and turned them toward the light. Her cuts were superficial and no longer bleeding. The deeper wound was only oozing a bit. A good washing and perhaps a small bandage was all she would need in the way of care.

Her hands felt small and very fragile in his. They were not the delicate hands of a woman of leisure, but callused from wielding a machete. Her nails were short, but evenly trimmed and clean. Off her island, she had a fragility, an odd tenderness and vulnerability that he had not suspected when he first laid eyes on her, but he felt it now, saw it in the open, trusting way she looked up into his eyes.

The room was incredibly quiet. In the stillness he became very aware of her nearness. The soft sigh of her breath, the warmth radiating from her, enticed him. He liked the way her hand felt in his.

Suddenly he imagined himself bending close and pressing her back against the goldenrod bedspread— imagined covering her lush, tempting mouth with his. He could almost taste her and knew she would be innocent, exotic. She was too tempting.

She was lovely and unattached, but no proper young miss would have ever allowed herself to be alone with him like this. Was it because Joya was so naive, or because he was Janelle's brother, that she trusted him so?

She did trust him and it did not matter why. She had put herself into his hands. If he were to kiss her or make any other improper advance, he would be taking advantage of an innocent.

He found himself wondering whether she might be the least bit attracted to him. Surely looking into a man's eyes as if she were about to drown in them was not a habit with her, but there was only one way to find out.

Trevor reminded himself that he was a man of prin-

ciple, a man of good conduct—a *gentleman*. He refused
to cross that line.

"Well?" Her voice, barely above a whisper, was as
soft as a tender caress. "What do you think?"

Confused, Trevor let go of her hands and straightened.
He looked away from the bed, away from temptation,
and cleared his throat. He took a deep breath and col-
lected himself.

"I think it's time I went to see what's keeping Mrs.
Billingsley. I will send Janelle up, too."

Thankfully, he did not break into a cold sweat until
he was in the hall.

Chapter 13

Joya had not been alone long when Mrs. Billingsley confidently bustled into the room, followed by a young maid who had barely left childhood behind. The girl, introduced to her as Betty, was dressed in a starched white apron. She carried a large pitcher and a roll of bandages, which she placed on a washstand before she quickly left again.

"Oh, you poor, poor dear," Mrs. Billingsley cooed. "Let me have a look at those cuts. Don't worry about a thing, miss. I've a knack at putting things like this to right."

As Mrs. Billingsley fussed and clucked over nothing, Joya sat patiently, content to let her mind wander back to her conversation with Trevor. Almost the entire time he had been talking to her, her heart had fluttered so erratically that she had barely been able to concentrate on a single word.

Whenever he was around, she noticed, her body had begun to do some very peculiar things. When her heart was not dancing to an erratic tune, she tingled all over. Her face felt flushed, her hands went cold, her knees weakened.

Since the day they had left tropical waters, the only time she ever felt warm enough was whenever he was near.

Could it be that she desired him? Could it be that she was falling in love?

She stared at Mrs. Billingsley's curly head of silver and white hair while the housekeeper bent over and gently dabbed a layer of fine white cloth against her palm.

"Mrs. Billingsley, as you are one of the elders here, would you mind if I ask you something? I'm not certain it wouldn't be more proper to ask Mr. Sims, since he might be older than either you or Mrs. Mandeville, but since you are here, and since I am very curious about something, I would like to ask you."

Mrs. Billingsley cleansed the second cut and smiled. Her cheeks were bright pink and ruddy, the rest of her complexion soft and doughy white. When she smiled, her brown eyes crinkled at the corners.

In the kindly woman's presence, Joya could not help but think of her mother. Clara, too, once served in a grand English house, just like Mrs. Billingsley. Knowing that gave Joya a sense of connection with the housekeeper, much more so than with Adelaide.

"I would be honored. What is it, dear?" A warm glow lit the housekeeper's eyes. Her mouth pursed into a neat little bow as she stood there so attentively.

"What does a woman feel like when she wants to mate with a man? Do strange things happen to her body? How does she know when it is time to marry? Is it when she desires a man and finds herself wishing that he will take her to his bed and do all the things that husbands do to their wives?"

Slowly, Mrs. Billingsley's eyes grew very round. The neat little bow of her lips unraveled into a gaping *O*. Her ruddy cheeks darkened to crimson, then went deep purple.

"Mrs. Billingsley? Are you all right?"

Joya was afraid that the housekeeper was going to die. She had seen it happen to an elderly woman in the village. One minute the crone had been dancing around the sacred ceremonial hut where the young maidens were taken to be initiated into womanhood. That woman had had just the same sort of strange, surprised expression before she sat down on the ground; and then she crumpled to her side and her spirit left her.

"Mrs. Billingsley? You are not dying, are you?" Joya was relieved when the housekeeper gasped and began to gulp air. At the same time, Janelle breezed into the room.

"What's wrong with Mrs. Billingsley?"

The housekeeper began to sputter. "I . . . she said . . . she . . . *You* talk . . . to her, miss."

With that, Mrs. Billingsley quickly gathered up the bandages, swept the room with her gaze and made certain nothing else was out of place, then left them alone.

As soon as the door clicked shut, Janelle sat down on the bed beside Joya. "Do you have everything you need?"

"Yes, thank you. The room is beautiful. Trevor said to tell you to have a dress made for me out of the draperies, but that is really not necessary. I'm happy with the one you have already given me."

Janelle frowned and chewed on her lip for a moment, watching her closely. "He wants me to have a gown made for you out of the draperies?"

"Yes, but I don't want one. Could we talk about Mrs. Billingsley instead? I am afraid I've upset her somehow." As Janelle leaned back on her elbows, Joya wondered whether her own eyes ever twinkled the way Janelle's did right now. It gave her a good feeling to see her twin so happy.

"Go right ahead, dear sister. I cannot *wait* to hear this."

"You see, on Matarenga, whenever one has a question or a problem, one seeks out an elder. They have lived long lives and therefore are very knowing."

"Why don't we just concentrate on what you actually said to Mrs. Billingsley for now?" Janelle suggested.

"I asked her to tell me what it feels like when a woman desires a man enough to want to lie with him. Does a strange sort of feeling come over her?"

Janelle quickly sat back up. "You asked Mrs. Billingsley about desire?"

Joya nodded. "Was that wrong?"

"I'm certain that you took her by surprise."

"In what way?"

"People usually don't speak of such things openly here. Especially to the servants."

"But why not? If people don't speak of desire, or ask questions when they are curious, how will they ever learn anything?"

Janelle appeared very thoughtful. She also looked as if she were trying hard not to laugh. "A good point. Whatever made you ask?"

Joya stood up to pace in front of the bank of windows, hoping to find a way to express her curious feelings. "You see, I had never really spoken to a white man until Trevor walked into our camp," she began.

Then she walked toward Janelle and noticed that her

sister's smooth brow was furrowed into deep thought lines.

"Trevor is not the cause of these questions you put to Mrs. Billingsley, is he?" Janelle asked.

Joya sat down on the bed again.

"That is the troubling part. Lately, whenever I have been alone with Trevor, I have felt very, *very* strange."

"How do you mean, *strange*?"

"Light-headed and dizzy. My heart pounds. My face grows hot. My hands turn cold. My knees go weak. I find I'm only afflicted whenever Trevor is near."

"You *only* feel this way when you are with Trevor?"

"Only with Trevor . . . and there is one thing more."

"I'm almost afraid to ask. What is that?"

"Just now I found myself wishing that Trevor would kiss me."

Janelle stared back at her sister, an experience not unlike looking into a mirror, but a somewhat distorted mirror. In Joya she saw herself, but not herself. Any discerning eye could see the many subtle differences: the fact that Joya had perfect vision, the way she walked and talked, the lighter color of her hair, her sun-darkened skin— characteristics that were all her own.

Different, too, was the expression of wonder and awe in Joya's eyes. Each and every new experience captivated her. Her unbridled enthusiasm and her innocence made Janelle feel much older and wiser. Her sister's mind was a *tabula rasa*, a clean or pristine state that had oft been the topic for discussion at her friend Cecily Martin's salon gatherings.

Joya could very well be likened to an open book, ready to receive the impressions of London civilization.

But now it appeared that what her sister was most impressed with so far was Trevor.

"Janelle? You are so quiet. Have I upset you, too?"

"No. You have not upset me." Janelle shook her head, trying to assure Joya that she was fine—while in actuality she was not quite sure.

Trevor was her brother, not by blood, but in all other ways. Joya her twin. Even though her sister had not grown up as a Mandeville, Janelle had assumed—falsely, she realized now—that Joya might eventually come to look up to Trevor as a guardian of sorts, if not a brother.

But now Joya was beginning to harbor deeper feelings for Trevor and, because Joya was almost an exact image of herself, the whole idea of her twin's attraction to Trevor and perhaps of his to Joya—if indeed he nurtured one—was more than a bit unsettling. It was greatly disturbing.

"Your forehead is all scrunched up, the way it was when you were seasick," Joya told her.

"You have given me much to consider, is all."

"Have *you* ever desired a man, Janelle?"

There it was again. Desire. And the image Janelle conjured was of Joya and Trevor locked in a fervent embrace.

"Can we talk about this tomorrow? I think I am coming down with a headache."

"Put my silly questions out of your mind." Joya hurried over to her trunk.

"I'll send Betty in with some more clothes for you," she said. "Perhaps you need help unpacking your things?"

"Oh, no. There is not all that much here, just a few things that are precious to me. My beaded bracelets and an anklet. A *pudong*, a native wrap. I have a ceremonial goat-hoof rattle, too, because it is necessary for every important ceremony. Some medicines. I can do this on my own." Joya was bent over her things, intently searching for something.

Janelle thought about how she liked to fancy herself open-minded and progressive—one who could debate politics as well as any man. A well-read, *forward*-thinking woman. Yet her sister's innocent inquiries had brought on a pounding headache.

She quickly decided retreat was her only option for now. Tomorrow was Tuesday, and Cecily always held a salon on Tuesdays. It would be the perfect opportunity to present her own dilemma as a topic for discussion. It would certainly prove a far more titillating subject than the usual debate upon the terrible conditions of women or the poor.

Joya was waiting by the door, holding something.

"Tomorrow morning, I have a meeting to attend," Janelle told her, hoping Joya would not mind staying home alone. "But I should be back by midday. In the afternoon, we will go to the dressmaker's and order your wardrobe. With Grandmama's dinner party set for two weeks from now, we'll have much to do to prepare."

She stood up and smoothed out her skirt. "Why don't you rest? We'll talk at dinner." Then as an afterthought she added, "Oh, and Joya, I think it would be best if we kept this conversation to ourselves. Do not bring up the topic of desire at dinner, especially in front of Grandmama."

Joya assured her that she would not and thanked her for the advice. Then she said, "I have found something for your headache. Go to your room and lie down and then place this over your forehead, between your eyebrows." Joya opened her hand. Lying across her injured palm was a small pouch made of some sort of reptile skin.

"What is *that*?"

"It is a lizard-skin amulet stuffed with pulverized shark liver."

"I think," Janelle began, forcing a smile as her stomach turned over, "a short nap is all I need." She quickly walked toward the door.

"Are you sure? This works very fast."

"I'm quite sure. You are sweet to be concerned." Janelle eyed the lizard-skin amulet in alarm.

"I may use it myself, then. As I said, I've not been quite right lately."

"You do that. I'll see you in a little while." Janelle closed the door behind her and leaned against the solid mahogany. She shut her eyes, afraid to admit that Trevor might have been right in his concerns about bringing Joya to London.

Chapter 14

Lady Cecily Martin had been in what she called her Chinese phase for two years. The cloying scent of incense lingered in every room of her London town house. The place had been done over with teakwood furnishings, dragons, lacquered ebony screens, and scarlet satin upholstery.

When Janelle was admitted to the familiar surroundings, she expected to find the rest of their group gathered there. Ushered into the drawing room, she found Cecily alone and dressed, as usual, in a heavily embroidered Chinese robe and wearing bangles up both arms. She was reclining upon her favorite divan, anxiously waiting to hear every detail of Janelle's excursion to Africa.

"I thought there was a discussion scheduled for this morning, Cecily. You should have sent word that it was canceled." Concerned, Janelle asked, "Are you ill?"

"No. I canceled the meeting because I wanted to talk to you alone. You have been gone for weeks and we have much to catch up on. And . . ." Cecily paused dramatically, "I have some very good news."

Janelle stripped off her gloves and laid them aside, happy to be in the comfortable presence of her dearest friend again.

"To tell the truth, I'm glad to have this time alone with you, for I too have some astounding news and I need your advice." Janelle, thinking of Joya, sat down amid a pile of huge, soft pillows gathered on the Oriental carpet.

Cecily's expression immediately became one of concern. "Is everything all right?"

"Something unbelievable has happened, but first, tell me your good news."

"Actually, it is good news for you. I have met someone who wants to become your patron. Not only is he interested in commissioning some paintings for himself, but he has many friends who consider themselves art collectors and he feels he can sell your work."

Janelle had always painted to fill the long hours of the night, when the horrors of her nightmares kept her awake. By bringing to life the haunting jungle scenes, she had hoped to face her fears and let them go. She had never thought of selling one of her works.

"Who is he?"

"An older gentleman, a friend of a friend. He attended last month's meeting—a resounding session on magnetism, by the way. Anyway, he saw the painting you gave me in the entry hall and demanded to know the artist's name. He said that if you have others, he could be instrumental in placing them."

"I've never sold a painting. I don't need the money."

"You could use it for charitable works," Cecily suggested.

"You told him the artist is a woman?"

"Yes, of course. He suggested you continue to sign them J. Mandeville." Cecily tucked her legs beneath her on the low reclining divan. The bangles on her arms tinkled. "He's a very personable, older gentleman, who by the way has a very, very handsome nephew with quite a reputation with the ladies in his district. The trouble is, the nephew is penniless. He is very anxious to meet you."

"My new patron or the nephew?"

"Your patron, Viscount Arthur, Lord David Langley. His nephew's name is Garr. Garr Remington."

"A title will certainly make things easier where Grandmama is concerned. If she ever finds out that *Viscount* Arthur is encouraging my work, her protest will be short-lived." Janelle thought for a moment, then said, "You don't think the viscount is only interested because of his nephew, do you? Perhaps he is only pretending to be interested so that he can bring this penniless but handsome rake and I together."

"I did not even hint that you were a woman until he was very committed. Now, I won't say another word until you tell me what stupendous thing happened in Africa. How are your nightmares? The insomnia?"

Janelle shook her head. "Gone—because of the most profound thing that happened on a small island called Matarenga."

She went on to tell Cecily about the great coincidence of Trevor's seeking out Dustin Penn on Matarenga, how she followed him to the island, and of the discoveries of both Joya and Osmond Oates's final resting place. Then she briefly outlined Joya's background.

"You must be delighted!" Cecily cried. "Why didn't

you bring her along? I cannot wait to meet this *tabula rasa*, this twin of yours."

"And you shall meet her. Soon, I hope. I left her at home today only because something has come up, something that I would have never expected."

"You look very baffled, my dear. What is it?" Cecily poured Janelle more tea. The bangles tinkled again—a sound that Cecily said always reminded her of fairies singing.

"I believe my twin sister is falling in love with Trevor."

"Why should that pose a problem? Your sister is no more related to Trevor than you are. Unless, perhaps, you are in love with Trevor yourself. Is that what's bothering you? Have you been harboring hidden feelings for him all along? There would be nothing wrong with that, you know."

"*Please*. Do not turn this into a Greek drama, Cecily. Of course I'm not in love with Trevor." Janelle stared at a huge statue of a laughing Buddha in the corner. "I suppose that I assumed Joya would come to think of Trevor as her brother, too."

Cecily leaned closer and lowered her voice to a hush. "Does the fact that she's attracted to him disturb you in an erotic way?"

"Heavens, no!" After last night's discussion on desire with Joya, Janelle was definitely convinced she was not as much of a free thinker as she professed to be.

"Then what *is* the problem, exactly?"

"Seeing them together will be a bit odd for me, don't you think?"

"If your sister were not your twin, would this bother you at all?"

"No. Yes. I'm not certain." Janelle propped her chin on her fist.

"You have to begin to think of her as an individual, not an extension of yourself."

"We are different in every way, except for our features."

"Does Trevor return her affection?"

"*Trevor*? Trevor is like his father. Instead of just his plants, he's in love with both the family business and his orchids."

"I think you might be forgetting that your brother is also a man."

"I have no idea if he is attracted to Joya," Janelle admitted.

"Do you have any objection to a union between them, aside from the fact that it might make you uncomfortable to see them together?"

Her friend's question brought her up short. Joya and Trevor actually together? What if her organized, structured, no-nonsense brother did begin to see Joya as more than an obligation or a nuisance?

The idea of Trevor falling in love, especially with someone like Joya, his opposite in so many ways, was intriguing. Indeed, the more she thought about such a match, the more she realized there was no reason why the two of them should *not* be together.

Trevor was the person for whom she cared most in the entire world, and Joya was her twin. Already there was a bond between all of them, one that became stronger every day.

If anyone needed a lighter heart and outlook on life, it was Trevor. And Joya, so spontaneous, so unpredictable, might be exactly the kind of woman he needed. The longer Janelle thought about it, the more she became convinced a match between them would be right.

"What are you smiling about?" Cecily leaned back, stretched her arm across the back of the divan, and plumped up a tasseled satin pillow.

"I believe that perhaps the greatest challenge of my life will be getting Trevor and Joya together."

"Joya, please don't hang out the carriage window. You might fall out on your head, or at the very least, you will be spattered with mud."

Joya felt Janelle tugging on her skirt and ducked back inside. This was only her second time in a carriage, and she had come to love the thrill of moving along above the ground. Beside her on the seat lay drawings of some of the places she had seen, drawings she intended to send home to her father.

"There is just so very much to see," she told Janelle. "It is hard for me to take in everything at once." On impulse, she reached over and squeezed Janelle in a ferocious hug. "Thank you so much for showing me London."

"You should be thanking me for getting you out of the dressmaker's alive." Janelle reached over and straightened Joya's hat and the satin bow tied beneath her chin.

"It was horrible. First that woman tapping her foot and making that *tsk, tsk* sound and then all of that talk about how the sun has ruined my skin. Then, when she came at me with all those sharp pins, yelling at me to stand still, wrapping me in fabric. Can you blame me for bursting out in a Matarengi war cry?"

"I'm certainly glad that Madame Fifi did not hit her head on anything when you began to scream and she fainted. I assure you that you will find those few moments of misery worthwhile when you see your new wardrobe. Madame Fifi is one of London's finest seamstresses."

Janelle looked out the window and smiled.

"Life with you is anything but boring, Joya. Ah, we're here at last. Now, come along and try not to get into any trouble between the coach and the door."

"Where are we?"

"You said you wanted to see where your orchids had gone. We are at Mandeville Imports." Janelle gathered her skirt when the carriage door swung open.

Joya wondered at her sister's ability to move so nimbly beneath so many layers of clothing.

"We've come to pay Trevor a surprise visit. Stir up his tidy schedule a bit. He is, no doubt, happily up to his neck in work," Janelle said.

"Trevor?" Joya put her hand to her breast and shrank back against the squab seat.

"Are you coming?"

Joya had not really seen anything of him except for a brief period at dinner the night before, during which time Adelaide demanded his full attention. She mustered the courage to step out of the carriage. As she approached the huge double doors and slowly read the Mandeville Imports sign high above them, she realized that she no longer had to be in Trevor's immediate presence to suffer heart palpitations. The mere idea that she was about to see him again had brought them on this time.

Inside the front office, Joya was introduced to Jamison Roth, a man with a long face who looked to be slightly older than Trevor, but not by many years. Janelle told her that Jamison was an accountant who had been in the Mandevilles' employ for a little over a year.

"Your sister is lovely," he said to Janelle.

Joya noticed he was staring at her but speaking to her sister.

"Why, thank you, Mr. Roth," Janelle said. "I'll take that as a compliment to myself as well. Ah, I see I've embarrassed you now."

He bowed to Joya and tried to offer her his chair. Too nervous to sit, she smiled, but declined.

"Mrs. Mandeville has graciously invited me to attend the coming dinner party at your home. Will you save a dance for me, Miss Penn?"

He was staring in a way that made Joya blush.

"Save a dance? How does one save a dance?" she asked.

"Just say yes, Joya. I'll explain later." Janelle snapped her fingers in front of the accountant's eyes. "Oh, Mr. Roth?" She snapped again. "Will you please stop staring at Joya like that. I'm beginning to feel quite neglected. Is Trevor here, Roth?"

"Yes, but he is with Lord Howard's solicitor just now. Perhaps I can be of help?"

"My sister is interested in seeing the warehouse, in particular her father's orchid shipment from Matarenga."

Joya listened to their exchange and thought Mr. Roth quite well-mannered and precise. She was certain that Trevor must value him as an employee, but when she looked into Jamison Roth's hazel eyes, which seemed intent upon roving over every inch of her, she experienced none of the symptoms that struck her when she was with Trevor.

"Perhaps Miss Penn would permit *me* to show her the warehouse?" He was looking at Janelle now, which gave Joya ample time to study him.

He was not as tall as Trevor, nor as solidly built and certainly nowhere near as handsome. He had a friendly enough smile, light brown hair, and a soothing voice, but he was no Trevor. She tried to hide her disappointment, for Janelle was considering his offer.

"I suppose if Trevor is too busy . . ."

"Too busy for what?"

Joya turned at the sound of *his* voice. Her heart skipped a beat when she saw Trevor framed in the doorway between the office and the great gaping warehouse behind him. An older gentleman entered the room with him, but she could not take her eyes off Trevor.

He made a commanding figure, so broad-shouldered, outfitted in a fine black coat and trousers. His skin was bronzed, his dark eyes vibrant and alive. His hair had been trimmed and tamed and overnight he had changed from an orchid hunter into an elegant Englishman, but he still looked very fine and very fit.

She could see now that there was no use comparing Jamison Roth to Trevor. None whatsoever.

Janelle stood beside the corner of Roth's desk. She answered Trevor when all Joya could do was stare.

"Too busy to give Joya a tour of the warehouse. She wanted to see what has become of her orchids."

Before he responded, Trevor bid the solicitor goodbye. Joya heard the other man say, "If you ever change your mind, Lord Howard might still be interested."

When he turned around again, he looked at her first, then Janelle.

"I don't have time to give tours." He appeared extremely uncomfortable.

"I would consider it a pleasure to escort Miss Penn," Roth announced. "I know exactly where the men put the crates from Matarenga."

Joya noticed that Trevor appeared to be worrying over something. "I asked about the orchids, but I see now that this was not a good idea. I should have remembered how very busy you are and how long you were away. You must have many very important things to do."

Her cheeks felt so hot that she thought she must certainly be glowing.

Roth took another step, one that brought him very close beside her. "As I said, sir, I would be quite happy to—"

"You have the new invoices to look over," Trevor quickly reminded him.

Janelle stood up. "Well, I see that I've created a dilemma that I must remedy. You are far too busy, Trevor. Please, stay on your schedule. We shall leave. Come, Joya."

Joya had not realized how desperately she had wanted to stay. She heard Trevor sigh. Then he set the papers in his hand on the corner of Roth's desk and said, "I suppose I can spare a few minutes."

Janelle sat back down. "Good."

"Aren't you going with us?" Joya began to panic at the idea of being alone with Trevor.

"I've seen this place before. I'll wait right here with Mr. Roth."

Roth's smile faded. Trevor let Joya slip past him into the massive interior of the warehouse. It was gloomy and far colder than outside and there was a foreign, musty smell about the place. The gaslights flickered on the walls as if lighting the huge room was too great a struggle.

Trevor seemed distracted as they walked between tall rows of crates and barrels stacked floor to ceiling. Two men came by, struggling under the weight of a huge gilt-framed mirror. Joya paused to watch. As the mirror passed, her reflection slid by. Not only did she see herself, but Trevor, who was standing behind her. Their eyes met in the mirror and held as the men carried the huge object past. His gaze, reflected back at her, was full of heat and something else she could not name.

The mirror was gone and the moment over before she could ponder what his hungry expression might have meant. Ahead of them, she recognized the orchid crate and the barrels stacked together, huddled on the loading dock like tired immigrants. When she recognized her father's bold writing slashed across the top and sides of the crates, she hurried over.

A wagon pulled into the open side of the warehouse that Trevor had explained was a loading bay. Three men rode atop more crates and barrels stacked in the wagon bed. The men hopped out, acknowledged them by tugging on the brims of their caps, and then began to unload the shipment. Joya watched with one hand resting protectively atop a barrel of orchids.

After an awkward silence, Trevor asked, "Would you like me to open it?"

Suddenly, she needed to see the orchids she had climbed over Mount Kibatante to find, needed to be reminded of the vibrant colors of Matarenga, the warmth of the jungle, the golden sunshine and warm, gentle mist. Of home, and her father. Perhaps for a few moments, she could hold those treasured memories and forget the chill that never quite left the summer air and all the strange new sights and sounds of London.

"I would love to see them," she confessed.

He called over one of the men wielding a crowbar and in seconds had pried off the top of a barrel. Thanking him, Joya reached inside and lifted away the dried moss and coconut fibers she had helped collect and pack around the plants. Beneath them lay the orchids, tired but alive.

"It's so sad, don't you think?" She looked at Trevor, who was standing across the loading dock watching the men work.

When he realized she had spoken to him, he turned. Suddenly she found it hard to see him surrounded by blossoms gathered from all over the world. He should be out collecting, free of his black coat and trousers, dressed in khaki. He needed to be living life the way she had first seen him, not shut away in this dark warehouse, buried beneath crates and paper invoices.

"Pardon me? What did you say?" he asked.

"It's so sad, to see them all packed together in there, away from the air and the sunlight."

"They are only plants, Joya."

"But they are every bit as alive as you and I." She bent over and inspected a few specimens, lifting away a bit more packing material. "At least most of them are. What will happen to them now?"

"Tomorrow there will be an auction. I've already put the word out to the Orchid Society members that Dustin Penn's latest, long-awaited shipment has arrived. The orchids will be sold and taken to conservatories like the one my father built at Mandeville House."

"I have not seen your conservatory yet. Will you show it to me tonight?"

"When I have some free time. Have you seen enough here?" He sounded so formal, so vexed, that Joya quickly turned away so that he would not see how he had wounded her.

"I'm sorry I bothered you, Trevor."

Practically at a run, she started back without him, weaving her way through the aisles of boxes and crates and barrels stacked to the ceiling, through the dark gloom of the warehouse interior. She hurried on without looking back.

The aisles became a maze of twists and turns. She went around one corner and then another. The hollow sound of Trevor's footsteps echoed behind her.

This is hopeless, she thought, after making another turn. She had somehow lost her way. Trying to catch her breath, she stopped and pressed a hand against a stitch in her side.

Suddenly, she felt his hand upon her arm, just above the elbow. She spun around and found herself looking into Trevor's dark eyes and saw the same expression in them, the same need she had seen in the mirror.

"Why did you run away like that?" His eyes were dark, piercing.

"I knew I was bothering you. I became lost," she offered lamely.

"Now you are found." Without any warning, he pulled her into his arms. She slammed against his chest, felt his strong arms close around her and was suffused with his warmth and solid maleness.

Before she realized what was happening, he lowered his face to hers. She went perfectly still. The only sound she heard was the sound of their breathing, the rush of her heartbeat echoing in her ears. His mouth covered hers. His lips, surprisingly soft, began to move. His tongue slashed across the seam of her lips. She gasped against his mouth, inadvertently giving him access. His tongue slipped in, explored, tasted.

His arms pressed her closer. She moaned, not in fear, not in protest, but from the sheer delight of the intimacy, the taste and scent of him.

Then just as quickly as he had grabbed her, he let her

go. Unbalanced by the power of his kiss, shaken by its stunning arousal, she stumbled back. He reached for her again, caught and held her arm until she was steady on her feet before he let her go.

"I'm sorry," he said. "I don't . . . I can't imagine what came over me." He looked fierce and began to rub his forehead.

"You kissed me!" She was stunned. All she could do was stare at his mouth and wonder at the magnificence of his kiss.

"I've never done anything like that before." He shook his head and appeared to be talking to himself more than her.

"You've never kissed anyone?"

"I've never been so impulsive. I've never in my life *grabbed* a woman."

As she watched, he seemed to shake himself and then draw himself up. His expression went from stunned confusion to one of cool, solid assurance. Tugging on the edges of his jacket, he cleared his throat.

"I'll take you back to the office," he said stiffly.

She was baffled. Was that *all*? Was he not going to say anything about the wonderful, incredible thing that had just happened to them?

Was this the way of it? After kissing, was one expected to go on exactly as if nothing extraordinary had happened at all?

"Fix your hat," he said.

"What?"

"Your hat. It has drifted over to the side of your head."

"Oh, no." Instead of making the repair easily, she tangled the ribbons in her hair and winced when she tried to unsnarl the whole mess.

Trevor sighed. "Let me."

He stepped close until they were toe to toe. Joya closed her eyes. Gently he tugged and lifted and pulled until her hair ribbon was free and the hat mounted correctly. Then, with the utmost care, he tied the satin ribbon beneath her chin.

Had his hands lingered after the bow was tied? Lost in a haze of confusing sensations, she could not say.

She whispered, "Thank you." Then, without a word, she followed him back to the office door. Trevor opened it and let her pass.

She stood in the center of the small office with her cheeks afire, feeling as if she had stepped out of a dream from which she never wanted to awaken.

There was no sign of Jamison Roth, only Janelle, who had found paper and pen and was sketching. She looked up, seeming to be inspecting them both closely. Then she slowly smiled.

"How was the tour?"

Before his kiss, Joya knew she would most likely have blurted, "Trevor kissed me!"

But now, having been kissed, having been in Trevor's arms and kissed so very well, she did not want to share the secret just yet. Perhaps if she held her silence, she might be able to hold on to the strange yet wonderful feelings gamboling around inside her.

"You two look as if you have had a shock. Was there something wrong with the orchids?"

"Nothing."

"Absolutely not."

Joya glanced up at Trevor. He was still frowning, his dark brows drawn together. He reached around her to pick up the papers he had left on the desk.

"I saw my father's orchids." She found it hard to get

the words out, to form a comprehensible thought.

Janelle suddenly went very still and appeared thoughtful. After a slight pause she said, "Well, then. It's time we went home." She came around the side of the desk and took Joya's arm. "Trevor, will we see you at dinner this evening?"

He shook his head, almost as if coming back from somewhere far away. "Not tonight. Please, remind Grandmother that I have a meeting."

"Joya?" Janelle hesitated, as if waiting for her to say something.

Adrift in the heady, intoxicating memories, Joya realized she was staring down at the raspberry slippers Janelle had loaned her. She mumbled good-bye and thank you to Trevor.

Janelle told her brother good-bye and led her out the wide double doors. When Joya finally worked up the courage to look back over her shoulder, Trevor still had not moved. Through the open doors, she saw him standing near the desk, frowning down at the papers clutched in his hand.

Janelle climbed into the carriage behind Joya and sat across from her. Something had happened between Trevor and Joya in the warehouse, something that had inexplicably changed them both. Her sister had walked back into the office stunned and disoriented, while Trevor's expression had alternated between puzzlement and distraction.

Now Joya, the same young woman who could not sit still before, sat in silence with her hands folded in her lap and a faraway look in her eyes. Janelle somehow sensed the turmoil bubbling inside her sister so greatly that it even left *her* feeling unsettled and jumpy.

"Are you feeling all right?" she finally asked Joya.

"Yes. Why?"

"You are so quiet."

"Perhaps I'm tired."

"Perhaps."

Janelle wanted to add that perhaps she was hiding something, but she let Joya keep her secrets.

"I was wondering if you might be suffering from that strange affliction that comes over you whenever you are near Trevor."

Joya shook her head. "Not that one."

"No?"

"It's . . . it's something I don't know how to put into words just yet."

"As long as you are all right," Janelle said.

Joya attempted a feeble smile and then she sighed. "I don't think this is anything that one dies of, but just to be certain, I am going to swallow a pinch of dried goat's udder with salt water when we get back to Mandeville House."

Chapter 15

Joya found it easy to compare Mandeville House to a cavern, for it was a dark, hollow-sounding place with too many rooms where servants appeared and disappeared like *jimbwa* through long narrow passages and back stairs hidden away in the bowels of the house. At night the place grew still and seemed to fill itself with shadows, silent sighs, and loneliness.

After sharing dinner alone with her sister, Joya had followed Janelle up to her studio where she viewed the many wonderful paintings her sister had begun over the past few months.

Scenes of the African jungle brought to life on canvas, the deep forest greens, emerald leaves shimmering with jewels of dewdrops, stark white and crimson splashes of blossoms tucked between the leaves—all of her sister's paintings brought the sting of unexpected tears of homesickness to Joya's eyes.

Janelle had seemed eager to closet herself in the studio high up on the servants' floor, so Joya excused herself and returned to her room, where she changed into her nightclothes.

With her nerves still on edge since her encounter with Trevor, she hated the thought of being alone in her room. On Matarenga, if she was not working with her father or camped out on a hunt, she often went to the village to sit with the Matarengi and listen to one of the storytellers impart a fable. Gathered around a central fire, the people would become bewitched by the story-teller and his tale, fascinated by both the message and messenger.

The villagers would laugh, gasp, even cry at the beauty, the magic and wonder of the story. Afterward they would talk about the drama, the characters' triumph and tragedies, and beg for another tale.

On Matarenga people were seldom alone. Families slept together in single-room *fadu* and did most of their living outdoors beneath the tropical sun. They did not hide or keep to themselves in huge boxlike rooms that shut out the light the way the English did. When her father was busy, Joya never wanted for companionship.

Now, isolated, pacing around her room in Mandeville House, Joya found she quickly lost her awe of the fine fabrics and the many gilded appointments there. She wondered how Trevor and Janelle could have spent their entire childhood growing up inside these walls.

From what she had seen of the city, she wondered whether the children of London had much opportunity to run and play freely or to climb and swim as she had done all her life. The only children she had seen alone on the streets had been begging, their gaunt faces withered, their eyes old before their time.

Abruptly she stood. She had to get out, to leave the confines of the room where she had done nothing for the past hour but pace and stare into the cold fireplace, thinking of Trevor, the taste and feel of his lips and the way his arms felt wrapped around her. She was confused, disturbed, and unsettled and could not shake her dark mood. The last thing she needed was to be alone.

She decided to venture out of her room and look for the conservatory, the glass room where the Mandevilles' orchid collection was housed. Perhaps, after a stop in the kitchen for a glass of warm milk, she would wander around until she found it.

She slipped one of Janelle's satin robes over her nightgown and tied the sash, then quietly left her room and trailed down the long, barely lit hallway.

Pleased that she had actually found her way to the kitchen, she was even more delighted upon finding Sims seated at a long table in the center of the room. He jumped to his feet when she entered, pulled his coat closed, and appeared surprised to see her.

"Good evening, miss." The old butler remained at attention. "Is there something you need? Shall I get Mrs. Billingsley?"

She shook her head and smiled, hoping to put him at ease.

"No, thank you, Mr. Sims. Please, sit down. I've come to have a glass of warm milk. My mother always said it calmed her nerves. I've never had nerves before. Do you think it will help?"

"It works for me, miss. I'm just having some myself. Milk, not nerves. I will pour you a mug."

"I need something to do, so I'll pour my own, if you don't mind."

Joya found a pan of milk still quite warm on a huge iron stove very much like the one her father had shipped all the way to the island for her mother. She smiled at

Sims until she saw him struggling to button his coat. His old hands were misshapen, his joints red and swollen.

"Do your hands pain you greatly, Mr. Sims?"

"It is just Sims, miss. Yes, indeed they do, but that's what one must expect of old age."

She left the stove. "I'm going up to get something that might help you."

"There's no need, miss . . ."

Before he could protest any more, she was off again—up the stairs, past the great, great ancestors, back into her room where she rummaged through her trunk until she found what she needed.

She lost her way back, ended up opening the door of a room full of books, backed out, and then finally reached the kitchen. Sims had her warm mug of milk already poured and awaiting her on the table.

She thanked him again, reached into the pocket of her robe, and pulled out a shriveled, mummified monkey's foot. Sims stared down at the object in her hand.

"It is for you, Sims. Take it."

He did not move. "What for, miss?"

"Everyone knows that there is nothing better than a monkey's foot for curing swollen joints. Well, some say a salve of pulverized lizard eye and hummingbird beak does just as well, but it is not used as often."

"I don't imagine so." He began wheezing desperately.

"Monkey is far easier to come by, you know."

"I didn't, miss."

She glanced at the larder, where a huge ham hung from a hook on the ceiling. "Well, at least on Matarenga it is. Go ahead now. Don't be shy. Take it."

"I don't believe—"

Before he could say more, she cried, "Oh, but you *must* believe, Sims. That's part of the magic."

"What should I do with it, miss?" He gingerly lifted the wrinkled, hairy foot between his thumb and forefinger.

She thought carefully, knowing how important belief in the magic of the cure was to the power of healing.

"You must wear it at all times. Tie a string around it and hang it from your neck. Keep it close to your heart and the healing will spread throughout your body with every heartbeat."

"Hang the monkey's foot around my neck?"

"That's right." Hoping to reassure him, she opened the front of her robe, shoved her hand down her nightgown and pulled out her own amulet pouch.

"I am never without this," she said, stepping closer to him and lowering her voice to a whisper. "This small pouch is filled with many charms. I have a red feather, some sharks' teeth, a shiny piece of rock from Mount Kibatante. Oh, and my mother's silver comb. They all bring me luck and help keep me healthy and safe."

He stepped back, held the foot out at arm's length and sniffed. "You certainly *look* healthy, Miss Penn. I'm to wear this . . . foot all the time, you say?"

"*All* the time. And *believe* in its healing power."

Footsteps echoed down the hall, coming toward the kitchen. Sims glanced in the direction of the door. "Our little party grows, it seems," he said.

When Trevor stepped through the doorway, his dark eyes reflecting the lamplight, the lower half of his face shadowed by a day's growth of beard, Joya's gaze went straight to his lips. Her breath caught in her throat and she prayed he could not know what she was thinking, that he could not hear the accelerated beat of her heart.

He paused on the threshold, obviously surprised to see her there.

"What have we here, Sims?"

Joya realized she was still holding her robe open and had one hand down the front of her nightgown.

"A monkey's foot and warm milk, sir."

Joya hastily let go of her amulet pouch and closed her robe.

"Poor Sims is all swollen," she said.

"Exactly where is Sims swollen?" Trevor locked his hands behind his back and looked at each of them in turn.

Sims held up his hands.

"I have given him a cure for his sore joints," she said.

"A mummified monkey's foot, sir," Sims added, showing the wrinkled appendage.

Joya offered, "Would you like a mug of milk, Trevor? Perhaps it will help you relax. You have a very pinched look about your mouth."

"No, no warm milk, thank you."

"I think I will finish the milk in my room," Sims said quickly, staring down at the monkey's foot as if at a loss as to what to do with it. Finally he recovered, shoved it into his pocket, and picked up his mug.

"Don't forget to tie it around your neck," Joya reminded him, happy she could be of help.

"Yes, miss." Sims excused himself and carefully stepped around Trevor, who moved to the center of the room, where he remained watching her.

The enormous kitchen seemed to shrink as she walked over to the table and tried to hide the way her hand trembled when she lifted the mug of milk to her lips. She sipped slowly, avoiding Trevor's gaze for several moments. When she finally looked up at Trevor again, she found he had not moved.

"Is Janelle asleep?" He set his tall hat carefully on the table.

Joya shook her head. "No. She is up in her studio working. She's very excited about someone she calls her new patron who wants to sell her work for her."

"A *patron*?" The creases between his brow deepened.

"She seems quite happy about it."

"Does Grandmother know?"

"Your grandmother retired early." She did not want to tell him why. When he said nothing in response, she added, "You were out very late."

She sipped more milk, hoping it would calm her sooner than later. Trevor continued to stare. The milk hit her stomach and began to tighten into a knot. She set the mug down, worried that she might throw up.

She remained silent, waiting for him to say something, studying him the way she might a new mountainside trail or jungle path, searching for signs of promise and discovery. A thrill raced through her. She was aware of his every move, his every breath. She was full of curiosity and anticipation.

He straightened his shoulders inside his perfectly fitted coat. "I want to apologize for what happened at the warehouse today," he began. "I've never done anything so ungentlemanly or impulsive. I've never done anything like that at all."

"Was that your first kiss, too?" She found that impossible to believe. "If so, I think you have what my father would call a natural talent for it. He says I have one for finding orchids."

"I've kissed women before, but . . ."

She nearly dropped her milk. "Who?"

He paused and blinked. "Joya, that's not the kind of a question a lady asks a gentleman."

"But you *have* kissed before?"

"Yes, of course."

"If you had kissed me in a gentlemanly way, would you apologize?"

He sighed. "Joya, you have an astounding way of confusing a man's thoughts."

"I don't mean to do that, Trevor."

"I'm sure you don't, but somehow you do it just the same."

"I am feeling a bit confused myself." It was her turn to sigh.

She placed her hand over her heart, where the lapels of the satin robe overlapped. His gaze slipped to her hand and lingered; then he looked into her eyes again.

"I just wanted to tell you that I am sorry I took such liberties with you today. It won't happen again."

She had no idea how she was supposed to respond, especially when she was actually hoping with all her heart that it would happen again.

"I really didn't mind at all, Trevor."

"You should have."

"Why, when it was so wonderful?"

"You should have been furious with me."

"But it was so delicious, like eating a ripe mango on a hot summer day. It made me feel hot and cold at the same time. Is that the way kissing always feels?"

"Please stop, Joya."

"Have I broken *another* rule?"

"Too many of them to name." He shifted uncomfortably, then picked up his hat.

She must have angered him somehow. She saw that much in the frustration on his face. He was going to walk out and leave her feeling all jittery and anxious and expectant, with no hope of any relief. She had to stop him.

"I was going to find the conservatory myself, but now here you are and you know right where it is. Will you show it to me now?"

"Are you crying?"

"No," she shook her head, blinking furiously.

"Yes you are. Why? If I have upset you—"

"It isn't you. Tonight I found myself wishing I were at home," she said softly. "Things were so much simpler there."

He seemed to soften, to relax a bit. He almost smiled as he shook his head.

"If you promise not to look so sad, I'll show you the conservatory."

She was relieved to have gained a little more time alone with him. "Thank you."

"This way."

He led her back through the maze of hallways to a room added onto the very back of the house—a room made of glass. Drizzle streaked the panes. Smeared halos of gaslight reflected from the courtyard behind the house.

He paused to light a lamp before they moved farther into the room. She could feel the change in the air as they moved into the close humidity stoked by the plants growing on beds of bark and the heat of the sun still trapped in the room beneath the domed glass.

The conservatory was lovely, a most magical place, especially with the mist falling outside. Crystal droplets gathered and ran down the panes of glass, shimmering with light.

Many of the orchids presented showy stalks of colorful blooms that bobbed in their wake as they passed by. When they reached the far end of the room, he turned to her again.

"You still look upset."

"It's the orchids. They look so very sorrowful here. Like prisoners all lined up in rows, forced to bloom, forced to live forever under glass. They will never feel the Kusi winds again or know the scent of the sea."

Suddenly, she felt as out of place, as trapped as the flowers, existing in a world that she might never fully understand. Adding that to what she had seen of the crate of orchids in the warehouse, she mused aloud, "I wish I had never learned what becomes of them. I wish I never had to see them like this."

He stepped closer and lingered before her. She looked up into his eyes.

"Think of the joy they spread." He had locked his arms behind him.

The only flowers she had seen thus far had been growing in regimented rows in parks and gardens. The English did have their own flowers. They did not need orchids from the tropics.

"Why go to all of this work to grow flowers where they don't belong?"

"They're thriving in here and they'll continue to grow and bloom as long as they are well treated," he said softly.

"But this is not their world. They should be in the jungle, where they grow wild and free."

"Are you feeling sorry for the orchids, or yourself, Joya?"

"A little of both, perhaps."

"Tell me what's wrong. I know it's more than the orchids."

She twisted her fingers together. Finding his nearness

disconcerting, she walked to the far end of the glass room and sighed.

"Everything is wrong. Today at the dressmaker's, when Janelle told me that you had meant for me to have a dress made of velvet material and not of your draperies, I was embarrassed.

"Later this afternoon, I took most of the cutlery off the table, thinking to save the maids having to wash all those extra spoons and forks. Your grandmother came down to dinner and was very, very upset. I was only trying to help."

"Where was Janelle?"

"In her studio. She has her work to do and cannot spend every moment with me, like a nursemaid. I don't want to upset all of your lives, but I have somehow offended Adelaide, and Janelle has much to do without having to show me all of London."

"You have only been here two days. Things will get easier."

"Will they, Trevor?"

"You're just feeling unsettled."

"I'm not certain that I will ever fit in." She turned around, rubbed her hands together and stared out into the night. "Everything is so different. I never imagined how much."

He seemed so calm, which was hardly fair, since her heart was jumping around inside her breast. Her hands were clammy, her nerves on edge.

"How do *you* feel, Trevor?"

There was no way in hell he could tell her how he really felt right now. His mouth was dry, his palms clammy. He was aroused by her very nearness, her walk, her tremulous smile. The sound of her voice. Even by the glisten of unshed tears in her eyes.

Trevor stared down at the lovely nape of her neck, at the wisps of fallen locks of hair that trailed over her shoulder. Thankfully she did not know of the fierce need rising up in him, a need he was fighting hard to deny.

She turned around again, tipping her lovely face up, and he was once more treated to a full view of those eyes and her lush lips.

"Why do you want to know?" he asked.

"I just wondered if you feel the strange way I do right now," she said softly.

He was only twenty-eight, but until now he had always thought of himself as much, much older than his age. Before he had kissed her this afternoon, he had been a level-headed and responsible man. He had goals—a well-planned, well-ordered life—and there was no room for a woman in it yet. But at this moment there was not one logical thought in his head.

He took a deep breath and waited for his confusion to pass. He had made a great error in judgment by bringing Joya out here tonight, and he found himself wondering when his good sense had taken a holiday. He certainly wished that his desire had gone along with it.

"I'm feeling quite odd," she whispered.

"Odd?" He took a step closer, stared at the open front of her robe, and discovered that he could see the gentle slope of her breast. Her skin, where it had not been exposed to the sun, was the purest ivory.

"I feel hot and cold. Empty and full at the same time. My heart is beating so very hard." She put her hand over the open seam of her robe. His eyes followed her hand. "Do you think there could have been something wrong with the milk?"

"No. I'm afraid not."

What made her even more alluring was the very fact that she was innocent of the way she could so easily seduce him without knowing what she was doing. She was not some calculating, husband-hunting young miss. Nor an experienced seductress.

Unlike her, he was perfectly aware of what was happening.

He should be the one strong enough to walk away, but all he wanted was to kiss her again. He tried to keep himself from touching her but failed miserably. He reached for a long tendril of her hair and let it slide through his fingers.

"How can you be sure there was nothing wrong with the milk?" she whispered.

"Because I had none of it and I feel the same way you do," he whispered back.

His heart was beating hard as a racehorse's at the end of a mile-long race. He felt hot and cold, empty yet full as he quickened with desire.

In the lamplight, beneath the shimmering reflections from the raindrops sliding down the glass roof, her up-turned face was radiantly alive and very expectant.

"I'm afraid I'm going to kiss you again." If only she would slap him, bring him to his senses. If only she would protest, or walk away.

"Like a gentleman?"

"No. But at least this time I'm giving you fair warning."

"Then don't be afraid," she whispered.

He was lost. He closed his eyes and let himself drift into the sensations she evoked and took his time kissing her. She went up onto her toes and leaned into him, offering her delicious mouth. He found himself thinking of mangoes, of summer sun and tropical breezes.

Her satin robe slipped open as the weight of the fabric pulled her nightdress off her shoulder, exposing the rise of her breast. He grazed her smooth, bare skin with his palm. Textured like silk, her skin tempted him to dip his hand below the neckline of her gown, to explore her bare back and then her ripe breasts beneath the sheer fabric.

He moaned and deepened the kiss and willed his hands not to stray. When her arms slipped around his neck, he wrapped her in a tight embrace and pulled her closer. She was soft and supple and yet very fit. Conditioned by the jungle, she was trim and lithe.

He found the idea of running his hands over every inch of her finely honed body more arousing than anything he could imagine. As he held her close and pressed his aching loins against her, she responded naturally. Without hesitation, she pressed back.

She opened her lips to let him gently explore with his tongue. He teased her until she moaned. He lifted his head, pulling back to look at her. Her robe slipped open further, down to her elbow, dragging her nightgown with it. The blush pink stain of her nipple teased him, tempted him.

He had already gone too far. He knew better, knew that he might have irrevocably changed the direction of their lives with this second chance encounter, and yet he was out of control and could not stop.

She was so very willing, so tantalizing, an exotic, golden-haired goddess that he had discovered in the depths of the jungle valley. One of his most precious finds.

He lowered his head, laved her nipple with his tongue, caressed it with his lips. She was panting. He felt her fingers tighten on his shoulders. She softly gasped and gave a little cry of wonder as she raked her splayed fingers through his hair, pressed his mouth against her breast.

Then, above their commingled, ragged breathing, he heard another sound, the slightest footfall upon the stone floor of the conservatory. As he lifted his head, he heard a muffled cry, then the sound of a clay pot shattering against stone. He and Joya turned as one and saw Janelle run from the room.

Joya pulled out of his arms, drew up the edge of her gown and robe, and stood there trembling.

"Oh, Trevor. Did she see us?"

"She saw more than that," he said, silently cursing himself, hating having hurt the one person who had been closest to him in all the world.

"She is very upset," Joya cried. "I can feel it here." She touched her heart. "I have hurt my sister terribly. *We* have hurt her."

"Let me talk to her," he said lamely, wishing he knew what to say, how to explain something to Janelle when he could not understand it himself. He had broken every rule in the book with an innocent who had been overly naive and oh-so-ripe for the taking.

He walked over to where Joya stood trembling amid the rows of orchids perched on their high benches. He saw the tears in her eyes, tears he had put there, and he felt like a cad.

"I'm sorry, Joya. It seems that all I am capable of doing is hurting you."

"I'm afraid we've both hurt Janelle." Her voice broke. "Perhaps *you* should go to her, Trevor. I do not know what to say."

"Will you be all right?"

She nodded.

Trevor finger-combed his hair and straightened his jacket. He would go to Janelle and try to make things right. If she hated him forever, he would certainly understand why, but he would never forgive himself.

Chapter 16

Janelle heard Trevor's footsteps on the uncarpeted stairs that led to her studio on the third floor. There was a hurried certainty in his steps, a pounding rhythm of purpose.

Surprise and shock had sent her running from the conservatory like a frightened sheep. She had recovered her composure, but she was still heartily embarrassed.

All around her, her paintings were gathered on every available surface; easels, tables, chairs, windowsills. Before Africa, her work had represented visions she did not understand, glimpses into a world she had never seen. Windows to her dreams. Now she treasured each creation, for the inspiration behind them had led her to her sister.

Trevor stepped into the studio without knocking. She faced him, outwardly calm, still flustered inside. Until tonight, her brother's private affairs had been his own.

She expected him to begin without hesitation, but he

did not. Instead, in a way she had never seen him before, he stood silent and uncomfortable.

"I'm sorry I walked in on you like that." She offered him a place to begin and shoved the bridge of her spectacles up her nose.

"I'm the one who is sorry. To have put you in such an awkward position. To have lost control. It will not happen again."

He crossed the room, pausing near one of her favorite paintings—the marketplace on Zanzibar. He ran both hands through his hair and sighed loud enough to be heard over the rain softly falling on the skylight.

"Are you saying that you won't make love to my sister again, or that the next time you will make certain I won't walk in on you?"

"I never should have touched her. Your having seen us only compounds my lack of judgment. I'm sorry, Janelle."

"I have compounded your lack of judgment? Joya is falling in *love* with you, Trevor."

She could see that her revelation disturbed him greatly. He smoothed his hand down his shirtfront as he looked away.

"She's falling in love with me?"

"Of course. You surely feel *some* affection for her, don't you? I never imagined you were the kind of man who would toy with an innocent young woman."

"I did not *toy* with her!"

"Joya is infatuated with you. She has no reference save the Matarengi and her parents' actions. She has no clear notion of what a young woman should or should not do with a man. She trusts you."

He walked to a nearby table and leaned his hip against it. She had never seen him look so miserable in his life.

"How do you know she is falling in love with me? Have you two actually *discussed* this?"

"We talked about it when she was settling into her room. To be honest, Trevor, at first I was uncomfortable with the notion of the two of you together. The fact that she is my twin made the idea very unsettling."

He pushed off the ledge and halved the distance between them. "Is that why you ran out of the conservatory?"

"No. I ran because I was embarrassed at having interrupted you. And, I was shocked at what I saw." She shook her head and sighed. "That in itself upsets me because I liked to think I was more unconventional," she mused aloud, frowning.

The corner of his lips lifted into a half-smile. He shrugged. "I'm happy to hear you are not as broad-minded as you professed to be. I was afraid that you might have been corrupted by Lady Cecily."

"Obviously not. Nor do I want to see Joya corrupted. Thank God it was *I* who walked in on you. Had it been one of the servants, or Grandmama—I hate to think what might have happened. You can rest assured I will be discreet where my sister is concerned, but if it had been anyone but me, she could have been ruined."

"You need not condemn me for kissing your sister. I'm already condemning myself."

"You did much more than kiss her." Janelle felt herself blushing at the memory of the passionate scene she had interrupted.

He spread his hands in a gesture of surrender. "I honestly don't know what came over me. Lately I seemed to have lost the ability to *think* around her."

"Why don't you simply admit to having feelings for her? What you are experiencing is an *emotion*—it is desire, Trevor."

"I'll admit I was intrigued almost from the moment I laid eyes on her. At first, I had the same misgivings as you, because she is your twin."

"From what I saw tonight, I would say you have gotten over any discomfort."

"Because you are both very distinct individuals."

He looked so uncomfortable that she wanted to spare him further anguish.

"I know very well that what I saw you two doing tonight had *nothing* to do with me."

He crossed the room, hesitating but a second before he slipped his arm around her in a most brotherly manner. "Thank God. You know I couldn't bear to lose you, Janelle, as a sister or a friend."

"There is no chance of that, but I must defend my sister's honor, Trevor. She has no one else."

He walked away. "I won't touch her again. I swear it."

"You don't have to go that far. I would welcome a match between you, for she is everything I would wish for you and more. You have had to shoulder so much responsibility that it has made you far too serious. Joya is full of life and spontaneity. She fairly *sparkles*. I think she is just the kind of woman you need."

He eyed her with suspicion. "Was that surprise visit to the warehouse today intended to bring us together?"

"I won't lie to you. It was."

"I would appreciate your not playing matchmaker anymore. I have too many responsibilities, too many plans. I cannot become entangled with Joya, or any other woman right now."

"When are you leaving for Venezuela?"

"Shortly after Grandmother's party, I hope."

"After what happened tonight, Joya will surely wonder why your ardor has suddenly cooled. What am I to say if she asks me why? Do you intend to tell her the truth?"

"Would she actually speak to you of such personal things?"

Janelle shrugged. "Women talk out their troubles. Who else can she speak to? You owe her an explanation."

"She will have one."

"When?"

"When the time is right. When I know what to say. I don't want to hurt her."

"Grandmother's soirée is in two weeks." She picked up a paintbrush and smoothed the sable tip. "It will be good for her to meet other men. After all, you are the first Englishman besides her father that she has ever really known."

Janelle suspected Trevor was feigning an indifference he did not feel when he turned away before he said, "Perhaps she will."

"All I ask is that you don't hurt her, Trevor."

"I wouldn't hurt her for the world." He looked back. "She's very concerned about *your* feelings right now."

"I'll go up and tell her good-night. I don't want this left between us." Janelle laid her brush down and wiped her hands on a rag.

Trevor bid her good-night and walked out the door. Janelle knew what it had cost him in pride to apologize. He was so rarely wrong, so forthright in his business dealings and in the way he treated everyone, that there was not much in his life he had ever had to apologize for.

He prided himself on being a man of honor and of his word. She had a notion that his feelings for Joya were much stronger than even he knew or could admit to himself, especially since he had been overcome by emotions powerful enough to cause him to lose all sense of propriety.

How far would he have actually let himself go tonight had she not walked in on them? Was he falling in love?

She doubted even he knew the answers.

Joya lay very still in the middle of her bed, dressed in her nightgown, eyes closed, hands folded. Aware of every nerve, every tingle, every shiver that ran down her spine, she had decided that if she did not move or speak, she might not lose the lovely experience of having been in Trevor's arms.

A soft knock sounded upon the door, then the door opened and she heard footsteps as someone approached the bed.

"Janelle?" she whispered.

"Joya, are you all right? Should I call a doctor?" Her sister ran to her side, took her hand, and began to chafe it.

"I am fine."

"Then why are you lying there like death? You gave me a fright."

Since the fluttering feelings inside her were almost gone, Joya sat up and looked at Janelle. "Are *you* all right?" she asked.

"Of course I am," Janelle said.

"I could not bear it if you were angry with me."

"I am not angry with you."

Suddenly Joya was off the bed. She took Janelle's

hand. "Please, don't be angry with Trevor, either. I am the one who is forever breaking the rules."

Janelle appeared very, very thoughtful. "But he knows them all far better than you."

"Oh, Janelle, hasn't such a *wondrous* thing ever happened to you?" Joya lowered her voice to a whisper and glanced at the door. "Haven't you ever been swept away with desire?"

"No, but from the radiant look on your face I am beginning to think I may be missing something."

Joya grabbed the edges of her robe and clutched the satin material tight in her hands.

"I never thought anything could be so very remarkable. Why, when Trevor kissed it me, the feelings inside me were stronger than when Kibatante stirs and shakes the whole island."

"Kiba-who?"

"His hands were so warm, his lips so sure. I only hope that someday very soon someone will kiss you and touch you as tenderly. I think that you English have far too many rules against something so wonderful. The strength of desire is very hard to resist."

"I don't think that you resisted very hard, Joya. At least not from what I saw."

Joya looked down at her hands and tightened the sash on her robe. There were some things one simply could not explain in words.

When she looked up again, Janelle was standing in front of the open window, fanning herself with her hands. A carriage was passing by on the street below. The sound of horses' hooves clacked against the cobblestones.

"Janelle, your face is all red. Are you all right?"

"I was not prepared to hear a lecture on desire tonight." She leaned out the window, took a deep breath, and then drew back inside. She crossed the room and took Joya's hands in hers.

"Let's not speak of this again." Janelle pushed her spectacles up and blinked. "Let's concentrate on Grandmother's soirée. Monsieur Renault is a Frenchman, an expert on dance who will be here in the morning to give you your first formal lesson."

"A dancing lesson?" Joya had no notion why anyone would need a teacher for something so natural and uncomplicated. Dancing came from the heart, from the rhythm of the drums.

"I can already dance," she assured Janelle. "I used to dance all the time on Matarenga. I have danced since I was a child."

"We'll call it a review, then. Grandmama insists."

"In the morning?"

"Yes, and the dressmaker wants another fitting tomorrow, too."

"Not *her* again."

"Don't look so fierce. Promise me that you won't frighten poor Madame Fifi to death. No more blood-curdling war cries."

"Perhaps just a short one, if she pokes me with pins again. When will I see Trevor?"

She did not like the way Janelle turned away with a sigh. Her sister was hiding something; she could feel it. She had caught a glimpse of reticence in her eyes.

"Trevor will be very busy for the next few days, but you are not to worry. We'll be busy, too, preparing for the party." Then, Janelle crossed the room and hugged her tight. "Promise me you will not let yourself be overwhelmed by desire any time soon."

"I don't know if I can make such a promise."

"Then tell me you will at least try."

"I'll try."

"Good. Now let's forget all about what happened to-night."

Joya was at a loss for words as Janelle straightened her spectacles, walked to the door, and bid her good night.

If she lived to be older than Otakgi she would never, ever forget what had happened in the conservatory to-night.

Chapter 17

With guest list in hand, Adelaide paused outside the door to the drawing room. Every morning for the past two weeks, the most deplorable torture of the tender sensibilities of Monsieur Renault, dance instructor, had taken place behind that door.

If she had not been paying the man a small fortune to teach Joya Penn how to dance, Adelaide might actually have felt sorry for the preening Frenchman.

Not only was Janelle's sister possessed of two left feet, but she had a habit of twisting words around until a person had no idea how a simple conversation could stray so far off the mark.

Nowhere in the house was she safe from Joya Penn. Lately the girl seemed to be everywhere, constantly putting her nose where it did not belong, upsetting the servants' routine. Even Sims had been acting peculiar, forever scratching at his shirtfront.

One way or another, Adelaide was determined to rid her home of Janelle's twin. But for now she had decided to concentrate on her dinner party as a means to that end.

How better to prove to Trevor that the girl was not right for him than to let her embarrass herself in front of their closest friends and associates?

Although there was no real evidence to support her suspicions, she was certain that *something* was going on between Trevor and Joya, simply because her grandson appeared to be going to great lengths to avoid the girl. He was never home anymore, not even for breakfast. Adelaide resented his absences. Dinner discussions about his business endeavors had always been the most stimulating highlight of her day.

Now because of Joya Penn, she was deprived of her grandson's attention and company, cut off from all he usually shared with her about Mandeville Imports, the venture *she* had single-handedly saved after her inept husband died before he could run it into the ground. She wished Trevor had never sailed for Africa or found Dustin Penn and his annoying daughter in the first place.

Adelaide was about to enter the drawing room when she sighed and thanked God that the Penn girl seemed to be unaware of the details of Clara Hayworth's past, and that Trevor would be sailing for Venezuela in a few days.

She had not encouraged her grandson to fortify his reputation and their great wealth just to have him throw it away on a nobody. She vowed to herself that one way or another, by the time Trevor returned with Queen Victoria's orchid, Joya Penn would be out of their lives.

As she opened the door, Monsieur Renault let go a high-pitched scream. The nervous, spoiled, little dog he carried everywhere, an obnoxious animal with curly white fur, had taken refuge beneath a chair. The dog raised its nose and began to howl in harmony with the oily-headed Frenchman.

"I am sorry, Monsieur Renault," Joya tried to yell over the racket, "but I'm never going to learn these English dances. If you want your toenails to stop turning black and falling out, then you must help me persuade Janelle and her grandmother to give up this crazy notion."

"Enough!" Adelaide slammed the door behind her. "Stop this noise." She glowered at the dog. It gave a short yelp and ran beneath the settee with its tail tucked between its legs.

"She has two left feet, Monsieur. I have told you all will be well if you remember to keep yours out from beneath them."

Joya looked as if she had been in a battle. Her long hair was mussed and tangled. One curl hung over her forehead and dangled across her face. Her right slipper was untied, her left sleeve pulled away from the shoulder seam. Her skin had faded, but no amount of almond paste was going to lighten it further before the party. She was staring down at her feet, turning them this way and that.

The Frenchman limped over to a chair and sat down with a groan.

"Joya!" Since Janelle was absent, Adelaide did not bother to disguise her displeasure.

"Yes, ma'am?"

"Where is your sister? I thought we had agreed Janelle would suffer through these lessons with Monsieur Renault."

"She left for a moment. She said she had something to see to in her studio." Joya looked down again and then up at Adelaide. "Ma'am?"

"What is it?"

"I don't wish to argue, but I do have a right and a left foot." She lifted her crinoline and skirt to her knees. "You see?"

Adelaide sighed. No stockings.

The Frenchman groaned and rolled his eyes. His little dog ran out from beneath the settee and jumped up into his lap.

"I suppose there is no need to ask how the lessons are coming along, Monsieur?" Adelaide asked.

He burst into a stream of French and waved his hands around.

"Just as I thought."

"*What* is just as you thought, Grandmama?" Janelle walked in and joined her sister.

"Monsieur Renault does not like the way I dance," Joya told her.

"According to the monsieur, you cannot dance at all," Adelaide looked down her nose. She waved the guest list at Janelle. "I see that you have added that Martin woman to my guest list."

"Lady Cecily is my dearest friend, Grandmama. Surely you do not object. I believe you said this was a welcome home party for Trevor and me. I can hardly retract the invitation."

Adelaide's head pounded. What more could she have expected from Janelle? She had never had much influence over the girl. Her choice of friends was appalling, but then, water always sought its own level. Janelle was, after all, only the daughter of a common botanist and his wife.

The girl had spent her early years either reading, whining, or suffering nightmares. She had been nothing but trouble since the night James had brought her to Mandeville House.

"Who are the other two you saw fit to invite without asking me?" Adelaide pointed to the names in question.

"Viscount Arthur is an art collector I met through Lady Cecily. The other man, Garr Remington, is his nephew."

Adelaide glanced over at Joya. "How *old* is this nephew?"

"Twenty-nine."

"Without a farthing, I suppose?"

Janelle's chin went up a notch. "Poor as a church mouse."

"Handsome?"

"I have never laid eyes on him."

"He'll be after our money," Adelaide snorted.

She looked the Penn girl over from head to toe. Getting rid of the chit might prove easier than she thought. "Joya, you should use this party as an opportunity to meet as many eligible young men as you can. Catch yourself a wealthy husband."

"I don't want just any man for a husband," she protested. "I want—"

"She wants to finish her dance lesson, Grandmama." Janelle quickly walked over to Monsieur Renault. "Come, Monsieur. I will play the pianoforte and you shall dance with my sister."

Adelaide watched Janelle position her sister for a dance. Janelle was hiding something. She could feel it in her bones.

Adelaide started to leave, then paused in the doorway and frowned. "I have enough on my mind without having to worry about what your friends might do, Janelle. Please make certain that they do not embarrass me."

Adelaide left the room hoping that Joya Penn would prove to be the greatest embarrassment of them all.

Joya turned to Janelle the moment Adelaide was out of earshot.

"I'll never learn these dances," she moaned. She threw a dark glance at Monsieur Renault. He was still seated upon the chair, kissing his little dog on the lips and muttering to himself. Nothing she did pleased the man. Was it her fault his shins were so very delicate? Should she be blamed because he bruised so easily?

"Come, I'll play the pianoforte and you can show me what you have learned," Janelle offered.

"I will not dance if he is going to keep hitting me on the ankle with that stick," Joya declared.

Janelle pulled out the stool at the pianoforte and sat down before she admonished him.

"Up, Monsieur Renault, and do not use that reed on my sister. She is doing her best."

"Her best? Her *best*? My furry little Jolie dances better," he said in heavily accented English. With a sigh, he kissed the dog and set her on the floor. She immediately ran to disappear beneath the settee.

Joya had no heart for dancing in the English manner. It felt stiff and unnatural, having to hold one's head just so, lift the skirt, dip, curtsy, and execute the steps of confusing patterns. Her dark mood did not make the lessons any easier.

She had rarely seen Trevor, even in passing, since the night he had kissed her in the conservatory. When she had last seen him, which had only been long enough to bid him good-bye one morning, he had behaved very formally.

Later, Janelle had tried to explain that Trevor was a busy man, that he had much to do after spending so much time in Africa. But Joya didn't understand why, if he desired her as much as she did him, he had not found some time to be with her.

And surely he did desire her, or why else would he have taken her in his arms and kissed her so deeply? Why had he put his mouth upon her breast?

"Joya?" Janelle called.

She realized she had her palm pressed over the amulet pouch hidden beneath the bodice of her gown. Monsieur Renault offered her his hand. His mouth was pursed into a terrible pout. He smelled of sour wine and musk on wool.

Joya tried to smile. Janelle began to play a lively tune. The dance instructor stepped to his left. Joya stepped to her right. Things were going well until Monsieur tried to guide her in a turn she had not anticipated. The man crashed into her elbow and she inadvertently knocked the wind out of him. The Frenchman gasped for air, doubled over, and sat down hard on the floor.

Janelle stopped playing. She was laughing so hard she did not rush to the man's aid. Joya quickly knelt beside him, asking forgiveness.

"Roll back and forth," she cried, remembering an old Matarengi cure. "Your breath will come back."

The Frenchman recovered without rolling, enough to curse in a mixture of French and English. The little dog was howling.

Joya looked up and thought she would die when she saw Trevor standing in the doorway.

She covered her face with her hands but she could hear his footsteps as he crossed the room.

"Trevor, thank God you are here," Janelle cried. "We are in desperate need of your help."

Joya finally dropped her hands to her lap and looked up from where she knelt beside Monsieur Renault. Trevor was frowning down at them. She thought him beautiful, even with his forehead all wrinkled and his dark brows pinched together.

"Are you purposely trying to *kill* the dance instructor?" he asked.

"That's not the way of it at all," she told him, hoping to smile. "I think that he's trying to kill me."

The Frenchman slowly rose to his feet. He straightened his cuffs, ran both hands over his oiled hair, and bowed to Trevor.

"Monsieur, I queet. Nothing you can do or say, no amount of money is worth thees . . . thees, torture." He snapped his fingers at the dog. "Come, Jolie." The poodle jumped into his arms. After pausing to collect his hat and bamboo switch, the monsieur was gone.

When Joya dared look up at Trevor again, he offered his hand. Embarrassed, she took it and let him pull her to her feet.

"I'm sorry," she said softly, unwilling to move away from him just yet. "I didn't mean to hurt him."

Janelle had left the pianoforte and walked over to join them. "Trevor, I have never been so glad to see anyone in my life. We have quite a dilemma brewing here. I hope you'll help us."

"I'm not staying. I've just come from a meeting nearby and stopped to collect some papers." He spoke without looking at Joya again. "I have to get back."

"Surely you can help for half an hour?"

"Impossible." He still refused to look in her direction.

She was already on the verge of tears after the fiasco with the dance instructor, and now Trevor was not even trying to hide the fact that he wanted nothing to do with her.

"Janelle, he has no time." She was afraid her voice would break.

"Nonsense." Janelle planted her hands on her hips. "Trevor, you can spare a few minutes. We've seen little enough of you these past two weeks."

"Please, Janelle," she whispered. "I don't need to learn to dance in the English style. I'll be happy just to watch the others. Trevor, be on your way. Please."

"If Monsieur Renault could not teach her, how do you expect me to help?" Trevor looked from Joya to Janelle and back.

Joya's shame intensified as Janelle continued to argue with him.

"Because you are far more patient than the monsieur and far less temperamental. Poor Joya has been subjected to both the instructor's switch and Grandmama this morning. She deserves a little kindness. Trevor, the party is tomorrow night. I would not ask if I were not desperate."

"You have no ulterior motive at all?"

"None." Janelle shook her head. Her curls bounced gaily. Joya had no notion how her sister managed to keep her hair perfect all the time. She also marveled at the way her sister seemed to choose her words so carefully when she spoke to Trevor and Adelaide. It was a trait she had not yet mastered.

"Your grandmother says I have two left feet." She looked up at Trevor and realized he had been staring at her.

He made no comment about her feet. "It isn't your fault that you never danced on Matarenga."

"Of course I did. I danced at the marriage ceremonies, whenever new children were born, even at the initiation rituals. I was only forbidden to dance at the full moon fertility ceremony."

"Trevor, why don't you dance with Joya for a few moments at least, see if there is any hope for her while I play?" Janelle started for the pianoforte again.

"A quarter hour only," he said as he set his hat on a chair.

"Let's forget the quadrille," Janelle suggested, "and concentrate on the waltz."

Trevor sighed. Joya waited for him to take her hand before laying the other lightly on his shoulder and stepping close.

"Please, feel free to yell out if I hurt you," she told him. "If you move fast enough, I may not step on your feet."

"Thank you for the warning." He fell silent while Janelle shuffled through the pages of music.

Joya was aware of the soft sound of his breathing, his hand upon her waist. His touch was solid and firm and nothing like Monsieur Renault's, which had as much substance as a butterfly's. Trevor smelled far better, too.

"Delicious," she whispered.

"Pardon me?"

The music started before she could explain and they began. Three seconds later, her foot collided heavily with Trevor's shin.

"I'm sorry." She pulled away. "Your grandmother was right. I'll never be ready by tomorrow night."

"You will do just fine. Perhaps we need thirty minutes." Trevor and Janelle exchanged a look Joya could not fathom. Her sister laughed as he shrugged out of his coat and draped it across the back of a chair.

"Now, shall we start again?" He held her hand tight, kept his arm about her, and continued with the same steps, forcing her to catch up when she faltered or lost count.

"You have to relax," he told her, "and let me lead the way."

They moved in time with the music—one, two, three, one, two, three, one, two—until she stepped down hard on his foot.

"I'm sorry," she mumbled.

Unlike the dance instructor, Trevor did not scream at her, nor did he stop dancing.

"Listen to the music," he told her. "Trust me not to run into the furniture."

"The monsieur told me to count inside my head."

"The monsieur is an idiot. Close your eyes and listen and I will take you where you need to go."

She closed her eyes and did not think about the room, the party, or her left feet. She thought only of Trevor and the thrill of being in his arms. She gave herself into his care, moved when he moved, followed where he led, and did not try to anticipate his steps.

"You see, you haven't stepped on me for a good two minutes," he said after a little while. His voice, so close to her ear, sounded deep and full and sent chills down her spine.

She nodded, listened to the music and let him waltz her around the drawing room, wishing the dance would go on and on forever. Gradually his hand tightened on hers. He drew her so near that she was leaning into him, dancing close to his heart.

Then, after what seemed too short a time, the song

ended and Trevor stopped. Joya opened her eyes and looked up into his face.

"I think that is quite enough." He was frowning again as he straightened his shoulders and stepped back. "You seem to have mastered the basic waltz steps."

She could see that he was not happy in the least. He was quite formal, but appeared confused.

"Thank you," she said, trying to hide her own turmoil and hurt, afraid that he could hear her heartstrings breaking.

As if aware of her pain, Janelle walked over to her. They stood shoulder to shoulder as Trevor picked up his coat and hat, gave them both the same even good-bye, and left the room.

"Did I do something wrong?" Joya asked after he walked out of sight.

"Not at all," Janelle said, smiling. "You did everything just right."

The evening of Adelaide's dinner party, Trevor was dressed on time but lingered in his room for a moment of solitude. He walked to his dresser, pulled open a drawer and took out a folded handkerchief. Then he carefully opened it to reveal a silver filigree hair comb with the letter *C* emblazoned upon it.

His mother's comb. The only part of her that he had ever possessed. His father had told him little about her, except that her name had been Carissa and that she was a lovely Italian aristocrat with beautiful dark eyes. She had angered her family when she married an Englishman, and when the beautiful Carissa died in childbirth in Italy, his father had to fight a host of Italian relations in order to keep Trevor and bring him safely home. Contact with any of his relatives on his mother's side had been severed.

After Carissa, his father never showed any interest in remarrying. Trevor often wondered whether that was because his mother had been so very exquisite that James never found anyone to compare.

Trevor ran his thumb over the silver *C* and tried to imagine the face of the woman who never held him, who had never sung him a lullaby.

It was not like him to give in to melancholy. Perhaps he felt low because he would rather be on the moon tonight than dance attendance on his grandmother's guests, but she had devoted her life to him and the Mandeville holdings. Where would he and Janelle have been without her?

As he rewrapped the comb and tucked it away, he knew that he had been skirting a hard truth. His obligations tonight did not disturb him as much as the knowledge that he had hurt Joya with his evasion and would, no doubt, hurt her even more when he left for Venezuela in a few days.

Janelle was upset with him now, too, for not having spoken with Joya about his plans. His sister had stopped him on the stairway not an hour ago and given him a severe dressing down. He had let her go on only because she was right. He *did* owe Joya an explanation, and he owed it to her as soon as possible. What he did not tell Janelle was that he had not spoken to Joya because he wasn't certain that he trusted himself to be alone with her yet.

He left his room, closed the door behind him, and then nearly jumped out of his skin when he turned and almost stepped into Sims, who had crept up to his door without a sound.

"Good, God, man. I could have killed you," he said, shaken.

Sims scratched his shirtfront. "Sorry, sir. Your grandmother sent me to find you. It seems that Miss Penn is missing and your sister is not yet dressed. *Mrs.* Mandeville requests someone find her. *Miss* Mandeville suggested you."

Trevor shifted, straightening his tie.

"You have no idea where she is, do you Sims? Miss Penn, that is."

"No, sir. The last time I saw her was earlier this afternoon, when she had Winters hanging by his knees from a rod the florist's assistants were holding over the stairwell."

"*What*?"

"Yes, sir. Winters hurt his back carrying extra chairs. Miss Penn said it was the only way to straighten him out again. She said it's the best back cure on Matarenga."

Trevor rubbed his eyes. Unfortunately, he had little difficulty imagining Winters hanging high above the marble floor of the open foyer. "He could have broken his fool neck."

"Actually, she cured him, sir. He says his back never felt better. He is trying to decide where to put a rod in his room so he can hang like a bat in private. He wasn't much for the crowd that gathered to watch, you see. It set the party arrangements back a good hour."

"Does Grandmother know?"

"Yes, sir. It was she who screamed and put an end to it all. The two florists nearly dropped the rod. But everything turned out all right."

"This time," Trevor mumbled.

"Now the little miss from Matarenga has gone missing, sir."

"I'll look for her, Sims. I have a feeling I know where she might have gone."

Chapter 18

A few moments later, Trevor stepped into the dark conservatory, closed his eyes, and breathed in the humid warmth of the air scented with the perfume of rare scented orchids.

"Joya?" He called her name softly, waiting for a response, but there was none. He felt a shaft of worry cut through him.

Could she have left the house to wander the London streets alone? He started to leave when he heard a footstep on the stone floor behind him.

"I am here, Trevor."

He walked in the direction of her voice and saw her when she emerged between two aisles of plants. The sight took his breath away.

Janelle had outfitted her sister well. Joya's gown of royal-blue silk exactly matched her eyes. The fitted waist emphasized her firm figure; the skirt belled over a crinoline, giving her the appearance of a china doll done up with bows and ribbons. Her hair was twisted into a simple style, one that, hopefully, would stand the test of time and dancing.

The only jewelry she wore around her throat was a single strand of pearls, with matching earrings. He had seen them on Janelle, and he knew they had once belonged to Stephanie Oates.

That his sister was not only kind but generous with her twin moved him.

"How did you know where to find me?" Joya did not venture closer.

He shrugged. "I know that this is the closest place to Matarenga that you have found here in England."

"I wanted to be alone."

She looked so beautiful that he stayed where he was, afraid to shorten the distance between them. Afraid that all of his resolve not to touch her might desert him and he would break his promise to Janelle.

"It's time to go, Joya. The guests will be arriving. Grandmother is looking for you."

"I'm afraid."

"Come, before you rub against a pot and get your lovely gown dirty."

"Could I stay in my room then?"

"No. I fear they would only find you another dress. Now, come along. There's no hope for it."

Her sigh, trapped beneath the glass dome, carried to him. He waited until she had reached his side before he spoke again.

"You look lovely tonight." He took her hand, telling himself that was all he would do, that there was no harm in that.

"Do I look good enough to kiss?"

Even in the semidarkness, he could see that she was finally smiling again. She was more than tempting. His arms ached to hold her, his lips to kiss her.

"We will not be kissing again," he said, unable to keep the regret from his tone.

"Why not?" Her smile instantly faded.

He took the coward's way out rather than go into a lengthy explanation of social mores. "I leave for Venezuela in four days."

He heard a small gasp and then, "So soon?"

"Not soon enough. You know about the race to find the Victoria orchid. I intend to win. Three years ago I was very close to an extraordinary find there, a new species that would easily qualify. With what your father has told me, I now know which side of the mountain and what altitude might be most likely to yield the plant I'm looking for."

"Take me with you." She grabbed his hand and carried it to her cheek. "I know as much about orchids as my father."

The touch of her skin made him want more. Gently, he pulled his hand away.

"I can't do that, Joya. You are better off here, with Janelle." *Well out of my reach.*

"I would be safer in the jungles of Venezuela than I am here in London. Please take me. I promise I will not cause any trouble."

He was sorely tempted to give in, seduced by an image of her aboard the ship and thoughts of trekking beside her through the jungle. To take her with him, without a chaperon, perhaps to put her in harm's way when her father had entrusted him with her safety, was unthinkable.

He placed both of his hands on her shoulders. "I can't take you, nor can I kiss you anymore."

There was a long silence before she asked, "Does this

mean you won't even dance with me tonight?"

He was thankful she did not argue. "Not at all. I look forward to it."

"That's something, then." She sounded disappointed, but resigned.

Thankfully, Sims chose that moment to appear in the doorway.

"You are both wanted in the drawing room. *Now*, sir. The guests are arriving."

"Thank you, Sims." Trevor turned back to Joya, wondering how, if Sims had not known where she was before, he had just found them. "Are you ready?"

"There is no way out of this, then?"

"None, I'm afraid. Don't worry. Just be yourself."

He did not tell her that there would not be a man in the room who would not think her a vision. Suddenly he wished he had thought to go over his grandmother's guest list and see how many eligible bachelors might be in attendance.

He turned to go.

"Wait, please, Trevor."

Joya bent over, grabbed the hem of her gown, and reached beneath her crinoline. The contraption was made to fold, which it did, as she raised it.

"What are you doing?" He turned his back before she fully exposed her legs.

"Janelle would not let me wear my amulet pouch around my neck, so I have tied it around my waist. I just want to squeeze it for luck."

Within seconds, he heard the sigh of her silk skirt as the fabric fell back into place again. He felt safe enough to turn around and offer her his arm as they started for the door. Then, above the rustle of silk, he heard something else—a distinct, rhythmic clacking that matched her steps. He abruptly stopped walking and when Joya did too, so did the sound.

"What is that rattling noise?" He was almost afraid to find out.

"My dog's-tooth anklet. It took the teeth of over five dogs to make it. To dance without one is to anger the gods."

Joya knew she would never forget this night as long as she lived. With her hand on Trevor's sleeve, she walked into the foyer, where he nodded to some of the guests just arriving, then they joined Adelaide and Janelle in the drawing room, where guests were greeted in a formal receiving line.

Joya was in awe of the ladies, young and old, in their lovely gowns and sparkling jewels and the gentlemen in severe, formal black evening wear.

The house had been transformed into a wonderland of cut flowers and draped garlands, ornate candelabra, and gilt-edged mirrors that reflected the light. The drawing room had been expanded by opening the folding doors that separated rooms that ran the entire width of the house. At the library end of the room, a long supper table awaited a midnight buffet.

None of the men, she decided early on, looked as fine as Trevor, even though they were all dressed in formal black trousers, waistcoats, and jackets. His shirt was blinding white in contrast to his coat and his tanned skin. He stood out among his peers, not only because of his height and the width of his shoulders, but because others were a collection of soft-bellied, pale men. Trevor looked as if he belonged out of doors, hiking a mountain trail or sailing at the helm of a ship.

It was good to see her sister smiling tonight. Janelle

was probably the happiest of them all, Joya decided. She did not know exactly *how* she knew, but she had been quite certain of it even before she had seen the sparkle in Janelle's eyes. Her sister had chosen a lovely lavender gown for herself, one with much simpler lines and fewer decorative touches than her own, one that suited Janelle's nature well.

When everyone was assembled, Trevor and Adelaide opened the dancing. Although she was dressed in her usual austere black silk, Adelaide looked younger than her years tonight. Slim and stately, she shone on Trevor's arm.

Since the opening dance was to be a quadrille, Janelle had told Joya earlier that she could excuse herself. When Trevor led Adelaide onto the dance floor, Joya gathered her skirt and hurried to the library end of the room, where she slipped behind a tall potted palm.

The musicians started—a piano, cello, and violin— and Joya was caught up in the lovely sight of the Mandevilles and their friends moving so gracefully around the floor. They made the intricate dance pattern appear simple.

"Miss Penn. How nice to see you again."

Nearly upsetting the potted palm, she whirled around and came face to face with Jamison Roth. It took a moment or two before she recalled Trevor's warehouse manager's name.

"Hello, Mr. Roth. What are you doing here?"

He blinked, as if taken aback by her question. She had not seen him come through the receiving line earlier.

"I just arrived. I have been invited to the Mandeville gatherings ever since I have been in their employ. Mr. Mandeville trusts me implicitly, I might add. I hold a very high position in the company."

Not liking the way he puffed out his chest, she turned around and peered through the palm fronds as Trevor danced by with a plump young woman on his arm.

"Miss Penn?"

"Yes?" She turned to find Mr. Roth staring at her expectantly.

"I just asked if you would grant me the next dance?"

Terrified at the thought, she looked between the palm fronds again. Janelle was dancing with an older gentleman who was a head shorter and she was laughing gaily. Adelaide had found a place at the side of the room where she could preside over the affair like a queen. Trevor was still smiling into the upturned, shining face of the plump young lady who could not take her eyes off him.

Joya could almost hear her father's voice in her ear. "Will you hide all night, girl? Get out there and take what you want. You are as good as the rest of them."

She took a deep breath, picturing the calm waters of the lagoon around Matarenga. Then she turned and looked at Jamison Roth. He was no taller than she. A bit heavier. And he had on quite sturdy-looking shoes. She squared her shoulders.

"Are you very strong, Mr. Roth?"

"I suppose. Why?"

"Then I think we should have that dance."

Adelaide's delight knew no bounds. Although her little affair did not qualify as a formal ball by any means, the more intimate group of fifty was a manageable number, given the size of Mandeville House. She had invited the wealthiest of the merchant class as well as a few fortune-hunting members of the aristocracy who needed to mingle with the rich but untitled, looking to refill their coffers.

She had succeeded as a hostess tonight despite the presence of Janelle's friend Lady Cecily Martin, who had arrived in an outlandish combination of clothing—a gold satin Chinese robe embroidered with dragons and clouds, and a pile of golden bangles upon both arms.

The woman had made a great show of arriving late in the company of a very effeminate-looking little man, who was outfitted in a garish violet brocade waistcoat. His title, Viscount Arthur, kept Lord David Langley from being a complete pariah. The man's nephew, Mr. Garr Remington, was far too handsome for his own good and rumor had it, a despicable rake.

Despite the trio, the evening was a success, which made her proud, but unfortunately, Joya Penn had not yet embarrassed herself and fallen out of favor with Trevor.

Adelaide took a glass of champagne from a footman, and thought, *I cannot complain*. Tonight fate had presented her with a simple means to get rid of the Penn girl with very little effort.

Early into the evening, she noticed that Jamison Roth could barely hide his lust for the girl and, being a woman who never let an opportunity slip away, she had immediately decided to do something with her new knowledge.

Now she had just returned from a few minutes of private conversation with Roth. She took a sip of champagne and her buoyant spirits faltered when Trevor waltzed by with the Penn girl in his arms.

It was his second dance with Joya, Adelaide noted. The girl's cheeks were flushed and her eyes closed. Even more disconcerting, Trevor had a faraway look in his eyes that made Adelaide quite thankful that she had not hesitated to take action and formulate a plan.

As she watched Trevor and Joya dance past, she was astounded at the girl's newfound grace. Obviously, her grandson was far more inspirational than the Frenchman.

Even she had to admit that they made a striking couple, but she had far too many objections to Joya Penn to consider a match between her and Trevor. She wanted nothing less than a titled young lady for her grandson, most certainly not anyone in any way connected to Clara Hayworth.

What, if anything, did the girl know of the woman who had raised her? Perhaps Joya was ignorant of Clara Hayworth's past, but Dustin Penn surely was not. As long as Trevor was associated with either of the Penns, the secret threatened to rear its ugly head.

For now at least, she could rest assured that Dustin Penn was on the other side of the world hunting for the Victoria orchid. Once the damned orchid was found by either Penn or Trevor, once Trevor could lay claim to the title that would be awarded for the prize, she would work to sever all Mandeville Imports ties to Dustin Penn.

For now, it would be enough to get the man's daughter out of the way.

Janelle tried to ignore the handsome man beside her, but was compelled to steal surreptitious glances. She had noted earlier that every other woman in the room, except for her sister, was doing exactly the same thing.

Cecily had warned her that Garr Remington was handsome, but she had not said anything about his looking like a Greek god. Next to Trevor, Remington was the tallest man in the room. His eyes were a clear, deep brown, his hair three shades darker, his lips full and inviting and usually smiling. For a man with a shady reputation and very little money, he seemed extremely carefree.

She had just succeeded in not looking at him for a full minute when he surprised her by leaning over to whisper into her ear. Gooseflesh rose on her neck as Garr's warm, teasing breath tickled her skin.

"Your sister is lovely," he whispered.

She turned to him, giving him what she thought was her coolest stare. Just as she had done with Jamison Roth, she said, "Thank you. I will take that as a personal compliment."

He laughed. "You may be twins, but *you* are by far the more beautiful."

"Now I know you are lying," she said, turning away again.

She could see Joya across the room dancing with an older gentleman who was both an old friend of the family and a member of the Orchid Society. Her sister, inspired by Trevor's tutoring session the day before, had overcome her inability to dance. She was making a successful introduction to the elite of London's merchant class, not to mention Cecily, who found Joya spontaneous and delightful.

Janelle was startled when Garr leaned close again. "I prefer a more serious, intelligent woman."

"Oh, please, sir. Don't insult me by feigning flattery." Janelle tried to turn her back on him.

"No, really," he insisted. "I speak the truth."

"Go away."

He showed no sign of leaving.

"I know exactly why you have come here tonight. I've had the truth from Cecily," she told him.

"I will make no excuses. I'm here looking for a wife," he admitted boldly.

"Rich?" She could not resist sliding another sly gaze in his direction, if only to see what shameless candor looked like on a man's face.

"*Very*, preferably. I have expensive tastes and no money. I'm the last in a long line of wastrels."

"You are handsome enough. You should do quite well."

"So you think me handsome?"

"In a manner of speaking. You probably are not as good-looking as *you* think you are, though."

"And you think me conceited."

"Most definitely." She thought she had finally insulted him and that at last he would leave her alone, but he did not budge. Instead he merely smiled an enticing, wicked smile that no man should be allowed to possess. She found herself wishing that she had not noticed the freckles across the bridge of his nose. She had hoped they were dust specks on her spectacles.

"I like an honest woman."

"Then let me be blatantly honest with you, sir. You are without a doubt *the* most conceited man I have ever met." She did not add that he was also the most handsome and certainly had good cause to be full of himself. "I have watched you all evening—"

"Why, thank you, Miss Mandeville. I had not dared to hope that someone like you would be attracted to someone like me." He made a deep courtier's bow.

"You, sir, are not the kind of man I would *ever* be attracted to. Besides, I do not have half the fortune you need, so you may as well move on in search of a more lucrative conquest."

She straightened her gloves and adjusted her spectacles. When he did not walk away, she found herself fighting a smile as she surveyed the room. He was a great challenge, indeed.

Then she said, "Do you see Mrs. Sutton's daughter across the room beside that urn? She has just turned eighteen. I can assure you that she is quite wealthy and sweetly submissive; not only that, but she has been gazing at you all evening."

"With which eye?"

A bawdy laugh escaped Janelle before she could help it. She pressed her gloved hand to her lips.

"I like you, Janelle Mandeville. And here I was beginning to think that your sister was the only breath of fresh air in the room. Do you know that at supper she told me, and everyone within earshot, that she is a far better dancer without clothes?"

Janelle laughed again and grudgingly admitted to herself that his reputation was well deserved. Rake or not, he was definitely charming. She could not help but like him.

"After many terrible days of assaulting her instructor's toes, my sister was convinced that she was going to maim every man who danced with her tonight."

Janelle watched Garr's interested gaze swing around to Joya and she suddenly sobered.

"Stay away from my sister, Garr. She is no match for you."

"If you are worried about my pursuing your sister, don't be. I find you far more desirable, softer on the outside but possessed of an inner strength and quick wit." He took a step closer. "You must be excited about attracting my uncle's patronage. He has not been this enthusiastic about discovering a new artist for a long, long time."

"If you must know the absolute truth, I am a bit nervous."

"Why?"

"I have not had many people acknowledge my work. Grandmother has virtually ignored it for she finds it a sore point. Trevor humors me. But Cecily has always been encouraging. I hope my paintings are worthy of your uncle's praise and support."

"Believe me when I say that I like you, Janelle Mandeville. Now I see that you have no airs or pretense, either. May I call on you tomorrow?"

"No, you may not. There is no use for it. That would be a great waste of time that you could spend on a more receptive quarry."

The sound of Garr's quick, deep laughter was as intoxicating as the sight of him. Janelle warned herself not to be taken in by his dark, seductive eyes. She tried to concentrate on Joya, who was dancing with a young married gentleman. With every turn, her sister scanned the room looking for Trevor.

Janelle saw her brother deep in the shadows near the back wall, where he could watch Joya dance without drawing attention to himself.

"What is going on in that mind of yours?" Garr wanted to know.

"Dance with my sister," she said, suddenly inspired.

He frowned. "You just told me to stay away from her. Besides, she does not fascinate me the way you do."

Janelle faced him squarely. "You misunderstand me. I would not let you marry my sister if you were the last bachelor on earth."

"Then why have me dance with her?"

"Humor me, please. The very next dance."

He was watching her carefully. She knew he was trying to discern the motive behind her request.

"I'll do it, but only because *you* ask." Finally, Garr left her side. She watched him make his way through the crowd around the edge of the dance floor.

When the music ended, Garr walked up to Joya and made a polite bow. Janelle held her breath until her sister accepted and Garr led her onto the dance floor, then she threaded her way through the guests and walked up to Trevor.

"It appears Grandmama's party is quite a success." She reached around him to take a glass of champagne off a tray as a footman passed by.

"Who is that dancing with Joya?"

She pretended not to be able to see her sister for a moment or two. "Oh, him. That is Mr. Garr Remington, nephew of Viscount Arthur, my art patron. He is looking for a wife."

"He is looking in the wrong place."

She quickly took a sip to hide her smile. A dark frown marred Trevor's brow. Janelle cleared her throat.

"That's just what I told him earlier, but he could not take his eyes off her. Actually, he was just asking me all about her. I hope I can keep her from being swept off her feet. After all, he is the handsomest man in the room. Cecily says he is quite the rake, though." Unable to resist, she dared to glance up at her brother.

"Why, Trevor, what's wrong? You look absolutely green."

Without a word, he handed her his empty glass and plunged into the crowd.

Trevor watched Joya waltz by in Garr Remington's arms and execute a perfect turn. When she smiled up at the man and said something that made Remington throw back his head and laugh, Trevor skirted the dancers and walked into the middle of the dance floor, blocking their way, forcing Remington to abruptly stop.

"Trevor!" Joya beamed up at him. "I haven't stepped on anyone for two hours."

"Good evening, Mandeville." Remington smiled and bowed grandly.

So nicely, in fact, that Trevor wanted to smash his fist into the man's even white teeth. He mentally chastised himself, and tried to regain some semblance of calm.

"Mr. Remington. I am going to dance with Miss Penn."

"Most certainly."

When Remington bowed and gave Joya over to him without argument, Trevor was surprised. He had expected more of an argument.

Once Trevor had Joya in his arms, he realized his great mistake in giving in to the first bout of jealousy he had ever suffered. To make matters worse, this was his third dance of the evening with Joya. Once more he had overstepped the bounds of propriety.

Thankfully, she had no idea that three dances denoted serious interest. He was certain there were others in the room who took note, but now there was nothing he could do but finish the dance.

That and hope that this insufferable inability to control his emotions was only temporary.

Chapter 19

It was almost noon the next day when Joya found herself going down to breakfast. Because the party had not ended until well past two in the morning, she, like the rest of the household, had slept late.

Refreshed after a good night's sleep, she hovered between euphoria and melancholy. Dancing with Trevor had been wonderful. Her discussion with him in the conservatory before the affair had been devastating.

Knowing that he would be leaving London soon made her miserable. She could not take her mind off him any more than she could last night. She had tried desperately not to let him know she was watching him, all the time wondering what she could say or do to make him either stay in London or take her with him.

He seemed to be in a dark mood all evening, alone even while surrounded by a houseful of family, friends, and business acquaintances. She suspected that concern over business was what had kept him so pent-up all evening. During their last dance, he had barely spoken two words to her.

She was looking forward to Janelle lightening her mood and was happy to find her sister beaming when she entered the breakfast room. Adelaide was there as well.

Joya greeted both women and went to fill a plate with ham, eggs, toast, and grilled tomatoes from an array of dishes on the sideboard. Behind her, a discussion of the success of the past evening's affair was going on. Even Adelaide, usually dour in the morning, was in a fine mood.

Joya had no sooner sat down beside Janelle than Sims appeared in the doorway.

"Excuse me, madam, but there have been quite a few gentlemen stopping by already this morning to leave calling cards."

Adelaide was watching him with her fork paused in midair. "Sims, *why* are you continually scratching your shirtfront? It has become an annoying, not to mention disgusting habit with you."

"Begging your pardon, but I itch, madam."

Joya smiled up at him. "How are your joints, Sims?"

"Much better, thank you, miss." He immediately started scratching again. "Well worth the rest of it."

"The rest of what, Sims?" Janelle wanted to know.

"The itching."

"Sims!" Adelaide laid down her fork and blotted the corner of her mouth with her napkin.

"Yes, madam?"

"You said gentlemen have already called?"

"Yes, madam. Quite a number of them wish to visit with Miss Penn. There was one asking after Miss Mandeville, as well."

Janelle's fork clattered loudly against her plate. Her complexion blazed.

"You two were such a success last night that I took the liberty to plan another, more intimate, social gathering," Adelaide announced.

"What?" Janelle, still stunned by Sims's announcement, turned to her grandmother. "What kind of social gathering?"

"Will I have to learn more dances? Or wear another corset and crinoline and stockings?" Joya was horrified to be faced with the prospect of such torture again so soon.

Adelaide sobered. "No more dancing. And I do not appreciate discussing undergarments at the table. Janelle, you look as if you are about to be ill. What is wrong with you?"

"Nothing, Grandmama."

There was something wrong. Janelle's voice was barely audible. Joya felt her sister's anxiety as if it were her own. She could not wait to speak to Janelle alone.

Adelaide, though, took Janelle at her word. "Good, because I have planned a country outing for day after tomorrow."

"You are going *outside*?" Joya had yet to see Adelaide leave the house, so she was shocked at the very notion of the woman planning an outing. Janelle was obviously as surprised.

Adelaide ignored the comment and blotted her lips with her napkin. "I thought that a day at the old Oates estate might be in order. A wonderful day with a grand picnic and perhaps some games. I plan to invite a few of the locals to add color. You, Joya, should see the property that once belonged to your parents. I am sure, Janelle, that you would have thought of this before summer was over. We can enjoy the old place and share the day with friends."

"Which friends, Grandmama?" Janelle sat back in her chair, her eggs growing cold.

"I have already spoken to Trevor, but of course he cannot be there. Too many things to attend to before his voyage, you understand, but I'll invite some young people to come along and perhaps even your friend Cecily can join us."

Joya wondered why Janelle was so surprised by Adelaide's generous offer. Her own joy was tempered, for if Trevor was not there, she would spend the day wishing it otherwise.

Adelaide tossed her napkin on the table. "It will be a wonderful day. I've much planning to attend to, so I will leave you two alone. Besides, I am curious to see which gentlemen you two have impressed so much that they have already returned."

Joya waited until Adelaide was out of the room before she turned to her twin. "Why are you so worried?"

"Grandmama does nothing without motive. I'm wondering what she might be up to."

"Perhaps she just wants to go outdoors," Joya offered.

Janelle shook her head. "I don't think so."

"Why did Sims's announcement upset you?"

"What do you mean?"

"When he said that a gentleman called for you and left his card, you turned all red and dropped your fork. Even if I did not feel it too, I can see by the look on your face that you are still upset. For no reason, my stomach feels very jumpy. More, even, than Monsieur Renault's little dog."

Janelle glanced over at the door and then leaned across the table. Joya leaned in toward her sister.

"I am afraid that the one man at the entire gathering that I should heartily detest has come calling on me. His name is Garr Remington."

Joya was well aware of who Garr Remington was. She would have had to be blind not to have remembered him.

"The big one. Handsome, like Trevor, although I find him not half as delicious. I danced with him once, that is until Trevor wanted to dance with me. Mr. Remington was very polite and said that he did not mind. I don't know why Trevor even bothered. He was in a very dark mood."

Janelle's face lit up with a smile. "Why don't we go upstairs and see if you have something appropriate to wear for a garden party?"

Joya loved the old Oates manor house on sight, not only because it was in the open where she could see the sky and walk through soft green grass and listen to birdsong again, but because it was so completely different from Mandeville House and the other soot-covered, brick-and-stone buildings crowded together on the streets of London.

It was a vine-covered, three-story dwelling that reminded her a little of her home on Matarenga. The house was still friendly and welcoming even though the roof had fallen in on some of the rooms and doves had taken up residence in the corners and eaves of the parlor. There was a sense of belonging, a spirit that lingered and made it seem a warm and happy place, despite the fact that the sky showed through the ceiling here and there.

Generations had no doubt taken joy in the place. Knowing that her true parents had once owned the house and loved it, that they had visited here and perhaps dreamed of making it livable, made it even more valuable in Joya's eyes.

She left the others seated around the remains of a picnic spread on fine linen on the lawn and walked around to the front of the building, wondering how much money would it take to rebuild the old house? Her father had told her she had funds in her English account, enough for whatever she needed. Did she have enough to put this house that Osmond and Stephanie Oates so loved back together?

While talking to Janelle earlier, Joya had learned that her sister dreamed of doing just that, but she had said that only time and money stood in her way. Joya knew that she, herself, had an abundance of money in the account her father had mentioned. But how long would she be staying in England?

She sighed and walked over to a tangled, climbing rosebush draped over a low garden wall. She carefully plucked an unfolding, pale pink bud and inhaled the rich fragrance. Everyone had been so kind to her this afternoon—Cecily and Viscount Arthur; Garr Remington; the vicar and his wife; and the accountant, Jamison Roth. Even Mrs. Sutton and her daughter, Penelope, who had been Trevor's plump dance partner.

Eventually, the conversation around her turned to political and social events that confused and bored her. She had no knowledge of such things. After luncheon, she decided to walk along the stone path that wound its way around the house to enjoy a few moments alone.

Her solitude was short-lived. She heard footsteps on the stone path behind her. Jamison Roth came strolling up to her, alone, smiling.

"Miss Penn. How nice to find you here. I was thinking that a walk to the old millhouse down by the stream would be quite enjoyable. Your company would make it even more delightful. Will you come?"

The others were lingering beside the picnic, some sipping wine, others watching an occasional, billowing white cloud drift across the open, deep blue sky. Janelle was laughing at something Garr Remington had just said. The pair seemed quite content together.

All morning Janelle had been by her side, showing her the house, making certain she was warm enough, asking if she was enjoying herself. Perhaps if she took the time to go walking with Roth, her sister might relax and, if Janelle got to know Garr Remington better, she would change her mind about him.

Joya turned to Roth and used a phrase she had heard the vicar's wife say over a hundred times that morning.

"Why, that would be simply delightful!"

Roth appeared much relieved and offered her his arm. Joya took it and felt nothing when she touched him. Again she sighed. Again she told herself not to dwell on Trevor. His mind was made up. He was leaving for Venezuela. Even if he were to stay in London, he had made it abundantly clear he wanted no relationship with her beyond one of friendship.

Sad inside, she lifted her face to the sun. Despite Adelaide's dire warnings against burning her skin now that it was paler, Joya drank in the familiar warmth, enjoying it as she might have enjoyed a hug from an old friend.

"Here we are," Roth said when they reached an abandoned stone millhouse beside a flowing stream. "There is a wonderful old grindstone inside."

"It's lovely," she said absently, her thoughts were on Trevor.

"Shall we go inside?" Roth smiled his mule-faced smile.

Joya shrugged. "Why not?"

• • •

Janelle looked into the charming face of Garr Remington and wished Joya had brought along a Matarengi potion that would quench his enthusiasm. The heated way he was watching her, coupled with his casual attempts to move closer, to brush against her as he reclined upon the picnic cloth and stretch out beside her, left her uneasy—for each time he touched her, she realized she wanted more.

As she gazed down into Remington's beautiful dark eyes, she reminded herself that this was certainly *not* the kind of man she should even be considering. He was too handsome, too experienced, too desperate for money. How could she ever expect him to be sincere? Or faithful?

Suddenly, she shivered, as if a dark cloud had passed over the sun, but the day was still perfectly fair with a light breeze. There was not a threatening cloud in sight.

"What's wrong?" Garr rose up onto his elbow, his face shadowed with concern.

Janelle scanned the small group seated not far away. She recalled seeing Adelaide walk off with the minister, his wife, Mrs. Sutton, and her daughter. Joya was nowhere in sight.

"Where is my sister?"

"Went for a walk, I think." Garr sat up and looked around, too.

"I feel there is something wrong with her."

"If you are worried, let's go find her."

A quarter of an hour later, Janelle had not yet found Joya. Nor had she seen Adelaide anywhere. Garr leaned against a tree, arms folded, more than willing to do whatever she wanted to do next.

At that very moment, Trevor came riding over a gentle rise that hid the sweep of road from view.

"Oh, thank heavens," she cried. "There's Trevor!"

"Trevor the wonderful," Garr said.

Janelle turned on him. "Trevor is my brother and I would thank you not to belittle him. He is everything you are not—serious, hardworking, caring."

When Trevor rode up beside them, Janelle reached up to stroke his Arabian's neck.

"I'm so glad you decided to join us." She was almost hesitant to voice her fears aloud, afraid he would scoff at her premonition.

He dismounted, nodded to Garr, and looked at the old house, then around the garden and lawn area. "I had forgotten how close this place was to London."

"We should come out here more often. It has been a very nice morning. The vicar is here, along with his wife. Grandmama invited Lady Cecily, too, among others."

"Where is she?" His gaze scanned the front lawn.

"Grandmama? She's walking with a few of the guests."

"Where is *Joya*?" Trevor asked sharply.

"I don't know," she admitted. "We've been looking for her, but we haven't been able to find her."

"You *lost* her?"

"I didn't lose her. I just can't find her." She could not withhold the inexplicable truth from Trevor. "I cannot help feeling that there is something wrong." She rubbed her hands up and down her sleeves, cold despite the sun. "I wish I knew where she is."

Trevor quickly whipped his horse's reins around a gatepost.

"Where have you looked?"

"Around the house," Janelle said, stemming a sudden

urge to cry and wondering where it came from.

"Remington, you walk to the edge of the wood. Call out her name. I'll go the opposite way. Did you follow the path all the way to the stream?"

Janelle shook her head. "Not all the way."

"I will." He left without a good-bye.

She wished that Trevor had brushed aside her fears as nonsense and told her not to worry. As she watched him hurry away from the house, Garr took her hand, his devil-may-care expression gone.

"Come, let's find your sister. Don't worry. I'm sure she is close by."

Joya could not shake the feeling that Jamison Roth was not as sincere as he seemed. She knew he was a trusted employee of Trevor's and that Adelaide seemed to consider him a dear friend of the family. Hadn't Trevor's grandmother said as much in the carriage on the way to the picnic?

Roth was acting very oddly just now, talking without pause, often glancing toward the door. The old stone millhouse smelled of mildew and mouse droppings. There were pigeon feathers all over the floor. A feeling of foreboding crept over Joya.

"This is the grindstone." Roth pointed to a time-worn stone wheel. He made no move to leave her side.

Joya shivered and rubbed her arms. "It's damp here. I'm cold. I think we should go back outside."

"Not yet," he said quickly.

Too quickly. He took a step toward her.

When she looked into his eyes, her stomach dropped. His face had taken on a hard, resolute expression. He was staring at her in a way that no one ever had before, as if he wanted to devour her and any objection she might have would go unnoticed.

Trevor's shipboard words of warning came back to her.

"Never be alone with a man."

Suddenly she did not want to be alone with Jamison Roth. She wanted to be outside, in the sunlight. His nearness and the strange look in his eyes made her skin crawl.

Without thinking, she had broken a cardinal English rule. Until now, she hadn't realized why it was so vitally important that one adhere to it.

"I think we should go back." She turned away from him and started for the door.

Roth reached for her and took her arm, alarming her even more.

"What is your hurry?"

"My . . . my sister. I don't like to leave her for too long." She yanked her arm out of his grasp.

His expression smoothed out at her mention of Janelle. "Your sister seemed perfectly happy with Remington."

"That is exactly why I need to go back. She . . . she does not welcome his attentions."

"She's a woman. No doubt she's just playing coy."

"What does that mean?" She tried to keep him talking while she slowly edged toward the door.

"Your sister is teasing Garr Remington, pretending not to welcome his pursuit when the exact opposite is true. Women do it all the time. Now, why don't you come here and give me a kiss?" He closed the distance she had gained between them.

"Why would I want to kiss you, Mr. Roth? I feel no desire for you. I cannot imagine kissing such thin, unattractive lips as yours. Besides, I have made a terrible mistake in coming here with you. Trevor told me that I should never be alone with a man who is not my husband."

"Trevor, eh? What if very shortly *I* am your husband, Miss Penn? It would be quite permissible then."

"Impossible. If that ever happened it would only be because I had lost my mind."

"Are you insulting me? Surely I am an exception to Trevor's rule. After all, I am a friend of the family. The account manager at the warehouse. I know firsthand that Mrs. Mandeville would welcome an alliance between us."

She had let his pasty white complexion and the smoothness of his hands fool her into thinking she was stronger. Joya attempted to shove him down and flee the millhouse, but he only stumbled back, then quickly regained his footing. He was on her in an instant.

"Let me go!" She shouted in his ear, trying to unbalance him again.

As she lunged for the door, she heard a rending tear and looked down. He held on to the shoulder of her gown so tightly that it had ripped the front of her bodice. The sight of her frilly chemise beneath the soft, muslin fabric sparked her temper. She slapped him across the face.

His mouth hardened. So did the determination in his eyes. He reached for her again. His hands tightened on her shoulders. His stare lingered on the rise and fall of her breasts beneath the torn fabric.

For the first time in her life, Joya wanted to hide her body. She twisted and kicked and tried to break his hold. She nearly succeeded until he shoved her up against the stone wall so hard that the air left her lungs in a *whoosh*.

Roth leaned into her and began to kiss her forcefully. She attempted to push him off, bucked and kicked, but there was no moving him.

When she tried to cry out, he bruised her mouth with his and mauled her with his hands. He began to force her down the stone wall.

"Why fight me? You want this. You know you do," he said against her mouth.

What she wanted was to hit him hard enough to knock out all of his front teeth, but he was holding her so close that she could not get free. Roth shifted, kicked a foot out from under her and she went down, banging the back of her head against the rock wall.

Seeing double, she tried to call for help as she pushed at him. *Not like this. Not this man.*

She had no desire to have him near her, let alone kiss or touch her intimately. If Kibatante was trying to teach her a hard lesson about desire, this one was *too* harsh. She mumbled a hasty promise to the god. She would keep the English rule. She would never, ever be alone with a man again.

Roth was on her, kissing her, pawing at the torn bodice of her gown, shoving her down into the dirt and the mouse droppings and feathers and then suddenly, he was gone. She heard a sharp cry, like that of an angry seagull, a strange, strangled sound—and she shoved herself up in time to see Jamison Roth go flying through the air. He hit the wall and landed in a heap across the room.

Trevor was standing over her, his chest heaving, his brows slammed together. He continually flexed his hands open and closed as if he could not wait to use his fists on Roth. First, though, he reached for her.

Joya let him pull her to her feet. His gaze shot to the

ruined bodice of her gown, then her bruised mouth, her tangled hair.

"Are you all right?"

"I broke the rule, Trevor, but you can be assured I will never do *that* again."

Roth was struggling to get to his feet. Trevor crossed the room, yanked him up, and planted a fist on his jaw. Roth went down again, but was still conscious.

"Is it my turn?" Joya wanted to hit Roth herself, but was finding it increasingly harder to stay on her feet. She began to sway and grabbed hold of Trevor's lapel. He made certain she was leaning against the old grindstone before he left her alone and pulled Roth to his feet.

"Please, don't hit me again, sir," Roth pleaded.

"You're right. I shouldn't hit you. I should kill you."

"Please. I'll never touch her again. I swear it on my mother's grave."

"There will be no chance of that, Roth. I want you out of here."

"I'll leave immediately. I promise."

"In case you don't understand me clearly, I want you out of England. Not only that, but if I ever see your face in London, or anywhere else for that matter, if I ever even hear your name, I will kill you. Make no mistake, I mean every word I say."

Nodding furiously, Roth was backing out of the mill as if he were staring into the eyes of Death. He kept his hands up in front of him, scant protection, as he shuffled backward.

When the man had cleared the door and was gone, when the sound of his running footsteps had faded, Trevor turned to Joya.

"I'm so sorry, Trevor. I did not think that I had anything to fear from Mr. Roth. This was all my fault," she cried.

"That man's behavior was absolutely *not* your fault."

"You saved me, Trevor."

"Look at you. I cannot let you out of my sight, it seems."

There was so much tenderness in his tone as he reached for her. That she wished that he really would not ever let her out of his sight. In fact, she thought that he was about to take her in his arms, but he did not. Instead, gently, carefully, he took the ragged edges of her gown and pulled them together.

She looked up into his eyes and could see that he shared her anger as well as her humiliation. Instead of throwing her transgression in her face, instead of pitying her, he shared her hurt. He truly, deeply cared.

"Thank you, Trevor," she whispered. Unable to resist, she threw her arms about his neck.

Adelaide looked at the watch dangling from a golden bow pinned to the cutwork bodice of her black gown. The time was right. She and her party had reached the old mill. Vicar Wilson and his wife, Eugenia, along with Henrietta Sutton; her flat-faced, husband-hungry girl, Penelope; and even Cecily Martin accompanied her. It was more than she had hoped for. She could hardly contain her excitement as they approached the door of the old millhouse.

Inside, all was quiet. She had purposely kept her voice low as they approached so as not to give their presence away. If all had gone as planned, she and her little entourage were about to discover the Penn girl and Roth in a tryst. The vicar would naturally insist that Roth do the right thing and Joya Penn would quickly be married.

Oh, glorious, glorious thought.

Leading the way, she stepped over the threshold of the millhouse, her heart pounding with such excitement that she felt short of breath. Two steps inside, she saw them in the shadows near the old grist mill.

Just as she had planned, that man had Joya Penn locked in a feverish embrace. The little wanton had her arms twined around his neck, and the man hot for the girl, was kissing her with great abandon.

As the rest of her party crowded in behind her, Adelaide noted with disgust that the girl's breast was cupped in his hand.

She gasped and then called out, "Stop!" with as much dramatic fervor as she could muster. "Unhand that young woman, you cad! This instant!"

Both Mrs. Sutton and the vicar's wife gasped. Vicar Wilson himself took Adelaide's arm to steady her.

The man swung the girl behind him protectively, shielding her from view before he straightened to full height. Adelaide was thinking that she had never realized the accountant was so tall when he spun around and she looked directly at the man's face.

Her breath left her in a rush. She took a faltering step back, made a grab for her chest. The trap she had set with Jamison Roth had not only ensnared Joya Penn, but her own dear Trevor.

Chapter 20

Trevor watched his grandmother crumple to the floor. As if on cue, a shaft of sunlight beamed down through a broken section of the roof, illuminating her silver hair. With the stark black silk gown pooled around her, her skin looked like blue-white crepe.

In a split second he took in the tableau behind her. It was a study of affronted sensibilities, with Vicar Wilson; his wife, Eugenia; and Mrs. Sutton and her homely daughter, whose name escaped him, all standing there gaping at him.

A few feet behind them, Lady Cecily Martin was not as shocked as she seemed to be amused. When Trevor met her cynical gaze, she merely lifted a brow as if to say, "Let's see how you get out of this, dear boy."

Joya moved first. Ignoring the state of her torn gown, she came out from behind him and ran to Adelaide's side, unaware of what the others must be thinking.

He rushed to stand beside her as she knelt down to minister to Adelaide. She waved her hands over his grandmother's prostrate form and began to chant loudly in Matarengi. When Adelaide's eyelids fluttered, Joya leaned over her and shouted, "Wake up, Mrs. Mandeville!" Then she started chanting again.

Trevor breathed a sigh of relief when Adelaide's eyes opened and she snapped, "*I am not deaf!* Stop shouting that gibberish."

"Oh, ma'am," Joya cried, truly relieved. "I am so glad to see that you are not as dead as you looked."

"Get away from me." Adelaide batted her hands at Joya. Trevor took a step back, putting his hand protectively on Joya's shoulder.

Vicar Wilson was kneeling on the other side of Adelaide. The vicar was a man in his early thirties with a beard, heavy brows and waving hair the color of weak tea. He demanded an accounting. He took the old woman's elbow and helped her up as he shot a dark, accusatory glare at Trevor.

"You have much to answer for, young man," the vicar said.

"I am not much younger than you are, sir."

"I trust you intend to make things right for Miss Penn." The vicar drew himself up and glared.

"I am already all right," Joya volunteered.

"Of course you are." Adelaide, quite recovered, was brushing off her skirt, smacking away mouse droppings and pigeon feathers, straightening her bonnet. "Why don't we go back to the garden and finish our picnic? Perhaps some croquet would be nice."

The vicar was staring in shock. "Madam, *you* may be willing to let this slight go because it was your grandson who has trespassed on this young lady's innocence, but *I* most certainly cannot."

"Oh, posh," Adelaide dismissed him with a wave of her hand.

"Nor can I." Mrs. Sutton, renowned for her ability to gossip, stepped forward, puffed like a stuffed partridge on a dinner platter. Her mouth was set in a stern line. "If anything like that were ever to happen to my sweet Penelope, I would do whatever necessary to salvage her reputation."

Behind her, the aforementioned Penelope had covered her face with her hands but was peering at Trevor through her pudgy fingers. He doubted that Penelope could ever find herself in this kind of situation, for she would never make a rational man lose control of himself the way Joya could. The young Miss Sutton definitely did not have Joya's charm.

The vicar refused to be ignored. "Trevor Mandeville, you have taken advantage of this girl . . . your sister's twin . . . when you should be acting as her guardian."

"He most certainly has not!" Adelaide snapped. "This is *not* what it appears. Tell him, Trevor."

"Trevor did not take anything from me," Joya announced. She had no idea why they were all so upset when for her, the worst was over.

She was holding the front of her gown together, which brought back the memory of Roth's attack and stoked Trevor's anger all over again.

If he had not happened along when he did—he refused to even contemplate what might have happened.

"Of course he didn't. If anything, I am certain you initiated this whole scenario yourself," Adelaide told Joya.

Before Trevor could argue, Joya said, "I broke the rule, you see, when Mr. Roth offered to show me the mill. I went out walking alone with him. Once we were here, I saw a horrible look in his eyes and I realized what a terrible mistake I had made."

"A horrible look in his eyes?" Mrs. Sutton had both hands pressed against her heart. She was trembling all over.

"Oh, yes. He was staring at me with something darker and far worse than desire. He looked as if he wanted to throw me to the ground and have his way with me. Then he lunged for me when I tried to escape. When I fought him, my gown tore.

"Why, I thank Kibatante that I am still fit from hiking the jungles of Matarenga. If I had not been wearing this huge skirt and all these ruffles and bows, and if I had had my machete, I could have done him in."

Trevor tried to get a word in, but she would not be stopped.

"If Trevor had not come along when he did, I cannot really say what might have happened, but I believe Mr. Roth would have used me in a most vicious, carnal way."

The young Miss Sutton swooned and hit the ground hard. Her mother knelt and began clucking over her. Cecily Martin sidestepped them both to move next to Joya.

"That explains your torn gown, but not the familiar way Mr. Mandeville was . . . touching you when we arrived," Cecily said.

"Why, that is easily explained." Joya looked up at Trevor with hero worship in her eyes. "He was kissing me back."

"Kissing you back?" Cecily was no longer trying to hide a smile.

"Because I kissed him first."

Trevor wondered how anyone could be so frustrating,

endearing, innocent, and wanton, all at the same time. The walls were fast closing in on him. His emotions were in a complete tangle, impossible to sort out. How did a man deal with feelings he had tried, at every turn, to deny?

He had spent the morning wrestling with worry over Joya's spending the day outside London without him along to watch over her. Rightly—given what had happened to Joya—he had not trusted his sister to do so, for lately Janelle had thought of nothing but her paintings and Garr Remington.

The import house had been shorthanded because his grandmother had insisted Roth be given the day off to "round out her little band of revelers," as she put it. Finally, giving in to worry, Trevor had left the warehouse and ridden out to join them. Thankfully, he had arrived just in time.

But after he had rescued Joya, why couldn't he have simply taken her directly back to Janelle? He should have known better than to spend even one second alone with her. Just as he had predicted on Matarenga, bringing Joya Penn to London had wreaked havoc on his life.

Now that he was rational and somewhat in control again, he knew that it was time to salvage the situation. He had to put an end to all of this nonsense. There was only one thing a man of honor could do. Only one way this little drama would ever end for the both of them.

He did not want Joya to be hurt any further —and if everyone went on any longer, she would surely understand that there was no other way out and he would spare her that. Trevor gave the vicar a silent, measuring stare before he turned to Joya and said. "Miss Penn, will you do me the honor of becoming my wife?"

"Oh no, Trevor!" his grandmother cried.

"Oh yes, Trevor!" Forgetting her torn bodice, Joya threw her arms around his neck again. Fortunately, he had braced himself.

"I will hold you to this, Mandeville," the vicar promised as Joya peppered Trevor's jaw with kisses.

"You have no need to worry on that score. We will marry as soon as I can obtain a special license," Trevor assured him.

At that, Adelaide swooned again, this time pulling Eugenia Wilson down with her.

Cecily Martin laughed, a loud, very unladylike laugh that came from the tips of her toes.

"Well done, Mandeville!" She thumped him between the shoulder blades. "May I be the first to offer you both my congratulations?"

Trevor sighed as he and Lady Cecily looked down upon Penelope Sutton and her mother kneeling beside her; then at Adelaide, who had already revived but was still pinning down the vicar's wife.

"Since there is hardly any room left on the floor, I'll go and see if I can find Janelle," Cecily said.

"Here I am, Cecily." Janelle stepped over the threshold with Garr Remington following close behind.

A quarter of an hour ago the terrible distress she had been experiencing had evaporated. Unable to explain her feelings to Garr, she had simply assured him, "Wherever Joya is, I feel the danger has passed."

From the look on Cecily and Trevor's faces just now though, she wondered whether her relief had been premature.

"Did you find her? Is Joya all right?"

"We found more than your sister, I'm afraid," Cecily said.

Janelle hurried over to Joya. When she saw the state of her twin's hair and her ripped bodice, she felt sick inside. Immediately, she turned to the one person she trusted most in the world.

"Dear heavens, Trevor, what happened?"

"Roth happened."

"Where is he?"

"Gone. Now I have to find a new accountant."

"But shouldn't you have notified the authorities?"

Trevor shook his head. "I took care of him myself in order to avoid any more scandal."

"From now on, when I get the feeling something is wrong with Joya, I will act upon it sooner." Janelle threw her arms around her sister. "Oh, you poor dear! Whatever came over Jamison Roth? I would have never imagined him capable of such behavior. I should have never left you alone."

It was all Garr's fault that she had not been with Joya. She shot the rake a dark look, but he merely shrugged and gave her his most devastating smile.

"We are going to be married," Trevor announced.

"Your brother did the honorable thing and immediately offered for Joya's hand," Cecily added.

"As well he should have," the vicar chimed in. "He saved her from Mr. Roth, but then took advantage of the poor girl himself. The scene we saw when we walked in was utterly appalling."

If what the vicar had seen was half what she had seen in the conservatory, then not only had she reason to be upset with him, but she knew Trevor had done the right thing by proposing in front of the others. He had immediately tried to rectify the situation in the only way he could have done.

Mrs. Sutton was a legendary gossip. Even dear Cecily

relished passing on a good story. Janelle ignored the vicar as she smoothed back Joya's hair and clucked over her torn gown.

Joya whispered, "Trevor and I are to be married." She continued to smile up at him as if he had hung the moon. Trevor, on the other hand, was staring out the open door.

Janelle wanted to talk to him alone, but she knew that he most likely needed time away from the accusatory look in the vicar's eyes, perhaps even from such bright excitement in Joya's. Obviously, her sister was not aware that Trevor's hand had been forced.

"Why don't you go on, Trevor. Take Garr with you. Have the footmen pack up the picnic and ready the carriages. I'll see to Joya."

His expression was one of gratitude. As the men stepped out into the blinding light of the warm summer day, she saw Garr clap Trevor on the shoulder and ask, "Don't you just love country outings?"

Joya watched Trevor leave. She had seen something in his eyes, something on his face that diminished her buoyant happiness. Janelle took charge.

"Let's see about fixing your gown. Cecily, now that Mrs. Sutton has Penelope on her feet, why don't you take them back to the front lawn? I'm sure Vicar Wilson would like to help Eugenia, and Grandmama as well." Janelle fussed with the front of Joya's gown; she pulled the edges together and had Joya hold them there.

Adelaide was now standing. There was some color back in her cheeks. The Sutton girl and her mother made their way out the door with the Wilsons.

Janelle quickly took the old woman's arm and led her grandmother to the door, where they spoke in hushed whispers. Joya watched the exchange between the two headstrong women. Adelaide was visibly upset.

Thankfully, the vicar returned, but he avoided meeting Joya's gaze as he offered Adelaide his arm and quickly escorted her out of the mill.

"Why is Adelaide so upset?" she asked her sister.

"She is worried about Trevor. And you. Don't concern yourself about anything." Janelle put her hands on her hips and frowned. Her spectacles had slipped down her nose. "A morning wedding, of course. We'll have an intimate gathering at the house following the ceremony."

Despite the aches and pains setting in from Roth's rough handling, Joya's happiness knew no bounds. She was going to marry Trevor and be his wife, his mate, forever. They would do all the things a husband and wife did together.

"I'll miss you," she told Janelle.

"Where are you going?"

"Trevor and I will have to live in isolation for a month."

"What are you talking about?"

Joya rubbed her aching shoulder. "On Matarenga, a man and his new bride always move into a marriage hut and are kept away from everyone for a month after the wedding. To ensure not only fertility, but a strong marriage. At the end of that time, they build a hut of their own in the village. Surely it is the same here, without a hut, of course, but the isolation . . ."

"In England things are quite different. As Trevor's wife, you will continue to live in Mandeville House, and unless Trevor plans a short honeymoon, which I doubt, you will not be going anywhere."

"No isolation?"

Janelle shook her head. "I am afraid not the way you mean."

Worry crept into Joya's heart the way the fog crept silently onto London's streets. How could a marriage survive without a fertility ceremony or the isolation of the marriage hut?

Gaslight flickered as Trevor walked down the hall toward his room, creeping along like a thief in the night. It was the eve of his wedding and he had no idea what he should be feeling, but he was certain it should not be doubt. He had been plagued with reservations ever since the moment he had proposed.

As he neared Joya's door, he slowed, lingering there, staring at the light escaping beneath it. What was she thinking tonight? Was she as nervous as he?

He smiled in the semidarkness. No doubt Joya feared English dancing more than she did the marriage bed, since she was familiar with Matarengi customs. The islanders regarded lovemaking as a natural act, not something to be whispered about behind closed doors.

Perhaps he would not be facing a terrified bride on his wedding night, but Joya was still a virgin—and he was inexperienced when it came to deflowering virgins.

He stared at the yellow glow of light smeared beneath her door, then he sighed and moved on. When he reached his own suite, he locked the door.

Earlier, when he had told Sims he did not wish to be disturbed, the old butler had again congratulated him on his pending nuptials. Between them, Sims and Mrs. Billingsley had issued enough good wishes to last him and Joya a lifetime. At least Janelle and his two most loyal retainers welcomed the match. His grandmother was another matter.

Since the scene at the mill Adelaide had taken to her bed, claiming shock kept her there. He suspected she was not as ill as she let on, for whenever he visited, she sat up, barked orders, and inquired about the business. After that she would enumerate all the reasons why he should not marry Joya.

He had no idea why his grandmother was reacting so vehemently to the union. He hoped that in time she would get used to the idea, just as he hoped that with time he would, too.

He shrugged off his coat and hung it on the back of a chair. Inside the front pocket was the folded license he had obtained yesterday. It allowed him to forgo the reading of the banns, which would have delayed the wedding for a month. Looking at the document now was a reminder that money did have its uses.

He reached up and rubbed the back of his neck, physically tired but too disturbed to sleep. The small window in his dressing room was open, admitting the cool night air along with the pungent smell of London, a place where too many men and animals resided together.

He opened the drawer where he kept his mother's comb, took it out, closed his fingers around the cold silver, and let it warm in his hand. He wondered whether Joya should wear it on their wedding day until he remembered Janelle's excitement over a special flower arrangement she was planning for Joya's hair. He put the comb back in the drawer.

His grandmother was right in one respect. Things had moved too quickly, yet he was still satisfied that he had done the right thing. Joya was completely innocent, a victim of Roth's wickedness. Who could have suspected the mild-mannered accountant had such a dark side?

Earlier that day, Trevor had gone around to the man's

address and found the rooms he had formerly rented empty. Hopefully, Roth had taken his threat seriously and had left London. Trevor did not want to go to the authorities, but he would not hesitate to do so if the man showed his face around any of the Mandevilles again.

Trevor had only himself to blame for his loss of control after the attack. He should have comforted Joya, not kissed her, but he was so relieved to have her safe that when she kissed him, he had stopped thinking. She had come so close to disaster, was so young and vulnerable, so beautiful and trusting that he gave into his relief.

She had been looking at him as if he were a knight in shining armor, but he was no knight. Nor did he have any idea how to be a husband, not any more than he could fly. He did not even have any secondhand experience to draw upon, no living archetype to mimic. He had been raised by a widow and a widower, and both individuals had avoided displays of affection.

Trevor sighed and hoped that doing the right thing would be enough. This marriage was for Joya's sake, so he would follow through no matter how much it might upset his own plans. There was nothing for him to do but the honorable thing, the right thing, and marry her.

Whether she would be any easier to protect after she became his wife was another matter.

Just down the hall, Joya sat alone in her room, suffering from restlessness and more than a touch of homesickness. If she were on Matarenga, she would know what to expect on the day of her wedding. She would be housed with her closest female friends and relations.

They would awaken early, take her from her house, paint her body with crimson and white paste from head to toe, outline her eyes with kohl, and tightly braid her

hair with clay beads and feathers. She would don a colorful *pudong*, a wrap woven of the finest, softest fibers,
one that had not been used before and would never be
worn by her again. In it she would later wrap their first-
born child.

The drums would start at dawn, calling the entire village to the beach, where a goat would be bled and a
bonfire would burn until far into the night. The sound
of goat-hoof rattles would fill the air, and the pounding
of the drums would intensify as she and her intended
mixed drops of their own blood into the *kujmbaa* potion,
which ensured long life and fertility.

Otakgi would bless them in the name of Kibatante and
after a long night of feasting, her husband would lead
her to the marriage hut, which he would have built by
himself in a secret location. For an entire moon cycle,
they would dwell alone and undisturbed.

She sighed and pulled her satin wrapper close, wondering where Trevor was now and what he might be
thinking. She slipped off the bed, wandered to her trunk,
and took out her mother's comb. Fingering the beautiful
filigree, she closed her eyes and envisioned Clara's face.

She would give anything to have her mother here with
her tonight, to advise and comfort her, to answer her
questions about English wedding customs. She would
forever miss the woman she had called mother.

Because Janelle planned for her to wear a spray of
orchids in her hair tomorrow, Joya put the comb away.
Just as she straightened, intending to try to sleep, there
was a soft knock at the door.

She opened it to find her sister standing in the hall.

Joya stepped aside. "Come in. I cannot sleep."

"I can't either." Janelle, too, was dressed for bed and
wearing a silk robe. She climbed up on Joya's bed and

patted the spot beside her. Joya's mood lightened immediately. Whenever she was with her twin, she felt at peace.

"I was sad, wishing my mother were here," Joya said. "And now you have come to remind me I'm not alone."

"I never knew a mother's affection," Janelle said wistfully. "You speak so highly of her. Clara must have loved you very much."

Joya nodded without hesitation. "She did. I hope I can be half as wise and loving when I am a mother. Which reminds me, will there be a fertility ceremony during the wedding ceremony? Of course, I'll perform the traditional one when Trevor and I are alone afterward, but is there anything of the kind at the chapel?"

"A *what*?"

"Fertility ceremony. The ceremonial bloodletting, the sprinkling of special magical powders. You know."

Her sister became very quiet and covered her lips with her hand. Her eyes grew very round behind her spectacles. Finally she dropped her hand to her lap.

"There will be nothing of the sort during the ceremony." She bit her lips and cleared her throat. "You say you will perform one in private, afterward?"

"Oh, yes. As a woman, it is my duty to dance and chant and to inspire my husband's lust. There is a traditional costume—not much of one by English standards. All the girls learn the chant and the dance of seduction at a very early age. My friends and I learned, too. Of course, I never told my mother."

"I'm certain Trevor will enjoy a little private ceremony like that on your wedding night. You should surprise him with it, though. Don't mention it beforehand. Is it really a very *small* costume?"

"Naturally. Your eyes are very round and merry behind your spectacles right now."

"I am so happy for you, is all. And for Trevor. Now is there anything else you are worried about?"

"As a matter of fact, there is one more thing. Do you think Trevor will take more than one wife?"

Chapter 21

"Don't you think it's time you joined your new bride?"

Trevor found Janelle watching him from the doorway of the library. He emptied the brandy snifter in his hand, set the crystal on a tray Sims had left on the corner of his desk, and stretched as she walked into the room before he began.

"She wanted some time alone and said that she would send Mrs. Billingsley for me when she was ready. Why can't I shake the feeling I should be worried about what's going on upstairs?"

She waved away his concern a bit too quickly before she said, "I'm sure Joya just wants everything to be perfect. Why are you frowning? It's your wedding day. You should be happy."

"Happy? It wasn't ever my intention to marry Joya or anyone else at this point in my life, and now I suddenly find myself a bridegroom. I'm not sure how to feel."

"There are some things you can't catalogue or categorize, Trevor, especially when fate intervenes. Joya loves you and even if you're uncertain about your own feelings, I know that soon you'll realize you love her, too." She looked down at her hands. "She is coming into this marriage in love with you. It would wound her deeply if she ever finds out that you married her because you felt you had no other choice. I pray you never hurt her."

"I can only give you my word."

"You gave me your word before and look what happened. I know you find her hard to resist. I just pray that your desire will be enough to hold your marriage together."

He sighed and came around the desk. Life had grown far too complicated of late. He knew how much Janelle had done for him over the past few days, making all of the wedding arrangements, dealing with his grandmother and Joya.

"Everything was perfect today, thanks to you. Joya looked radiant. The orchids in her hair were a lovely touch and they actually stayed in almost all day. And I noticed that she didn't even rattle when she walked."

Janelle laughed. "I can't believe I succeeded in getting her to leave her dog's-tooth anklet at home."

"You must have been very convincing."

"I reminded her she would have other occasions to wear it. When she balked, I told her that some English think it's actually bad luck to wear dog's teeth to a wedding."

He found himself laughing. "You were right about having a small celebration. It was a welcome diversion to have a few close friends gathered for dinner this evening."

"I hope you did not mind my asking Cecily and Lord

Langley to join us. They certainly helped keep the conversation going."

"I just wish Grandmother had been in a better mood."

"Grandmama will come around eventually. I think she is upset because your marriage to Joya was not her idea. She must still be very embarrassed about the scene she witnessed at the mill."

He rubbed his hand over his jaw. "It was irresponsible of me, but we were only kissing, Janelle."

"Your spontaneous reaction to having saved my sister?"

"Something like that. I hope you are right about Grandmother coming around." He ran his hand through his hair. When was his new bride going to send Mrs. Billingsley after him?

Uncomfortable with indecision, he tried conversation. "I heard Lord Langley tell you that he has two more friends interested in acquiring your paintings."

Janelle nodded. Her eyes shone with pride. "To think that my work is actually becoming sought after is very exciting. Don't ever tell the viscount, but I would happily *give* my paintings away. The fact that his friends actually pay for them is a pleasant reward for the joy of doing something I love so."

"And you've had no nightmares?"

"None since we found Joya. I'm ecstatic over this marriage between you. It will keep her with us forever."

Just then, there was a soft knock at the door. Trevor called, "Come in."

Mrs. Billingsley stepped into the library. Her cheeks were bright as two beets, her brown eyes huge.

"She's ready, sir," she announced. Sims was hovering in the hall behind her.

Trevor felt his face heat up. Now that he had taken

the vows that gave him the right to touch her, to hold her, to have Joya completely, he found himself nervous as an untried youth. His collar felt too tight, his mouth too dry. Anyone would think he was going to the gallows instead of his wedding bed.

"Thank you, Mrs. Billingsley." Both the housekeeper and Sims were beaming at him as if he had already accomplished a tremendous feat. He dismissed them for the night and closed the door.

Since the scene at the mill, he had wrestled with the notion that he would be married, with his needs and his wants, with the fact that Joya was going to be his wife. One of the hardest things he had ever done was to write to Dustin Penn and relate the circumstances behind his proposal and marriage to Joya and apologize for his behavior. He was not looking forward to Penn's response.

He had gone over and over his own plans and debated his future. Although his voyage would naturally have to be postponed, he was still determined to return to Venezuela and search for the Queen's orchid. His grandmother was of the opinion that he should not give up on the hunt, but he knew there was no way he would leave England if Joya was with child, no way he could leave her alone the way her true father had left Stephanie Oates.

No matter what transpired in their bed tonight or on any other night before the voyage, he was determined to take every precaution against getting her pregnant.

"Trevor?" Janelle was staring at him expectantly.

"Are you going up yet?" He forced himself to sound calm.

She shook her head, took off her spectacles, and carefully folded the stems. "No, I think I'll sit here alone for a while. I've always loved this room. It smells of brandy and tobacco and old leather."

He gave her a kiss on the cheek. "Good-night, then. And thank you for everything."

"Good night." The more he studied her, the more he thought she appeared to be fighting for control. She was, he supposed, like most women. Weddings made them emotional.

As he closed the door and stepped into the hallway, he thought he heard her add, ". . . and good luck."

After Trevor left the room, Janelle poured herself a splash of brandy and then curled up in one of the deep armchairs near the hearth. There was no need for a fire tonight, for Joya's wedding day had been warm and sunny, the most beautiful of English summer days. Except for the fact that Grandmama had made only a brief appearance for dinner, the festivities had been quite successful.

The only thing that hampered the day for her was that she could not stop musing over Garr Remington. Even now she found herself thinking of him in ways that made her cheeks burn and her heart flutter.

As Trevor and Joya spoke their vows, she imagined standing before a minister with Garr, her hand in his, staring up into his dark, laughing eyes and hearing him pledge his troth in rich, deep tones.

Impossible, ridiculous thoughts. Even with his notorious reputation, he had never pressed her for more than companionship and friendly conversation, which led her to believe that he was not interested in her as a conquest. Perhaps because of that realization, lately she had found herself wondering what she would do if he ever did try to kiss her.

She had purposely not invited him to the wedding supper, but all evening long she had missed his company, his gregarious nature, his witty banter.

Dear heavens, was she falling in love with him? With a rake who would never be true? A penniless fortune hunter?

Taking a sip of the heady, richly scented liquor, she let it warm her to her toes and closed her eyes. How could she, who had always prided herself on her independent nature and her level-headed logic, be falling in love with a man like Garr Remington?

Perhaps the direction of her thoughts was unconsciously driven by what was happening to Joya tonight. Even though she was not trying to dwell on what was going on upstairs, being emotionally connected to her sister, she found it hard to concentrate on anything but the sensual pleasures that Garr Remington could surely give her.

After a few more sips of brandy, she found herself enticed by seductive, erotic images, and tried to imagine what it would feel like to have Garr's hands on her body, his kisses on her lips, her throat, her breasts. Her mind had strayed into dangerous and forbidden territory. What would it be like to have him touch her in that most intimate of places?

"Get hold of yourself, Janelle," she said aloud. Finishing off the last of the brandy, she stood. The clock on the wall chimed ten, still a ridiculously early time to retire when sleep would no doubt elude her tonight.

Working in her studio would be a much better way to spend the next few hours, she decided. At least working, her mind would be well occupied with something other than Garr Remington. She hoped.

As she turned out the light and closed the door behind

her, she could not help but chuckle. Surely by now, Joya's rendition of the fertility dance of the Matarengi had begun.

Trevor stepped into his dimly lit suite and closed the door, but when he went to turn the key in the lock, he found it missing. He took a step, stopped, and looked around his room in shock. His usually uncluttered, well-ordered sanctuary had been transformed. Tall potted palms filled every available space. A golden, gossamer fabric shimmered from the ceiling above his bed to drape the huge four-poster like mosquito netting. Various blooming orchids from the conservatory had been brought up and interspersed with lit candles on every tabletop and even the mantelpiece.

If he had not known better, he would have thought he had stepped through a magical portal into a jungle paradise.

Since there was no sign of his bride, he uttered her name softly. He walked over to the bed and slowly pulled back the golden netting.

His heart thundered, stirred by the notion that tonight he would no longer have to worry about convention or containing his desire for Joya. Janelle was right. Fate had wanted them together and now, for better or for worse, she was his.

He looked down at the empty bed and frowned.

"Joya?" He straightened and glanced around the room.

"Undress, please, Trevor. I cannot begin until you do." The sound of her voice came from his dressing room. He started to walk toward the door that connected the small anteroom to the larger chamber.

"You cannot come in here!"

"Why not?"

"Because you cannot see me yet. It will ruin everything."

"When and how did you get all these plants and candles up here?" He had left the room not an hour before dinner. Everything had appeared to be quite normal then.

"I drew a sketch of what I wanted the room to look like and gave it to Sims and Mrs. Billingsley. How do you like it, Trevor? Do you feel as if you are back on Matarenga?"

He stared at the cold fireplace hearth crowded with orchids and pots of pothos vine. The chandeliers were draped with blossoms and trailing greenery.

"Well, to be perfectly honest with you—"

"I am *so* happy with what they have done. I feel *so* at home."

He sighed. If she felt comfortable, perhaps the rest of the night would go smoothly.

"I think it looks like . . . Matarenga." He scratched his head. "When are you coming out of there?"

"After you take off all of your clothes and lie down on the bed."

Despite his misgivings, he had already worked his necktie loose. Any preconceived notions of what his wedding night might be like went out the window.

He sat down and took off his shoes and socks.

His fingers fumbled with his collar. He removed it and went to work on the studs down the front of his shirt. Finally he managed to free his arms and slipped his shirt off. Instead of folding it as usual, he tossed it across the back of a nearby chair.

A soft rhythmic rattle issued from the dressing room. Dog's teeth.

He desperately fought with the buttons at his waistband.

"Are you ready?" The teeth rattled again.

"Not yet."

His hands faltered. He was already fully aroused. Who could blame him? He had not had a woman for weeks, and now the object of his desire was demanding he strip off his clothes and climb into bed.

Damn. She was actually making *him* nervous. He was beginning to feel as if he were the virgin here. He stepped out of his trousers, then shucked off his silk stockinette drawers in one fell swoop. They missed the chair and hit the floor. He hurried over to the bed. Lying atop the counterpane, he decided his erection might frighten Joya, so he slipped beneath the bedclothes and covered himself to his waist.

"I'm naked." He had to clear his throat. "And I'm in bed."

The light in the dressing room was extinguished. He heard footsteps accompanied by the rattling of something much louder than a dog's-tooth anklet and could not resist lifting aside the edge of the filmy netting.

His breath caught in his throat when Joya appeared wrapped in a crimson and saffron *pudong*, a much smaller *pudong* than he had seen on any of the women on Matarenga. Slung below her navel and knotted on the side above one hip, it barely reached the tops of her thighs. Her lovely, full breasts were completely exposed.

Her body, in the few places where it had not seen the sun, was creamy white. She had let down her hair so that it fell in long, flowing golden waves past her shoulders. He couldn't recall ever being with a woman whom he had not had to coax out of her clothing.

Joya did not walk, but appeared to glide into the room, pausing after each step to thrust out her hip and shake it to the beat of the clacking rattles she held over her head.

Clack, step, shake. Clack, step, shake.

Slowly, seductively, she inched her way over to the bed, weaving through the sea of palms, illusive, enticing, pausing now and again to lean forward and shake her shoulders. Unabashedly wanton, her gaze locked with his. She never looked away.

His mouth went dry. His palms ached. His erection throbbed. He wanted her so bad his teeth hurt.

She was driving him over the edge and she was nowhere near him. He was afraid that if she kept this up he would leap off the bed, plunge into her, and spill his seed. His well-laid plans for the future would fly out the window right along with his preconceived notions of their wedding night.

Clack, step, shake. Clack, step, shake.

"Stop!" He sat up, calling out with more force than he had intended. The entire household had probably heard him.

The rattling slowly faded away. She dropped her hands to her sides. "What's wrong, Trevor?"

"Nothing, I just . . . wanted you to stop, is all."

"Why have you covered yourself like that?"

"I didn't want to frighten you."

"Are you deformed?" Dancing forgotten, she walked the rest of the way to the bed. The clacking was softer now that the rattles hung neglected.

"No, I'm not deformed!"

"Then why are you hiding your body?"

"I happen to have a modicum of modesty."

"Is it painful?"

He started over, gently this time. "What is that . . . that dance that you were doing?"

"The Matarengi fertility dance. Did you like it?"

He nearly choked. "Fertility dance?"

"Janelle assured me that it would be best to surprise you."

"*Surprised* doesn't come close to describing the way I feel right now. I'll remember to thank her."

She laid the rattles on the side table and sat down on the edge of the bed, casually, without a trace of embarrassment, as if it were perfectly normal for her to sit beside him for an intimate little chat wearing no more than a scrap of crimson and saffron across her pelvis, and with her breasts fully exposed. She was as relaxed as if they did this every evening of their lives.

For the life of him, he could not stop staring at her bare breasts. They were firm and high with blush-pink nipples, and the sight of them was slowly rendering him speechless.

She ran her finger over the satin counterpane that covered his thigh and then looked into his eyes.

"Should I finish?"

"Finish?"

"The dance."

"No."

"Do you think I have done enough to ensure fertility?"

I hope not. He picked up one of the rattles with a slim piece of tree branch for a handle. The sound came from the curved hoof pairings of some beast all strung together. There were green parrot feathers woven into the colored beads that banded the handle.

"Goat hooves," she volunteered.

He set the rattle back down.

"Joya, there is something I have to say."

"Don't worry, Trevor. I have heard it said that many men worry about the size of their . . . well, their manly staff, but since I am still a virgin, I probably will not know the difference, if that is what you are trying to tell me."

He drew himself up against the headboard.

"There is nothing wrong with my . . . manly staff, Joya."

"Oh, good." She sighed, leaned over, and laid her cheek against his heart.

Her warm breath tickled his nipple. When she began to run her fingernails up and down his chest, he gently took her by the shoulders and nudged her into a sitting position again.

"If you keep doing that, I will never get this said."

"Then tell me what it is you have to say, Trevor, for seeing you there all warm and naked and dark and handsome is making me melt inside. I want to climb beneath the sheets with you."

He tried to pull his thoughts together so that he could deliver the well-rehearsed speech he had outlined over the past few days. She needed to know that he was still planning to leave for Venezuela, and because of that, he intended to take every precaution against her becoming pregnant.

But then she shifted and propped her knee higher upon the bed, treating him to the sight of her entire thigh. The *pudong* gaped open. His gaze shot to the mirror on the opposite wall. In its reflection, he could see up her sarong. Just as he had suspected, she was not wearing a stitch beneath it.

"Trevor?" She had reached for his hand and was holding it tight.

"Yes, Joya?"

"This is the happiest day of my life."

Her eyes were shimmering with unshed tears, her

dimples enticing, her smile bright as the sun over the lagoon around Matarenga. The idea of taking time to outline their future, to try to stress to her the importance of the work schedule he expected to keep, and to add that he fully intended to leave her very soon all seemed absurd now that this moment was at hand.

All he wanted right now was to keep the radiant glow on her face and the happiness in her eyes and, lord help him, he felt as if he would move heaven and earth in order to do so. Tomorrow would be soon enough to explain to her how things were going to have to be.

"Come here," he whispered, pulling her close so that he could kiss her.

She willingly came to him, lifting her face until his lips touched hers. Then she opened to him like an orchid bud as it is coaxed into bloom by the sunlight, slowly revealing more and more until its alluring beauty is fully realized.

She scooted closer, climbed up him as it were, until they lay bare breasts to bare chest and then she wrapped her arms around his neck.

He kissed her slowly, deeply, exploring with his tongue, teasing her lips, teaching her to kiss him back, to taste and nip and savor.

When he touched the satin-soft, translucent skin over her breasts, he was reminded that no matter how strong she seemed, she was still very feminine, very fragile. He let his hand trail over her firm midriff to her navel and circled it with his fingertip. She shivered. He found the knot that held the scrap of fabric, her *pudong*, in place.

As if by magic, it came loose immediately and became no more than a bloodred and saffron stain against the ivory satin counterpane. Joya sighed. He could tell she was smiling against his lips.

"I have waited so long to be deflowered. To be initiated into the rites of womanhood by my husband. There was a time I thought I would never marry."

He pulled her over him, tugging, sliding, edging her around until he had slipped the bedclothes out from beneath her. He tucked her beside him and did not bother with the covers again.

"I am so very, very lucky that I have a husband now, and that it is you. I dreamed of you once, you know, when I was a girl."

"You mean you dreamed of marrying someone *like* me."

She shook her head. "Oh, no. I saw *you* in my dream. I know it was you."

It was impossible, but he was not about to argue anything with her just now, for she had begun to kiss him, to take the initiative and practice what the last few moments had taught her.

He was delighted to note that she had learned her lessons so well. His hand fell to her breast, and his lips soon followed. When he took her nipple between his teeth and gently teased it into a tight bud, she moaned and writhed against him, thrusting her hips much the way she had done during the seductive dance.

He had never, ever wanted a woman so badly. Hell, he thought, he had never, ever wanted *anything* as badly as he wanted his warm and oh-so-willing wife. Her breasts filled his palms, tempted him to lave and lick them. When he did, he felt her fingers tangle in his hair at the nape of his neck. She whispered his name over and over again, pressing him to her breast, urging him to take more.

He slipped his hand between them, moved down to touch her between her legs, was shocked when he felt her slick and wet, indeed, ready to be deflowered. Slipping his fingers inside her, he stroked and teased and stoked the fire within until she clung to him and cried out breathlessly.

"Oh, Trevor, do it now, please. I don't think I can wait any longer!"

Fantasies flitted through his mind, thoughts and images of her touching him intimately, her lips on him, tasting, bringing him to the edge of release—but she was still an innocent, no matter how much she had heard or what she thought she knew of lovemaking. After Venezuela there would be time, plenty of time, to get to know one another in so many, many ways.

His breath came in ragged bursts as he eased himself up and over her, hung suspended between her legs before he nudged them wider with his knee.

"Open for me, Joya."

Like the fragile, erotic petals of an orchid flower dripping with dew, she blossomed. He pressed against her honeyed warmth, found entry, eased into her. He heard her breath catch, felt her shudder beneath him.

"Are you all right?"

"It hurt a bit, just then."

He waited, suspended in her and over her for what seemed like a lifetime and a heartbeat and then she seemed to sigh and relax. He moved again, slowly, bit by agonizing bit. She moaned low in her throat and clutched him tightly against her and he drove into her, granting her utmost wish. She gasped and held perfectly still.

"Trevor?"

"What?"

"Am I deflowered?"

"Yes." He barely managed to get the word out.

"Is that all? Is it over?"

"No . . . there's a bit more to come."

"Oh, good. Show me."

"I will," he whispered. "I will."

From what she had seen of his staff before he slipped inside her, Joya thought it a miracle that she and her husband actually fit one another. A miracle indeed, she decided again, when he pronounced her deflowered and then assured her there were more delicious delights to come.

He was moving inside her now, sensuously rocking and stroking her with his member. She wanted to cry out, but was afraid that she would awaken the entire household. No wonder the Matarengi insisted upon a marriage hut hidden in the jungle. No wonder. So many things were fast becoming clear.

She could not lie still with Trevor working such exquisite magic. She began to rock with him, locked safe in his arms. He was moving faster, and as she felt the urge building inside her, she followed him, certain he would never lead her anywhere she did not want to go.

His brandy-scented breath was warm against her neck, comforting and soothing. She moaned, unable to hold back the sound that filled her throat.

He took her even higher, toward a pinnacle that she never knew existed. She answered every thrust, flew with him until they reached the summit together. Then, unable to hold back, she took the lead, went before him, cried out again. Her climax rippled outward.

When Trevor abruptly began to withdraw, she gave a cry of protest, wrapped her legs around his waist, trapped him between her thighs. He called her name, in ecstasy or protest she could not tell, as he drove into her.

Still shuddering with her own release, she felt his seed fill her and smiled, satisfied that she had brought him to fulfillment.

Her happiness knew no bounds. Now she was a woman, utterly and completely. Seductress, sorcerer, wife. She was part of the grand scheme of all natural things. She was part of the earth and the sky and the waters and the great mysterious plan that Kibatante had designed for all of the earth's creatures.

Trevor awoke at his usual time, shortly after dawn. The first thing he saw when he opened his eyes was sheer gold netting flowing from a hook above him, then the palms and orchids, burned-out candle stubs and melted wax everywhere. With his mind still fogged from sleep, he thought he was in the jungle until he felt the warm naked body pressed against his side. He looked at Joya snuggled against him.

Exhausted, he put his hand over his eyes and rubbed them. Not only was his new bride inquisitive, but she had been very inventive last night. Afterward, when she finally fell asleep in his arms, he had lain awake thinking about the obvious consequences of what they had done together.

Joya lay sleeping on her stomach, naked, vulnerable, beautiful. He lifted a strand of her hair, tempted to kiss the nape of her neck, but was afraid that if he woke her, she would want to make love yet again.

What good were his intentions to keep her from becoming pregnant now, when he had already lost control?

His trip would definitely have to be postponed,

at least until her monthly came—or did not come. His seed might have already taken hold.

Although he didn't find the idea as startling or as objectionable as he had thought he would, until he knew for certain whether Joya was actually with child or not, he wanted to keep the rest of his life on course.

Carefully, he sat up so as not to disturb her, swung his legs over the side of the bed, and moved stealthily to his dressing room. If he hurried, he would arrive at the warehouse close to his usual time.

Within minutes he was dressed and ready. With his shoes in hand, he tiptoed across the room and turned the doorknob, but the door would not open. He tried again and then remembered he had not seen the key last night. Someone had locked them in from the outside. If this was some kind of prank, he was not laughing.

The bedclothes rustled behind him. He turned around and found Joya sitting up, dreamy-eyed and smiling. She was completely at ease even though she was bare to the waist and lovely in the soft morning light.

"Good morning, Trevor. What are you doing with your clothes on?"

"Going to work. I tried not to disturb you."

"Work?" Her smile faded, taking her dimples with it.

"The door is locked from the outside. Do you happen to know anything about this?"

She crossed her arms below her breasts and was frowning fiercely.

"Joya?"

"Perhaps Sims locked us in."

"And why would Sims do that?"

"Because I asked him to."

Trevor walked over to the bed. He tried but could not resist touching her. He traced his hand along her cheek, her collarbone, the swell of her breast. Then he pulled the bedclothes up, covering the tempting sight, and tucked them beneath her arms.

"I know you have what you consider a perfectly reasonable explanation as to *why* you would ask Sims to lock us in."

"Of course I do. On Matarenga it is the custom for a newly wed husband and wife to go to a secret location in the jungle and live together for a month in a marriage hut. Since we are not even moving out of Mandeville House, I thought that we should at least stay together undisturbed."

"For how long?"

"For a month, of course." She looked up at him through lowered lashes. "To insure the success of our marriage."

Their marriage, Trevor decided, was already far more successful than he had expected it to be at this point.

"I have to go to work to ensure the success of our business ventures, so that none of us starves. Speaking of starving, I'm hungry for breakfast. Did you and Sims have some sort of plan worked out that would keep us fed while we were locked in?"

"Breakfast will arrive at eight o'clock. Although it will cause me great worry, I'll tell him to let you out, but only because you think it is so necessary to go to work today."

"It won't be eight o'clock for another hour and a half."

She pulled back the covers invitingly. "Good. I think I know what we can do to fill the time."

Chapter 22

Adelaide stepped outside her room for the first time in days and stood in the long hall listening for signs of life. The house was quiet as a tomb. As cold, too. The late afternoon weather was just as dismal, cool, gray, and dreary. She would have been warmer in bed, but had tired of sitting in her room feeling ignored and abandoned, and so she decided it was past time she stopped feigning illness and took an active part in ridding her home of Trevor's wife.

Trevor's wife. The very idea that he had married Joya Penn made her mad enough to spit. Worse yet, the entire mess was the fault of her own stupid scheme gone awry.

She started down the hall, leaning heavily on one of her husband's old canes, not because she needed it, but because she thought it would garner her more sympathy. There was nothing wrong with her that fresh surroundings and a bit of activity would not cure. The fact that she grew tired earlier each evening and that her left hand was numb now and again did not bother her as much as knowing she had failed.

She would give Trevor the world if she could. Hadn't she always done right by him? Hadn't she raised him to take the helm of Mandeville Imports?

She had always wanted what was best for her grandson, and what was best for Trevor was not some upstart little baggage from Africa. He might think he wanted Joya now, but he would soon forget her.

Even if she was a tad ill, she refused to die until Trevor was free to live his life the way she had always planned it.

Today the upstairs hall seemed longer and darker than she remembered. She told herself to have Sims's head for not lighting the lamps. One would think he had to pay for the gas.

She stacked her hands on top of the cane and paused to catch her breath, ignoring the heaviness in her chest.

Damn Trevor for letting the chit get to him. He was hot for the girl now—no doubt Clara Hayworth had passed on all the tricks she had used to seduce men.

She wondered whether Trevor thought himself in love with his new wife. She had seen the undisguised desire in his eyes last evening when he and Joya had come to her room to pay a short visit. Her grandson could not take his eyes off the girl. He had been caring and solicitous toward her: ushering her into the room with his hand possessively riding her waist, sharing the settee, vulgarly sitting shoulder to shoulder, thigh to thigh.

She could not help but notice the way their hands touched and their eyes met and held. It was enough to make her want to scream with frustration.

When they left her, she had to calm herself by remembering that the girl was young and impressionable, while she herself was possessed of the kind of fortitude it had taken to keep Mandeville Imports afloat all those years after her husband's death and again after James proved to have no head for business. She had managed to hold on until Trevor had assumed the responsibility.

Surely, after all she had accomplished in her lifetime, she could triumph over a simple, backward girl that Clara Hayworth, housemaid and whore, had raised.

She started walking again and slowly made her way along the hall and then the stairs. When she was halfway down, Sims appeared at the bottom of the wide staircase. She shooed the old butler away when he offered to help her, but he remained two steps just below her until she reached the foyer.

"I don't know why you are watching me like that," she snapped. "If I fall, I am likely to kill you on the way down."

"Would you like tea in the drawing room as usual, madam?"

"First I would like a word with my daughter-in-law. Have you seen her?"

He was quiet for a moment, obviously hesitant to tell her where Joya was. Good, she thought. The girl was up to something and Sims, the old coot, was protecting her.

"Well, man?"

"She is in the kitchen, madam."

"I thought I told her to stay away from the servants."

"I'll go and get her, madam, if you would like to wait in the drawing room."

"Don't try to dismiss me like some unwanted caller. I'll find her myself, thank you, Sims. I have not been in the kitchen for years."

"Then I'll just go ahead and announce you, madam."

"You will do nothing of the kind."

When she stepped into the kitchen, tiring after the long walk, she found Joya happily chatting with Mrs. Billingsley and the cook, a rotund Hungarian woman with a peasant's stocky build, a head full of black hair and the shadow of a moustache on her upper lip.

The two women were perched on tall stools near a workbench where Joya stood up to her elbows in bread dough. An apron smudged with bits of dough was tied over her dress. Flour smeared her face and dusted her hair. There was a dirt smudge across the bridge of her nose.

The girl was boisterously laughing and talking, punching at the mound of dough as the other women looked on. A fire glowed in the huge fireplace as pots of aromatic foods simmered on the stove. Adelaide didn't appreciate the warm and cozy scene in the least.

Mrs. Billingsley and the cook jumped to their feet as soon as she walked into the room. Joya looked up and smiled.

"I'm learning to make bread," she announced, completely unaware that she had overstepped the bounds of propriety by miles.

"We'll give you some privacy, ma'am." Mrs. Billingsley was apparently ready to grab the cook and slip out of the room.

"Stay." Adelaide felt a heady surge of power when both serving women visibly paled and remained rooted to the floor.

Joya's smile slowly faded. She pulled her hands out of the dough and tried to wipe them on her apron.

"You have absolutely no idea how improper your behavior is, do you, Joya?"

The girl's cheeks flamed. Adelaide glanced at the housekeeper and cook. Both women were obviously very uncomfortable. Adelaide was greatly pleased.

"Is there something wrong with making bread?" Joya asked.

"You have no idea how *not* to be an embarrassment to him."

"How is this embarrassing to Trevor? This is honest work. A wife should know how to cook for her husband."

"We have servants to do that. You should be learning how to direct them to do the menial tasks, not associating with them. You should be neatly dressed, with your hair combed, ready to receive callers."

She walked closer to Joya, looking her over from head to toe. "What if someone came to pay a visit and found you looking like a scullery maid? What others think of you reflects upon my grandson. I thought you cared about Trevor."

Joya spread her hands wide. "I love Trevor with all my heart. Where is the shame in baking? There is no one here to see me but Mrs. Billingsley and Cook. No one is coming to call."

"Which is another problem. You have no friends. You have no ties to London society or even to other wives of wealthy businessmen."

"I have not been here long enough to make many friends, except for Lady Cecily, who has been very kind."

"Lady Cecily is not worth discussing."

"This morning I finished repotting the orchids as a surprise for Trevor."

"Perhaps that is how your dress and your face became soiled, which doesn't please me in the least."

"I'll try to do better."

When she was certain the girl was upset, she decided to go for blood.

"I'm sorry, Joya, but you are not a fit wife for my grandson and definitely not the one *I* would have ever chosen for him. Nor are you the woman Trevor would have chosen for himself—if he had a choice at all. He may have felt obligated to marry you after that little scene at the mill, but that doesn't mean he has to put up with your backward notions forever. You can be certain I will tell him about this when he gets home tonight."

"I didn't think Trevor would mind my baking bread or I would have never asked Cook to teach me."

"That is just the trouble. You never think of the consequences of any of your actions. You weren't thinking that day in the country when you went into the mill alone with Roth. Nor were you thinking when you seduced Trevor after he came to your rescue. Or perhaps you were," Adelaide mused. "Perhaps you knew *exactly* what you were doing."

"I simply kissed Trevor, that is all."

Knowing when to play the winning hand, Adelaide glanced over at the housekeeper and cook and then looked at Joya again. She lowered her voice, feigning embarrassment.

"This is not something we need to discuss here. Clean yourself up and meet me in the drawing room." She turned to the housekeeper. "Mrs. Billingsley, have Sims bring us tea and scones."

Joya shook with anger and humiliation as she untied the apron that Cook had loaned her and set it aside. Adelaide was old and therefore to be respected. Her status as Trevor's grandmother gave her a position of authority in the household. But did it also give her the right to be cruel?

The woman had belittled her in front of Mrs. Billingsley and the cook and caused them both undue embarrassment. To what purpose?

"Don't worry, dear." Mrs. Billingsley handed her a wet towel. "She hasn't been feeling well lately, is all. I'm sure she did not mean half of what she said."

Joya wiped her face and hands. Even if Adelaide meant only half of what she had said, it had been more than enough to wound. What had she meant by Trevor's having been obligated to marry her? How was that possible?

She thought back to the incident, to the kiss she had given him after he rescued her. They had kissed before—at the warehouse and then in the conservatory—yet he had not proposed to her. What made him obligated at the mill? Why suddenly ask her to marry him if he did not love her? Was there a rule about marrying after a third kiss that she didn't know anything about?

He desired her enough to deflower her, and afterward they had shared wonderful, blissful nights of passion. At least they had been wonderful for her.

Her hands were shaking by the time she paused outside the drawing room to smooth down her hair. Plagued with insecurity, she would rather ride a goat than face Adelaide again.

The woman's tirade had breathed life into doubt already haunting her. For the past two weeks, Trevor had found one excuse after another not to make love with her.

At first she had thought it was because he was working too hard and was exhausted, but last night, hoping to inspire him, she danced the fertility dance again. She had been thrilled when she rekindled his desire and he took her to bed. But at the moment of his climax, he completely surprised and humiliated her by withdrawing from her and spilling his seed on her belly.

Later, she had lain in the dark beside him, crying silently, trying to fathom why he would rather waste his seed than make a child. This morning he had slipped away without saying good-bye.

Because she already feared she was somehow failing him, she had gone to Mrs. Billingsley and the cook to ask for help. Repotting the orchids and rearranging the conservatory had not been enough. She had wanted to surprise him with some very productive, domestic accomplishment.

Sims stopped her before she entered the drawing room. He was holding one of her new shawls when she got there.

"I had the upstairs maid bring this down in case you were cold. You've not ever grown used to our weather. Now that it's grown chilly, I thought you might need it," he explained.

His thoughtful act of kindness was all it took to release the raw ache building inside her. She bit her lips together and blinked furiously, fighting back tears as she reached for the shawl.

"Thank you, Sims," she whispered. "You are too kind."

"There is tea waiting inside, and Cook sent along a plate of your favorite cookies."

She opened her eyes wide as they would go and blinked faster. "Thank her for me," she said.

She knew Cook and Mrs. Billingsley must have told him about the humiliating scene they had just witnessed when he added, "Don't worry, miss. Mr. Mandeville will be home soon and all will be well."

When Sims left her standing outside the door alone,

Joya whispered the words of an old Matarangi battle cry. There was no hope for her if she showed any sign of weakness. She squared her shoulders, prepared to face Adelaide and ask some questions of her own. Her mind was crammed with doubt and questions. She held her head high, but she would still rather ride a goat.

She had just stepped inside the drawing room and sat down on a chair opposite Adelaide's to pour herself a cup of tea when the door opened and Trevor strode into the room.

One look at her husband set her heart plummeting. She was forced to set the teacup down before the amber liquid sloshed over the rim. His expression was preoccupied, just as it had appeared so often of late. He greeted her and then his grandmother.

"Trevor. How nice to have you home early for a change. You are just in time for tea." Adelaide looked as if she were about to say something more when the door opened again and this time, to Joya's relief, Janelle came breezing in.

Janelle crossed the room, greeting them all before she settled herself in a wing chair near the fire.

She had spent a most pleasant afternoon at Cecily's with five other women discussing the suffrage movement and the women's rights conventions that had been taking place for the last three years in America.

Garr Remington had arrived just as the meeting ended and the ladies were taking their leave. He had charmed and teased and persuaded her, against her better judgment, to let him see her home. Despite her misgivings and a twinge of disappointment, he had behaved like a perfect gentleman all the way.

"I have a surprise," Trevor said, claiming everyone's attention.

Something had not been right with her brother of late. She could see it in his eyes, but had not had any opportunity to speak to him alone. That, she supposed, was part of the problem. Trevor was never at home anymore. Just now, he was looking at Joya wistfully, as if she were a confection he was not allowed to indulge in— and Joya, well, Joya was not looking at Trevor at all. Her sister was clutching her shawl and studying the teacup on the table before her as if she had never seen one before.

Trevor pulled two stiff vellum envelopes from his jacket. One was open. The other he handed to Adelaide.

"In two days, the members of the Orchid Society along with their wives are invited to attend a reception given by Prince Albert." He looked at Adelaide. "Grandmother, you have been invited to represent Father because of his role in conferring with Joseph Paxton on very early conservatory designs."

"How wonderful." Janelle knew that court receptions involved complicated protocol and so really did not envy them a bit.

The sound of Joya's cup rattling against the saucer drew all eyes. "I cannot go," she announced firmly.

"Are you all right?" Janelle took her sister's cup before she dropped it.

"I won't do it." Joya shook her head vehemently. "I cannot."

"She's right," Adelaide quickly agreed. "It will be too much for her."

"Nonsense," Janelle said.

"Joya, what's wrong?" Trevor was all concern. He

tried to take her hand but Joya refused, knotting her fingers in her lap instead.

Janelle watched her grandmother and Joya exchange a look that she neither understood nor cared for. Trevor was watching his wife closely, obviously in the dark as well. Something was going on and she did not like it in the least.

"Are you sure you're all right, Joya?" Janelle asked. "The prince's invitation is a great honor. One you shouldn't turn down."

"I *won't* go. Not even for the queen," Joya said adamantly. Then she finally looked at Trevor. "Please, don't make me do this."

Joya had gone incredibly pale. When she sat back down on the settee, she turned directly to Janelle.

"Will you please go in my place? If you pretend to be me, no one will know that Trevor's wife has refused the prince's invitation."

"That is an excellent idea." Adelaide picked up a scone, broke off a piece, and popped it in her mouth. "As long as the two of you are not side by side, and without your glasses, Janelle, no one will know the difference."

"*I* will know the difference," Trevor said firmly. He was scowling at Joya. "I want you there with me," he told her.

"I can't go," she whispered. "I won't."

"Are you really that uncomfortable with the idea?"

Joya reached for his hand, held it between both of hers, and begged, "Please take Janelle in my stead. It will only be for a few hours."

Adelaide brushed crumbs off her black skirt and got to her feet. "Janelle, come with me and we'll talk about what you should wear."

Janelle started to protest, longing to talk to Joya first and determine what was upsetting her so, but one look at her sister's face and she decided it was better to leave her alone with Trevor.

Sims was summoned to clear away the tea tray. Adelaide and Janelle left the room talking about the advantages of satin over silk. Joya was finally alone with Trevor.

Alone and at a loss as to how to begin.

Taking tea in the Mandeville drawing room always reminded her of the day she first arrived. She still felt as out of place as a goose egg in a hen's nest. Looking around the room now, she was reminded of how very far she was from her old life and her old home.

If it were not for Trevor and her love for him, for the fact that she was now his wife, she would go to her sister and tell her that she loved her dearly but that she was going home, back to the island where she belonged.

"What's wrong, Joya?"

When she looked into his eyes she almost said that nothing was wrong. But avoiding confrontation would not ease her doubts and fears, nor would it answer her questions.

"Were you obligated to marry me, Trevor?"

"What are you talking about?"

That he did not deny it outright gave her the answer, but she wanted to hear it from him.

"*Were* you?"

"Where did you get that notion?"

"*Were you obligated?*"

"I did what honor dictated."

"What does that mean?"

He reached for her hand. She pulled it back.

"Joya, after Roth attacked you and I was comforting you—"

"By kissing me."

"My grandmother and the others walked into the mill and saw us. There was nothing else for me to do but marry you."

"But why? When Janelle saw us in the conservatory you felt no such obligation."

"Janelle would never tell anyone what she had seen. But that was not the case with Mrs. Sutton and her daughter or even the vicar and his wife. Gossip would have spread, word would have gotten out, and your reputation would have been tarnished." He must have known she did not completely understand, for he added, "Everyone there would have told others and had I not married you, your good name would be ruined."

"You married me to keep my name clean?"

"Yes."

"So that none of them will tell anyone what they saw at the mill?"

"I am sure Mrs. Sutton could not wait to spread the word, but I made everything right by marrying you."

"You married me thinking that if Mrs. Sutton or the vicar's wife tells anyone what they saw, that people would then say, 'Of course he kissed her, she was to be his wife.' Is that it?" The English were nearly incomprehensible people.

"Something like that. Why are you crying?"

When he reached over to wipe a tear off her cheek, she was too numb to avoid his touch. He cupped her chin and swiped the tear with his thumb. The simple gesture made her feel even more vulnerable. She felt as if they were standing at a crossroads, staring down two unmarked trails that neither of them had ever explored. One-way roads with no return.

"So you thought that you had no choice." The very idea that he had been trapped broke her heart.

"I did, too, have a choice."

"No. You are a man of honor. You would never let me walk around with a soiled name. You are the kind of man who would want to make things right, and so you married me."

"I *wanted* to marry you."

She shook her head. She would never believe that now, especially after what Adelaide had told her. Something else dawned on her just then.

"You did it because you felt guilty, didn't you? Because you broke the rules, and so did I, and we were caught."

He shook his head, tried to deny it. "I did *not* feel guilty."

"You would never, ever have asked me to marry you."

"That is not true—"

"Look me in the eye and tell me that you wanted to marry me before that day in the mill."

When he did not answer immediately, she knew it was because he was choosing his words wisely.

"I won't lie to you, Joya. I had no plans to marry so soon but—"

"You had no plans to marry at all."

"Yes, but we *are* married now. Are you unhappy? Is that what this is all about?"

Joya stood and walked to a table by the window. Twilight filled the sky. It was the hour when the lamplighters walked the streets. Darkness gathered.

She faced him again. Her legs were shaking so hard she had to put one hand on the table for support. He had not moved from the floral-patterned settee, a dainty curve-legged piece of furniture that he dwarfed.

"I was happy at first, so happy to think that you loved me. Now I see that I was thinking like a foolish child because I was so ignorant of your English ways. How was I to know a man would ever ask for a woman in marriage, not because of love or desire, but because some ill-mannered, heartless people might spread gossip about her?"

"Joya, please stop this and come over here to me."

"No." She shook her head, not trusting herself to take a step closer. "You asked if I was not happy. I'm trying to tell you that I'm not. I have no friends of my own. I don't dress to receive callers. I don't even have any callers. I'm not allowed to make bread. Or get dirty."

"What in God's name are you talking about?"

"Last night, you wasted your seed. If I am not even worthy of having your children, then I want to end this marriage and go back to Matarenga. At least there, when a man wants a wife, he is honest enough to admit that it's either because he wants to bed her and make many children, or because he needs another wife to help with the work. It isn't a sin there to kiss before marriage. It isn't even a sin to lie with a woman before marriage. Your English would say there is no honor on my island, but there is—it's just not this tangled kind of honor that has to do with gossip and the tarnishing of names. Marriage should be based on an exchange of goods, or love, or best of all, both. You didn't pay for me, Trevor. You don't love me. You married me for honor. What good is an honorable marriage without love? What good is anything without love?"

She could see by the troubled look in his eyes that her argument was lost on him. He stood up and crossed the room until he was near enough to touch her, but he did not even try. When he spoke, his voice was very, very low, so that only she could hear.

"What happened to you between the time I left the house this morning and now?"

She shrugged. "I grew up," she said sadly, fighting back tears. "Please, be honest with me now, Trevor."

"If it's honesty you want, so be it. I married you because I thought I was doing what was right for you, but it was no sacrifice, for almost from the moment I laid eyes on you, I have desired you. You are the only woman who has ever made me lose control of myself, my thoughts, my emotions. It's because I can't keep my hands off you that we came to this.

"It is true I had no intention of marrying you before that day at the mill, but we *are* married now. There are things I have to do in the next year, plans I made long ago concerning the family business, and I still intend to sail in search of the queen's orchid. That is why—as you so colorfully put it—I 'wasted my seed' last night. I'm trying to take precautions to keep from getting you with child until I return. I'm leaving the morning after the queen's reception."

Afraid her heart was about to rip in half, she laid her hand over it and felt her amulet pouch beneath her gown. Did Kibatante's guidance and protection extend this far from the island, or had the god abandoned her long ago?

"On our wedding night, and then for many nights afterward, you didn't seem concerned about fathering a child," she reminded him. "Now you are."

"You were far too persuasive for me to resist on our wedding night. When your monthly came two weeks ago, and I knew for certain that you were not with child, I decided to renew my resolve."

"Without telling me why." Now she knew why he had not wanted to make love lately. She began to hope that from now on, while he clung to his damned resolve, that he found it cold and lonely.

"I was afraid if I tried to explain, that we would argue—and I was right, for that is exactly what is happening now. I didn't want to leave you upset when I left for South America."

"You say you are going to Venezuela after the reception?"

"Yes."

"I will leave for Africa then."

He looked stunned. "That is out of the question. You are my wife. Your place is here."

"I want to go home."

"Joya, we're married, for better or for worse. I'm determined to see that this marriage succeeds."

"By sailing away? Where is our marriage on your list of priorities, Trevor? Will you work to make it succeed after you no longer have to worry about your plans for the Mandeville business? After you have gone halfway around the world searching for the queen's orchid? I think that this marriage of *obligation* is last on your list. I don't want to be married to you anymore."

It was a lie, but her heart was breaking. She was hurting and wanted to hurt him back.

"Please, let's stop this, Joya."

"I want to go to my room now." Unable to get warm, she pulled the shawl closer.

"The woman I met in the jungle on Matarenga would not give up so easily. She wouldn't run."

"But that's just the problem. I'm not that woman anymore, am I? I don't know who I am anymore. Let me go, Trevor."

He ran his hand through his hair and sighed, but did not move. She was pressed up against the table, unable to step around him without touching him. She was measuring the distance to the door when he surprised her by taking her in his arms.

She stiffened, determined not to give in to the urgency of his kiss, not to be moved by passion and forget all that she had heard this afternoon. Instead she concentrated on the things he had just admitted and the things Adelaide had said earlier.

She imagined that her heart was made of rock, of stone as hard and sharp-edged as a coral reef. She refused to feel anything.

Bewildered, Trevor raised his head and looked down at the unresponsive woman in his arms. Joya's eyes were open but her stare was blank, as if she were looking right through him. She had not responded to his kiss at all.

Desperation almost made him want to shake a reaction out of her. He looked at his hands, at his fingers tightened on her upper arms. Afraid to lose control, afraid he might be capable of doing something he would forever regret, he abruptly let her go and backed away.

She flew by him and out the door without looking back.

The shattered look on her face kept him from going after her. He had hurt her deeply, but God help him, he had only been honest. Obviously he should have told her the truth long before now.

He picked up the shawl lying on the floor and balled it up in his hands. The clock on the mantel chimed seven. He would give her time to have a good cry, then go to her after she had calmed down. They would talk things over rationally.

There would be no more discussion of her leaving.

Chapter 23

Thirty-three-and-a-half minutes later, Trevor walked in the door of their suite. The orchids had been returned to the conservatory weeks ago. Now even the gold gauze that had been suspended from the ceiling over the bed since their wedding night was gone. So too were the palms, ferns, and vines. The room looked inordinately bare.

"Joya?" He called her name. Emptiness echoed around him.

Sims stepped out of the dressing room, his arms piled high with a rainbow of new gowns.

"She is not here, sir." The old butler's tone was cool, even brittle.

"Where is she?"

"Moved back into her old room, sir. Down the hall. I think one more load should do it." He walked past Trevor and out the door. No sooner had he disappeared than Mrs. Billingsley stormed in. She gave Trevor a tight-lipped smile and a nod and went straight into the dressing room.

He walked over to the bed, leaned a shoulder against a bedpost, and stared down at the embroidered counterpane. Behind him, Mrs. Billingsley was crossing the room again. When he glanced over his shoulder, he saw that she was carrying a stack of frilly undergarments. The moment she cleared the doorway, Janelle walked in. His suite, it seemed, had become Piccadilly Circus.

"What in the world is going on?" Janelle demanded.

"Ask your sister."

"I have a terrible urge to sob for no good reason, which leads me to believe it is Joya who is very, very upset. Where is she?" Janelle looked around the room.

"I believe she has taken up residence down the hall."

Sims walked in again and went straight to the dressing room.

"What's going on here?" Janelle followed the butler. "What are you doing with those hatboxes?"

The look Sims gave Trevor would have chilled a Lapplander. "I am doing your sister's bidding, miss. She is no longer comfortable in this suite, with *him*, so she has moved back into her old room."

Trevor watched Janelle's eyes widen and was just thankful that she waited for Sims to leave before she closed the door and turned on him.

"What did you do to her?" she demanded.

"What makes you think this is my fault?"

"My sister believes you hung the moon and the stars. At least she did yesterday. Now she's moved out of your suite and I want to know why."

"She wants to leave me and go home to Africa." He sighed, rubbed the back of his neck, and sat down wearily on the edge of the bed. "I was fool enough *not* to lie to her when she asked me if I had been obligated to marry her."

"What made her ask in the first place?"

"I have no idea."

"What exactly did you tell her?"

"The truth."

"In other words, you were typically yourself—honest, cool, and above all, very businesslike."

"I'm afraid so. She's not happy that I'm leaving for Venezuela, either."

"I hate to admit it, Trevor, but I am almost glad she wants to leave you. I thought that the two of you were perfect for each other. I thought that perhaps she could teach you not to take life so seriously. Above all, I had hoped she could teach you how to love, but I can see now that just the opposite is happening. You are not changing—Joya is. You have no idea what my sister can give you, nor what she needs from you."

"And what's that?"

"I'll tell you what it *isn't*. It isn't money or a detailed business agenda. Nor is it a list of things you need to accomplish or orchid classification. She loves you, Trevor and that is all she wants from you in return."

Down the hall, Joya sat in a tall wingback chair with a thick wool blanket wrapped around her shoulders. She was staring into the flames of a low-burning fire, trying to pretend that Mrs. Billingsley was not fussing and personally overseeing the upstairs maid as the girl put her clothes away.

When someone tapped on the door, Joya sat up. "Mrs. Billingsley, if that is Trevor, please tell him to go away."

"With pleasure," Mrs. Billingsley mumbled.

Joya turned her back to the door and listened to the

housekeeper as she spoke to someone in hushed whispers.

"It's your sister, ma'am."

Joya sighed. Janelle, no doubt, had come to plead Trevor's case, but she could not lock her sister out.

"Show her in."

The housekeeper and the maid left them alone. Janelle drew a footstool up close beside her chair, took Joya's hand, and sat down.

"Thank you for taking my place at the reception." Joya had no other notion of where to begin.

"I am happy to do it if you insist."

"I do," Joya assured her.

Janelle took a deep breath and looked over at the door, which was still closed. "There is no use pretending I don't know what is going on here. I just spoke to Trevor and I know you are upset about more than the reception."

"I'm so confused. I have never felt so lost. But, then I have never been married before or in love with such a stubborn, goat-headed man, either."

"I do know that he hurt you and that he's sorry," her sister said.

"Did he send you to apologize?"

"Oh, Joya, he did not send me. It's just that I love you both and I don't want to see either of you hurting."

"Why have *you* never married?"

"Because I love my freedom and my friends. Thanks to our parents, I have money of my own, so I can be independent." She shrugged. "Marriage would mean giving over control of my life and my freedom to a husband and I am not ready to do that."

"Have you ever really been in love, Janelle?" The answer was important to her. She watched her sister closely as Janelle thought long and hard. When she looked up, there was confusion and more than a hint of fright in her eyes.

"Actually, I'm afraid I may be losing my heart to Garr Remington."

"Why are you afraid?"

Janelle shrugged. "For all the reasons I just named. Besides, he is not in love with me. He's only after money. Having never been in love, I'm not at all certain what true love is."

"You and Trevor are very much alike. His father never remarried after his mother's death, did he?"

"No."

She was musing now, searching through threads of thoughts and ideas, trying to weave them together. "My mother and father were deeply in love until the day she died. I know what a happy union can be. I think that is why I'm so confused and sad now. What Trevor and I have is not a marriage, not when he was forced into it by obligation."

"Did Grandmama tell you that Trevor felt obligated to marry you?"

Joya looked down at the edges of the blanket that she had balled up in her hands and wished she would feel warm. If she admitted the truth and told Janelle all the hurtful things that Adelaide had said, she was afraid that her twin might feel obligated to confront Adelaide and defend her.

Joya did not want to be the one to destroy a lifetime of family ties, so she omitted much of the story.

"I will never belong here, Janelle. Just as you would never feel at home on Matarenga, no matter how much we both might want to be together."

"I will not believe it," Janelle cried.

Joya shook her head. She had to make Janelle understand somehow. "Here you have Cecily and your friends. You are wise because you know the stories and the music, the songs and the history of this place. You know your way about the city. You feel safe and confident because you understand the customs and the clothing and the language and why people do and say what they do. And you have your work. How much would you know or have on Matarenga? If I took you deep into the jungle, how long would it take you to learn to survive on your own? A week, or a month? A year? Maybe two?"

"I would be forced to learn."

Joya shook her head. "You would be lucky to survive a few days. Even if you did, that does not mean you would be happy away from all you have ever known."

There was a wistful look in Janelle's eyes when she said, "I would be terrified. Without help I would be lost and frightened out of my wits."

"Perhaps now you can understand. I have tried. Given more time, I would eventually learn some of what I need to know, but to be a good wife it seems that I must learn everything at once in order not to shame Trevor. To make things worse, suddenly I find that I have a husband who did not really want a wife."

"He understands this will take some time. What he doesn't realize is that he loves you."

"You think all it takes is more time for him to grow to love me? Or to realize that he already does? What if he never changes? What if he can't?"

"He told me that you wanted to go home. I didn't really believe it until now, hearing you talk like this."

As soon as Janelle said the word *home*, Joya's eyes filled with tears.

"I do want to go," she whispered. "That makes me a coward, I suppose, but I cannot stay."

Janelle reached up and hugged her. "You're not a coward. I'm as much at fault as Trevor. I should have spent more time with you. I thought that encouraging your relationship with him would be the best thing for both of you—because you already loved him so and because he needs someone like you in his life. I did it for selfish reasons too. I wanted to keep you here with me. I never stopped to think that you might not be happy or that you might never hear sweet declarations of love from my brother."

Joya had given Trevor her heart, her love, and he did not know what to do with it. He had wanted her body, desired her in a carnal way and most likely still did, but he did not really love her. He might never love her as she loved him. She had to get out of this house, out of this marriage, and away from London before she lost her own ability to love.

"My mother taught me that love was the single most important thing in the world. She said that love gives us the power to do anything we need to do. I believe that, Janelle. I always will."

"Then how can you leave him? You love Trevor, Joya. You are his wife. Why not use that power to teach him how to love?"

"Because my love for Trevor is so one-sided. He sees me as an obligation and our marriage as a duty. If I stay here, he will only become bitter and soon resent me. I will grow to hate England, and my love for him will slowly drain away along with the person I was on Matarenga and the person I really am inside. That is why I must go home, even though it will break my heart to leave him, and you, behind. I have to leave to save us all."

Behind her spectacles, Janelle's eyes glittered with tears. "Promise me that you will at least stay until after the reception and Trevor sails. I can't bear the thought of your leaving as soon as tomorrow."

"Because you've asked, I'll stay until Trevor leaves for Venezuela, but then I am afraid that nothing will stop me. Not even you."

Her sister hugged her and then left her alone. Joya shrugged off the shawl. Her heart ached but her mind was made up. Coming to England had been a mistake and so was her marriage. If being desirable to a man makes me this miserable, she thought, then it is far better to live out my life alone on Matarenga. At least there she knew who she was and how to survive. Here, she was hopelessly lost and so was her heart.

She glanced at the door, afraid that Trevor might try to talk to her again. She could not bear it if he did. He was, after all, her husband. No doubt the English had quite a list of rules against wives leaving their husbands and sailing off to Africa.

But Trevor did not come to see her that evening, and as she turned down the light and climbed into bed, Joya did not know whether to feel relieved or brokenhearted.

Trevor worked like a man possessed, going over figures with his new head accountant, setting up shipping schedules, and making last-minute additions to the load of trade goods that he would carry to Venezuela. As long as he was going on the expedition, he was determined to make the trip profitable.

In one way the voyage was already costing him far

too much. He could only hope that the damage done to his marriage was not irreparable.

On the day of the Orchid Society members' reception at St. James's Palace, he left the warehouse earlier than usual so that he could bathe and change into formal attire. His wife had successfully avoided him for the past two days, taking her meals in her room and refusing to see him. Janelle had told him that if he wanted to save his marriage, that he should think long and hard about it and then tell his wife that he loved her before it was too late. He had wrestled with the idea day and night, but he would be damned if he was going to shout professions of undying love through a door.

As Sims admitted him, Trevor stepped into the foyer and then handed the butler his hat.

"Is my sister upstairs?" He suspected Adelaide and Janelle were in the process of getting ready.

"No, sir. Miss Mandeville left shortly after breakfast. She has not returned."

Trevor halted just short of the staircase. "She's not home yet?"

"No, sir. Your grandmother is upstairs, with her maid."

He was almost afraid to ask after Joya. Sims had made it very clear without a single word that the rift between them was obviously all his fault.

"And my wife? Is she still locked in her room?"

There was a long, contemplative pause before Sims admitted, "I believe I last saw her in the library."

Trevor thanked Sims and hurried upstairs. He started to knock at the library door but stopped himself. It was his library and his house. He'd be damned if he'd beg admittance.

She was seated at a small writing table beneath the

window, drawing. When he closed the door behind him and walked toward her, Joya put her pen down, folded her hands on the table, and waited. If she felt anything at all for him, she was doing a damned good job of hiding it.

"Have you seen Janelle?"

"Not since breakfast."

"Sims said she has not come in yet. Do you know when she was due to return? We cannot be late."

"I think she is with the viscount somewhere. She said something about delivering one of her paintings to a grand house in the country."

He picked up one of her drawings, a very detailed, wonderful likeness of Sims. Replacing it, Trevor noticed that there were also black-and-white line portraits of Mrs. Billingsley, Cook, and his grandmother. Joya had been working on a sketch of the library when he walked in.

"These are very, very good."

"Thank you. Since I arrived I've been making a collection of drawings of things I have seen and places Janelle and I visited, of people, carriages, and cathedrals. I will show them to Papa when I go home."

His stomach fell to his toes.

"Joya, you cannot leave, damn it." *Very badly put*, he decided the minute it was out. He cleared his throat, as uncomfortable with the lump forming there as he was with the raw ache in the vicinity of his heart.

When she finally looked up and their gazes locked, he realized he had forgotten how very blue her eyes were. She quickly looked away and read the tall standing clock beside the door.

"You do not want to keep the queen waiting," she said.

"Janelle's gown will fit you if you've changed your mind—"

Before he could tell her that he wanted her beside him tonight, not Janelle, that he missed her in his bed, she interrupted with a very cool, very sure, "I cannot go."

Dismissing him, she picked up her pen, dipped it into a pot of ink, and began drawing again.

"If Janelle stops in to see you, please tell her for me that she needs to hurry."

"I will."

He lingered, longing to say something, anything, that would make things right. He knew of contracts, of shipping schedules, of the price of tea from Rangoon, teakwood from China, rice from the Philippines, and tobacco from America. He could classify and identify every orchid species known to man. He could hack a trail through the jungle as easily as he could waltz around a ballroom.

But until he knew he meant them, until he was certain he would not hurt her ever again, he could not say the words his wife needed to hear.

Joya waited until he closed the library door and then pressed her hands to her lips and tried to gather her scattered thoughts.

She had not seen Trevor in two days and with every passing hour she had missed him more. How in the name of Kibatante was she going to find the courage to leave in a few days, knowing she would never, ever see him again?

Her hands were shaking as she gathered her drawings together. The clock chimed the half hour. Joya drew aside the curtain. A light mist had been falling all afternoon and now it had turned to a hard rain.

Suddenly, a different kind of emotion shook her, a wave of anxiety and frustration, along with something more, a confusion she could not describe. Her thoughts were immediately centered on her sister. *Where was Janelle?*

Just as she was about to leave the room, the library door opened again and Sims appeared. She admired his uncanny ability to move through the house without making a sound.

"You look very upset, Sims.

"Miss Mandeville has not yet returned. I am afraid she will not be here in time to go to the reception."

"I hope she is all right," Joya said, glancing out at the rain-soaked street again.

"Mrs. Billingsley said that Mrs. Mandeville is growing anxious. She is concerned your sister's delay will ruin the evening."

"*Anxious* is probably not the right word, is it, Sims?"

"No, madam. She is in the midst of throwing quite a tantrum."

Joya frowned. What if Janelle was detained until well after time to leave? Adelaide would never forgive her sister.

"Couldn't Trevor simply tell the queen that his wife has taken ill?"

Sims shook his head. "This is, perhaps, the most important thing to ever happen for the Mandevilles." He was staring at her as if trying to silently communicate some unspoken thought.

"Why are you looking at me like that?"

"If I might be so bold as to make a suggestion, madam?"

"Surely. What is it?"

"You could go in your sister's stead. No one would be the wiser."

"You mean that I should pretend to be my sister pretending to be me?"

"Exactly. I can have Mrs. Billingsley tell Mr. Mandeville and his grandmother that Miss Mandeville has returned and is dressing, while you slip into her room where Mrs. Billingsley will attend to you herself."

"But I will still have no idea what to do when I get to the palace."

"Simply watch and do what everyone else does."

"What if I don't go along with this plan?"

"I hate to think what Mrs. Mandeville will do if Miss Mandeville, in some form or another, does not appear."

As dusk gathered, rain beat down on the roof of a hired carriage stranded a few miles from London. The conveyance sat at a lopsided tilt, its rear left wheel mired in a muddy field bordering the country road. Inside, Janelle sat opposite Garr Remington, thinking that if looks could kill, he would surely have died a mercifully quick death by now.

"I could murder you for this, Garr."

"You mean to say you would rather be curtsying to the queen than stranded with me? Think of how romantic this is, the two of us alone here in the countryside while the coachman is off searching for someone who can help him hoist the back wheel out of the muck and the mire."

"*You* should have helped him. Perhaps we would already be on our way."

"What? And get dirty?"

"You are the most infuriating man alive." She crossed her arms and glared at him.

"A short while ago you told me that your *brother* was the most infuriating man alive."

"I've changed my mind. Now I'm certain *all* men are equally infuriating."

"It is not my fault that the owner of Nevillewood is an idiot with more money than sense." He stretched out, crossed his long legs at the ankles, and seemed perfectly content with the situation.

She wished he had not mentioned the estate of Nevillewood or its owner. The house was a fine example of Georgian architecture complete with formal gardens and wonderful furnishings. The viscount had sold one of her paintings to Lord Covington, the owner of the estate, and had invited her to accompany him—not as the artist, of course—but as a friend, when he delivered the painting.

Of course, Lord Covington had no notion that she was J. Mandeville, so when she asked him what he thought of the idea of women pursuing the arts, he gave her his most blunt and honest opinion. He had been so blunt and so honest that she almost told him that he had just paid an exorbitant amount for a painting that she, a woman, had produced. But she held her tongue when she remembered just how far her percentage of the price would go to feed the poor of London.

"Stop scowling," Garr ordered. "I thought it rather cleverly put when Covington said the only art that women should be allowed to engage in is the fine art of seduction."

"You would. How did you happen along in the first place?"

"If you must know, I begged my uncle to let me meet him there and drive you home. It isn't my fault we hit a rut and the driver has left us stranded."

"I am beginning to suspect you paid him to leave. Especially since he seems to have disappeared altogether and we are alone out here in the dark."

"Are you afraid, Miss Mandeville?"

She stuck her chin out at him, as a show of bravado. "Of course not."

"You don't sound positive."

"I am more afraid of the tongue lashing I'll get from Grandmama when I get home."

"If you had your own home, you would not find your-self embroiled in your brother and sister's marriage squabbles, nor would you be having to jump to your grandmother's tune."

"I do *not* jump to her tune. She drives us mad at times, but I love my grandmother. She raised Trevor and me after his father died."

"I didn't say you don't love her, just that you are old enough to marry and establish your own household."

"No, thank you." She realized what she had inferred and felt her cheeks blaze. The interior of the carriage was growing darker by the moment, which made her increasingly uncomfortable.

"That was not a proposal. When I propose to you, I'll do it properly."

"And I will politely refuse."

"There is no way you would be able to turn me down."

"You are a pompous ass."

She turned aside and looked out the window. The rain had become a downpour. Dear God in heaven, what had she been thinking when she let the viscount talk her into returning to the city with Garr? Now she was not only caught in a highly compromising situation, but she was never going to get back to Mandeville House in time to attend the reception in Joya's place.

When she turned away from the window again, she was startled by the sight of Garr on bended knee, wedged into the confining floor space between the seats.

"What are you *doing*?" She braced herself, prepared for an attack.

"I'm proposing. Give me your hand."

Chapter 24

"You're as ready as you'll ever be, ma'am." Mrs. Billingsley stood back and surveyed Joya from head to toe, nodding in satisfaction as she reached out to straighten the sleeve of Janelle's chosen gown. A three-foot-long train attached to a loop that hung from her wrist made walking a greater challenge than the crinoline.

"I can't see a thing through these spectacles," Joya complained, squinting, then crossing her eyes. Nothing helped. "They make me so dizzy I am afraid if this train doesn't topple me over, these spectacles surely will make me fall."

"Janelle would not be wearing them if she were posing as you, so take them off as soon as you can and give them to Mr. Mandeville to carry."

They were still in Janelle's room, where Mrs. Billingsley had helped her change into the formal gown that her sister had planned to wear. Joya walked over to the mirror. The housekeeper and Janelle's maid, Betty, had done her hair to perfection. She prayed the intricate tucks and curls would stay in place for the entire evening. Thankfully, her skin had faded somewhat, and Mrs. Billingsley had bemoaned the fact that the almond paste they had applied had no time to work. A layer of face powder helped to hide what Adelaide always referred to as her heathen skin coloring. Mrs. Billingsley told her not to worry, that she was supposed to look like herself anyway.

Dressed in the English finery, she took one last look in the mirror. The image brought to mind the first time she had seen Janelle and had so admired her sister's clothing. She remembered wondering what it would be like to be a proper English miss. She knew now that clothing did not make one English. Far from it. She doubted that she would ever truly belong, even if she lived here for the rest of her life.

She took a deep breath and turned away from her reflection. Mrs. Billingsley politely reminded her that she still pronounced some words slightly differently than Janelle did. Together they decided the less said, the better. Still, she would have to communicate. She wondered how long she would be able to hide the truth from Trevor.

A quick knock at the door startled her so badly that she jumped. She would have her answers soon enough.

"Don't worry. That'll be Sims," Mrs. Billingsley whispered as she hurried across the room.

To Joya's relief, the housekeeper was right. Sims stood at the threshold, gave her the same thorough once-over that Mrs. Billingsley had, and then smiled. "You are wanted downstairs, *Miss* Mandeville. They are waiting for you."

Joya saw him wink before he left. She reached for her small amulet pouch, tied around her waist beneath her gown. Closing her eyes, she touched the amulet and whispered a hushed prayer to Kibatante, asking for guidance and protection. She thought of her mother and asked for her to help, too.

"Come, ma'am," Mrs. Billingsley whispered. "There's no putting this off any longer."

Trevor watched Janelle slowly descend the stairs. She clung to the banister, walking very cautiously, carefully placing each step. Except for what he thought was a bit too much face powder, his sister looked delightful tonight. She resembled Joya more than ever, lovely in a pale lavender gown. Mrs. Billingsley had worked wonders, somehow even managing to make his sister's skin a shade darker beneath her powder.

When she reached the bottom of the stairs she took off her spectacles, folded the stems, and handed them to him. "Please carry these for me, will you?"

He slipped them into his pocket. "Are you ready?"

Sims brought her wrap and handed it to Trevor, who slipped the heavy velvet cape over her shoulders. "The rain has stopped momentarily, so we will not get drenched," he said.

Without comment, she nodded and took his arm. Together they walked past Sims. The butler wished them good evening before he closed the door behind them.

Adelaide was already seated inside the carriage. Trevor helped Janelle up and then waited until she was settled before he climbed in and sat beside her.

"It took you long enough," Adelaide snapped. Impatience and anxiety had sharpened her tongue.

When Janelle offered their grandmother no more than

a soft-spoken apology, Trevor stared at her. "Are you all right?"

There was a long, silent pause before she said softly, "Yes. Why?"

"You don't seem yourself."

"She is not herself," Adelaide reminded him. "She is supposed to be your wife. This is a foolish situation at best, but at least this way I won't have to spend the entire evening worrying about being embarrassed."

"I would thank you to remember that Joya is my wife, Grandmother," Trevor reminded her firmly. He was more than uncomfortable with this entire charade now that it was under way. There seemed to be something about Janelle tonight, some indescribable essence that she exuded that made her seem too much like Joya. It was more than disturbing.

And what of Joya tonight, he wondered. Would his wife stay shut up in her room? Would Mrs. Billingsley see to it that she ate dinner?

His thoughts were interrupted when his grandmother asked Janelle, "What kept you so late? I feared you were not going to be ready in time."

"I'm sorry you worried. I mean, *were* worried."

Trevor continued to watch Janelle closely. Something was not quite right. She was visibly uncomfortable and far too quiet. "Are you certain you are all right? Are you coming down with a cold?"

"I am fine." She sat with her hands folded demurely and spoke without looking at him.

Trevor folded his arms. Shifting with the sway of the carriage, he frowned in the semidarkness, certain that something was definitely wrong with his sister. He had no idea where she had gone or with whom she had spent the day, but that was not unusual. He rarely questioned her about her comings and goings. Now he found himself wishing he had.

He wondered if her strange demeanor had anything to do with Garr Remington? If the man had done something to hurt her, then the rake would pay the consequences. Unwilling to speak about such a volatile matter before Adelaide, Trevor decided to wait until he and his sister had a moment alone, and then he would try to get to the bottom of her submissive silence.

Joya, trapped in the charade, had to force herself to breathe. When the carriage hit a deep pothole in the street, she was thrown against Trevor and practically landed in his lap. Ever the gentleman, he helped her back to a sitting position, but all the while he watched her closely.

She was grateful for the darkness and for the fact that she had been there to hear him defend her to Adelaide. *My wife*, he had called her. Hearing him say those words had filled her with a bittersweet longing. If only he had spoken his marriage vows out of love and pride and not some sense of obligation or duty. If only he knew how to love her along with his desire, then their marriage might have stood a chance.

The carriage reached St. James's Palace, and soon they were inside a huge hall mingling with the crowd assembled there.

Trevor naturally introduced her as his wife, Joya Penn Mandeville, to many members of the Orchid Society. Not one person among them had not heard of Dustin Penn. Everyone was very much in awe of her father's reputation and discoveries and held him in great esteem.

The society members included men wealthy enough to hire hunters willing to risk their lives for enough money. There were orchid hunters in the far corners of Mexico, Brazil, Peru, Madagascar, India, Africa, and New Zealand.

Before she realized what she was doing, she was discussing many of her father's most famous finds and even the exciting news that John Lindley, one of the founders of the *Gardeners' Chronicle*, was undertaking an intensive study of the genera and species and was working on a series of monographs of all orchid genera identified so far.

It was not until she looked up and saw Adelaide standing nearby, tight-lipped and watching her with barely concealed anger, that she realized through her excitement and knowledgeable comments that she had given herself away.

Just then, an announcement was made at the far end of the hall. Queen Victoria and Prince Albert had arrived. Trevor pulled her close just as the crowd started to move into a receiving line.

"What made you change your mind, Joya?"

She was vastly relieved at having been found out.

"How did you know?"

"*When* did I know is more the question. I thought something was wrong with you, or rather, with Janelle, on the ride over. I was almost certain when you fell over me in the carriage, but it became evident when you were able to add so much to the conversation. My sister knows next to nothing about orchid classification and nothing at all about your father's most famous finds."

He glanced over at Adelaide, who was headed toward

them. "Grandmother looks as if she has swallowed a bad beetle," he said.

When he actually chuckled softly, Joya almost smiled. Oh, how she wished they could turn back time to the point where things had been uncomplicated by honor and obligation.

"When Janelle did not come home, Mrs. Billingsley and Sims suggested I take her place," she said.

"Where *is* Janelle?" His expression instantly darkened with concern.

Joya had not intended to cast Janelle in a bad light. As yet she was not overly alarmed about her sister. "I think I would feel it if she was in any real danger. She went to the country with the viscount to meet a man who bought one of her paintings. I have no idea why she did not return on time."

Before they could say more, the crowd began moving in a calm, orderly fashion, the way the tide slowly creeps toward shore. There was no stopping the inevitable.

Joya grabbed his sleeve. "Oh, Trevor, I am so afraid I will do something wrong."

"You will be just fine. You look absolutely beautiful tonight. Something told me it was you the minute I saw you on the stairs. I should have listened to my heart."

When Trevor's admission brought her to a complete standstill, the woman in line behind her walked right into her. Joya apologized and then Adelaide appeared and fell into step alongside them.

"So, it *is* you," she said. The lines around her mouth deepened as she pursed her lips.

Joya's heart clinched. Trevor tightened his hand on her arm. She decided that having to perform in front of

Adelaide made her more nervous than the idea that she was about to meet Queen Victoria.

As if he knew what she was thinking, Trevor whispered, "Stay calm. Watch the other women. You will be just fine."

"That's what Sims told me to do." She felt for her amulet pouch through the many layers of clothing and for the moment felt safe. Her mother's comb was inside the small pouch. If Clara did know that she was here, what must she be thinking of her daughter who was about to meet the queen?

Joya swallowed. It was too late to turn back now.

"You are breaking my heart, Janelle," Garr said.

"I am about to break your head."

"I can't properly propose if you don't give me your hand. Please, have some pity on me. My knee is killing me."

"Don't be ridiculous. Get up off the floor and behave yourself." She had scooted as far into the corner of the seat as she could.

"Not until you accept."

"Why on earth would I accept a proposal from you, of all people?"

His smile was devastating. "Because you have never had a more exciting offer, I can guarantee you that."

"I have turned down suitors one hundred times more worthy. Besides, you are not even a suitor. I was actually beginning to think that you were my friend."

Earlier that afternoon she had found herself hoping at least that much was true, that they really could be friends, for she truly enjoyed his company and his easy banter. Right now, though, she could hardly think of anything clearly with Garr on the carriage floor staring up at her.

"What better reason to marry than friendship?"

Janelle thought of Joya and Trevor and of the uncontrollable desire that had brought them together. Hunger for one another had been the catalyst behind their marriage—and where had desire gotten them?

Garr took her hand before she could stop him, then rose to make a place for himself on the seat beside her.

"What are you thinking about?" he asked.

"What of love?" She said it before she could stop herself.

"Ah. Love. Is that what you are looking for in a husband?"

"I'm not even looking for a husband, especially a fortune-hunting rake."

He leaned closer, until their shoulders barely touched. Rain beat down like a hoard of wild Saxons dancing atop the roof of the carriage. It was almost completely dark now. The pungent scent of the rain-soaked, newly plowed fields filled the air.

"Would you marry me if you loved me?" He leaned so close she could feel his warmth all along her side.

"No." It was unimaginable. If she loved him he would have the power to break her heart.

"I think you might already love me," he whispered.

"Think again, Garr."

"Shall we find out if there is any hope?"

Before she knew what he was about, his lips touched hers. They were warm and sensual, surprisingly soft. She put her hands on his shoulders, on the fine forest-green wool of his well-tailored coat, intent on pushing him away—until she felt his tongue slide over her lips.

Something deep inside her fluttered, tugged at her, and then unfurled. She shivered and waited to see what might happen next.

He urged her gently, teasing her with his tongue until she opened to him and allowed him to deepen the kiss. She could feel his tongue moving against hers, something so heady, so delicious that she went weak and light-headed all at once. A soft, throaty moan escaped her without warning.

Garr slipped his arms around her, pressing her to him.

"Your heart is beating—" he whispered.

"I hope so, else I would be dead." She wondered whether one could die of such glorious feelings.

"If you had let me finish, you would know I was about to say that your heart is beating like the wings of a caged dove."

"Is that what you say to all the young women you seduce in the dark in broken-down carriages?"

"Only half of them."

"What do you say to the other half?"

" 'Your heart is beating like the wings of a trembling butterfly.' "

"I prefer the dove reference."

He reached up and slipped off her spectacles, carefully folded the stems, and pocketed them.

"Let me kiss you again, Janelle."

She sighed, knowing she was already lost.

So he kissed her again. And again. Long, slow, luxurious kisses that did nothing to quench the thirst building inside her. He asked permission to touch her breast. She thanked heaven it was dark so that he would not see her cheeks flame when she said yes. Gently he cupped her; tenderly he massaged her breasts but did not attempt to remove her jacket, nor did he even try to slip his hand beneath the fabric.

Janelle closed her eyes, wanting to tell him to stop, unable to even think of the word. He kissed her again as his hands worked their magic on her, caressing her breasts, touching her cheek, her hair. She was lost and she knew it. In one tiny corner of her mind she was thinking, *so this is the desire Joya tried to describe.* This *is what brought my sister and Trevor to such an unhappy conclusion.* She understood at last, but even that newfound understanding could not temper her own response to Garr.

Suddenly, it was Garr and not she who put an end to their lovemaking. She had wanted it to go on and on forever.

She was breathless. Her hair had come loose. A long, heavy strand was hanging alongside her cheek. Melted butter had more substance than she right now. If he wanted more, she could not resist.

"I do not want a quick tumble in a carriage from you, Janelle. I want a lifetime. I will not take you this way, although I know good and well that you would let me. I want you to be my wife."

Oh this is rich, she thought. The man was holding back favors until she agreed to marry him.

He looped her wayward curl around his finger, used it to draw her to him, kissed her lightly once, twice, thrice. Then he let go of her hair and moved back across the carriage. Once more, he leaned back, stretched out, folded his arms, and crossed his ankles.

She felt cold without him, almost bereft. There was not a sound but their breathing inside the carriage. His was calm and steady; hers ragged, uneven, desperate.

It was too dark to see Garr clearly, but she could still make out his brilliant, triumphant smile.

"Well, Miss Mandeville, what will it be?"

It was nearly Trevor and Joya's turn to be introduced to the queen. *In a moment*, she thought, *this will all be over*. With a lump in her throat and fear in her heart, she waited, reminding herself over and over that the queen was only a woman, a sovereign of the British Empire, yes, but still a woman, flesh and blood. A mother. A wife. There was nothing to fear.

A mere introduction could not be half as difficult as hacking a trail through the steaming jungle to get over Mount Kibatante.

The couple before them bowed and curtsied, and then it was Adelaide's turn. Joya watched Adelaide curtsy, and then Trevor made a polite bow, and then she found herself standing face to face with Queen Victoria.

She executed a low, perfectly acceptable curtsy. Then the queen spoke directly to her.

"Mrs. Mandeville, we have heard that you were raised in Africa."

"Yes, Your Majesty."

It did not do much for her already jumbled nerves to realize that everyone in the room was watching and trying to hear the exchange. Victoria had not taken the time to actually converse with more than a handful of Orchid Society members as they passed through the long reception line.

"What is your opinion of London, now that you are here?"

"What do I think about it, do you mean?"

The queen nodded. She was far younger-looking than Joya had imagined and she seemed so very, sincerely interested that Joya thought surely it would be all right to be perfectly honest with Her Majesty.

"I think there are too many rules."

A murmur rippled through the crowd. The queen raised her head and glanced around sternly, and a hush immediately fell over the room.

Out of the corner of her eye, Joya saw Trevor move closer and she smiled. For some reason, the queen seemed very, very interested now. Perhaps Adelaide would finally have something to be pleased about. Trevor might have been obliged to marry her, but tonight she would do the Mandeville name proud.

"Which of Our rules would you have done away with, Mrs. Mandeville?" The queen was attentively awaiting a response.

Joya took a deep breath. "Well, most definitely the one that obliges a man to marry a woman when they break Rule Number One. I believe Rule Number Two is far too rigid also."

"I don't believe We are familiar with Rule Number One or Rule Number Two."

Joya found it odd that the queen did not know her country's social strictures by heart.

Trevor bowed slightly. "Your Majesty, if I may—"

"You may not," the queen said. "Please, enlighten Us as to Rule Number One and Rule Number Two, Mrs. Mandeville."

Joya smiled and looked around. Since everyone appeared so intent upon listening, she spoke louder.

"Rule Number One is never be alone with a man who is not your husband, and Rule Number Two is always wear enough clothes for modesty's sake. Cover yourself from head to toe."

Joya feared Her Majesty was growing overly warm in

the crowded room. The queen's face had reddened considerably.

"Why would you have Us do away with these two particular rules?"

"Rule Number One is too easily broken, especially when one is overcome with desire, which is a very unpredictable thing, Your Majesty, as surely you know, seeing as how you already have seven children. And as for Rule Number Two—" Joya raised her arm and indicated her gown's heavy train. "I think wearing too many clothes is *very* unnatural. If it had not been for my mother and father, I would have been half naked when Trevor found me."

Joya waited politely for the queen to respond. There was not a sound in the room. She wanted to smile up at Trevor, but did not wish to offend the queen by looking away. Nor did she want the others to think she was gloating over her good fortune.

"Most enlightening, Mrs. Mandeville."

"Thank you, Your Majesty."

Joya curtsied again. The queen was looking very thoughtful, but Joya suspected Her Majesty smiled very little. No doubt the business of running an empire and seeing to so many children was not easy. She had seen enough on her sojourns through the streets of London to know there was much work to be done here.

Trevor touched her arm, signaling her that their time was done. Although she would have liked to discuss other English customs with the queen, she did not want to monopolize Her Majesty's time.

She and Trevor moved on briefly to Prince Albert, who encouraged Trevor in his hunt for the queen's orchid. Joya smiled up at Trevor. He appeared to be clenching his jaw.

"Are you all right?" she asked, thinking perhaps he had been as nervous as she.

He nodded absently, scanning the room. There was a hard look in his eye, as if he were braced for a fight.

"Oh, Trevor, I will never forget this night," she told him.

"I doubt anyone who is here ever will either."

She smiled at Lord Godfrey Howard and his wife, one of the couples she had met earlier. Lady Howard turned her back. Lord Howard frowned, shrugged at Trevor as if to say, "I'm sorry, there is nothing I can do," and turned away as well.

It was not until she had experienced the same reaction from three more couples that Joya realized no one was willing to acknowledge her. Looking around, she discovered that Adelaide had disappeared.

"Trevor?" He was wearing the same fierce expression as he had on the night he had walked into her father's orchid camp—fierce, daring, and very stubborn.

"Trevor, what is it? What have I done?"

"Nothing. You have done nothing, absolutely nothing, to be ashamed of." When he looked down at her, cupped her cheek, and smiled, it nearly broke her heart. "You are one of a kind, Joya. No one will ever take that from you."

Panic welled inside her. Despite his denial, she knew she had done or said something terribly wrong, something that had offended everyone in the room.

She tugged on his sleeve until he leaned close enough for her to whisper, "Are they upset because the queen chose to speak to me for so long?"

"Something like that."

"Please, Trevor," she begged, on the verge of tears

and hating herself for such weakness. "Do not treat me like a child."

"Lift your chin, Joya. Pretend you are facing down a horde of cutthroat pirates invading Matarenga."

She scanned the room. Adelaide was still nowhere to be seen. No one was bothering to hide their displeasure, not even the Howards, who had been so charming to her earlier. Couples either cut her directly by turning around when she looked their way, or openly stared at her without hiding grim expressions.

She had done something quite terrible and Trevor, as her husband, was now obligated to defend her.

"No one will even acknowledge me. Why?"

He lowered his voice. "You were a bit indiscreet, is all, when you spoke of being half naked."

Preoccupied with thinking of an excuse to exit the room, she decided to try to make him leave her side.

"I'm thirsty," she blurted.

"Then come with me to the refreshment table."

"I . . . I need to go to the ladies' salon. I will look for Adelaide."

He put his hand beneath her chin and gently forced her to look up into his eyes. "Are you certain you'll be all right alone?"

She smiled. "Of course. I will remember the pirates."

"Good. Show these people what you are made of. I will meet you over there," he pointed to a long buffet table. "I'll be waiting for you with a glass of champagne."

Joya stared up at him for as long as she dared.

"Do not be long," he told her.

Without another word, she turned away. She had to escape before it was too late, before she was too blinded by tears to make her way through the room. The crowd parted. Couples stepped aside to let her pass as if the mere touch of her skirt might infect them with the plague.

The Secret

Chapter 25

Joya had no sooner escaped from the reception room when Adelaide grabbed her arm and pulled her into an alcove tucked into the long hall.

"You have ruined us," Adelaide hissed.

A wave of nausea, brought on by nerves and the pungent scent of the older woman's perfume, made Joya's head swim. She could think of no response, giving Adelaide ample time to continue her tirade.

"You have ruined Trevor's chances for a royal appointment, whether or not he finds the queen's orchid."

"I am sorry, I did not mean—"

"You should have never come here in the first place."

When Adelaide moved closer, backing her against a window seat, Joya's self-protective instincts took over. She stood her ground, squared her shoulders.

"If you recall, I didn't want to come tonight."

"You should have told us that you and Janelle had switched places again. You should have stayed where you belonged, and I don't mean at Mandeville House. I mean in Africa!"

Afraid someone would overhear, Joya lowered her voice. "I know that now, better than anyone."

"Trevor has had to waste time coddling you ever since you arrived. At the very least, your sister should have been watching out for you, not Trevor, but Janelle has been too worried about furthering her own interests. Haven't you noticed she has all but deserted you since you arrived?"

"She has her own life to live. I do not want to burden her," Joya said, sincere in every word.

"Poor Trevor could have married someone worthy. With our money, he could have found a titled wife, someone who would have raised his social standing. Now, as long as he is bound to you, his chances are completely ruined. You are an embarrassment to the Mandeville name."

Joya had had no notion that the old woman truly hated her so badly. No wonder Trevor had no belief in the magic of love or the power of it. She, who had been raised by two people with no blood ties to her at all, had fared far better than he—for she had grown up loved and cherished, not groomed to further someone else's dreams.

Adelaide loved only two things, the Mandeville name and money. Trevor excused his grandmother because she had spent her youth fighting to keep the family business alive so that he could take it over. Being a man of honor, he believed he owed everything to his grandmother. She might have raised him, but Joya doubted that the woman had ever let Trevor see this embittered, angry side.

Joya knew that it was useless to try to defend herself. Besides, her own mind was already made up.

Life in London was as complicated as Trevor had warned her it would be. No matter how much she learned of Londoners and their ways, there would always be some new pitfall. She would never fit in here. It would be better for her to banish herself, the way an unworthy wife on Matarenga would be banished.

Trevor had done the honorable thing by marrying her.

Now she must do the right thing and give him his freedom.

Adelaide's eyes had narrowed. She was watching Joya closely. "What little scheme are you concocting now? I suppose you are planning to run to Trevor and tell him everything I've just said."

"You will not have to worry about my harming the Mandeville name again. I'm leaving London tonight. I'm going home."

The smug, satisfied smile on Adelaide's face was chilling.

"Then you had best go now, before Trevor finds out and tries to make some noble, misguided effort to stop you. I will go back and tell him that you'll be along shortly. By the time he suspects anything, it will be too late. Tell our driver that you have a headache and must return home. We'll have to find another way back, which will take even more time. I would expect that by then you will be gone."

Adelaide did not wait for a reply as she stepped out of the alcove and headed back to the reception room.

Forgetting about her train, Joya stumbled and nearly fell to her knees, but a kindly stranger grabbed her elbow just in time. She adjusted the loop over her arm and paused once to look back at the door to the reception room. Reminding herself that her father would expect no less, she held her head high and never looked back as she walked down the long corridor toward the door.

Adelaide did not bother to hide a smile as she watched Joya trip over her train. She would bide her time, make certain the chit had left the building and was well on her way before she sought out Trevor.

He would, no doubt, be very upset when they returned home and he found the girl gone, but in time she would convince him that he was better off without Joya Penn. Once and for all, he would be able to get on with his life. He could begin his search for the queen's orchid and, once he found it, hopefully make up for his wife's social blunders. Then he could forget orchid hunting forever and concentrate his efforts on diversifying the business.

Things would be far, far easier for him without his wife. Eventually he would forget the girl.

No one need ever know that Joya had left him, either. She was already prepared to spread the word that the girl had been high-strung and nervous, so ill that they had been forced to have her confined at a sanatorium on the continent. After word of her conversation with the queen had spread, no one would doubt it.

Adelaide reached up, touched the numb right side of her face. Her damn cheek had been tingling off and on since her confrontation with Joya in the kitchen. Ah, well, she thought, shrugging off any concern, she was bound to have a few aches and pains at her age, but she would let nothing diminish her triumph tonight.

Trevor downed his glass of champagne and then the one that he was holding for Joya. The longer he waited, the more incensed he became, not at her, but at those who had openly cut her.

At least Joya was honest. There *were* too many rules here, too many silly notions and restrictions, society's little dance steps that had no bearing on a person's true worth.

The hurt he had seen in her eyes was affecting him more with each passing moment. He set the champagne glasses on a passing footman's tray and was about to go looking for his wife when one of the queen's ladies-in-waiting walked up to him and requested he join Victoria. He bowed and thanked her, then immediately made his way back through the crowd.

He was genuinely surprised when Queen Victoria made a great show of greeting him. "Tell Us about your wife, Mr. Mandeville. We are intrigued."

He quickly told her—without indicating that Joya had actually been kidnapped—of how she had been raised by Clara and Dustin Penn on Matarenga. He reminded the queen that Penn was famous for the various orchid discoveries he had made over the past twenty years and then added that Mandeville Imports was now the exclusive brokerage for Penn's orchids. He added that even now, the famed hunter was searching for a unique specimen worthy of her name.

"Ah, yes," she sighed. "Dear Albert's little challenge to all of you orchidologists."

"The entire Orchid Society is taking that challenge quite seriously, Your Majesty."

She nodded. "Just as the planned exhibition is important to Our husband, so too is finding Our orchid." Her level stare met Trevor's. "We would hate for him to be disappointed."

"I'm certain a worthy blossom will be found before the exhibition opens."

As the queen casually scanned the crowded room, he was inspired by the notion that nothing she did was without purpose.

"We found your wife charming, Mr. Mandeville," she said.

Bless her heart, he thought. Victoria had raised her voice so that the compliment carried to everyone gathered around them, guests who were trying hard not to appear to be eavesdropping.

"I think so, too, Your Majesty. Thank you."

"Please tell her that We enjoyed speaking to her very, very much. Such honesty is refreshing." She lowered her voice so that only he could hear. "A bit shocking, mind you, but refreshing."

Trevor never knew relief could feel so overwhelmingly wonderful. He bowed and backed away from the queen, then scanned the room for Joya, expecting to find her waiting near the refreshment table. He wanted to share what the queen had said, to put her mind at ease.

There was no sign of her anywhere, but he saw his grandmother reenter the room. Anxious to locate Joya, he went to ask Adelaide whether she had seen her.

To all the hypocrites now able to nod and smile at him, even to those who tried to engage him in conversation, he turned a cold shoulder.

No one would put tears in *his* wife's eyes and get away with it.

Joya had quickly changed into her plainest gown and had just left Trevor's room when Sims walked up to her in the hall. He looked at the casket trunk under her arm but made no comment.

"Is my sister home, Mr. Sims?"

"No, madam. She is not. I am concerned, for it is not like her to stay away so long without some word."

She touched the old man's sleeve.

"Don't worry. I would feel it here"—she touched her heart—"if she was in real danger or any harm had come to her."

He looked at the trunk again. "Are you moving back into Mr. Mandeville's room? May I send for the maids to help with your things?"

She shook her head. There was little time to tarry.

"Good-bye, Mr. Sims."

"Good-bye? I thought you had just returned, Mrs. Mandeville."

"I am going back home, to my island. I have left a note for Trevor in his dressing room. My marriage is over, Mr. Sims, and I am banishing myself. He can take a second wife now, a suitable Englishman's wife. I will miss you, and would enjoy nothing more than a long good-bye, but I must hurry. By the way, how do I reach the docks?"

"It's too late to take a train. You can't think of going alone."

"I am and I will."

"It is far too dangerous."

What could be any worse than what she was already going through?

"Mr. Sims, don't look so anxious. I will be fine. I have my amulet pouch and my charms."

"Although I don't want you to leave, I am considering ways to help you escape, madam. After all, it was you who cured my affliction. I am forever in your debt."

"You may keep the monkey's paw."

"Nothing I say will persuade you to stay, will it?" He looked old and tired and sighed heavily, shaking his head at her.

"No, it will not. Will you please tell Mrs. Billingsley good-bye for me? I'm afraid I might cry."

"Of course, madam." He reached for her trunk, took it from her, and started down the hall. "Come with me. I'll order Joshua to take you to Bristol."

It was pouring rain again by the time Trevor had finally secured a carriage for himself and his grandmother. As they pulled up before Mandeville House, the hired conveyance creaked and swayed unmercifully. He was coming out of his skin.

He had wasted precious time waiting for Joya after Adelaide told him she had seen his wife in the hallway and that Joya had assured her that she was fine and would join them shortly.

But she had never returned to the reception room. By the time Trevor went in search of her and concluded that she had left the palace alone, he was frantic. When he finally learned that she had commandeered his own driver and carriage, the information did nothing to lessen his anxiety. He was further detained until he located a cab for hire.

"I don't know why you are so upset." His grandmother spoke over the sound of the pouring rain as they negotiated the front steps. "I am sure Joya is safe in her room. It was certainly insensitive of her to leave without telling you."

Trevor stopped listening the moment Sims opened the door.

"Did my wife arrive safely?" He handed the butler his hat and cape, then helped his grandmother with her things.

"Yes, sir, she did," Sims said.

"I told you." Adelaide frowned down at the water spots on her skirt.

Trevor was headed toward the staircase when Sims added, "She put a note in your dressing room, sir, before she left again."

Halting in midstride, Trevor turned around. "Before she *left* again?"

"Yes, sir." Sims cleared his throat, hovering on the brink of some uncertainty.

"Where did she go?" Trevor felt a sense of deep foreboding when he noticed that Sims looked entirely too pale.

"Banished herself, sir. So that you can take a second wife."

"*A what*?"

"A second wife, sir."

"I suppose it is probably for the best, Trevor, dear," Adelaide said, brushing off her shoulders and shaking rainwater droplets off her skirt.

Trevor's panic mounted. He could not breathe. He reached for the neck of his shirt, unfastened his collar, ripped it off.

"For the *best*?" He stared at his grandmother, then turned to Sims. "Did she say where she was going?" He was afraid he already knew the answer.

"Home, sir. To her island."

Trevor's long-pent-up emotions, like the evils released from Pandora's box, spiraled out of control. He splintered in two, as if watching himself and yet still inside himself, and there was nothing he could do to rein that other self in.

"When did she leave? Was she alone? Tell Joshua to bring the carriage around. I won't fire him until morning."

The sound of his own voice echoed around the foyer, but for the life of him, he could not stop shouting. Standing beside the massive round table in the center of the entry, his grandmother pressed her fingertips to her temples.

"Calm down, Trevor, please. You are making my head pound."

"Joshua drove her to Bristol in the carriage, sir. I insisted upon it only because she was determined to leave. I did not think you would want her out alone and on foot. I hope I did the right thing."

"Of course you did not! You should have stopped her. You should have tied her up and locked her in her room."

"I did send her by carriage, sir, instead of train, hoping to delay her."

Trevor flung his collar to the floor and ran his hands through his hair, certain he had become a stark raving madman. "What about Janelle? Couldn't *she* persuade Joya to stay?"

"Miss Mandeville is not at home, sir."

"I suppose she never returned?"

"That's right, sir."

"Damn it! Damn it all to hell."

Helplessness stoked his panic and rage, at himself, at Sims, at Janelle, at the world at large.

His wife had left him. He had to get her back.

·   ·   ·

Joya's note lay on his dresser beneath his mother's silver comb. He picked up the filigreed hair ornament, circled his thumb over the letter *C* and tried to recall having left it out of the drawer. The piece was precious to him, so much so that he always put it away.

Laying the comb aside, he lifted the ragged-edged piece of drawing paper torn from a larger sheet and stared down at Joya's writing. The letters were smudged, uneven, and cramped. He imagined her toiling over every word. Her good-bye to him was pitifully brief.

Dear Trevor,

I am going back to Matarenga. Your grandmother is right. I am an embarrassment to all of you. I have shamed you too many times. In London, I have lost myself somewhere. I love you, but I cannot be a good wife here. You need someone who keeps all of the rules.

I have left you the one thing I cherish most in the world—aside from you and Janelle and Papa. My mother wore this silver comb in her hair until the day she died. It has been my good-luck charm. Now I hope that it will become yours.

Be careful always, Trevor. Your loving wife,
Joya

Another violent surge of emotion threatened logic. As he stared down at the note, the wavering script blurred. He sighed, rubbed his eyes, then reread the line about *her* mother's silver comb.

Frowning, he set aside the note and picked up the hair piece, turned it over in his hand, and stared at the bold letter *C* entwined with grape leaves. The comb seemed a bit more tarnished than he recalled. When he looked closely, he could see that here and there it was pitted with black spots.

His hand actually trembled as he pulled open his dresser drawer. Inside, all of his things were still in place and neatly folded. Immediately his hand went to the pile of handkerchiefs. Even before he lifted them, he knew what he would find.

Beneath them lay his mother's silver comb, mono-grammed with a *C* entwined with grape leaves; a comb identical to the one in the palm of his hand.

A few moments later, Trevor found Adelaide in the drawing room. She was slumped against the armrest of the settee. He had recovered his composure somewhat before he presented both combs.

"You do not seem shocked or surprised over my find-ing a second comb, or over Joya's leaving. Why is that, Grandmother?"

"Because I am sure there is some simple explanation for the comb. As for Joya, obviously she was very un-happy here."

Her words sounded a bit slurred, but he was not about to let her persuade him to postpone the discussion be-cause she had taken too many sips of champagne.

"These combs are identical. One belonged to my mother, one to Clara Penn, the woman who raised Joya on Matarenga. How can that be?"

She shrugged, staring at a point across the room. "How should I know, dear? There were probably many, many of those old combs fashioned years ago."

He shook his head. "Father told me that he had a set of combs made *especially* for my mother, but that she had lost one. Before she died, she made him promise to give me the one remaining. Now Joya has given me a second and it is identical to my mother's, down to the letter."

"Your father walked around with his head in the clouds and you know it. Perhaps he embellished the story for you. I greatly doubt he had that comb especially made for your mother."

"Look at me, Grandmother."

She put her hand to her forehead. "I am tired, Trevor. Please, help me up to my room."

There was a knock at the door. Beyond frustrated, Trevor shouted, "Come in."

It was Sims. "Your horse is ready, sir."

Trevor focused on Adelaide again. "I'm going after my wife. When I come back, I want the truth. About the combs and about why you told Joya that she was an embarrassment to this family."

"I've nothing further to say about either," Adelaide grumbled.

"We'll see. For now, just pray that I find her."

With that, he swept past Sims and left his grandmother sitting alone.

She would pray all right. Adelaide waited until Trevor had left the room before she closed her eyes and prayed that he would not find his wife and that the chit was gone for good.

Seeing those two silver combs in his hand had left her terrified. The dark secret still hovered in the room. All she could do was pray that if she held fast, the truth would stay buried and that Clara Hayworth would not reach out of the grave to ruin everything.

She hoped to God that he never learned the truth.

• • •

Janelle awoke with a start and looked around the interior of the carriage. It all came back to her in an instant, where she was and how she had gotten there.

How many hours had passed since she had fallen asleep on the cold, cracked leather of the upholstered seat? It was still dark outside and it was still raining.

On the seat across from her, Garr slumped with his arms folded, his chin resting on his chest, snoring softly.

She kicked him in the shin. He jumped to his feet, hit his head on the roof of the carriage, and sat back down.

"That wasn't fair," he complained, rubbing the crown of his head.

"None of this is fair. I have let my sister down. Not only that, but my brother is no doubt scouring the countryside looking for me by now. If I ever find out that you planned this . . ."

"You are thoroughly compromised. We must marry."

"We will do nothing of the sort. If and when we get back to London, you will take me directly home. Cecily will vouch for me. I'll tell my family that I spent the night with her. If I have to, I will claim I drank too much wine and passed out. Better a lie than the truth."

"Is the thought of marrying me really that horrible?"

He actually sounded very pitiful. He was an actor worthy of Drury Lane. In truth, the experience had not been bad at all. She had dozed off wondering what it would be like to have a man like Garr truly fall in love with her, to have him make love to her.

Impossible. Ridiculous.

"Well?" He was still waiting for an answer. "Do you really find me so disgusting?"

"I should," she mumbled.

"But you don't, do you?"

"I doubt any woman could find you disgusting. But I

am still not about to ruin my life by marrying you. All you want is my money."

"Damn your money, Janelle." He moved over to the seat beside her again.

"Get back on your side," she warned.

"Doesn't the fact that I did *not* seduce you when I very well could have prove that I care for you?"

She sniffed.

"Janelle, do you believe in love at first sight? I fell in love with you the night we met at your grandmother's party. But you don't believe me, do you?"

When she suddenly realized that deep within her heart she desperately wanted to believe him, she almost frightened herself to death.

Chapter 26

Like a madman, Trevor rode through the countryside to
Bristol. Intermittent downpours had turned the roads into
muddy quagmires. He had hoped that he would come
upon Joshua and his carriage on the way, but luck was
with Joya. He did not pass them anywhere.

When he reached the wharf, he went from ship to
ship, combing the docks. Frantic, angry, belligerent to
ships' captains and innkeepers and anyone else who
crossed his path, he got nowhere. No one had seen Joya.
If they had, they would not admit it.

As the gray light of dawn crept over the sodden landscape, he walked into a grog shop and caught sight of
himself in a mirror on the wall.

No wonder I can get no cooperation from anyone, he
thought. He looked beyond despicable, with wild eyes
and a night's growth of beard. Spattered with road mud,
his clothes were rumpled and damp. Somewhere along
the way he had lost his hat, and his hair stuck out in
matted clumps. Why would anyone trust a man in such

a sorry state? Who would turn a woman over to him?

He ordered a mug of ale, drank it without pause, and, fortified for the long ride home, threw his coin on the bar and walked out. There was nothing he could do now but return to London and send back a search party of stevedores as soon as he reached the city. If his men could not find Joya, he would take his already-outfitted ship and sail to Africa.

For once in his life, he had no plan for his future save one—to get Joya back. During the long, desperate hours of his search, when reason and control had entirely deserted him, he had clung to one single hope—that he would find her again. When he did, he would never let her go.

It was nearly noon before he walked into the breakfast room at Mandeville House, right into the midst of an argument between his sister and his grandmother. They were so involved that they did not notice him standing there in the doorway.

"You, like your sister, are nothing but a little whore." His grandmother's face was florid, her lips tight, almost as if she were in pain as she glared at Janelle.

He had never heard Adelaide use such a venomous tone in his life. When he stepped over the threshold and made his presence known, his grandmother started, then stared at him in shocked surprise.

"I didn't know you were here," she said, cornered.

"Obviously not. You have slandered my wife and my sister in one breath. I would like to know why."

Janelle was pale and silent as a stone. Even her spectacles could not hide shadows the color of old bruises beneath her eyes. She looked exhausted and at the same time furious. When she realized he was alone, her disappointment brought tears to her eyes.

"You did not find Joya?"

He shook his head. "No. But I sent my men back to Bristol. If they can't find her, I will leave for Africa. Where were you last night?"

"At Cecily's. I will explain later."

His grandmother snorted. "Why bother? None of it is the least believable."

"Grandmama told me some of what happened last night at the reception, Trevor," Janelle said. "I take it Joya left without knowing the queen did not take offense?"

"She came home, packed, and left me a note."

"Did she leave one for me?"

Janelle looked crestfallen when he told her that Joya did not.

"Trevor, eat something," Adelaide encouraged.

He pulled out a chair, sat down wearily, and stared across a sea of china and silver and a tall epergne filled with fresh flowers.

"Do you seriously think I could eat anything right now?"

His grandmother had often been stern, but never, ever had she sounded so cold and heartless before. Adelaide kept pressing her fingertips against her cheek.

"You must eat," she said again.

"I'll have coffee."

"You should rest. You need a bath."

"What I need is the truth, Grandmother. Joya did her best to fit in, but obviously you made her feel inadequate. Last night you told her she was an embarrassment."

"Why are you looking at me like that?" His grandmother's hand fluttered to her breast.

"I am beginning to think I don't really know you at all."

Janelle went to the sideboard, poured him a cup of coffee, and dished up a plate of eggs. He was thankful that breakfast was always a casual affair without servants present. He would not have to put off questioning his grandmother for the sake of privacy.

"Tell me about the combs, Grandmother."

"I told you all I know last night. Please, do not continually badger me over a silly piece of silver."

"What combs?" Janelle looked at each of them in turn.

Trevor reached into his coat pocket and withdrew both silver pieces.

"That is your mother's comb, isn't it? I thought you had but one," she said.

"I did, until last night." He quickly explained Joya's having left the matching comb with her note.

He had had hours on horseback to ponder why his grandmother had never fully accepted Joya, why she continually doubted his wife's ability to adapt. He had also tried to unravel the mystery of the two combs and could not shake the feeling that somehow everything was connected.

"I have the feeling you were lying to me last night and that you're lying now, Grandmother. Why?"

The look in her eyes reminded him of that of an old fox caught in a snare. Ever since the floodgates opened last night and his emotions had begun to run wild, he had experienced a full spectrum of feeling he never knew he was capable of.

As he looked across the table at the woman who had raised him, nurtured him, and instilled pride in the Mandeville name and a sense of responsibility to all that name meant, he became desperate to understand why she would lie to him now.

He took a sip of black coffee, then carefully placed the cup on the saucer. Then he looked at his grandmother and held his silence until she met his eyes.

"Please, Trevor." She was trembling. "I am not feeling well."

"You are strong as an ox."

"No." She shook her head. "I am not. Not anymore."

"Tell me the truth, Grandmother."

She was obviously very afraid of whatever it was that she was hiding. Did he really want the truth, after the long night had left him feeling so raw? His heart had taken one beating; it did not need another.

He needed to find the right words. He had to discover the one thing he could say that would move her enough to tell the truth. He had to reach her heart. He glanced over at Janelle, who nodded in encouragement.

Trevor took a deep breath. "Grandmother, whatever you are *not* telling me cannot be as bad as a lie left between us. You are the only mother I have ever known." He looked down at his hand, then forced Adelaide to look him in the eyes. "I love you, Grandmother."

As he spoke the words that were never heard uttered aloud in this house, words as foreign on his tongue as Chinese, he knew he had reached her at last. "Please, if you love *me* at all, tell me the truth," he urged.

"The truth will ruin you," she whispered.

"Let me be the judge of that."

She closed her eyes and spoke in such a low voice that he could barely hear her.

"When your father was very young, barely eighteen, he had an affair with one of our upstairs maids. When she became pregnant by him, he moved her into a room of her own somewhere in London. She had the child, but could not afford to even feed the newborn on her own. She gave him up, into my care."

"Me," Trevor whispered.

He looked down at the twin combs in his hands, thinking of all the times he had tried to picture his mother, the Italian aristocrat. The beautiful, dark-eyed, exotic woman was nothing more than a figment of his imagination, a fabrication his father had invented for him. He could barely swallow.

Adelaide drew a ragged breath. "James found a position for your mother as housekeeper for the Oateses. He felt obligated to place her with his friends. Even though she had sworn never to contact you or tell anyone about you, I was terrified that somehow, someday, you would find out, or worse yet, that someone else would discover that you were the son of a servant and use it against you."

Trevor traced the *C* with his thumb. "Clara Hayworth. Clara Penn. She kept her bargain."

"Yes, apparently." Adelaide turned to Janelle. "She worked for your mother, Stephanie Oates. It was Clara who handed you over to James the night you were born."

"And then she stole my sister," Janelle whispered.

Adelaide nodded. "Clara disappeared that night. We never knew where she went or why. I tried to discourage James, but he scoured London for her. Of course, I was relieved that he never found her, but always, *always* I feared that she would come forward one day and try to ruin us. Thus my aversion to Joya. At first I was afraid Joya knew that Clara was your mother. As time went by, it became apparent that if the girl did know, she was not telling Trevor. I feared that she or her father might use the information against us somehow."

Trevor thought of the day he had stood over Clara Penn's grave on Matarenga and wondered how a house-keeper could have had the nerve to steal someone's child. He had looked down upon his own mother's grave and condemned the very woman who had given him up to save him from starvation.

Then Clara had taken Joya to raise and love as her own. She taught Joya everything about life and love that *he* should have learned from her. He knew of honor and loyalty to a business and a family name. He knew how to make money. But what did he know of the kind of love his mother had for him? The kind that Joya had offered him?

Janelle was wiping tears off her cheeks. "Do you think Dustin Penn has any idea?"

Trevor shrugged. "I don't know."

"I need to lie down," Adelaide said, pushing away from the table.

Of course, Trevor thought. His grandmother would try to avoid any more of such an emotional scene at all costs.

Placing one hand on the table to steady herself, Adelaide looked up at him. Her lower lip trembled. "I cared more for you than I ever cared for my own son. I hope someday you will understand and forgive me."

Before he could respond, his grandmother pushed away from the table and stood up. She took three steps in the direction of the door and collapsed in a heap on the breakfast room floor.

Two hours later, Janelle slipped out of Adelaide's room and found Trevor sound asleep on a chair in the hall outside the bedroom door. Gently, she touched his shoulder. He immediately awakened and rubbed his tired, bloodshot eyes.

"How is she?"

"Not good. The doctor says she had an apoplectic fit. Even if she lives, she will never fully recover."

He rested his elbows on his knees, propping his forehead on his hands. "I caused this."

"You cannot blame yourself, Trevor. The doctor said that she has been failing for a long time. I just thank God that she told you the truth before this happened. If Dustin Penn doesn't know that you were Clara's son, then Grandmama would have taken the truth to her grave."

The doctor, a thin young man who appeared far too fresh-faced to be credible, stepped out of Adelaide's room and closed the door silently behind him. He nodded as Trevor stood and introduced himself.

"Mr. Mandeville, has your sister given you my prognosis?"

"She has."

"I don't expect your grandmother to survive."

"How long does she have?"

"That's hard to say. I've made her comfortable and given instructions to your housekeeper. If you'll excuse me, I have to leave now, but I will try to come back later this afternoon. I can see myself out." He bowed politely and made his way down the hall.

Janelle put her hand on Trevor's sleeve. "You look exhausted. I want my sister back, too, but you won't find her if you kill yourself trying."

She was waiting for Trevor to respond when the sound of voices raised in argument echoed up the stairwell.

"What now?" Trevor was already hurrying down the hall.

Janelle ran after him, her heart pounding, for she recognized Garr's voice above the others. By the time they reached the foyer, Joshua, the coachman, was nursing a bleeding lip. Cook was brandishing a rolling pin and Sims was waving the ancient Saxon sword over his head. The three of them had Garr pinned against the wall.

"What's going on here?" Trevor demanded. "Sims, put that sword down before you kill Cook with it. Joshua, take Cook back to the kitchen. I can handle this."

"He's a madman, sir," Sims warned. "The scoundrel brought your sister home at quite a shameful hour this morning. Now he demands to speak to you."

Janelle was tempted to grab Cook's rolling pin and clobber Sims for his revelation and then bash Garr for showing up. Before she could say or do anything, Trevor was closing in on Garr.

"You had better explain yourself, sir, or I'll unleash all of them on you after I've finished with you myself." Trevor was already shrugging out of his rumpled jacket.

Janelle grabbed his arm. "Please, don't hit him, Trevor. If anyone deserves the honor, it should be me."

"I would prefer we all sit down and discuss everything in private," Garr suggested.

"Five minutes," Trevor snapped.

Janelle had never seen her brother so unhinged when he said, "Show him into the drawing room. Now."

She hurried Garr through the doors and showed him to the settee, but he would not sit.

"What are you doing here?" she whispered frantically, while Trevor calmed the servants lingering in the foyer.

"I came to make things right."

"I will not marry you, even if Trevor tries to march us to the altar. I refuse."

He reached for her. She took a step back and held up her hands. "Stop it, Garr. Don't touch me."

"I want you, Janelle. I love you."

"You do not even *know* me."

"I know what I want and I know that you want me."

She crossed her arms and tried to deny the truth. "Oh, that's a fine basis for a marriage. I have seen what happens to a union founded on desire. My sister ran away last night."

"Our marriage will be different," Garr countered.

Trevor chose that moment to walk in. When he slammed the door, Janelle winced. Perhaps Garr would not sit down, but she could no longer stand. Her knees were wobbling.

Trevor was in a fine fury. He bore down on Garr, who surprisingly, was not cowed.

"Isn't it enough that our grandmother is upstairs dying, that my wife has run away, or that you have dishonored my sister's name, Remington? How dare you have the nerve to show up here unannounced, demanding to speak to me when you should be running for your life?"

"I'm not a coward. All I ask is that you both hear me out." Garr spoke in a low, evenly measured tone that only seemed to rile Trevor.

Trevor ran his hand through his wild, matted hair and sighed. "Four minutes."

"I have come to ask for your sister's hand."

"No!" Janelle was on her feet, looking from one to the other.

"Obviously she objects," Trevor said. "And so do I. Good-bye, Mr. Remington. I'm sure that Sims is loitering in the foyer, waiting to see you to the door."

"We spent the night alone in a carriage. Your servants all know now that I delivered her home early this morning. Doesn't her good name mean anything to you?"

"Of course it does. That's why I wouldn't let her marry you, even if you were the last man on earth and she got down on her knees and begged me. You are down to two minutes, Remington. Give up and leave."

"I only have two things left to say."

"One minute each, then."

Janelle clasped her hands and closed her eyes. Surely Garr would not tell Trevor what had passed between them in the carriage. Surely he would not be so cruel.

"First, I am far from impoverished. Secondly, I am in love with your sister."

Janelle shook her head. Impossible. All of it.

"What are you saying?" Trevor demanded.

"It's true that I came to London to find a wife. Whether she was rich or not, it did not matter to me. I have recently inherited not only a title, but a very sizable estate from a distant cousin in Cornwall. The only stipulation in his will was that I marry and beget heirs so as not to end up childless as he did. Viscount Arthur and Lady Cecily both agreed to keep the truth a secret and helped me fabricate the story that I was penniless in order to save me from any fortune-hunting young misses and their families."

Trevor shook his head as if to clear it. "You are saying you are wealthy *and* titled?"

Garr spread his hands and shrugged. "There are far worse fates. I am also an incurable romantic." He turned to Janelle. "I told Lady Cecily and my uncle that I was not going to marry anyone unless I loved her and she loved me. My future wife had to take me without money and overlook my soiled reputation. I wanted to marry a woman who loved me despite any shortcomings, real or imagined.

"I did not plan last night's little escapade, Janelle, but I am not unhappy it happened. Now I know that you love me, even if you won't admit it to yourself or your brother. Will you marry me?"

"Well, Janelle?" Trevor glared, impatiently awaiting an answer.

She looked over at Garr, who was smiling his devastatingly handsome smile, looking every inch the scoundrel that he supposedly was not.

"Life with me will never be boring, darling," he promised.

She crossed her arms. "What about my art?"

"There is a wonderful end room on the upper floor of the manor house with windows on three sides. It would make a perfect studio."

"I am a free thinker, you know. I will not be molded or tempered into a simpering, acquiescent little wife."

"The very idea gives me indigestion." He sat on the settee beside her. Only a few inches separated them.

"I will want to attend salons at Cecily's," she warned.

He lowered his voice to a more intimate level. "Whenever we are in town, I would expect you to do so."

"My grandmother is dying. I must be here for her."

"As well you should be." Garr reached up and brushed a lock of hair off the corner of the lens of her spectacles. "Family is important."

"And there is Joya, too. She has run off to Africa." She was staring at his mouth, fascinated with his smile, remembering the way his lips tasted.

"I have always wanted to see the world," he whispered.

From behind them, Janelle heard Trevor say, "I'm leaving, but I'm ordering Sims to come in here brandishing that old sword in three minutes, no more, no less."

As soon as the door closed behind him, Janelle leaned into Garr's embrace.

"Three minutes is not very much time," she warned him.

As he lowered his lips to hers he whispered, "I am counting on a lifetime."

Chapter 27

Joya, her father, and half a dozen bearers had been living at the orchid camp for two weeks when two more of the men from the village arrived with replacement supplies and a packet for her father. She asked if there were any letters for her. He frowned, then looked away and shook his head.

"Damn it, girl. I'm sick to death of your asking if Mandeville has written. It is time you either went back to him or let me write and tell him to take steps to divorce you."

When she first returned, her father had fully explained the English meaning of divorce. Matarengi banishment meant that she and Trevor simply lived apart forever. Divorced, their marriage would be forever severed according to the English laws, cast off as if it never was. That was a stark reality she could not yet face, even though she was certain that she would never go back.

She was torn between being thankful and feeling hurt

that neither Trevor nor Janelle had written. Anything they had to say would surely break her heart.

She wiped the sweat off her forehead, adjusted the *pudong* tied around her waist, and watched billowing white clouds scud across a crisp blue sky. Since she had come back to the island she had never been as happy or as miserable in her life. What she had almost become in London was not as easy to strip away as English gowns and petticoats.

As loath as she was to admit it, she had been forever changed by her experiences in England. Although she still loved Matarenga and its people and was more than comfortable here, she feared she would never be as free nor as innocent as before she left.

She missed Trevor and Janelle desperately and even Sims and the other servants. But during a few brief, shining moments of each day, when the island soothed her with its incredible peace, she was convinced she had made the right decision. That was enough for now.

"What are you afraid of?" He scratched behind his ear and adjusted one of the gold rings in his earlobe.

"Nothing. Everything." *Of severing all ties to Trevor forever.*

"I've never seen you run from anything in your life, girl. I can still remember when you were no higher than my knee and Umbaba and some of the others dared you to jump over the falls. You did not even hesitate to go flying off the edge of the cliff into the pool below."

"You made me stay out of the water for three days."

"You scared years off my life."

"We never told Mama." She smiled with the memory of their secret.

"You still love him, don't you?"

"Yes." Closing her eyes, she tried to picture Trevor's

face and remember the sound of his voice. Even Matarenga could not protect her from her own memories.

"I am going upriver," she told her father. "Where you found the epidendrum yesterday. There are hours of daylight left."

"It's the best specimen I've come up with in weeks. I'm thinking of sending it on to Mandeville. Maybe he'll consider it for the queen's orchid." Then he sighed and rubbed his hand over his eyes. "I don't know why I should bother. I ought to go back and murder the man for what he did to you."

"Trevor did not do anything, Papa. I have tried to explain that to you. We were not meant to be together, that's all."

The orchid her father had found most recently was definitely lovely. Perhaps, if Trevor had found nothing compared to it in Venezuela, he could present the Matarengan find to the queen and make amends.

"I will return before dark," she promised in Matarengi.

Joya did not care to dwell on Queen Victoria, or the night she had made a fool of herself in Her Majesty's presence. She waved to her father and signaled a halt to Umbaba when he started to follow her. She needed time to herself and started down the trail alone.

A few miles from camp, she paused on the bank of the Terurai River. The water was stained by mud carried down from upstream, where rain clouds covered Kibatante's mountain peak.

She swatted at a pesky mosquito on her thigh, wiped the back of her arm across her forehead, and watched tree branches and coconuts bob their way down to the lagoon. A flash of white on one particular log riding the current caught her eye. As the rough-barked trunk floated closer, her excitement mounted. Unless she was mistaken, three huge orchid blossoms were blooming on a plant attached to the tree.

She speared her heavy machete into the ground before she waded into the water. As the tree trunk floated nearer, she became convinced the blooms were the finest and some of the largest she had ever seen, and well worth the effort it would take to recover them.

She stretched and dove beneath the surface of the river and began swimming with strong, sure strokes toward the log.

LONDON
A few weeks later . . .

"Sign here, Mandeville. Here. And here." Lord Howard's solicitor dipped the nib of a pen into an ink pot and handed it to Trevor, who nodded in understanding. "Lord Howard instructed me to tell you that we are most happy you changed your mind and decided to sell. We plan to take possession of the warehouse in a week. Will that give you enough time to have your personal things moved?"

Trevor nodded and glanced around the office. The sale agreements lay on his great-great-grandfather's desk. He looked down at the scarred wood used by generations of Mandevilles and, oddly enough, felt not a shred of remorse. In fact, for the first time in his life, he found himself excited by the prospect of the future.

The last of the documents was signed when one of his stevedores poked his head around the edge of the open door.

"Sorry to interrupt, but a shipment from Matarenga

just arrived, sir. Ye said ye wanted t' know the minute one ever came in."

"Thank you, Bart." Trevor laid the pen down, blotted the last of his signatures, and then handed the page over to the solicitor. "If that's all for now, I have pressing business on the dock."

The solicitor stood, tugging on the hem of his coat. "In two weeks, the amount agreed upon will be transferred into your account."

"I don't need to be here?"

"No, Mr. Mandeville, you do not. If you don't mind my asking, what are you going to do now that you will no longer be working?"

Trevor looked through the open door, out toward the shipping bay where loaded wagons arrived full and left empty. There was a shipment from Matarenga on the dock. He prayed that it would contain a letter from Joya, or at the very least her father, for there had been no word from her since the night she disappeared.

Had she even received any of the letters he and Janelle had written? If not, she had no way of knowing that Adelaide had fallen ill and had died two weeks later.

Letters be damned. His greatest fear was that perhaps Joya had never safely returned to Matarenga at all.

"Mr. Mandeville?"

Trevor remembered he was not alone. "What did you ask?"

"What are you going to do now?"

"I am going to do something I have long wanted to do. I am going to hunt orchids." *And my wife.*

The crate, stained with watermarks and muddy handprints, had been set off to one side of the loading bay. He could imagine Joya supervising the packing and

Penn's bearers carrying it over the mountain trail and across the beach to the sailing canoes.

Bart handed him a hammer to pry up the lid. Trevor noticed his own hands were shaking.

"Orchids?" His new accountant came strolling over with a handful of bills of lading. Trevor was tempted to tell all the men gathered around to go away and leave him alone. They were intruding upon a private moment.

What a pitiful creature he had become, coveting the arrival of a crate, but it was all he had of Joya now.

He took off the lid. Even touching the dried husks and moss seemed part of an intimate ritual that he should be undertaking alone.

"Just orchids," Trevor said, chastising himself for his fantasies.

"Do you think it's the one you have been waiting for?" Bart asked. Trevor looked up. Three more men were hovering nearby. Everyone at the warehouse had been waiting for Penn to find an orchid that would win Prince Albert's competition. They all hoped to play a part, no matter how small, in the discovery of the queen's orchid.

Excitement mounted as Trevor pulled out the last of the husk material then carefully lifted a piece of burlap wrapped around the first plant. Once the material was folded back, the others crowded in.

A *Phalaenopis*, it was a bicolor plant with a spray of blossoms, each one as huge as a man's hand, each one gold in the center tapering to the purest ivory at its ruffled edges. It was indeed an orchid worthy of a queen's name.

"There is a letter here, sir." His accountant reached into the crate.

"Do you think that could really be it, sir? The queen's orchid?" One of the young men asked.

"It's a wonderful find," Trevor admitted. "The loveliest I've ever seen."

The accountant handed him the folded letter. When Trevor recognized the uneven script, his heart jumped. He refused to read it in front of the others. He had no inkling how he would react to whatever Joya might have written.

Balancing the orchid in one hand and the letter in the other, he told them, "I'm going to keep this orchid under lock and key."

Unable to wait, he went straight to his office, pulled out the chair, and sat down at Great-Great-Grandfather Mandeville's desk. He carefully put the blooming orchid aside and opened the letter.

Relief swept through him when he saw the brief, unsigned note in Joya's childish hand. She was safe.

Dearest Trevor,
   This one is fit for a queen. I hope that it brings you everything you desire. Tell Janelle that I miss her and that I love her.
   J.

When the letters blurred and ran together, he laid the letter aside and picked up the gold and ivory orchid. All he could think of was his own bright, precious flower, one he had possessed for such a short time. Throughout the weeks that Adelaide hovered near death, Trevor had spent his days putting together the sale that would rid him of his responsibilities to the Mandeville holdings. He spent his nights missing his wife.

Despite the fact that Janelle had married Garr Remington and they had taken up residence at Mandeville House until everything was settled, the house had become nothing more than a tomb for him. He felt like a man who had never seen the sun and so he did not miss it—until Joya left and took the sunlight with her. He found himself thinking about her and wondering how he had ever existed without her.

He lifted the orchid. That it had a heady fragrance made it even more precious. Unwilling to leave it unguarded, he rewrapped it carefully in the burlap to keep the plant from freezing as he made his way home across London.

"This is all she wrote?" Janelle turned her sister's letter over in her hand and wished there had been more. Upon his return, Trevor had come directly to her studio to show her the beautiful orchid that even she could appreciate—and Joya's note.

For months she had waited for some word from her sister in answer to her own letters. Every time Trevor had written to her, Janelle had included a letter of her own in the packet.

"Are you crying?" Trevor moved closer and put his arm around her.

"Oh, Trevor. I was convinced she hated me. If I had only been here to take her place at the reception, if I had only spent more time with her instead of being so wrapped up in my own little world, then she might still be here with us."

He sighed and walked across the room. "I have tortured myself with 'if only', too. I never realized how much she meant to me until it was too late."

"There is so much I still want to share with her, Trevor." Not the least of which was news of Adelaide's death, and the announcement of her own hasty yet completely wonderful marriage to Garr.

Joya was suffering, of that Janelle was certain, but she was hesitant to tell Trevor of her unfounded intuition. If he did believe her, he would only torture himself with worry. Until he had rid himself of Mandeville Imports and the rest of his responsibilities here, there was no way he could go after Joya.

Although her own future with Garr and their good fortune seemed assured, a continual sadness inhabited her heart.

"The fire has gone out. It's freezing up here." Trevor looked over at the small coal stove in the corner of the room. The skylights in the ceiling were covered with snow, the glass a thin protection from the cold.

"Garr should be home from his uncle's soon. I was just going downstairs for tea."

Before they reached the second floor, Garr met them on the stairs. Unmindful of Trevor, he greeted her with a kiss and then asked, "What's wrong, darling?"

"Trevor has received a letter from Joya. She is on Matarenga, which is a relief, but she did not mention having received any of our letters. And she sent a wonderful orchid."

"At least now you know she reached the island safely. Oh, before I forget, there is a footman in royal livery in the foyer. It seems he has a letter for you, Trevor, and since he was commanded to wait for a reply, Sims has him sequestered on a chair and is standing sentry over him."

•   •   •

For the second time in his life, Trevor was ushered into Queen Victoria's presence, this time for a private interview. He had been commanded to bring the orchid with him and realized the instant he had read the queen's summons that news of its arrival had certainly traveled fast.

"Mr. Mandeville," the queen said, "thank you for coming. We must say that you appear a bit surprised to be here again."

He nodded. "I am, Your Majesty. The orchid arrived not three hours ago."

"You are wondering how We heard of it?"

"To be honest, yes, Your Majesty."

She smiled. "There are no secrets in England, most especially where something to do with Us is concerned. Now, let Us see this precious bloom."

Trevor carefully unwrapped the orchid and held it out so that Victoria might view the wonderful cattleya.

"Have you named it?" she asked expectantly.

"I have, Your Majesty." What he was about to do would cost him a royal appointment and perhaps the Queen's censure, but his heart had been dictating to him ever since he set eyes on the orchid.

"I have named it for my wife, Your Majesty."

The queen frowned, pursed her lips, and sat in thoughtful silence as Trevor counted his heartbeats. Then, slowly, her expression changed and she smiled.

"Your lovely island girl. How does she fare?"

"Your Majesty, I honestly do not know. She went home to Africa weeks ago."

The queen looked enviously at the orchid in his hands, touched the ruffled petals with her fingertip. Then she looked into his eyes.

"We are a bit disappointed, and I'm certain the prince will be, too, but there will always be more orchids. Your wife is a rare treasure. Go after her, Mandeville. Do not let her get away."

Chapter 28

Through hand signs, the Matarengi on the beach made it known to Trevor that Joya and her father were at the orchid camp. He wasted no time starting out after them.

As anxious as he was to see his wife again, the beauty of the island often distracted him. Each time he rounded another bend in the road or reached the top of a rise, he stopped to take in the panoramic views of the turquoise lagoon, the waves breaking on the outer reef, the sunset on the far horizon.

During one such stop, Trevor closed his eyes, took a deep breath and made a swift and silent prayer for his grandmother, hoping that she was at peace, hoping she knew he had forgiven her. Then he shouldered his pack and moved on.

The afternoon of his second day on the trail, at a point where he could see the river rushing through an open section of bottom land in the valley below, the lilting sound of Joya's laughter floated to him on the Kusi trades. At first he thought he was hallucinating. He let the sound infuse him and sing through every pore.

He pictured Joya as he had first seen her, with her blond hair a wild halo about her head, her skin sun-kissed and glowing, so vibrant, so free, so much a part of the island.

She laughed again, calling out in Matarengi. He took up his machete and hacked his way through the thick undergrowth, cutting away fronds from giant tree ferns and tall stems of yellow ginger.

He stopped when a flash of ivory in the trees caught his eye. Sheathing his machete, Trevor gazed through the jungle growth. What he saw almost stopped his heart. A few yards away, Joya was up a towering acacia tree, perched on a thin limb, stretching to reach an orchid. Umbaba waited at the base of the tree, ready to break her fall.

Trevor made his presence known, waved at the younger man, and then held a finger to his lips. Thankfully, Umbaba did nothing to alert Joya, but the look he gave Trevor was not welcoming.

Trevor doubted the man held any regard for him, especially if Joya had told her friend all she had been through in England. He tried smiling. Umbaba glared but did not give him away.

Up in the branches of the tree, Joya chatted away, climbing ever higher. When Trevor saw how far she had gone, he almost forgot to breathe. One false step and she would break her lovely neck.

He set down his pack and his rifle and, quickly signing his intention, convinced Umbaba to step back, then took the man's place beneath the tree. Concentrating on the orchids, Joya never looked down.

With his heart in his throat, Trevor watched her pry

off three plants and drop them into a burlap bag at her waist. Satisfied with her prize, she began the climb down.

Umbaba called to her, directing her descent. Joya felt around with her feet, choosing footholds as she worked her way down, using staggered limbs as steps. He had no sooner decided she was actually going to make it safely to the ground when she gave a short, high-pitched squeal and came flying through a series of limbs that gave beneath her weight.

She landed in Trevor's arms with enough force to knock him off his feet, but he cradled her so that she suffered no injury when they hit the ground in a tangle of arms and legs, burlap and crushed specimens.

Stunned, she looked up at Umbaba. When she realized that someone else had caught her, she whipped around and recognized Trevor. She gasped and jumped to her feet, her first words to him in Matarengi. Then she shook her head, as if to clear it.

"What are you doing here?" she cried.

"I am here under royal orders from the queen."

"The queen sent you? Did she like the orchid? Did she send you back for more?" She adjusted the faded trousers tied low around her hips and brushed her hair out of her eyes.

"She loved the orchid. She also told me that you are a rare treasure and that I should not let you get away. She told me to go after you."

"Is that why you came? Because of an obligation to the queen?"

He tried to pull her into his arms, but she stepped out of his reach.

"I came after you because I want my wife back. My first wife. My *only* wife."

"But I was a terrible English wife."

"I don't want an English wife. I want you." He indicated Umbaba with a nod. "Can you ask him to go back to camp?"

She was staring into his eyes the way she had on the day he had saved her from Roth, as if he had hung the moon and all the stars. She spoke to Umbaba and after a long, heated conversation, the native finally left.

"You were about to tell me why you want me back instead of looking for a proper English wife," she reminded him.

Trevor was desperate to hold her in his arms. "I prefer not to shout," he said, lowering his voice. "You'll have to step closer."

He held his breath until she moved close enough for him to take into his arms. When he felt her arms slip around him in return, he tightened the embrace. Tenderly, he kissed the crown of her head.

She was alluring, totally captivating even though dressed in nothing more than what he had found her in before—mud-stained, ragged trousers that came up to her shins, and a thin, time-worn linen shirt knotted over her midriff. He smoothed his hand over her slim waist, traced the swell of her hip, and kissed her fully.

Now that he had her in his arms again, everything else he had come to say could wait, save one.

"I love you, Joya. I need you in my life forever."

In disbelief, she leaned back in his arms so that she could look into his eyes.

"Are you certain, Trevor?" Had he at last come to believe in something he could not see, something he could not classify, or order, or categorize?

"I am very sure. I love you and from now on I plan

to tell you so many times a day that you will beg me to stop. I want you beside me. Always. My life was so empty without you that I saw no reason for what I was doing anymore. There was no purpose to those long hours of work. Money meant nothing compared to you. The night you left I searched for you and when I couldn't find you, I was like a madman. I felt things I never thought I was capable of feeling. I was lost, and I've been lost, and will be until you tell me you will come back to me."

She searched his eyes and saw the truth in them. Blinded by tears, she went up on tiptoe and brought her lips to his. It felt so good, so very right to have his arms around her again.

She loved him desperately and knew she always would, but still she found herself wondering . . . *at what cost*? She took a deep breath. There was no denying her love for him, but she did not think she could ever endure what had happened to her in London again.

"I cannot go back with you, Trevor," she whispered. "Even though I love you with all my heart, I cannot live in London."

He smoothed back her hair, kissed her cheek, her eyelids, the tip of her nose.

"You won't have to live in London. But wouldn't you consider a few visits to see your sister?"

Janelle. That part of herself that she had sought for so long, only to lose her again.

"How is she?"

"Well and happy, but missing you terribly. Obviously you didn't get our letters."

"*What* letters?"

"I sent you letters and so did Janelle. Your sister wrote to you nearly every week."

She thought of the expression she had seen on her father's face whenever she had asked whether there had been any letters for her, and found that she was more hurt than angry that he had deceived her again.

"Papa must have kept them," she realized with a shake of her head. "But what of Mandeville Imports, Trevor? How can you manage your family's business if you are not in London?" The hope that had quickly blossomed began to fade. What kind of a reaction would Adelaide have to a reconciliation between them? "And what does your grandmother think of your coming after me?"

"I have sold Mandeville Imports and all the rest of it." Before she could respond, his handsome features darkened and his eyes were shadowed with sadness. "Grandmother had a stroke the day after you left. She died two weeks later."

"Oh, Trevor, I know you loved her. Could it have been my fault? I thought she would be so pleased by my leaving."

"You aren't in any way responsible. The doctor told us she had been failing for a long time. She was too stubborn to let it show. There is much to explain, much more to tell you, but right now, all I want is you."

She could not resist him any more than she ever could. She gave in to some very persuasive, long, hot kisses, sighing when he slipped his hand beneath her shirt and grazed the curve of her breast with his fingertips. He began to nuzzle her cheek and whisper in her ear.

"What would you say if I suggested that we make love beneath that acacia tree over there?"

Trevor was certain his lovely little wife was just about to acquiesce, for she was eyeing the ground below the tree, when suddenly a twig snapped behind them and Dustin Penn's voice rang out.

"Take your bloody hands off my daughter, Mandeville."

Trevor heard Joya sigh, "Papa."

It was, indeed, her papa, and he did not sound any more welcoming than he had the first time Trevor saw him.

"I mean it, Mandeville, get your hands off her and step away."

Joya pulled out of his embrace. Before Trevor was able to turn around she snapped, "Oh, Papa, put down that gun, for heaven's sake. Do you honestly think I would let you shoot Trevor?"

Dustin Penn chose to ignore her.

"Hands up, Mandeville, and turn around slowly."

"Penn, have you lost your mind? She's still my wife."

"Not here she's not. She banished herself."

"Papa, I've changed my mind. I want to be *un-banished*."

Trevor winced. *Un-banished?* He slowly turned with his hands in the air. Not only was Dustin Penn holding a gun on him, but they were surrounded by a host of Matarengi bearers armed with spears and shields.

"I'm sure we can sit down and talk this over like reasonable men."

"I strive never to be reasonable *or* normal, Mandeville, so don't insult me."

Suspecting that Penn enjoyed playing the role of great white hunter, Trevor decided to hold his temper and humor him. The situation was ridiculous. He would be damned if he took the orchid hunter or his threats seriously.

"You hurt my girl, Mandeville." Dustin Penn kept the gun trained on him as Joya walked over to his side. "Now you will have to pay the price."

"Papa, please. Put down that gun. It doesn't matter that I'm not a good English wife. Trevor doesn't care."

"I *never* cared about that," Trevor added quickly. "Don't tug on his arm, Joya. Not while he's got that rifle pointed at me."

"Where did she get the notion she wasn't good enough?" Penn held firm and ignored Joya the way he might a pesky fly. The gun never wavered.

"From my grandmother, unfortunately. I had no idea that she wanted Joya out of my life so desperately. She did everything she could to make Joya feel insecure, for a reason that made sense only to Grandmother until the night Joya left and the truth was finally revealed. Don't shoot me, Penn. I want to show you something." Trevor slowly reached into his pocket. "These will help me explain—" He pulled out the matching silver combs and held them in the palm of his hand.

"Mama's comb?" Joya walked away from her father, concentrating on the identical silver pieces in Trevor's hand. "Why, there are two of them!"

"That's right," Trevor said, handing them both to Joya.

"They are just alike, Papa, except that one is not as tarnished." She turned them over and over.

Penn finally lowered the gun. "What are you up to, Mandeville?"

"I am hot and I am hungry and I am trying to win my wife back, Penn. Do you think we could go to your camp where I can sit down and explain?"

• • •

This is the way it should be. This is where he belongs.

Back in the orchid camp, Joya watched Trevor accept water from one of the men. She could not take her eyes off him. *This is the way he should always be*, she thought over and over. Gone were his somber dark clothes, his shining waistcoat, his stiff collar and tall beaver hat. Gone was the preoccupation that had never left his eyes in London. He was dressed in his khaki clothes, sun helmet, leather gaiters, and muddy boots. Here he was vibrantly alive, free of the heavy responsibility he had shouldered as the heir to the Mandeville business fortune.

She decided that he actually enjoyed sparring with her father. There was not only a twinkle in Trevor's eye, but a smile hovering about his delicious mouth.

"You were about to explain something to me, Mandeville, so I'll thank you to quit staring at my daughter and start talking."

Joya could not believe her eyes when Trevor actually winked at her. Then, in an instant, his smile faded. He held out his hand for the combs. She gave them over to him, as curious as her father was about what he was going to say.

"It was a stroke of luck when Joya left me this comb the night she ran away," he told them. "If she had not, I would never have known that Clara Hayworth was my mother."

Penn came up off his camp stool to stand over Trevor. His frown was fierce. Doubt and suspicion filled his eyes.

"What are you saying? How dare you make such a claim?"

"So you *didn't* know."

"Know what?"

"That Clara Hayworth Penn, your wife, was *my* mother."

Joya gasped.

"Don't be ridiculous," her father yelled. "How could she have been your mother? Your father was James Mandeville. My Clara was only a housekeeper for the Oateses." He sank back down onto the stool, slapped his hands on his thighs, and shook his head.

Joya grabbed her amulet pouch. It had felt so empty since she had given Trevor the comb. Afterward, she had sorely regretted leaving the memento behind.

Was he telling her now, that because of that comb he had discovered that Clara, the woman she thought of as her mother, had given him life? She shook her head and whispered, "How could that be?"

She listened while he told them everything Adelaide had related to him the morning after he had found the second comb. She tried to imagine her mother being wooed by James Mandeville, then having to live in shame in a shabby room somewhere in London. She pictured Clara starving, fearing for Trevor's life if she did not give him up to Adelaide and James.

Trevor did not look at her until the end of his tale and then he said, "I swore to myself that I'd never make you cry again—and now I have already broken that vow."

He turned to her father, who was still sitting in stunned silence. Trevor said, "Shoot me if you must, Penn, but I'm going to hold my wife."

"Why is it every time you come to this island, you upset our world with some revelation from the past?" Her papa rubbed his eyes. "Clara never even told *me* she had worked for Mandeville, let alone that she had a son by him. It appears that she kept her promise to your grandmother and took the secret to her grave."

Joya let Trevor enfold her in his warm embrace, knowing his loss was far greater than hers. He would never, ever know what a truly wonderful mother Clara had been.

Each lost in their own thoughts, they fell silent until Joya suddenly remembered all the letters she had never received.

"Why did you keep Trevor's and Janelle's letters from me, Papa?"

Her father never flinched. Nor did he even try to deny any wrong. "I would do it again," he said almost proudly. "I was determined not to let them hurt you any more, girl. At least not here, on *my* island, where I have a say about it."

"You'll never change, will you Papa?" She knew he had acted out of love. He had only tried, in his own way, to shield her from the pain of missing Janelle, of what Trevor's letters might have done to her. Just as Clara had done that by agreeing never to tell Trevor that she was his mother, hoping to save him from humiliation and shame.

How often, she wondered, are family secrets kept, how often are the wrong choices made, all in the name of love? Her father had been wrong, but stubborn defiance remained in his eyes.

"You were very lucky this time, Papa," she told him, "that things have worked out between us."

"Someday, Mandeville," he told Trevor, "when you have a daughter, you'll understand why I did it. You will be willing to do anything to assure her happiness."

"I won't forget this, Penn. If I am lucky enough to ever have a daughter, remembering what you've done might help me be a little more understanding and a little less of a tyrant."

Her father obviously knew he was in the wrong, for he held his temper and tried to change the subject. "So the orchid Joya found pleased the queen, did it?"

"*Joya* found it?" Trevor frowned.

"She damn near drowned taking it off a log in the middle of the river. I thought it the finest I've ever seen." Her father was beaming with pride at her accomplishment. "Did you receive the royal appointment? Should we be calling you Sir Mandeville? Or Lord Something-or-other?"

"Neither," Trevor said, but he was smiling.

Joya was crestfallen. If the queen had not granted him an appointment, even though she thought the orchid stunning, then it had to have been because of her social blunder.

"Oh, Trevor, I'm so sorry."

He quickly reassured her that the queen had actually found her charming the night of the reception, then he related the story of his second private audience with Victoria.

"The queen loved the orchid, and Prince Albert accepted it for the exhibition. He was upset that I did not name it for the queen, for it was the loveliest orchid anyone has ever seen. There was only one person in the world I could have named it for. I call it *Phalaenopsis joyata.*"

"You gave up a royal appointment to name it for me?"

"I would give my life for you, Joya."

She could barely see him through the tears in her eyes. Despite the fact that her father was watching, that she was a banished wife, that she would never, ever be an English lady, she kissed Trevor.

When the kiss ended on a sigh and a promise, he told

her, "There is nothing I wouldn't do for you, Joya. Nothing I wouldn't give up to have you, for you mean more to me than anything in the world." He cupped her cheek, smiled down into her eyes, and added softly, "I have another surprise."

"Haven't you said *enough*?" her father grumbled.

Ignoring him, Trevor smiled secretively. "Janelle is waiting for us at the beach house."

"Janelle is *here*? On Matarenga?" She hugged him tight. "Janelle is truly here? Oh, we must go back! There are still a few hours of daylight left—"

"Not enough," Trevor said.

"We've got to pack up our shipment first. We can leave in the morning," her father added.

She stared at them both as if they had lost their minds.

"But *Janelle* is here. She's waiting for me."

"We can't leave until dawn, Joya," her father said.

"He's right," Trevor added.

She looked from one to another. "I liked it better when you two did not agree." Then she told Trevor, "You can put your pack in my tent."

"Don't think you are going to sleep with him tonight, either," her father added, eyeing his rifle.

"Papa! He's still my husband."

"Not according to Matarengi law. You have banished yourself and told the whole village. You are on Matarenga, so you must respect the Matarengi custom. I don't have any idea if there's a precedent for reversing a banishment."

"Why does the world have to be so full of rules? It is simply not fair," she argued.

"You are the one who banished herself," her father reminded her.

Trevor obviously was not happy, either.

"Do something," she urged.

He turned, took one look at her father and shrugged. "As he said earlier, it's his island."

Chapter 29

It was, indeed, her father's island.

As the hunting party journeyed home the next day, Joya noticed he had been acting very mysteriously. That morning her father had sent a runner ahead with a note to her sister to let her know that they would be back by sundown. All day long he had been far too jovial, continually whistling and smiling.

She wished Trevor were as happy. He had been in a black mood since last night when her father had adamantly refused to let them share a tent. He would, he promised, consult with Faruki, the high chief, to see if anything could be done to remedy her self-proclaimed banishment.

Trevor had told him he was being ridiculous, that once they were off the island, he could take his rules and do something unmentionable with them, but her father could not be moved. He argued that to go against Matarengi law would show disrespect and insult the natives.

He warned Trevor to be patient until the situation was resolved, *if* it could be resolved.

Just as she had done the last time Trevor journeyed down the mountain with them, Joya felt compelled to watch him all day.

Trevor walked beside her as they came off the hillside trail that ended on the beach. The wind had stopped and the air was thick with humidity. Parrots and monkeys kept to the highest boughs of the trees and taunted them. It was all Joya could do not to run ahead.

"Oh, Trevor, I cannot wait to see Janelle."

"It appears that you will not have to," he said, nodding in the direction of the shoreline.

Unable to contain her excitement, she grabbed his hand and started tugging, urging him to run. "Is that Garr Remington beside her? What is Garr doing here? And is that . . . it can't be . . . is that *Sims*?"

For the first time that day, Trevor actually smiled. There was a secretive sparkle in his eyes.

"I will let your sister tell you why Garr thought he should come along. As for Sims, well, he refused to be left behind. I can see you are about to come out of your skin. Go to meet them."

She kissed him on the cheek and ran down the beach toward her sister, who began waving. Breathless, Joya ran up to Janelle and hugged her so hard she nearly knocked off her sister's spectacles. They were both laughing and crying at the same time. She welcomed the mysterious, innate sense of peace that always flowed through her when she and Janelle were together.

They hugged and cried awhile longer, and then, wiping away her tears, Joya remembered Sims and Garr. She kissed the old retainer on the cheek despite his ob-

vious embarrassment, welcomed him, and thanked him
for coming to Matarenga.

"I have never seen you outdoors, Sims."

"Mandeville House was sold, madam. I've no longer
any foyer in which to lurk."

"You may lurk around our home for as long as you
like, Sims."

"Thank you, madam. And might I add that you have
never looked lovelier?"

"You may say it," she told him, "but I won't believe
it."

"You *are* quite a sight." Garr reminded her she had
not greeted him properly yet. "I'm trying to imagine my
wife in an identical ensemble."

"Please, don't," Janelle laughed.

"Your *wife*?" Shocked, Joya watched them exchange
a very intimate smile. "You two are married?"

He slipped his arm around Janelle's waist. "Very. We
were married shortly after her grandmother died."

"Don't stare so, Joya," Janelle teased, then she leaned
close and whispered, "I did not want you to be the *only*
one of us to experience the heady delights of desire."

"I . . . I don't know what to say." Joya could not stop
staring at all of them. To have them all here on the island
seemed like a wonderful dream.

"Just say congratulations," Trevor advised, "and then
we had best get over to the house. I see your father
talking with the high chief."

"What's wrong, Trevor?" Janelle asked. "You look
terribly angry. Oh, dear!" She quickly turned to Joya.
"You two did make up, didn't you? You must forgive
him, Joya. He truly does love you."

"Yes, I know, and I love him," Joya reached for Trevor's hand. He did, indeed, look very upset as he

watched her father and Faruki with their heads together in the garden. "Papa is upset because I banished myself and it seems that we must appeal to Faruki to make things right again."

"Our marriage is no longer recognized here, it seems," Trevor clarified.

Garr laughed. "*Now* I know why you look so out of sorts."

"I'm certain there is some remedy, sir," Sims commiserated.

"Oh, there's a restorative," Garr laughed, "but it appears my dear brother-in-law is not allowed to get his hands on it at the moment."

Jungle drums pounded frenetically, drowning out the sound of the sea. Torchlight wavered on evening air scented with frangipani and ginger. Trevor's mood had gone from bad to worse all afternoon. Shortly after a riotous evening meal during which everyone insisted on talking at once, Dustin Penn had asked Joya to accompany him to Faruki's *fadu* to plead her case for reversing her banishment. Janelle went with them.

Now, alone with Garr and Sims, Trevor was growing more and more impatient for them to return.

"You do not take well to commands, I see," Garr quipped.

Trevor rubbed the back of his neck. "No. I don't. This whole thing is utterly ridiculous."

"No doubt," Sims said sagely, "as ridiculous as some of our customs must have seemed to your wife, sir."

"No doubt," he admitted. "What do you think they are doing out there?" he asked no one in particular.

"Quite a party from the sound of it." Garr walked to the window and stared at the black, shimmering sea and the star-filled sky above it. "Here comes Penn. And he's alone. What do you suppose he's done with *my* wife?"

Trevor assured him, "There's no need for *you* to worry. Janelle is not his daughter."

Both of them met Dustin Penn at the door.

"You are to come with me," Penn told them.

He was not smiling, which bothered Trevor.

"What's going on, Penn?" Trevor looked past him. Joya was nowhere in sight.

"Follow me." Penn was decidedly more than secretive.

Garr looked at Trevor and shrugged. "What choice do we have?"

"I should take Joya and leave," Trevor groused.

"Joya is waiting for you with the others."

"*What* others?"

"I believe, sir, that we should go." Sims was suddenly there, standing at attention beside the door. The drummers intensified the beat. All three men were waiting for Trevor.

He looked at Garr, then Sims, then Dustin Penn.

"Why do I have the distinct feeling that there is something going on here and I am the only one who doesn't know what it is?"

"What do you think, Janelle? How do I look?"

Joya stood perfectly still and waited for her sister to pass judgment.

"I am relieved to see that your breasts are covered. It's not that I am embarrassed, mind you, but I am not certain I want Garr to see you exposed any more than I would want Sims to drop dead of shock." She adjusted her spectacles and stepped back. The dim nut-oil lamp in the native *fadu* made it difficult to see. "Does that paint itch? I would think there are some parts of your body they would have left undecorated."

Joya looked down at the chalky, rose-hued body paint the native women had smeared over her arms, legs, neck, face, and every other visible part of her.

"It is beginning to harden." When she smiled the paint around her mouth and eyes cracked.

"I cannot wait to see the expression on Trevor's face when he sees you."

"Do you think he will be pleased?"

"I think he'll be . . . speechless. Whose idea was this?"

Joya dropped her gaze to her hands and admitted, "I have always wanted a Matarengi wedding. I cannot help but think that this time, our marriage will succeed. We'll be blessed by Otakgi, the wise man, and the fertility ceremony will surely assure children in our future."

"What about the marriage hut?"

"Of course we'll have a marriage hut. Although Trevor won't have built it."

"So I will not see you for a month?"

Joya's heart sank. "I never thought . . . oh, Janelle, you don't have to leave yet, do you? Trevor and I haven't had a chance to speak of plans or the future. I don't even know if he intends to stay here on Matarenga after our month of isolation. He promised me that I did not have to live in London."

"Joya, calm down. Garr and I have no set plans. If you get upset you will make your paint run, or melt, or something. You know, you really are the most delicate shade of rose." Janelle reached out and straightened one of the many strategically placed strands of shells around Joya's neck. "Trevor intends to devote his time to orchid hunting. His hope was that you would accompany him everywhere. He has kept two Mandeville Import ships and a seasoned crew of men. You will see the world together."

"Could any woman ever be happier than I am?" Joya mused aloud.

"I would say I have made an equally happy match," Janelle assured her, as one of Umbaba's wives came to the door of the *fadu*.

"They are ready for us," Joya told Janelle.

"Then let's go. Am I to do anything?"

"Here," Joya said, handing her a goat-hoof rattle. "Everyone must make a joyful noise."

Standing alone, bathed in the light of a roaring bonfire on the beach, Trevor watched as a bent and wizened old man shuffled toward him. Beside him, Garr lifted one foot and tried to shake sand out of his low-cut shoe. On Trevor's other side, Sims was paralyzed, staring at the natives surrounding them—in particular, at all the bare-breasted women.

"I think, sir," he said as an aside to Trevor, "I will remain here on Matarenga when you leave. Perhaps Mr. Penn is in need of a good butler."

Trevor turned to Sims and shook his head. "This is only the first of many stops in a world full of various exotic and stimulating sights, Sims. Are you certain you don't want to explore other options before you choose a place to settle down?"

"I take your point, sir, and a very good one it is."

The diminutive, wrinkled old native was standing before Trevor now, staring up at him in silence. The intensity of his stare made Trevor look away. Unfortunately, his gaze touched upon a group of men down the beach who had just slit a goat's throat and were letting the blood pour into a huge bowl.

Garr stopped brushing sand off his pant leg and turned Trevor around. "I am not certain, but I think that might be your wife coming toward us."

Trevor swallowed. A woman covered from head to toe in rosy pink paint and a native *pudong* was walking slowly toward him. Her hair was woven in long, tight braids, decorated with beads and feathers. Thick strands of tiny shells hid her breasts. Dog's-tooth anklets and bracelets chattered and clacked with her every step.

There was no mistaking his wife. She was walking toward him from the opposite side of the circle of villagers. Dustin Penn led her across the sand while Janelle walked beside them shaking a goat-hoof rattle above Joya's head. By now all of the villagers were shaking rattles and chanting.

Joya's smile was brilliant, even by firelight.

"I would say congratulations are in order again, sir," Sims told him.

"Thank you, Sims."

Dustin Penn placed Joya beside Trevor.

"This time you will do it right," Penn said before he stepped back.

Because Joya seemed to be waiting expectantly for Trevor to say something, he said, "You look . . . lovely," though he was not quite certain exactly what one should say to a bride covered in pink paint.

"Thank you, Trevor. I would kiss you but it isn't proper," she said softly.

"I take it we are being married by this small, very old personage standing before us?"

"We are. That is Otakgi."

"He's a witch doctor." Penn chuckled.

"I would not have missed this for the world," Garr said as he took Janelle by the hand and pulled her close.

There was much singing and then everyone began to jump up and down in time to another chant. When Joya explained it was a ceremonial dance, Trevor suddenly understood exactly why she had never mastered the quadrille.

The wise man went into a trance and mumbled for what Trevor thought was an hour before he was handed half of a small cocoanut shell filled with something warm and thick and red that Trevor refused to dwell on.

Both his and Joya's palms were pricked with a lethally sharp blade and drops of their blood mingled in the bowl with the goo already there. The old man made a sign instructing Trevor to drink up. When he tried to refuse, a hush fell over the crowd. Joya looked as if her heart would break if he refused, so he gave in and tried to convince himself that there were worse things, surely, than drinking goat's blood. After he swallowed, he very much doubted it.

What felt like hours of singing and dancing and chanting went on and then the old man began to sprinkle them with a powder finer than sand that he took from a leather pouch.

Joya was beaming. "Dried flamingo heart and fruit-bat claw. It will assure everlasting love and fertility," she explained. "Now the wedding feast will begin."

"I cannot *wait* to see what is on the menu," Garr chuckled.

Trevor squeezed Joya's hand. Over her head, he frowned at Dustin Penn. "And *then* what?"

If he did not get to sleep with his wife tonight he was going to kidnap her and swim out to one of the small islands in the middle of the lagoon.

Joya's eyes were shining. "After the feast, we will be led to the marriage hut. I hope you do not mind that we will be alone there for a month. I know that you probably have everything all planned, but Trevor . . ."

He put his finger over her lips, effectively silencing her.

"Actually," he said, bending close, "I was just wondering if a month alone with you will be long enough. Perhaps we should make it two."

Janelle leaned close to Garr, her own heart full of joy as she watched her twin smile up into Trevor's eyes.

"What are you thinking?" Garr whispered low.

She slipped her arm around his waist, just as he had done hers. "I'm just so relieved and happy that they are together again at last. What are *you* thinking about? It has certainly brought a wicked gleam to your eye, Garr Remington."

"I was just wondering if we shouldn't have a Matarengi wedding ceremony. Or perhaps we could just let the old man sprinkle some of that bat dust on us."

"For fertility? Actually, Garr, it's a little too late for that."

"Are you saying what I think you are saying?"

"Mmm. We're having a baby."

"I hope," said Sims, who was lurking very close behind them, "that we have twins."